Entwined

A MONARCH SERIES ROMANCE

LEIGH ADAMS

Entwined

Copyright © 2021 by Leigh Adams

All rights reserved.

ISBN: 9798584994761

No part of this publication may be reproduced, distributed or transmitted on any form or by means including electronic, mechanical, photocopying, recording or otherwise, without the written consent of the author except for the use of brief quotations in a book review.

This book is a work of fiction. Names, characters, businesses, places, events, and incidents are products of the author's imagination or are used fictitiously. Any resemblance to actual events or locales or actual persons, living or dead, is purely coincidental and beyond the intent of the author or publisher.

EDITOR: Missy Borucki

PROOFREADING: Michele Ficht; Janice Owen

COVER DESIGN AND INTERIOR FORMATTING:

T.E. Black Designs; https://www.teblackdesigns.com

COVER PHOTO: © Lindee Robinson Photography

COVER MODELS: Kailey Marie and David Turner

Dedication

To my mom.
You taught me the meaning of unconditional love
and what it means to be a mom.
You are the rainbows in the sky,
and the butterflies that fly.
You will be in my heart forever . . .
Until we meet again.

CHAPTER *One*

SIENA

Two suitcases, a cardboard box, three trash bags, and a laundry basket. That was all it took to pack up everything important to me.

"Text me when you get there," I heard Nev say from behind me. I turned around, her eyes shimmering with tears threatening to spill over.

"I will," I promised her, taking the pillow she was still clutching. "I *will* be back. I'm just going to go to my grandparents for a little while. It's not going to be forever."

Nev sniffled, tucking her hair behind her ears. "I know." She pulled her sweatshirt closer to her body, crossed her arms over herself, and shivered at the crisp morning air. It was still dark outside, the sun trying to fight against the darkness. My eyes scanned the tall structure behind her, the glow from her apartment window the only light illuminated above us.

I wanted to get on the road and start the long journey, knowing the drive along the coast would take me hours longer. But I knew the scenery would help clear my head. To clear my mind of the disaster my life had become in San Francisco. So, as much as I wanted to get to Grams and Pops, I wanted to get there with some semblance of the old me, the one whose life hadn't collapsed around her. With a tight hug, I let Nev go and watched as the city I loved faded into the background, trying not to cry as I drove away.

If anyone had told me ten years ago that I would move back in with my grandparents at the age of twenty-six, I'd have laughed in their face. Moving back to my childhood home after leaving a city, an apartment, a job, and the man I was in love with—correction, thought I was in love with—seemed crazy. Not only crazy, but stupid too. Who in their right mind would leave all that behind?

That would be me, Siena Giuliana Moretti. The jury is still out on the level of crazy and stupid.

I was rolling down Highway 101, windows down, music blasting, and the heat on, providing warmth against the cool air blowing off the ocean. Five hours into my drive, I pulled my long brown hair into a bun on top of my head while I danced to the song on the radio, turning the volume up, feeling the drums pound through the bass of my speakers.

Then a love song came on.

And while it was tempting to turn the station, I didn't. I swiped at the few tears that fell, and with an angry huff, I pulled off on the side of the road, stifled the music, shifted into park, and cut the engine. I was all alone on the side of the 101. All alone.

"FUCK! FUCK! FUCK!" I screamed at the top of my lungs, slamming my fists against the steering wheel, gripping the wheel till my knuckles turned white. "Why me?" I cried, letting the tears flow freely.

The tears came fast and hard as I cried uncontrollably, my body spasming from the onslaught of emotion. I hadn't cried in four days. And I wouldn't even call what I did real crying. It was more like a tear here and there. But somehow, driving down the 101 on a beautiful morning, wind in my face and the ocean in view, mind free to think as I made my way down the highway, and a ballad playing on the radio, I couldn't hold back the tears. I was feeling sorry for myself.

Who wouldn't be feeling the same way if they were in my shoes?

Relationship: Broken.
Career: Standstill.
Heart: Shattered.

My thoughts jumped to San Francisco and the fiasco that my life had become. I quit my job as a chef and waited on pins and needles, hoping for a call back from a restaurant. *Any* restaurant. I had sent my resume to several places before I got this wild hair up my ass and decided to go back home. At the time, I'd been living on Nev's couch for almost two weeks, feeling like a complete and total loser. She was working and living her own life, while my ass had melted down and become an official part of her sofa. Even though she swore up and down on our friendship that I could stay as long as I needed, and even though she swore on her favorite Gucci bag that I wasn't a burden, I had to get out of San Francisco.

I was on the verge of a nervous breakdown, feeling suffocated and trapped, crushed by concrete buildings and memories of my ex, Tim, the lying sack. I did the only thing that felt natural to me. I called my grandparents and asked if I could come home.

I'd promised Nev I'd be back, even showing her *proof* with my stack of resumes and sent emails. I knew I couldn't leave San Francisco behind for long. I had everything I had ever dreamed of in that city. Well, before Tim went and took a giant shit all over it.

I knew I shouldn't dwell on things, but I was in a deep, dark fucking hole, trying to climb my way back out. Something would turn up. It was just a question of *when?*

One more minute, Siena, I told myself. One more minute, then I'd get back on the road.

I lifted my head and wiped my face. The crying jag had drained me, and the pounding behind my eyes promised a mother of a headache. I popped an emergency aspirin and thought of the one thing that might help right now. "Coffee," I told myself, rubbing my temples.

♥ ♥ ♥

Fresh latte and a warmed blueberry scone in hand, I leaned against my car, looked at the ocean, and inhaled a deep cleansing breath. The waves crashed, and the birds soared overhead. At that moment, I wished I were flying with them. Not a care in the world. No shitstorm to clean up, no worrying about the past or the future. Just flying free, enjoying the moment.

I tried to clear my head and focus on the present. Some things were constants in life. For me, that was family and friends—cooking, coffee, and California. I could never go a day without them. Even though it broke me to leave San Francisco, I was surprised by how many things I could give up. One thing was for sure though, I could never *not* have my California scenery. Whether it was the beaches of San Diego or the bays of San Francisco, being near water was a *must*. Even if I never had an oceanfront view, having the ocean within driving distance always brought me peace of mind.

I fished out my cell to call my grandparents, another constant I was ever so grateful for.

"Hi, hon," my grandmother sang as she answered my call.

"Hey, Grams." I kept my gaze on the ocean waves.

"How's the drive going?"

"Fine so far. Just stopped for a caffeine fix."

"You making good time?"

"Yeah. I'm just outside of Santa Barbara."

"Oh! You've been driving too fast." She was right. I had texted her when I'd left. There was no way I'd have made it this far without breaking the speed limit.

"You know I get my lead foot from you," I teased. Driving

fast brought me a sense of freedom—more like escape—as I left the Golden Gate in my rearview.

Grams's laughter echoed through the line. I could picture her smile, eyes lighting up with happiness, crinkling around the edges. "Don't I know it." An audible sigh followed, then she said, "Well, I used to anyway. Been slowing down a bit in my old age."

"You're not old, Grams. Age is just a number."

"Old enough to know better, but still young enough not to care."

"Totally," I laughed.

"You just be careful and take your time. No need to rush and be reckless."

I sighed, rolling my eyes in amusement. "Yes, Grams."

"Don't sass me, young lady. I can hear you rolling your eyes through the phone."

She knew me all too well. "Love you, Grams."

"Love you more, *Cara*." My eyes pricked at the word.

I smiled as I ended the call, looking at the picture of my grandma and me on my screen.

Hours later, I was finally in San Diego County. It had been a while since I'd been to Monarch, but the familiarity of the land called to me like a beacon. As I turned off the main street onto the two-lane road that would take me to the winery, I embraced the familiar smells of earth and nature. No longer was I surrounded by car exhaust and concrete, but by the simplistic, serene scent of fresh air perfumed with grass, orange blossoms, and tilled earth. All the fragrant aromas that reminded me of my youth.

The hills glowed green under the setting sun, rows and rows of vines stood in greeting. Some of these were the same vines planted by my great-great-grandfather's hands, the very man who had bought this land and established Moretti Vineyards.

Two buildings stood at the top of the hill. The tasting

room located on the south side of our property offered the best view of the winery, something our customers always admired. My grandparents' house was set in the north, offering a glorious view, but inset so it wasn't visible to our visiting guests. The natural fieldstone work, a mixture of tans, grays, and browns, offered a great contrast to the light brown stucco and dark brown shutters.

Night-blooming jasmine and orange blossoms that lined the edges of our wraparound porch sweetened the air. Sophia Moretti, my Grams, was waiting in her chair on the front porch, just like I knew she would be.

"Oh, *Cara*! Let me get a look at you." She grabbed my face between both her hands. Her golden-brown eyes twinkled, misted with tears, her hair perfectly set in place, makeup impeccably applied. "My beautiful girl. Welcome home, *Cara*." She kissed me once on each cheek in welcome.

I sighed into her. She smelled like lilacs, and my breath hitched as I took in her familiar scent. The screen door squeaked as my grandfather came to join us.

"Ah, Siena, my pride and joy. How I've missed you!"

"I've missed you too, Pops." He wrapped his arm around me, pulling me to him and into the warmth of his embrace.

"Come. *Mangia, mangia*. Dinner's waiting." Grams maneuvered us inside.

Sitting down to homemade lasagna complete with an antipasto salad, garlic bread, and the winery's delicious chianti, my grandparents asked about my drive and brought me up to speed about the winery and how things had changed since I'd been back. Pops had taken over the responsibilities of vintner since Joseph's retirement after suffering from a stroke. I knew they wanted to talk more about me, about the real reason for my abrupt visit, but I was exhausted.

"I will tell you everything tomorrow. I promise. I just want to crawl into bed."

A look of worry passed between them. "I'll get your stuff," Pops said.

"Just the two suitcases right now. I'll get everything else tomorrow." I walked out with him, his quiet presence a comfort.

"Jenny can't wait to see you," he said as we mounted the front steps.

"I know. We're supposed to have a girls' night soon. Lauren and Audrey too."

"That'll be nice." My grandmother waited at the base of the stairs.

"Yeah. It will." My eyes felt heavy, my face puffy. I sighed with fatigue.

I kissed them goodnight and, taking the suitcases from Pops, climbed the stairs, making my way to my childhood room. I texted Nev to let her know I'd arrived safely, then opened the window that overlooked the vineyard. Being in the comfort of home freed some of the tension. The natural scents that made me feel so loved, so warm, eased my mind. Spring at the vineyard was exactly what I needed.

♥ ♥ ♥

"A SIMPLE, YET DELECTABLE BREAKFAST," POPS COMPLIMENTED me with a wink.

"She sure has found her niche, hasn't she? A wonderful chef with a promising future."

"I don't know about that now," I said around a mouthful of pancakes.

"And why's that?" Grams questioned.

I rolled my eyes dramatically. "It's obvious, isn't it?" I'd just finished telling them how Tim had betrayed me with someone from work, shattered my heart, and ruined my life. There was no way I could continue to work at his family's restaurant with a daily reminder of his infidelities. I told my grandparents every gruesome detail except one, the only piece of information they didn't need to know because I knew how much they would worry. I just had to figure out how to fix that one little problem.

"Not to me," she rebutted.

"Or me," Pops agreed, slapping his napkin down.

"Just because that low-life, piece of shit did you wrong . . . Did what he did . . ." She wagged her finger at me. "It doesn't have anything to do with your cooking or your ability to run a restaurant," she added matter-of-factly.

"No. But doesn't it say a lot about me?"

"How so? Just because he didn't keep his dick in his pants doesn't mean there's anything wrong with you."

"Grams!" My eyes bugged out of my head.

"What? Like he's never heard the word *dick* before," she scoffed. Pops laughed so loud, and soon Grams and I were laughing uncontrollably too.

When he caught his breath, my grandfather agreed, "Your grandmother's right. On both counts. Besides, Tim was a slimy piece of shit."

"*Pezzo di merda*," Grams said with a curt nod. "A complete weasel. Beady little eyes, pointy nose." She gestured to her own, trying to imitate a weasel.

Images of Timothy's face floated through my mind as I tried to recall what I'd found attractive about him. "You are kind of right, I suppose," I said, miming her movements. As hurt as I still was, it felt good to mock the asshole.

"*Si.*"

"In any case, I'm swearing off men. Don't want 'em. Don't need 'em. Not gonna waste my time on anyone but me, myself, and I."

The phone rang, interrupting our dramatic mocking of Timothy and my new pledge.

Pops wiped his mouth with his napkin. "Perfect time for me to get out of here, away from the man-bashing."

"Perfect way to get out of dish duty!" I called at his retreating back.

His footsteps echoed in the hall a few minutes later. "That was the new owner of the Grayson's property."

"I thought they were going to rebuild," I said, handing Grams a dish to put away.

"Oh, they were. But someone made an offer they just couldn't refuse. Said it was enough for them to retire without the hassle of rebuilding and running a business at their age."

"Good for them," I said.

There was something odd in Pops's voice as he brought his mug to the counter to rinse out. "Blaire, the new owner, wants to come by and introduce himself in a few days."

"Blaire? As in Blaire Enterprises?"

"Yep."

"As in Allan Blaire?" I asked, shocked.

"That's the one."

"What the hell is he going to do with it?" I asked, surprise still registering in my voice.

"Don't know. Guess I'll find out when I talk to his son." He shrugged, placing his mug in the dishwasher and bidding us farewell as he headed out to the vines.

Allan Blaire was a property tycoon. Blaire resorts were known for their luxurious accommodations in some of the biggest hotspots in the US. What could he possibly want with an old burned-down inn in Monarch? And who the hell was this son of his? Coming in to do his dirty work, most likely.

I pulled out my phone and did a quick Google search.

Oh, shit.

CHAPTER *Two*

MICHAEL

Okay, It's official, my dad hates me. All I ever wanted was to run our New York hotel or the property in Florida. But *no*. Allan Blaire kept New York and gave Florida to my younger brother, Matthew, the golden child. The favorite. After all, Matthew Allan Blaire was named after our father. I was never the favorite son. Shit, I wasn't even his second favorite. And there were only two of us.

I had just hung up with my dad.

All details.

All directions.

All business.

He didn't care about my feelings or what I wanted. He just shipped me off to San Diego to take care of the new project on his ever-expanding list of takeovers and acquisitions. And it wasn't even *San Diego*, San Diego. I googled the area he was sending me to. Monarch. More like bumfuck Egypt.

So, here I was, exactly where I did *not* want to be. In a damn rental car. At least it was a Mercedes. There was absolutely no way I was going to be stuck driving around Nowhere, USA in a Prius.

My dad and his third wife, Stephanie, had honeymooned in Hawaii after they eloped, then stopped for a couple of days in San Diego on their way back to the East Coast. Where they found this town, I had no fucking idea. Apparently, they went to Podunk, San Diego, and had a fuckin' blast after someone mentioned wine tasting a short distance from the resort where they were staying. My father and wife number three were probably totally shitfaced when they decided they just *had* to buy this property and redevelop. At least this latest trophy was older than all the other women he'd dated or married, even if she were fifteen years younger than him.

Not sure why my dad decided to get married again. He wasn't too keen on marriage and preferred relationships where there was always an "out." A safe out that didn't include alimony or financially supporting a woman in any way, shape, or form. He already had two alimony payments to deal with—one to my mother and one to wife number two. Wife number two had been a fucking gold digger for sure, but that didn't seem to bruise his ego. The fact she had only been after him for his money didn't bother him in the least. If I remembered correctly, my father said, "She may have been after my money all along—but if that's the case, I just paid for a divorce from an expensive hooker. She won't get a dime more from me."

My dad was a bastard. I didn't like him, but I respected him as a businessman. He was shrewd, innovative, and a hell of a negotiator. He never took no for an answer and knew how to get exactly what he wanted.

Every. Single. Time.

In business, he was someone I admired and aspired to become. In every other aspect, I did my damnedest to avoid becoming anything like him.

There were a few things I was thankful for when it came to my dad though. First: the Blaire name. It was the one thing that made me who I was. My mom had kept it since she never remarried, but I think it was out of wanting to keep the connection to Matthew and me, not my dad. Second: his business savvy inspired me to create an enterprise just as he had. Third, my brother. Even though we had a somewhat awkward and tense relationship, I loved him. He was my blood, and he helped lessen the tension between my father and me. And, finally, Mom. I wasn't a mama's boy by any stretch, but I wouldn't be where I was if it weren't for her.

After my parents divorced when I was seven, I lived with her. Matthew stayed with Dad. For what purpose, I don't know, and I always wondered why Mom didn't fight to keep him. But I never had the nerve to ask her why they split us up. I was around nine or ten when one of my friends told me they probably split us up because it wasn't fair for one of them to have both of us. It always made me think of that story from the Bible about the two women who had to go before King Solomon to fight over the baby. At least they didn't have to decide whether to saw us each in half. Although maybe that would've been better all around.

Maybe if I had lived with my dad, I'd be closer to him and we'd have a better relationship, like Matthew did. But that option was trapped in the past. What I had now worked. I didn't have to like everything about my father to have a successful working relationship with him. Keeping it strictly business between us worked just fine.

I had watched my father go from relationship to relationship since I was a kid. And while, right now, I seemed to take after him, I didn't want to be like him when I was his age. I didn't want to be an old man marrying woman after woman. Women who only cared about my name and my bank account. I didn't much believe in marriage, and after seeing all his failed attempts, it wasn't difficult to imagine why. Keeping things breezy and easy in the relationship department was the best thing for me. That's why I called things off with my ex. She had gotten too serious for me, and I had to break up with her before the shit hit the fan. No need to dwell on that though. I missed the sex, but I didn't miss *her*.

My phone rang and broke into my reverie. Mosby's picture illuminated my screen.

"Hey, Mos."

"Whew! I'm just about finished with the designs. Getting ready to finalize them before sending them off for proofing," she said.

"How they looking?"

"I think Allan will approve But, you know him. There's going to be some minor tweak, something he *just has to change*."

"To put his own fuckin' signature on it."

"I just hope it's not gold urinals. Again."

The distinct sound of rifling pages filled the line, and I visualized her going through her designs one last time to find *that one thing* he'd want to fix. Mosby always liked the challenge of beating my father at his own game.

"When do you think they'll be approved and ready for me?"

"Hmm. Depending on how things go, maybe next week or the week after. I'll keep you posted."

"Thanks. You know anything about this place I'm going to?"

"Not too much. Just what your dad told me about it being the next up-and-coming area in southern California."

I scratched at my beard. It was growing in nice, but I was getting sick of it.

"Why?"

"'Cause it's in the middle of fucking nowhere. And because this idea came out of left field."

"Guess there's an opportunity for major growth—wineries nearby, cute little town. Got a great deal for it too, master negotiator that he is. All I know is Stephanie loves it there. She's really excited about it."

"Figures he'd do some major show of love for his new bride. Old man hasn't learned his damn lesson. Bet they'll be divorced within three years, knowing him."

"Don't be so pessimistic."

"He can't keep a marriage together to save his life."

"I think he might actually keep this one. He's totally in love."

Mosby's defense of Dad's rushed marriage surprised me. "It's not only a question of his feelings but hers. Probably after his money like every other broad."

"I don't know, Blaire. I think she's genuinely besotted with him too."

"Looks can be deceiving. And considering hers . . . well, let's just say, she reminds me a lot of wife number two."

"Don't say that. She was a bitch. Total gold-digging whore. I'm just thankful your dad snapped out of it and came to his senses. Everything about her grated on my nerves. But Stephanie is good people. I like her."

"Yeah. Well, good for you." I couldn't help my sarcasm. I was used to my father's philandering ways. And while he claimed to have been faithful, there wasn't a bone in my body that took him at his word. I couldn't imagine that he'd been any more loyal to them than he had my mother. And if he could cheat on the mother of his children, why wouldn't he cheat on everyone else?

"You're such a dick. I'm telling you I've got a different feeling about this one."

"I wouldn't know since I only met her a handful of times before they got hitched."

"Maybe if you tried, you could mend that bridge." That was Mosby, ever the optimist. She'd been like that since I met her in college. Even knowing all the crap I'd been through and dealt with about my father, she always tried to help me stay positive.

I grunted. "Fat chance. I wasn't even invited to the wedding."

"Well, they did elope. Stephanie told me the story. It sounded so romantic. She had stars in her eyes."

I grunted. "More like dollar signs."

"She comes from her own money, you know."

"I know it doesn't hurt to have more money."

"God, you really don't give the man a break. You need to fix this relationship, Michael. Before it's too late."

I rolled my eyes. "Yeah, well, I've learned the hard way to keep Allan Blaire at a fair distance. Any mending he wants done will need to come by his effort, not mine."

"Jesus. You're a hardheaded son-of-a-bitch."

"Yeah, I am. But he conditioned me to be this way. Besides, it's best that he and I focus on business and not personal matters."

"Whatever you say, Michael. You know I always have your back."

"I know you do—and I appreciate it."

"Of course." There was a beat of silence as she waited for me to say something more. But I was done talking about my relationship with my father. "All right, then, as soon as I get the approval, I'll send the designs your way."

"Sounds good."

"You got everything else taken care of out there?" Mosby asked.

"Yep. The trailer comes the day after tomorrow, I think. I'll be in San Diego until it gets delivered. The demolition crew and everyone else is lined up, ready for the go-ahead. I just need the green light from Allan. Should be within the month."

I heard the faint clicking of a pen. "Sounds like everything's under control. Let me know if there's anything you need me to do."

I hung up and drummed my fingers against the steering wheel in time to the song on the radio. Dad was three thousand miles away, and he was still irritating me. I couldn't let anger and old resentments get to me now. I needed to let this shit go, get my head back in the game, and focus on the project, not the bullshit surrounding it.

I rolled down the window and breathed in the salty air,

counted to eight, and exhaled slowly. Deep full breaths to get my anger in check, the way my shrink taught me to do, and focused on the road in front of me.

I loved my job. I really did. I loved building and creating. Nothing I could do about my boss—I was stuck with him unless I wanted to set out on my own, start from the ground up, and try to build my own empire. I'd miss working with Mosby though. And Matthew. Even though I resented him a little, he was still my brother.

I looked at the ocean as waves crashed onto the sand—wave after wave coming into the shore. My anger dissipated. *Keep it going, Michael, get your shit in check.*

I checked the clock. I was making decent time. I scanned ahead as far as I could see, trying to find any glimpse of a billboard for coffee. At this point, I'd settle for gas station sludge. With the pounding inside my head from my hangover and an acute bout of irritation brought on by thoughts of my father, I needed caffeine. Driving and breathing in the clean, salt-laden air, my thoughts drifted back to last night—drinking and male bonding with Jax.

And thank god for him. Jax O'Halloran was one of my best friends from college. We tried to see each other at least once a year. When my father told me I was going to San Diego, I left with a few days to spare so I could hit up Jax and hang with him before I had to make my way down to the claustrophobic hellhole I'd be stuck in for the foreseeable future.

There was a Starbucks and a quaint little shop that boasted "liquor." I pulled into the lot, considering both as I stared at the ocean before me. All I wanted was to get to the hotel ASAP. I'd have to settle for an espresso. I could always have a stiff drink or a beer after I checked in.

Coffee in hand, I walked to the edge of the road and found a post to sit on and watch the ocean waves. The gulls swooped down from high in the air and waddled along the sand. The smell of the beach—salt, fish, and sea—wafted up to my nostrils. The wind blew cool and crisp, the briny air relaxing me. I had the most spectacular view before me, and I felt at peace. Everything was going to be all right. Everything would work out. Somehow, someway, I would find a way to get everything I wanted out of life.

Unless Allan Blaire found a way to fuck it all up.

Again.

CHAPTER Three

Siena

I got to the tasting room a little after ten o'clock. Another familiar space that brought me comfort. Things looked the same as I remembered. Dark wooden floors. A small but cozy bar and tasting area lined with chairs. Tables made of old wine barrels surrounded by stools offered seating and conversational spaces.

The clean scent of lemon lingered in the air. The counters and tabletops were meticulously cleaned. I checked the bar, making sure the wine bottles were organized in a fashionable way and that glasses were set up for efficient pouring.

Jenny got in about thirty minutes later. She was one of my best friends and had worked for us for years. We chatted for a few minutes before the customers began arriving. That we hadn't seen each other in over a year meant we had a lot to catch up on. *A lot* to talk about.

The girls—Jenny, Audrey, and Lauren—knew most of my story already, at least the highlights. But I didn't want to have to retell it over and over and over, so I figured I'd rip the bandage off and tell it *once* when we had girls' night.

It felt good to dive right back in at the winery, and I knew my grandparents appreciated having me around. Pops had his meeting with the new owner next door, so I didn't expect him until later, but his absence made me wonder what would happen with the old property that was once the only inn in town.

Five o'clock came quicker than I expected. Closing time was officially six, and there were still a couple of customers finishing up.

Four people sat nearby. Two women wore flowy dresses, perfect for the cool spring day, a guy in a dress shirt opened at the neck, and another who wore a polo shirt and baseball cap. I freshened their waters and cleared away their appetizers.

With the rush over, and all but Baseball Cap and Dress Shirt gone, I looked around the almost-empty room. Jenny came back, and I placed my phone facedown on the lower ledge of the counter, turned toward her, ready to get the dirt, pick her brain, and make her spill the beans. After all, she was one of us, so she'd have some idea of what was going on. I urged, "So tell me . . ." I paused for dramatization. "Have you heard anything about this Blaire guy?"

"The what guy?"

"Not the what. The *who*. Blaire."

"Nope."

"Allan Blaire, the hotel guy who bought the Grayson property?"

"Oh, hmm." I imagined thought bubbles above her head. "Never heard of him."

"Ugh," I huffed out in defeat. I wanted information about this guy and his intentions. Not just because I was nosy, but because I wanted to make sure it wasn't going to affect my grandparents or the winery. I needed to get a leg up on him, to figure out how to handle the situation in case I needed to step in on their behalf. My Google search a few days earlier hadn't been promising.

"What's wrong?"

"Nothing." I slapped the rag against the counter in frustration. "He's some property tycoon who bought the Grayson property, and it's going to be a freaking disaster." I put my hand up by my face and added out of the corner of my mouth, "And by freaking, I mean *fucking*." Seeing as there were still a couple of stragglers in the room, it would be uncouth if any patron heard me using profanity.

Jenny laughed. "Why do you say that?"

"Because the guy's probably planning to build a new hotel there."

"And?"

"And he builds huge hotels."

"There was a hotel there before, right?"

"Yeah. Well, an inn technically. But that's not the point."

"So, what's the point?"

"If he does, it's going to be a huge monstrosity. Right next to the winery!" My voice was bordering on shrill.

"Doesn't sound like such a problem to me. It could be good for business."

"It's not just that."

Dress Shirt got up and said goodnight. I thanked him, then wiped down the counter where he had been sitting. Leaning toward our solitary customer, Baseball Cap, I asked, "Can I get you anything else?"

"Thanks, I'm almost done," he answered, not looking up. Clearly, he was trying to keep to himself. He looked vaguely familiar, and I started going through the celebrities who were *HOT* right now, trying to place him.

"Do you know that guy?" I mouthed the words at Jen.

She peeked over at him. "No," she mouthed back.

"I think he's famous."

"Maybe."

"I know him from somewhere. Movie. TV show. Something."

She shrugged. "So, what's the other problem?" She looked

quizzically at me. Now it appeared Jenny was trying to read *my* thought bubbles. "Wait." She held up her hand. "Before you start, is there more than one more problem?"

I blurted out, "First, he builds these massive, thirty-story hotels. Second, they're completely outrageous! Every single one of them is over the top."

"So, you've been to one? And didn't like it?"

"No," I said exasperated. "But I googled them. And him!" I picked up my phone and pulled up my browsing history. "Just look at him," I insisted, shoving the phone into her hand.

"Oh, he's hot!"

I snatched the phone back and tried to lower my voice. "Not him!" I admonished, and clicked the back button, then shoved the phone into her waiting hand. "*Him.* The other picture was one of his sons. *That's* Allan Blaire. You know, Blaire Enterprises? E Properties and Hotels?" I grimaced.

Jenny began fanning herself. "He's really *hot*!"

"Hot? He's an *old man*!"

"Not him, his son! Sorry, I went back to the other page." She turned the phone back toward me, revealing one of the most handsome faces I'd ever seen.

Rolling my eyes in exaggeration, I conceded, "He's all right, I guess."

"You guess? His dad's pretty hot too. For an older man."

The solitary man laughed, making me jump. He held up his almost-empty glass, saluting "cheers" to us. His cap shadowed his eyes, but he had a great smile and a deep, sexy laugh.

I hadn't realized we were talking loud enough for him to hear. I looked around, double-checking that we were the only ones left. His lips quirked up. I covered my mouth in embarrassment when a giggle escaped. He turned his hand over in a "go ahead" movement. And so, on I went.

"Regardless . . ." I looked upside down at his pictures on the screen. Jenny was furiously scrolling through them. "I guess he is pretty hot," I said, pointing to a particular shot of the younger Blaire. "Too bad he's probably as egotistical as his father."

I heard the stranger choke as he almost spit out his wine. "Wow," he said, rubbing his hand over his trimmed beard.

"Whoa, look at this one!"

My eyes bugged out of my head as a half-naked picture stared back at me. "Give that here!" I snatched the phone back, wiping it on my boob before stowing it in my back pocket. "You can't use my phone for ogling men, Jen!"

"Why not? He's a gorgeous specimen. Did you see those abs? And that smile? Ooh-wee." She fanned herself again.

"Well, he may be gorgeous and easy on the eyes, but his hotels are a different story."

"Why?" Jenny asked.

"He turned this cute hotel in Maryland into an atrocity."

"An atrocity, you say?" the man asked, officially joining in on our conversation.

"Okay, not an atrocity like it's ugly. But atrocity like by demolishing it, they eradicated everything unique about it. It was quaint, maybe a little old and outdated, but they didn't even try to preserve any original charm. Now, it's just this huge white box." Two pairs of eyes stared at me. "It's super glamorous and luxurious, don't get me wrong. But seriously, what are they trying to do, be the next Four Seasons?"

The only response was an audible clearing of the man's throat. Jenny tilted her head in confusion.

"You know how it is out here," I continued, desperate to prove my point. "People like the serenity, the setting, the off-the-beaten-path feel. It's picturesque . . . quiet . . . peaceful. Our guests want to hear the birds chirping, see the squirrels and chipmunks running up the trees. Nature in all its glory, you know?"

Neither answered, so I persisted in my diatribe. "Tourists

come here for the beautiful, relaxed atmosphere. The sun rising over the hills in the morning and setting over the vineyard in the evening. No one's going to come to Monarch for Blaire's hotel." I spared a glance at Baseball Cap.

The man's lips were pressed tightly together, but he nodded in seemingly obvious agreement.

"All Blaire wants to do is bring the city life out here. That's not what people want. Definitely not what we need. San Diego's less than thirty minutes away. If people want a big city or downtown feel they drive there to get that, right?" I put my hands on my hips. My head swiveled between them.

"I guess so," Jenny answered meekly.

"But they always come right back."

"Do they?" the man asked.

"Yep," I answered.

"What about you?" He looked directly at me. "Is that what you did? Left and came back?"

"Me?" I pointed at myself. "Oh, no." I picked at an invisible piece of lint.

He leaned back in his chair. "Then why do you say that? How do you know?" His eyes held me in place.

"I did technically come back. But just for a couple of weeks or so." His silence unnerved me. "I actually came down to help my grandparents. But I'm not staying forever."

"Huh," he said with a slight nod.

"So, when do you meet Mr. Blaire?" Jenny drew out his last name into some kind of sexual word that made me shiver.

"I don't know." I turned back, grabbing a rag. "But I know guys just like him—filthy rich womanizers. Probably thinks the women out here will throw themselves at his feet because he's got a big name and an even bigger bank account. That they'll drool over his every word and hop into his bed at the snap of his twiggy little fingers. Like he's some big-shot celebrity or something. Allan Blaire has an ego the size of a redwood. I doubt the apple falls far from the tree."

"A redwood's a big tree then?" the man cut in again, the corners of his mouth twitching.

I snorted. "Only the biggest. He probably thinks he doesn't need to answer to anyone because he works for *Daddy*. Just tells people what to do, and they do it. Doesn't value anything or anyone other than his money."

"Don't you think you're a little harsh?" Jenny countered. "You've never even met the guy."

"If you'd done the research I did, you would've come to the same conclusion. Trust me."

The man grunted. "You must have been quite busy with Google. Probably doesn't leave much time for a social life."

I scoffed, checking the contents of the opened bottles. "I had to google him. I had to make sure I was right. And I was. This guy's just not a good fit for Monarch. He's going to ruin everything. As for a social life, I'm swearing off men. Maybe for good."

"Perhaps you should meet him first. Hear him out. Maybe you'll be pleasantly surprised," he prompted.

"Yeah," Jenny agreed, taking the empty seat next to him. I hadn't realized I'd absentmindedly moved closer toward him.

My head popped up. "Are you siding with him? You know as well as I do that if they build another huge-ass hotel like all the others in their portfolio, it'll ruin the vibe around here. But don't worry. If I have my way, things won't work out, and he'll be running back to New York with his tail between his legs."

"So, what do you do, besides google people you've never met before and then verbally slaughter them?" he asked.

He had backed me into a corner. "Well, I—" I fumbled, trying to form an answer.

"Actually, Siena is a chef." Jenny stepped to my rescue. "She's going to open her own restaurant."

"Ah." He seemed impressed, which helped ease the frustration I felt. "So, you cook?"

"No." I felt the breath snatched out of my lungs. *What the* hell was *Jenny* doing? She looked between us. "I should say, Siena doesn't just cook. She *creates*. Masterpieces, I might add." She winked at me. If her smartass grin could speak, it would have said, *This is what best friends are for. Number one wing-woman right here. You can thank me later.*

"What kind of masterpieces?" He inched forward, intrigued.

"C'mon, Jen. Don't exaggerate," I begged. This was embarrassing, even though I was secretly enjoying every second of it. *I am a hell of a chef. And this dude is hot as hell.* Maybe I should let her do her thing, see what happens. I laughed inwardly at her attempt to play matchmaker and help me get over my slump. To get over Tim.

"You do." Jenny brushed me off. "She's an excellent chef. And baker, I might add. She makes brownies that'll make your toes curl." She laughed flirtatiously. "At least they do mine." She wiggled her feet in demonstration.

"Hmm," he said, glancing from Jenny's feet to my reddened cheeks. He looked like the guy from the new cop show on TV. I rolled through the alphabet, trying to conjure his name.

"She can make *anything*. Brownies. Cookies. Cupcakes. I mean *an-y-thing*."

"Sounds like quite the talent."

"Not only that, but she makes her own pasta." Jenny leaned forward like a conspirator sharing a dirty little secret. "All homemade, from scratch. And oh my god, she makes the most amazing sauces you've ever tasted."

I laughed. Here she was pitching my culinary skills to a total stranger. Where was she when I needed her in San Francisco a couple of weeks ago? Next, she was going to invite him over for a taste test.

"What else can she do?" His words seemed innocent enough, but there was a hint of flirtation in his question. Jenny looked from him to me, and I could tell she was pleading for me to flirt right back. *Uh-uh. No way. Swearing off men, remember?* I silently reminded her with my telepathic skills.

"I can do almost anything," I said matter-of-factly, not falling into her trap. "I've honed my skills both at home and in the kitchen as a chef. Now, I guess"—I threw my hands up—"I'm finally ready to run my own place."

"What I meant was, what do you do besides cook?" He swallowed his final sip of wine. I couldn't tear my eyes away from his mouth.

Do. Not. Answer. Him! my brain ordered me.

"So, a restaurant, huh?" he asked when I ignored his question.

"Yeah." Why did I sound breathless? He appeared genuinely interested, although I couldn't figure out why he cared. "I guess I just got tired of doing what someone else told me to do every day of my life. Working for someone else in their place. Doing whatever *they* demanded. Never having any real say-so, you know?"

"Yeah," he agreed, looking into his empty glass.

"I want to create my own masterpieces. Not someone else's. My dishes will mean something to me. Way more than something off a menu that someone else decided on. Does that make any sense?"

"I *totally* get that," Jenny agreed with a sigh.

"Me too," the stranger concurred.

"My dishes will be unique, inspired by local flavors, using fresh products grown by the people who live and work in the area. Farm to table. Fresh from our garden to your plate. A farmer's market type of cuisine," I explained.

What am I doing? I was sharing my ultimate dream with a stranger. I couldn't for the life of me figure out how this guy could get me to share such personal things without even knowing him.

He nodded. "Sounds good."

"She's gonna be a sensation," Jenny said, hopping off the stool.

"Growing up, I thought I'd go into the family business. But things change, you know? I've always loved cooking and baking, so I figured if it wasn't going to be this"—I looked around the space—"then I should go after my passion and open my own restaurant."

"What if you don't get it?" he asked.

"I won't settle until I do."

He cocked his head slightly. "Do you always get what you want?"

I considered a moment. "Yeah." A smile crawled across my face. "Mostly, anyway." I felt Jen cheering me on, visibly excited that I seemed interested in this guy. A complete shock to even me. However, as fun as flirting might be, I would not get involved with anyone after everything I was still healing from.

He laughed. "Yeah, me too." His self-assured tone made me way too tingly.

Pops came through the open doors. *Perfect timing*, I silently thanked him.

"How's it going?" Pops asked with a kiss on the cheek. "Jenny." He kissed her cheek, too. "How are my girls doing?"

"Great. We've just been having a pleasant chat with—I'm sorry . . ." I gestured to our stranger. "I didn't even catch your name."

"Michael."

"Pops, this is Michael. Michael, this is my grandfather, Salvatore Moretti."

"Michael!" Pops bellowed, extending his hand. "It's a pleasure to meet you."

"You know him?" I asked. Jenny looked at us in turn like she was watching a tennis match.

"Well, unofficially, yes." Pops looked at me, then back to Michael. "But this is the first time I've met him in person."

I was thoroughly confused.

My head pinged between him, Pops, Jenny, and back again.

And then it *clicked*.

My mouth dropped open.

This could *not* be happening!

CHAPTER *Four*

SIENA

MICHAEL AIDEN BLAIRE—*BLAIRE WITH an E*.

I was mortified.

He slid his empty glass toward me, a bit forcefully, a Cheshire-cat grin on his face. I snatched it up before it crashed to the floor. I grabbed a rag and wiped the counter, watching Michael speculatively.

"Mr. Blaire is the new owner of the Grayson place," my grandfather answered the unasked question. He had no idea what had just transpired.

I swallowed the huge lump in my throat.

Michael took his cap off and ran his hands through his hair. "Well, actually, my father is the new owner. I'm his son. You know, the guy who thinks he can get any woman he wants."

I felt my cheeks get hot. That's why he had looked familiar. He wasn't a celebrity, but he was infamous. It all came together. He was dressed too casually for a business meeting, but yep, same chiseled jawline, same mouth from the pictures I'd seen in my search. And now that he'd taken off his hat, the eyes were the same rich, velvety chocolate orbs from the internet.

Pops cleared his throat, looking back and forth between us. "Mr. Blaire, let's grab a table."

"Sure. But please, call me Michael."

"Will do," he agreed and turned his head to me, wagging his eyebrows. "Siena, grab us a bottle of wine and a plate of apps, will you?"

"Okay," I whispered, thoroughly embarrassed as Michael slid off his stool.

"Great introduction, by the way." Pops laughed as he slapped the counter before following Michael.

"Oh, shut up." I scowled, watching as the two of them laughed like they were the best of friends.

Michael Fucking Blaire.

I felt Jenny bump me with her hip. She smiled a huge I-told-you-so grin. "As much as I don't want to leave right now, I have to get going."

"Yeah, sure." I was occupied with my own thoughts. How the fuck was I going to get my foot out of my big mouth this time?

"I'd love to stick around and see what happens next, the impending fireworks and all, but . . ." Jenny looked back to where Michael and Pops sat, her smile wide.

"Oh!" I huffed. "Get outta here!" I steered her forcefully toward the exit, laughing despite my screwed-up situation. I grabbed her arm playfully. "What the hell just happened?"

"Ooh wee. I don't know. Fate?" She kept grinning.

"Yeah, right."

"Fate's twisted sister? That was definitely *not* what I was expecting."

I shook my head. "Me neither."

"Keep me posted," she added with a smirk. And with that, Jenny sauntered out.

I tried to mind my own business but shamelessly attempted to eavesdrop on the two men in the corner. I hoped Pops would invite me to sit down with them when I was finished. My intuition was telling me Mr. Mogul wanted something more than just to introduce himself and be neighborly. When I finally made ready to leave and walked over to check on them, under the guise of offering more food and wine, of course, I was politely, but completely, brushed off by Pops. Michael barely spared me a glance and looked irritated that I had come over at all.

This asshat was in *my* space. *My* place. And he had the nerve to regard me as the intruder? I was ready with a smart-ass comment, but my grandfather simply kissed my hand and told me he'd see me back at the house.

♥ ♥ ♥

I barreled through the front door in a huff, ridiculously pissed off. The slamming echoed in the foyer as I closed it forcefully with my foot. The nerve of him. Ignoring *me*? Blowing *me* off? I tore into the kitchen, opened the fridge, and started hauling out veggies to make a salad, slapping them down on the counter, and then banging cupboards open and slamming them closed. I was in my own headspace and was being so loud, even for me, that I didn't hear my grandmother come in.

"What's all this ruckus?" Hands on her narrow hips, she glared at me before she moved around me, getting down the pots and pans to make dinner.

"Ugh!" I shouted. "Pops is down there talking with Michael Blaire!"

"And?"

"And he's awful. Just fucking awful, Grams."

"Why? What'd he say?"

"Not much before Pops came in. Then, off they went. Together. To talk in the corner like old friends. And I wasn't even included."

"Do I sense some jealousy?"

I tore the lettuce with relish, wishing it were Michael's

head that I was ripping from his body. "No," I fumed, pouting.

"Then what's got you so mad?" she asked, gathering some herbs and garlic for the salmon.

"I'm not mad. I'm embarrassed." The reality caused me to deflate a little. She didn't say one word. Just grabbed a knife and started mincing the garlic. "Okay, maybe I am mad a little too," I admitted.

"With Pops?"

"No. With Michael Blaire." My lips curled into a sneer just saying his name.

"About what?"

"He didn't tell me who he was."

"Was he supposed to?"

"Yes. No. I don't know!" My hands flew up with a mind of their own. "But it was humiliating!" I buried my head in my hands, not wanting to admit the ugly truth.

"Did you tell him who you were?"

"Why would I? Clearly, I worked there since I stood behind the counter and all. Not to mention, the nametag." I pointed to the tag still pinned on.

"Hmm." That was all I got from her. I considered her question. Should I have introduced myself? No, that would've been weird. Why would I introduce myself to a customer?

I took a deep breath and waved my hands, trying to put my thoughts into an explanation. "So, Jenny and I are sitting there talking, and I go off about Blaire and how he builds outrageous hotels. How he's an egomaniac. And *dickwad* is just sitting there, der-dee-der, not saying anything, totally egging me on."

"What do you mean *egging you on*?"

"He was asking questions and staying in the conversation."

"Maybe he was trying to get to know you."

I snorted. "Yeah, right."

"Or maybe he was just trying to be polite."

"C'mon, Grams. He was trying to get me to shove my foot in my mouth, which I did. Excellently, I might add." The memory brought an embarrassed blush to my cheeks.

"I'm going to play devil's advocate here. It sounds to me like there was more to it than trying to wheedle some smart-ass retort from you." She cackled, amused with herself.

The back door opened, announcing Pop's return. I waited until he came through the doorway before I sprang. "What was that all about?" I whirled. All my calm immediately switched to outright irritation.

He ran his hand through his full head of black hair. "What was what?" Pops asked, pretending to be oblivious to my frustration.

"Don't play coy with me. Michael Blaire in the tasting room? You rushing off to talk with him?" I crossed my arms.

"I told you I had a meeting scheduled with him."

"That was supposed to be earlier."

"He called and asked if we could push it back. Said he got tied up with something."

"You didn't say he was coming *here*."

"He asked if it would be all right for him to come by. I didn't think it'd be a problem. Figured he wanted a glass of wine at the end of the day. Plus, it made it easier for me."

"And?"

"And what?"

I squinched my eyes. "And what did he want, Grandpa?"

He looked from me to Grams and back again, rubbing the back of his neck, noticing I didn't call him *Pops*.

"I can't believe it." I smacked my forehead. "I totally thought he was just some random guy hanging out drinking wine. Not the new owner next door!"

"Well, you sure put a kink in things," he said.

"Don't worry, Pop. I'll fix it."

"Before dinner?" His eyebrows were raised in consideration.

"What do you mean *before dinner*?"

He shrugged, absentmindedly walking to the sink, "I invited him to dinner."

"Oh. My. God. You didn't!"

"I sure did." He laughed as he washed his hands.

"Are you shitting me, Pops?"

He turned his head. "No, ma'am."

"What the hell?"

"Well now, don't you worry your pretty little face." He pinched my cheek. "Turns out he wasn't able to make it after all. Said he still has a lot of work to catch up on."

"Oh, you!" I poked him in the ribs. My body sighed with relief.

"But it is good to know what kind of reaction a man can still get out of you." He roared with laughter at my expense again. Typical Pops. He looked at Grams. "Oh, Sophia, you should have seen them. All flustered with each other."

"Pops! No, I wasn't. No, we weren't," I admonished him. He waggled his eyebrows again. "Now don't you start with that crap," I warned.

"What? Who? Me?" He pointed to himself, feigning complete innocence.

"Yes, you." I nudged him again in his ribcage.

"Ooh, that one hurt a bit." He rubbed his side. "Well, you're going to have to fix your hullabaloo at some point. He's our neighbor now. And we're going to be doing some business with him."

"What do you mean?" Grams and I asked simultaneously.

"He wants to purchase some of our land."

"What!"

Pops covered his ears. "He wants to buy the area closest to his."

"Why?!"

"Because he wants more land. He made an offer on the winery, but I told him we weren't interested."

"I knew it! I *knew* it!" I slapped my hands on the countertop.

Grams chimed in, "Calm down, Siena. Let's hear all of it before you blow a gasket."

"Fine," I huffed, leaning over, feeling like the wind was knocked out of me. I turned around and leaned against the counter. "He's an evil man, I'm telling you." I shook my finger at him and squinted my eyes in distrust while waiting for Pops to finish his story.

"He actually made an offer to buy the winery," he said, filling a mug with coffee, "but I told him no. So, he asked to buy the strip of land closest to him. The part that was damaged in the fire last year, along with Barney Grayson's hotel."

"And what'd you tell him?" I demanded.

"I said I needed to talk to my wife and granddaughter. That this is a family-owned and operated establishment. And that we needed to decide as a family."

"What'd he say?" My squinted eyes displayed my complete distrust and disdain.

"He said he understood and told me to take all the time I needed."

"Yeah, right! That guy's a snake in the grass. He's not to be trusted."

Grams looked at me, admonishing, "You don't know that, Siena." She turned to Pops. "What was his offer?"

He retrieved a piece of paper from his shirt pocket, unfolded it, and set it face up on the kitchen table. My eyes bugged out of my head. So did Grams's. "That's the reaction I wanted to have, but I tried to play it cool," Pops chuckled.

"Holy shit!" I exclaimed as my grandma shouted, "*Merda santa!*" and began fanning herself.

"I know." Pops took a seat at the table.

"What's he trying to do, buy our land, or buy your silence?"

"I think he's just trying to make me an offer I can't refuse," Pop teased, with a hint of the *Godfather* in his voice. "Said there was more in it for us if we'd agree to sell the winery." He laughed nervously. "It would cost a hell of a lot to rebuild that area to what it was, and we still have enough land and vines to do everything we need."

"Plus, it would give us some breathing room," Grams added.

"What does that mean?" I asked.

"Nothing," Pops interrupted with a stern look at her.

"What?" Silence filled the air. "What?" I asked again, giving them both a look that demanded an answer.

"Nothing for you to worry about, Siena." My grandma patted my cheek to placate me.

"I'm not buying that BS." I looked from one to the other again.

"It's not *nothing*, but it's nothing huge," Pops started. "It's just that we've been struggling a bit financially."

"What?" I whispered. "What do you mean? Why didn't you tell me? Why didn't you say anything?" I sat down next to my grandfather, feeling defeated and on the brink of tears.

"We've been through this before." I felt my grandma's hand on my shoulder, felt her gentle squeeze trying to reassure me. "Look at me, Siena," she prompted. I turned toward her, tears stinging my eyes. She took my face between her hands. "*Non ti preoccupare.*" She leaned in and kissed my right cheek. "Don't worry," she repeated, kissing my left cheek.

"Like Grams said, we've been through this before, and we've always survived. You don't need to worry that anything's going to happen. We will pull through like we always do. But selling this land could take away some of the stress." He smiled at Grams.

"Maybe you're right."

"And we wouldn't have to worry about redeveloping that area. It might sting a little to sell part of our land, but it would help us financially, and it's not like we need it to survive. We've got more than enough."

It made sense and hearing their perspective helped me feel a little better. "I will support whatever decision you guys make."

"You're a part of this winery. You're a partner in all this, Siena." Grams's hand still rested on my shoulder.

"Even though I declined your offer to take it over?" I looked between them.

"*Si*," she said.

"*Sempre*," added Pops, grabbing our hands and kissing the tops in turn. "My favorite girls."

"Thanks, Pops." I squeezed his hand. "Grams." I squeezed hers too. "I trust you to make the right decision and will support you. Even if that means selling to a weasel."

"He's not a weasel. Timothy's the weasel, remember?" Pops joked. Grams and I laughed.

"Okay, he's slightly less awful than *that* weasel."

"Well, then," she contemplated, looking at Pops. "I guess you won't mind helping me plate some leftovers for him."

"Sure."

There was a mischievous twinkle in Grams's eyes. Pops winked at her. "And then you can go with me to take them over."

"No. Absolutely not!" I told her. "And what was that?" I chastised Pops, pointing at him.

"What?" He faked absolute innocence, rubbing his eyes. "Must be some dirt in my eyes or something."

"Yeah, or *something*."

"Now, Siena. That man is over there all by himself. The least we can do is be neighborly and bring him some home cooking," Grams insisted.

"You can. I don't have to."

"You most certainly do. You are a representative of this business."

I rolled my eyes.

"And this family," Grams added. Her words got to me.

"Fine. But I'm doing this out of sheer obligation and guilt. Not because I agree or care what he thinks."

"That's my girl," she said, then whispered something to Pops that earned a chuckle.

"Whatever you two are up to, stop it now," I warned. My thinly veiled and empty threat made them laugh harder.

♥ ♥ ♥

POPS DID THE DISHES WHILE WE PLATED THE LEFTOVERS AND took them to Michael. Even though I could see the Grayson's, or should I say *Blaire's* property from the top of our hill, we took my car. The tree-lined, winding lane took us to the base of our vineyard, the path set on both sides by long-matured Mediterranean olive trees. Something about driving under a canopy of trees calmed me.

And then we were at the threshold of the enemy. And I felt nervous. I didn't know why I was. Or why I even cared. So what if I made a complete fool of myself earlier? It's not like I had to interact with him daily. And, if need be, I could very well steer clear of him for the next few weeks or months. Or however long it took me to put my life back together.

His trailer sat in the dark, only a faint light coming from the windows. I could barely make out the ruins of what used to be Grayson's Inn in the darkness. Knowing it was gone, even though it was dated and a bit worn, made me sad. It reminded me of how much I'd lost recently.

Grams handed me the packed dinner while she fluffed her hair. I smiled at her vanity. She knocked on the door while I held the bag, irritated at a nervousness I didn't want to feel.

When the door opened, I almost dropped the bag. *What in the actual hell?* My breath caught in my chest, and I swear I felt my heart stop. *Oh, holy hell.*

Illuminated by the dim light behind him, Michael Blaire looked like absolute sin. He'd had a beard earlier. Now, he had a cleanly shaven face. And he was absolutely gorgeous. Chiseled jaw, angular cheekbones, tanned skin, black coiffed hair. He looked like someone I'd want to see endorsing Moretti wines: mouthwateringly delicious. I immediately wondered if he smelled as good as he looked—a mixture of hot sex and unadulterated manliness. I halted my thoughts. A man? Now? After what Tim did to me? *Fuck no!*

Grams broke the silence. "Mr. Blaire, I'm Sophia Moretti. Siena and I just wanted to bring you some food. Since you couldn't make it for dinner at our place, we figured you might enjoy some leftovers. Grilled salmon, asparagus, broccolini, potatoes, and a side salad. All fresh and homemade with love." She smiled up at him.

"Thank you. That's truly kind of you, Mrs. Moretti."

"Oh please, call me Sophia." She patted her hair. Was my grandma blushing? I swear I could see the pink in her cheeks, even in the darkness. "Siena made everything." She hip-bumped me, urging me to say something.

I snapped out of my shock and awe. "I just assisted."

"Oh, now. You did almost all the work."

"It was a team effort." I held the bag out for him, hoping it would bring an abrupt end to this.

"Ms. Moretti," he said, finally acknowledging me, "how delectable this all sounds." He looked at me, down to the bag, then back up to my face.

"It can be reheated whenever you get hungry." He cocked his head and grinned, raising one provocative eyebrow. Was he playing with me? I jiggled the bag, silently willing him to take it and bid us good night.

"I'm always hungry," he said, his eyes meeting mine as he slipped the bag from my grasp. His hand brushed against mine. A surge of electricity shot through me, and I shamefully wondered, *Are you hungry for me?* He licked his lips, seemingly reading my wayward thoughts. I couldn't look away, his eyes kept me captive. What power did he hold over me? What was I getting myself into with him? *Nothing, Siena. Absolutely nothing. Except maybe for a little fun, a little release.* I shook my head, trying to get these thoughts out of my head.

"All right, Grams." Intense heat rose from my chest to my cheeks. I grabbed my grandmother by the hand. "Clearly Michael . . . uh, Mr. Blaire has things to do. Remember, Pops said he had a lot of work?" I needed out of here. Now.

His hungry eyes appeared to switch to a look of annoyance almost instantaneously. He cleared his throat and addressed my grandmother. "Thank you again, Sophia. Mr. Moretti told me what a fine cook you are." He waited for what felt like forever before finally looking at me again. There was an iridescent sparkle in his eyes.

"All right, Grams," I said again, feeling like a cat backed into the corner with nowhere to run. I tugged on her hand.

"Ms. Moretti," he bade me farewell as he shut the door.

As I climbed back into my seat, I glanced at Michael's door. Who was this guy? And what was he really up to?

I tried to keep my thoughts on the problem at hand. But the sound of his voice made me tremble with desire. And those eyes made my heart race.

Fuck my life.

CHAPTER Five

MICHAEL

I CHUCKLED TO MYSELF AS I sat down on the sofa in my trailer, grabbed the beer I had just popped open, and took a swig. Things were rapidly getting more and more interesting around here.

Earlier that morning, I'd received a very curt and formal call from my father asking how things were shaping up. All I could report was that I'd be meeting with the owner of the winery. He immediately requested that I do a little more R&D about the Moretti family and look into the winery's value because he wanted to make an offer on that too.

After meeting with Sal Moretti, I was ninety-nine percent sure he would never consider selling. I didn't begin our conversation with the idea of buying the place outright, but when the opportunity arose, I subtly felt him out about selling. He told me the winery was a "family business" owned and operated by the Moretti family since inception and that he wasn't willing to give it up. In the short time we'd spent together, I could see how much the place meant to him. But my father genuinely believed everyone and everything could be bought—for the right price. I asked about the area that was partially destroyed from the fire, and, after Sal told me it'd take a lot of funding to recoup the loss, I offered to buy that portion if he was interested.

I hoped that maybe, just maybe, getting additional land would be good enough for Allan Blaire. I wasn't looking forward to delivering that bit of news. At all.

Then there was Siena. One look into those hazel orbs and I knew I wanted her. Just my luck, she turned out to be the granddaughter of the man I'd have to build a working relationship with. The man I knew my father was going to want me to grind down to the stump until he conceded to sell.

I couldn't figure out if it was sheer dumb luck or some fucked-up twist of fate that had brought me here. It wasn't like I had to deal with Siena Moretti directly, but after meeting her and hearing what she had to say about my father and his hotels—and me—I didn't think I'd be able to steer clear of her.

She was a shit talker, that was for sure. And although she wasn't that far off base about my father or his hotels, she had jumped to conclusions about me way too fast. She'd made up her mind before ever laying eyes on us. I didn't know if I could blame her, but she had hit a chord inside me that I didn't particularly like having struck, especially by a total stranger.

There were people in the business world, people I had met and dealt with, and even many whom I hadn't, who I knew vehemently disliked my father and his tyrannical ways. Many times, I couldn't help but agree with them. But this was business. And if there was one thing my father taught me, it was that, in business, sometimes you had to be the shark and not the bait.

I had kept my calm after listening to Siena berate my father and me. I had kept my head level and cool. At first, I was seriously amused by her. I thought she was funny, spunky, and feisty. Something about her attitude got my attention. Her energy called to me, and I couldn't take my eyes off her. She was incredibly beautiful. I had kept my staring, and the eye-fucking, well hidden. One look at her though, and I couldn't help myself. There was some kind of serious pull. At least on my end.

Honestly, all I had wanted to do was introduce myself to Mr. Moretti and to let him know what I'd be doing over the next several months. Sal, as he insisted I call him, was truly down to earth and easy to talk to. Siena, on the other hand, was a fighter, and I didn't know yet if this battle of wills was going to be fun, entertaining, and exhilarating . . . or a royal pain in my ass.

Sal had invited me over for dinner that evening, presenting the invitation under the guise of meeting his wife and partner, Sophia, but I didn't know if that was truly the reason or if he was setting me up for another inquisition by Siena. It wasn't that I was afraid. I just had more pressing things to deal with regarding the hotel.

I regretted declining the invitation after looking in my minifridge. Beer, beer, and more beer. In the cupboards, coffee and some crackers. If I was going to live and work out of this shoebox, I'd have to get at least some food that would sustain me through the long and tedious hours and months—*dear God, please not years*—ahead of me.

I found myself sitting at the table, rubbing my temples, and contemplating whether I should go out and try to scour something up for dinner or just stuff a bunch of crackers down my throat and call it a night. After taking another look at my food options, I grabbed a beer and sat down on the tiny excuse of a couch in the sitting area. At six foot one, the firm and unforgiving sofa wasn't exactly the most inviting or even comfortable option. Nothing in this tiny excuse of a trailer was comfortable. But I guess when you're being paid the big bucks, you have to just suck it up.

I tried calculating the timeframe in my head. How long would I have to be out here living like a goddamned sardine? Much too long. There was no knowing when the job would be finished. Something always came up when building something new: unreliable contractors, wrong materials being delivered, damaged inventory, sucky crewmen, shitty workers. The list went on and on.

I sat up, trying to accept the inevitable: I'd have to stick it out because I had no choice. Business was business. And this was my job.

I had just popped the top of my beer when I heard a car. I didn't know who in the hell would be out here this time of night. I listened for the car to circle around and leave. Instead, I heard two doors shut, then a brisk knock at my door.

As luck would have it, it had been Sophia Moretti, a sweet, petite, beautiful woman, bringing me dinner. And apparently, luck was going to strike me twice today. I decided to accept fate's little twist in tonight's agenda. It seemed I didn't have a choice here either—our paths were destined to intertwine. Sophia had brought her granddaughter along.

I couldn't help but flirt. It came naturally to me. Flirting with a beautiful woman was just part of who I am, and the idea of making Siena squirm, seeing how she reacted to me, was just too good an opportunity to pass up. I got a reaction all right. I could see it in her eyes: the slight dilation and the big doe-eyed look that crossed her face. It was what I'd been shooting for. Even if she did more-than-slightly despise my father, and even if she was trying to derail our hotel plans, there was enough of a response to see there was something between us. She was like a deer caught in the headlights of my rented Mercedes. This was going to be a challenging game for both of us. The only question: *Who was going to come out the victor?*

Life certainly had a crazy way of twisting and turning. Fate? *Maybe.* Destiny? *Perhaps.* Or maybe life was just warming up its throwing arm to pitch me a healthy serving of kick-me-in-the-ass karma? Fuck if I knew. But what I did know was that I would enjoy the ride as much as I could as long as I was stuck here.

My phone rang. *Shit.* It was my dad. He was going to be pissed when I told him that he wouldn't get the winery. I didn't want to deal with him right now, but knew he'd just keep calling if I didn't answer. I took another swig and settled into the cushions, knowing the conversation wasn't going to go in my favor. As usual.

CHAPTER Six

Siena

I COULD HAVE SWORN MY grandma was smirking on the quick ride back home. But each time I turned to look at her, her face was deadpan serious.

"Michael seems nice," she finally said when we walked into the kitchen.

"Nice?" I scoffed. "There's nothing nice about him."

She crossed her arms and beamed.

"He should have told me who he was right from the get-go. Instead, he just let me ramble on and on, making a complete fool of myself."

"Well, it's not his fault you acted like a fool, is it?"

"No, but . . ." I looked out the window. I could barely make out the lights of his trailer. It was hard not seeing the familiar glow of the inn. "He could have said something."

"You could've too," she said simply. "Night, honey." She kissed my cheek and left silently.

I continued to stare out the window, nothing on my mind except a pair of rich, dark-chocolatey eyes. I huffed in frustration. Sleep was not going to come easy for me tonight. I had the feeling I would dream about Michael's handsome face.

I decided I needed to work out my frustration in the form of baking. Something yummy and comforting. *Something warm and gooey*, I thought as I rummaged through the pantry. Something deliciously sweet. *Brownies!* I finally decided, grabbing the ingredients I needed.

I also decided I needed to try to make amends with Michael Aiden Blaire. If he was going to buy part of our land, that meant having business dealings with my grandparents. But the fact that he was interested in purchasing the business raised my hackles. I was irritated, pissed off, and worried all at the same time. I couldn't believe they wanted to buy our winery. I couldn't imagine why they'd have any interest in anything in Monarch.

Sure, Monarch was beautiful. Stunning. Peaceful, serene, natural. But it was also just wineries, orange groves, and family farms surrounded by the Cleveland National Forest to the north, and the Cuyamaca Mountains to the south. In no way at all was this area even remotely suited for a Blaire hotel. Something as flashy as that would change everything the families in this area loved about calling Monarch home. Not to mention the tourists who came for the relaxed and easy-going feel our town was known for. Of course, I admitted to myself, those folks *would* need a place to stay. But a fucking Blaire hotel? No way.

I couldn't afford to have my grandparents get played by Michael or his dickhead of a father. In fact, I had to be extra cunning and win him over so I could make sure he didn't screw them over himself. He needed to understand who he was dealing with. I wasn't just some bimbo with big boobs and no brain like he was probably used to manipulating.

I was determined to charm him. *Kill 'em with kindness.* And in this case, my kindness was going to be chocolatey decadence. If my big mouth couldn't make peace, my brownies could. There'd be no way he'd be able to deny me now.

♥ ♥ ♥

THE NEXT MORNING, WITH MY FRESH-OUT-OF-THE-OVEN brownies wrapped on a plate and a mason jar of iced cold milk, I made my way back over to him. I had to steel myself, pump myself up, give myself a pep talk like I would for an interview. "Okay, Siena Moretti. You can do this. All you gotta do is be nice and smile. Let your baking do the talking." *Let your baking do the apologizing is more like it,* my subconscious said back to me. *Shut up!* I told it.

I retraced the same steps I had taken the night before. Fifteen feet from my car to his door. Three knocks. I waited, checked my watch. It was nine in the morning. Surely, he was awake by now. I knocked twice more, waiting for the door to open.

"Come in."

I hesitated a moment before doing as instructed. On a round wooden table where he sat, papers were laid out in some kind of order. What order, I couldn't tell. I lifted the plate of brownies and jar of milk in advertisement. "I brought a peace offering." Silence. "Homemade brownies." Nothing. "Chocolate? They're delicious." Still nothing. *Fucker!*

"Sure," he said, nodding toward the plate. "Set them wherever." He jerked his head back toward the ridiculously small kitchenette.

Not even a polite *Thank you.*

What a DICK!

Inside, I wanted to scream, but for my grandparents' sake, I plastered a smile into place and walked behind him to the counter. Attempting a cheerful tone, I asked, "Don't you want one? They're still warm." I hoped the enticing, rich smell would waft to his nostrils and make him peek up. Still nothing. Trying again, I placed one of my decadent squares onto a napkin and took it and the cold milk to him. "Here. Take a break. Indulge a little."

"I don't have time to take a break. But thanks."

"Look, I'm sorry," I huffed.

"About what?" he said without looking up.

"About what I said."

"What you said?"

"Yes, what I said," I repeated, my irritation already starting to get the best of me. Was he playing stupid on purpose?

He spared me a glance. "Which part exactly?"

"I didn't mean to insult your father."

"But you did mean to insult me?" he asked, setting his pen aside, finally looking at the deliciousness in front of him. Was that a smirk I heard in his voice?

"Ugh, you are insufferable, you know that?"

"Well, I guess that's a step up from . . . Now, what was it you called me before?" He cupped his chin and tapped his finger to his lips. His eyes grew wide in remembrance. "Oh, yes . . . *An egotistical maniac who thinks he can get any woman into his bed.*"

"Is that what you're mad about?"

"Not particularly. I would agree with that statement." A deep chuckle escaped him.

I quickly took the six steps that separated me from the door. "You self-absorbed, conceited . . ." I all but shouted.

"What?" he prompted.

"Jackass!" I spat as I reached for the doorknob.

"Oh, so now I'm a jackass?" His sexy tone stopped me dead. I dropped my hand as I turned to face him. Slowly, never taking his eyes off me, he pushed up from his chair and walked toward me in silence. His walk, I noticed, was more like a stealthy prowl as he edged around the table. And fuck me if I wasn't a little turned on.

"I-I," I stammered, my feet frozen in place, my heart pounding. My back against the wall next to the door put me in prime position as he came in for the kill. *Kiss me. Kiss me.*

He leaned down, his lips barely an inch away from mine. He whispered, "You . . . were supposed to be apologizing."

I had no words. The sexual pull racing through my system stole my breath. With nowhere to go, I shifted, trying to create space between us. I was afraid he'd smell the lust emanating from my skin.

"I-I *am* sorry," I faltered, wringing my hands together to have them do something other than reach out and touch him.

"I appreciate your attempt. And your brownies."

He reached out to me.

Touch me, please.

He opened the door, shaking his head. "But I'm not really a fan of chocolate," he said as he ushered me out. "Thanks all the same." And with that, he promptly shut the door in my face.

Knocked completely from my arousal, I stared at where he had just been. When I finally came to my senses, I stormed off and walked the entire way back home. I didn't even realize I had left my damn car at his place until I went to hang my keys up and they were nowhere to be found. They were still on his fucking counter.

♥ ♥ ♥

Back at the house, the walk had done nothing to calm my insane anger. I was even more pissed off now than I had been before. Grams and Pops sat at the kitchen table, finishing breakfast. "Ugh, that man is insufferable! What is his problem?" I stomped over to the coffee pot.

"Aside from him overhearing you badmouthing him yesterday?" Pops asked, not looking up from his newspaper. "Probably nothing."

"He shouldn't have been eavesdropping!"

"I don't think he was eavesdropping. He probably just overheard you. You know you're loud."

"What?!" I shrieked. *Ah, he has a point, I guess.* We all started laughing. I was definitely the pot calling the kettle black. Yes, I was loud. We all were. It was in our nature, in the Moretti genes. None of us had a quiet bone in our body.

I took a seat at the table, grabbed a piece of toast from the stack, and buttered it, a bit of the wind knocked out of my sails. "Well, shit. What should I do? Why do I even care?"

"What you should do is make peace with our neighbor. Especially since he's going to be over there for the next year or so," Pops reminded me.

"He's an asshat."

"Asshat or not, he's our neighbor now. We can't afford to make him our enemy, Siena," Grams reminded me.

"He wouldn't even accept my apology."

Pops raised an eyebrow.

"Or my brownies," I grumbled.

"What do you mean *or your brownies*?" Grams asked.

"I made 'Let's make peace' brownies, and he's all 'I don't like brownies. I don't like chocolate,'" I imitated him, bobbing my head, using a deep baritone moronic voice.

"Who the hell doesn't like brownies?" Grams spouted.

"Right?" I looked at her, then over to Pops, and we all started laughing again.

"There's something up with him." They exchanged a look, and Pops raised his eyebrows at me. I glared back. "Now, don't get started with that crap again. I have sworn off men, remember?"

"I'm just going to suggest you try again," he said. "Maybe without a bribe."

I scoffed. "Seriously, who doesn't like brownies? Something is wrong with him."

My mind was running in circles. I couldn't figure out how I would get on Michael's good side without losing my dignity again. I grabbed a windbreaker and made my way to the vines.

I walked the rows, touching and talking. I believed wholeheartedly in talking to plants and treating them like friends.

Something Pops had instilled in me when I was young. I reminisced back to the lesson from my childhood.

"The plants respond to your voice. It makes them happy to hear from an old friend, just like people. Talk to them, Siena. When you work, share your stories and your life. And they will respond in kind. You will see them grow and flourish, just as Grams and I have with you."

Looking back, I didn't know whether or not he was blowing smoke up my skirt, but I talked to plants just the same. Everything appeared to be going well. The weather forecast looked favorable, and the plants looked healthy. I wrapped up my inspection, bid my friends farewell, and made my way to the tasting room.

My grandfather's words about making peace with Michael ran around and around in my head while I worked. He had a valid point about Michael being our neighbor. Pops was always one to make peace, not war. And since I didn't intend to move back home for good, I knew I had to make amends with him. I had to follow my grandpa's mantra.

As I was taking a glass from one of the last customers, a devilishly tall, dark-haired man caught my eye. I felt a flutter in my belly as I did a double take, then immediate embarrassment over being excited about seeing Michael. But it wasn't him—just another tall, dark, and handsome stranger.

Michael was a mixture of pleasure and pain. Pleasure because he, like Jenny had pointed out, was a "gorgeous specimen." Pain, well—he was just a pain in my ass!

The man walked to his female companion, wrapped an arm around her, and kissed the side of her forehead. Her smile was so full of love as she looked at him. It made me heartsick for all I'd lost recently.

"Penny for your thoughts?" Jenny bumped my hip with hers.

"Huh? Oh, no," I laughed. "Just lost in my head, I guess."

"About?"

"The winery. Life. Love. Michael Blaire." I sighed, leaning against the counter.

"Ooh," she crooned, "let's focus on that last one!"

"Uh. No, thanks!"

"Well . . ." She tapped her chin, thinking. "Life and love always make good topics, but they're a little deep for me right now. So that leaves the winery or Michael Blaire."

I rolled my eyes. "I am not discussing *him* at work."

Jenny's eyes widened as a deep voice inquired, "Talking about me again?"

CHAPTER *Seven*

SIENA

I TURNED TO FIND MYSELF face-to-face with Michael and swallowed the lump in my throat. Just my luck! *Play it cool*, I commanded myself. *Don't be a bitch. And for goodness' sake, don't bring up the brownies.*

"Ha ha," I said, rolling my eyes. "Not this time, anyway."

"Mm-hmm." He wiggled his eyebrows.

"Eavesdrop much?" I joked.

"Just a coincidence, I guess."

"Mm-hmm," I imitated him.

He chuckled. "Either that, or you just have a big mouth."

Jenny burst into laughter. "Oh, man. He's got you there!"

"You're both hilarious." I rolled my eyes, wiping the counter.

"I can step away if you two want to continue your *private* conversation about me." Michael's eyes sparkled mischievously.

"We were *not* talking about you," I answered emphatically. *Yet*, my subconscious added. *Shut up!* I told it.

"Okay, okay." He held up his hands. "If you say so. I guess I have to believe you."

I tucked the rag into my back pocket. *Okay, this is going all right. Friendly banter. Nothing serious. Don't let him know you're pissed about the brownies!*

"I don't believe you. But . . ."

I cut him off with a sharpening of my eyes and a flare of my nostrils. He roared with laughter. And so did Jenny.

"You two are insufferable. You know that?"

"Not the first time she's called me that," he told Jenny. "She also said I was full of myself."

I narrowed my eyes at him. "And I don't think I was wrong. Look at you, sauntering in here, thinking you're all that. Making eyes at the help."

"Who you calling *the help*?" Jenny demanded jokingly.

I turned to her. "Shut up. You know what I mean. But you"—I turned, pointing at Michael—"you know exactly what you're doing."

He winked. "That, I do." I heard Jenny's girlish giggle.

"This is pointless," I grumbled.

"She did call me *hot*, though, remember?"

"She did, didn't she?" Jenny agreed, looking back and forth between us.

"You are incorrigible," I said.

Michael rested his chin in his hands. His grin was endearing, but also wolfish and devouring. "Ahh, more compliments. Keep 'em coming."

I chuckled. I could see why so many women could fall for him. "I think you also might be a bit bipolar."

"What?" Jenny and Michael echoed one another.

"You were pretty rude earlier." I raised my eyebrows. "Unbearable. Mean even."

"I know," he admitted as he splayed his hands over the counter and then drew them up, crunching his fists so his knuckles popped. "You caught me at a bad time. I was already pissed about something else with work. Then you came in and reminded me that I was still a little pissed at you from yesterday. I just couldn't separate the two."

"Is that an apology?" I asked.

"I'm not saying you're entirely wrong about my father. Or

me, for that matter. But you know how it is, I can talk crap about my old man, but no one else can."

"I guess you *do* have a point," I agreed, knowing I was the same way regarding my family and friends.

"I was hoping we could call a truce. Put it all behind us." He cocked his head to the side. "Start over?"

Jenny nudged me. I could telepathically hear her screaming *Say YES!*

I sighed, knowing when to admit defeat. "Okay."

He cleared his throat and straightened his shoulders. "Hi, I'm Michael Aiden Blaire." He held out his hand, beaming a megawatt smile.

"Seriously? Why you gotta be all fancy?" I harassed.

"Because that's my full name. Even my business cards say so."

I laughed, extending my hand. "Nice to meet you, Michael Aiden Blaire. I'm Siena Giuliana Moretti." I flared my best Italian.

"Beautiful name for a beautiful woman."

"Knock it down a few notches, Romeo," I teased, subconsciously willing him to keep going.

He laughed. A deep, rich, beautiful laugh. And that smile. *A total panty-dropper*, I could hear Jenny say through our unspoken looks.

"All righty then. Our truce is agreed upon."

"You got it," I agreed.

He smiled as he turned and walked away. He'd only taken a few steps when he turned back. "Ms. Moretti?" he crooned.

"Yeah?" My cheeks heated again at the way he said my name.

He sauntered back over, leaned seductively onto the counter, and said in a low, come-hither voice, "I think I might have something you want."

The hairs on the back of my neck broke out. "You do?"

He didn't break eye contact. "I do."

I swallowed the lump in my throat, heat rising in all the best parts of my body.

"Your keys." He slid them to me with an utterly arrogant smile plastered on his perfectly chiseled face.

I cleared my throat, trying to form the words to answer. "Oh, right. Um, thanks." I smiled sweetly and shoved them into my pocket.

"Any time, Siena." He winked and walked away.

I swear I could hear him whistling as he left.

Damn fate to hell.

♥♥♥

4:22 A.M. SATURDAY, AND I WAS WIDE AWAKE. I DIDN'T EVEN need the alarm I had set in the off chance I didn't wake up from the heavy consumption of wine the night before. Pops had kept pouring, and I had kept taking. I had been in a mood, that was for sure. Despite my attempt to drink away the memories, Michael's chocolate-brown eyes and perfect smile kept flashing through my dreams.

I couldn't escape him.

He was tormenting me.

While Michael and I had called a truce, I still didn't fully trust him. How was I supposed to when I felt he had ulterior motives? I couldn't let my guard down or let him in yet. I had to play the defense for now. Keep my friends close and my enemies closer. And while Michael might not realize it, right now, he was the enemy.

The fog of my dreams disturbed me and heightened my anxiety. My heart was beating erratically, and I felt tight all over. I couldn't sleep, and I had nothing to do for the next few hours. So, I did what any sane person would do. I went downstairs, started a pot of coffee, and proceeded to stare at the walls.

I sat and waited, listening to the slow, steady trickle of the freshly brewed elixir of the gods. Impatiently counting the drip, drip, drip of the last drops as they fell into the pot.

By the time I had my first sip of the delicious eye-opening liquid, my heartbeat seemed to have returned to normal. I drummed my fingers against the kitchen table, trying to get my mind off Michael and onto something less annoying. *What to do? What to do?*

Thirty minutes later, I had a frittata ready for breakfast but couldn't put it in the oven until my grandparents were up. *What to do? What to do?* I thought again, leaning on the counter. My restlessness was palpable. A good solid workout was all I could think of to do at this hour. I rushed to my room, threw on my running gear, and wrapped my hair into a ponytail.

A run around the perimeter of the property, while the night was just beginning to fade, would be a great way to burn off some steam and repressed energy. Or, in my case, frustration. I made my way quietly back down the stairs and mapped out the route in my head. A twenty-five-minute run would do just fine. It'd allow me to clear my mind, relax, and get back in time to put breakfast in the oven and then shower.

The damage from the fire a year ago brought me to a halting stop. Instead of shrubbery, trees, and other green foliage separating our property from Grayson's, there was nothing left except a destroyed plot of land. Just dirt, charred debris, and a scorched structure of what used to be the Grayson Inn. I had to admit, it had been rundown and old, but there was something cute and quaint about it. I hadn't seen the damage up close and personal since I'd been home, unless you counted the other night when Grams and I took Michael dinner. But the darkness had concealed the pathetic and deserted sight of the ruined property.

Seeing everything in the early morning light hit me like a ton of bricks. As I scanned the wreckage, my heart twisting in my chest, I realized how lucky my grandparents were not to have been caught in the crosshairs of the disaster. Some of their vines had been damaged, but overall, they were fortunate. Unlike the Graysons.

Michael's trailer stood to the right of the dilapidated edifice. It was a bandage slapped over a wound, a superficial cover hardly hiding the ugliness of the blackened structure. When he was finished building, and the wound was healed, what would stand in its place? Images of the other Blaire properties zoomed through my brain. I had to find out what his plan was.

This land had a ton of potential, I thought, mindlessly doing some stretches. It was too bad Allan Blaire was the one who had bought it to develop. He did have beautiful properties, but the Blaire idea for hotels, and their history of ignoring the local ambiance, would hurt something deeply beautiful and serene about our town. Ideas started rushing through my head: a gazebo with a pond, walking paths with lush greenery all around, a beautiful stucco building that wasn't flashy or outrageous.

A quick movement in Michael's trailer brought me springing back to attention. The curtains in the window moved as if they'd just been pulled shut. *Shit! Oh. My. God.* I was standing there right in the open, looking like a goddamn prowler.

Despite knowing I probably wasn't that lucky, I hoped he hadn't seen me. I took off down the stretch of road separating our two properties. At least I could honestly say I was out for a run if he asked me what I'd been doing. That was the truth anyway, right? And the only reason I stopped was to see what was what in actual daylight. I wasn't trying to peek in his windows or anything.

Wild thoughts passed through my head as I jogged away: *Does he sleep naked? Was that why he moved the curtains? Because he needed to cover himself? Hmm.*

CHAPTER *Eight*

MICHAEL

I'D BEEN UP SINCE 5 A.M. I was used to staying up late and waking early, but it was so goddamned quiet out here that it was disturbing. I was used to the noises and lights of New York. But here, the lack of noise was eerie. There was nothing to listen to, nothing to look at. Except darkness. I had to admit the sunsets over the surrounding mountains were breathtaking, but aside from that, once the sun had set, it was just me, alone with my thoughts.

And my thoughts recently were consumed by a doe-eyed brunette with a mean streak.

Having nothing better to do, I called Mosby. I got her voicemail. *Probably at the gym working out.* I scrolled through my inbox, looking for something to read and take my mind off the gorgeous woman with hazel eyes.

Every time I started thinking about Siena Moretti, I wondered what her mouth would feel like. What her body would feel like. What she would feel like pressed up against me. And then I'd start thinking about what she'd look like as I slowly stripped off her clothing. *Don't go there, Blaire.*

I glanced at the clock. "Fuck it!" I threw the blankets off. I wasn't getting back to sleep now, especially in this lame ass excuse of a bed. All I was going to do was give myself blue balls. As it was, I was already sporting some serious wood.

I looked out the window across the rows of grapevines. The sky was on fire with soft clouds scattered across the electric pinks, yellows, and oranges cascading just above the mountains' peaks. Just as gorgeous as the sunsets, I noted and completely different than the scene from a New York high rise. I turned away to grab a shirt and shorts, throwing them over my shoulder. I started a pot of coffee and made my way to the other window. If I took a quick run, the coffee would be ready when I got back.

"Holy fuck." There she was. Bent over, glorious ass in perfect view. Goddamn, she was flexible. Just as I imagined she'd be. I automatically dragged my hand across myself, feeling my hard-on in my grasp. "Shit." The curtain was open—wide open. And I was standing there stroking myself. I yanked it shut and prayed she hadn't seen me. *What the fuck is she doing out there?* I peeked back out the window. Still there.

I dressed quicker than I ever had in my life. Triple-checked to see where she went. *Shit! Where'd she go?* I ran out the door.

It didn't take long to catch up, considering I sprinted like a fucking Olympian to find her. "Hey, neighbor," I called out behind her. My lungs were on fucking fire, but I tried my damnedest to keep my breathing under control.

She stopped abruptly and turned. She brought up her hand to shield her eyes from the morning rays. "H-hey." She seemed nervous.

"Nice morning for a run, huh?" My words came out in puffs from the chilled morning air. *Could I sound any more pathetic?*

"I suppose." Her breaths were coming out in clouds of white too.

"I couldn't sleep. Woke up at about five. It's too damn quiet out here." I was fucking rambling, making small talk. *Get your shit together, Blaire.*

"It's one of the perks of Monarch. Quiet. And solitude."

I could've sworn she added the last part just for me. Well, if she wanted to be alone, she shouldn't have been bending over in front of my window where I could get a perfect view of her perky ass. "Yeah, well . . . the quiet woke me up." I was aiming for lighthearted conversation, something other than business. That seemed a bit of a touchy subject with us so far.

"What do you want, Michael?"

"What do you mean?"

She shot me a look of amused frustration. "Why are you making small talk?"

"Just trying to be neighborly." I turned up my smile, flashing my pearly whites, knowing very few women could resist it.

She lifted her chin and arched a perfectly shaped eyebrow. "Uh-huh."

"I am."

She scoffed, resting a hand on her hip. "Doubtful. Something's up."

"Nothing's up." *Other than my cock a minute ago.* I held my hands up in surrender. "I saw you outside and decided I might as well join you." I didn't add that her voluptuous backside had me running out the door just to follow her. That I wanted to see up close and personal what that perfectly plump rump of hers looked like. To watch it shake and rise, bounce with every step she took while jogging.

"Well, that's too bad." She smirked. "I'm just about done." She looked at her nails, one of those classic things women do when they're trying to brush you off.

"It's okay. I'll just pick up where you leave off." I wasn't about to let her get off that easily. *Come to think of it . . .* I chuckled at my own joke.

"What's so funny?"

"Nothing," I lied. "Just thinking about how kismet this is."

"Kismet?"

"Yeah, you know . . . Destiny?"

She rolled her eyes. "I know what *kismet* means, dummy. How is *you* chasing after *me* during my morning run destiny?"

"I saw you out my window. That part is kismet. Me running after you? Well, that's just me being sociable."

"Uh-huh." A tiny chuckle escaped her.

Thank god. I had to keep her talking. Get her to see me for the person I am, not the douchebag she thought I was. "What were you doing?"

"Just looking."

I quirked an eyebrow, hopeful. "For me?" I forced my laugh, so she'd know I was flirting, as was in my good nature. I was joking . . . teasing . . . trying to make her laugh. But part of me hoped she had been looking for me.

"Don't flatter yourself, Blaire. I was looking at the property." She shooed me off, adding, "I was *not* looking for *you.*"

I didn't believe her. Maybe it was my own egotism. Then again, maybe she was telling the truth. "Well, what'd you think?"

"About what?"

"Duh." I rolled my eyes in jest. "About the property."

"Duh," she returned with a smile. "That it burned down."

"That's it?"

"That. And how sad it is there's nothing left of what used to be." The hurt in her voice got to me.

"Well, technically"—I tried to sound upbeat—"there are still a few beams that didn't totally get scorched."

She looked away in the direction of the old property. I could feel the sadness emanating from her.

I didn't know what was happening or what to do. So, I did the only thing that felt natural. I reached out and laid my hand on her shoulder. "Hey, what's wrong?"

Her eyes were brimming with tears. "Oh. God. This is just stupid." She pressed her eyes with her fingers, wiping her tears. "Ugh. You wouldn't understand."

"I can be a very understanding person."

She scoffed as her head shot up. "Yeah, right."

I chuckled. Okay, she had me there. "I think at times . . . sometimes . . . I can be empathetic." I brought my hand to her shoulder again, trying to get her to trust me and to open up. "Try me."

I didn't understand why I wanted her to tell me her feelings but standing there, watching the tears in her eyes, affected me. I didn't want to be the cause of any woman's tears. Damn women and their tears—suckered me every single time.

She breathed in, and I watched as her chest rose with a deep inhale. "I guess the easiest way to explain it is that I feel like a little bit of history was destroyed in the fire. The Grayson family was a staple in this community, and now they, and their inn, are just"—she lifted her hands in a simple, hopeless gesture—"gone." It was a genuine, emotional movement mirrored by the look in her eyes.

"I understand that."

"You do?"

"I think so. Anything that's been around and meant something is bound to stir up feelings and emotions if it's taken away. Especially if it's so sudden."

She sighed. "Yeah."

"It's tough to lose something. Especially when it symbolizes something or means a lot to you."

A small smile turned up at the edges of her beautiful lips. "Huh."

"What?"

"I guess you kind of do understand."

"See. Told ya."

"We've dealt with fires before. And other things you can't control because of good ole Mother Nature. But this? This just hits too close to home." She visibly shuddered.

"Hey." I took her hand. "Be thankful your property was saved, yeah?"

She looked at her hand in mine, then into my eyes. God,

those eyes. They shimmered in the bright morning light, glowing with flecks of gold in a sea of mossy green and earthy brown, mirroring the beauty of the area at sunrise.

"I guess that's the silver lining. I don't know what I'd do. What we'd do . . . if anything happened to the winery. It's been in our family for generations. It's everything to us."

"Your stamp on the community. Yeah, I get that too."

She broke contact, taking her hand from my grasp. She chuckled, looking at me as she wiped her hands on her thigh. "Sorry, sweaty hands."

"Right." I hadn't even noticed until she pointed it out. I didn't even care. "Are you feeling better?" I asked, hoping she wasn't going to cry again.

"Yeah. For now, I suppose."

She started walking and I fell in step beside her.

"So, let me ask you . . ." She peeked up at me. "What exactly are your plans?"

"Well, maybe some coffee and breakfast back at my place." I smirked at her.

She laughed. "No, thanks, Casanova. I've already got plans."

I feigned shock and brought my hand to my heart. "That hurts. And after I joined you for a morning run?"

"Oh, please!" She pushed me playfully. "You joined me of your own choosing. I didn't invite you."

I inhaled sharply. "You wound me again." I chuckled. "Can't a guy catch a break?"

"You? Nope." She considered her words a moment. "Maybe I can give you a break this once."

My ears perked up. "Really?"

"Yeah. Agree not to build your stupid hotel first."

I knew she wasn't joking, but seriously? Her and my dad. I couldn't seem to escape the wrath from either of them when it came to this place.

She laughed and rolled her eyes. "I know you can't pull out now. But wouldn't it be nice?"

"Nice for you, maybe. Not so nice for me." I wish it were that easy. *Then, I wouldn't have to be fighting with two people on opposite ends of the continent about this goddamned property.*

"Why's that?"

"You don't know my father. I hate . . . Ah, never mind." I didn't want to get into things regarding my father with her. That was another touchy subject that seemed best to avoid—especially considering my recent conversation with him. Maybe someday we could discuss him. But not today. I didn't have the energy to talk about Allan Blaire.

"I know enough about him," she sighed, looking up into the sky.

"Yeah. Well, let's leave that beast alone. It's such a nice morning. No need to spoil things."

"Right. Anyway, back to those plans of yours," she said, walking again.

"I was thinking we finish up here and—"

"Cut the crap, Michael. I meant the hotel. Not coffee and scones with you."

"Mmm, scones." I laughed at her sigh of exasperation. "Okay, okay." I held up my hands in defeat. She wasn't going to give up. She was persistent as hell, and instead of brushing her off, I figured it might help to give her a glimpse. "Overall picture? Luxury rooms and amenities. Very posh. Very upscale."

"And you're probably going to install a string of tennis courts."

"Maybe."

"And a huge pool."

"Naturally."

She stopped us again. "Probably multiple pools. And hot tubs."

I laughed. "Have you already seen the plans? I haven't

even seen them yet. How is it you seem to know more about them than I do?" I teased. She was pretty spot on. I'd give her that.

She rolled her eyes and threw her hands up. "Typical. Just typical." Her mood was shifting. *Shit.*

"Typical of *most* hotels, Siena."

"No." She narrowed her eyes at me. "Typical of E Hotels. Come in, take over, and bulldoze everything with only one goal in mind."

"And what's that?" I couldn't take my eyes off her. Even if she was spitting mad at me.

"Just selfishly build whatever you want because that's what you want, never once considering other people or the community you're building in. And you always get your way." She huffed, crossing her arms across her beautiful chest.

"Hey, money talks, honey. And why are you blaming me for my father's ideas?"

"Because you're the one implementing them."

"That's my job. I don't design the buildings. I just execute the plans." I could feel my blood pressure rising. "And I do a damn good job of it," I added. Why did our conversations always come back to this?

"Even if it's at the expense of the people who live and work here?" she spat back.

I was getting frustrated with her—her and her fucking opinions. Something about her pulled me to her. And that mouth. Goddamn, that mouth. Never failed that at some point that mouth was going to spit fire and fury at me. I couldn't help it. Something about her was magnetic, and I was like a moth to a flame.

"What are you talking about?" I asked.

"Your fancy hotel with your fancy amenities. Pools, health spas, tennis courts, beauty salons." Her hands were flying as she grew more and more intense. "A fancy bar where all your rich guests will go to drink and party."

I grabbed her hands and held them. "Is that what you're worried about?"

"Wh-what? What are you talking about?"

"All the things we will offer our guests. That we'll take away business from you?"

"I-I . . ." She yanked her hands out of my grasp. "I can't think when you're holding my hands."

I wiggled my eyebrows at her. "Nice to see I *do* affect you."

"Oh! Shut up!" She shoved me. "Get over yourself, Michael. I'm Italian," she sneered. "I need my hands to talk."

"Ah. Okay. Please," I said, turning my hand over. "Proceed."

She scoffed. "You're annoying. I don't remember what I was saying."

I smirked. I knew I was getting under her skin. And for some sick and twisted reason, I was enjoying our sparring match. "You were saying," I began for her, "you don't like the fact our hotels offer our guests the best amenities available."

"That's not what I said. It's not about that."

I kept quiet. I knew when to keep my mouth shut. Most of the time. I wasn't about to dig the hole even deeper for myself. I needed to politely wait for her to finish what she wanted to say. Then, I could figure out a way to fix it. Or finagle her over to my side.

She threw her hands up again, in that true virtuoso Italian spirit. "It's all too much. Why can't you build something simple and natural? I don't get why everything has to be done so outrageously."

"We want to offer the best things for our guests, Siena. Isn't that what you and your grandparents aim to do?"

"I guess."

"You guess?" I scoffed. "Please."

"Okay, yes. That is our goal."

"Then give it a rest. People in glass houses shouldn't throw stones."

Her eyes bugged out as she put her hands on her hips, elbows sticking out. "I am *not* throwing stones!"

I laughed at her. Standing there like she was, she knew I had her.

"Ugh! Whatever, Michael!"

"Now, now. Don't get your panties twisted."

"Ha!" She stuck a finger in my face. "They're not twisted, 'cause . . ." She caught herself, trapped by her sensuous mouth, and, hopefully, her dirty mind.

"'Cause why?" I raised a brow. She had piqued my interest. My imagination was running wild over her slip of the tongue. Mmm, her tongue. I couldn't keep my eyes off her mouth now as my mind wandered. *Thong? G-string? Commando?* My eyes rolled heavenward. *Oh, dear Lord!*

"Nothing," she brushed me off, not finishing her sentence.

"What?" I asked as I silently begged, *Please, please, please finish the sentence.*

"Anyway," she evaded, and started walking again.

I couldn't help but try to sneak another peek to get a good, solid look at her panty line. Or lack thereof.

Oh, damn. No line.

I smiled after her, adjusted myself . . . again . . . and followed where she led.

Her grandparents' house stood a short distance away. The stonework was incredible and provided an impression of strength and stability, fortified with what I had already learned from the three of them was unconditional love. A strong structure that held all the memories of their family, their history, their legacy. Three archways enclosed the balcony on the second story, pillars dissecting the arches.

I wondered which window was hers. Wondered if the inside of the house would feel just as warm and welcoming as it looked on the outside. I detected a flowery perfume sweetening the air, a hint of night-blooming jasmine that must have just closed its buds with the sunrise. It was mixed with the hint of orange blossoms, the same smell I couldn't help but notice every time I drove through the area.

We stood awkwardly, neither of us knowing what to say next. I didn't want to continue the debate over the property. And, I was fairly sure, despite her fiery nature, she was probably at her wits' end about it right now too.

She looked at the house, then back at me. "I guess this concludes our time together. I'll just . . ." She kicked at the dirt. "See ya around."

"See ya around? Come on, Siena. We're not breaking up."

The corners of her mouth twisted into a hint of a smile.

"We haven't even had our first date yet," I teased.

"God, you are so ridiculous." Her eyes sparkled with amusement.

"All right then."

"Don't you mean '*all righty*'?" she joked, air-quoting the words.

I winked and leaned in close, looking her square in the eyes. "All righty then," I corrected, wiggling my eyebrows.

She laughed, shoving me playfully. "What is it with you and that phrase?"

I grabbed her around the waist and pulled her toward me. She didn't push me away. She looked up at me, blinking.

"Damn, I love your eyes," I said without thinking.

She groaned, burying her head against my chest. I felt her breath and her breasts, hot against me.

I couldn't help it. Her body against mine was getting to me. I lifted her face so I could look her in the eyes. Fuck, I wanted to kiss her so badly in that moment. But I didn't know what she would do. Kiss me back? Or kick me in the nuts? I decided not to risk it . . . this time.

What we did from here was yet to be determined. Meeting her was serendipity. It had to be. And, of course, my impromptu plan of chasing her down this morning didn't hurt. I couldn't stop thinking about the lack of a panty line I'd spied on our run. And her mouth—her beautiful, pouty, full mouth—I wanted to sample. *Focus, pal.*

"I gotta get back." She pulled away. "Breakfast. Chores. Work."

"I will bid you *addio* until next time." I pulled her hand to my lips and kissed it.

"'Kay," she said softly, smiling at my use of the Italian word for goodbye.

"Siena?"

"Yeah?" The word was barely a whisper.

"See ya around."

I didn't wait for her to respond, grinning as I jogged off.

CHAPTER Nine

SIENA

THE WEEKENDS WERE OUR BUSIEST days at the winery. We were only open Thursday through Sunday, but we got plenty of business—first-timers and our regulars who were like family. While our winery was family-owned and operated, and while it was on the small side compared to chain operations around the country, we produced a variety of wines that appealed to almost every wine enthusiast.

A little after two o'clock, I offered to go with Pops while he led a tour. He could've taken them on his own, and vice versa, but I knew he enjoyed working as a team. Jenny and Grams could hold down the fort back in the tasting room while we were gone.

This afternoon, our group consisted of four couples who were taking a weekend getaway in San Diego to celebrate their friend's birthday. Vickie, the birthday girl, her husband, her three best girlfriends, Joanna, Clara, and Georgie, and their husbands formed a semi-circle around me. We were gathered on the patio of the tasting room while I explained the history of our winery.

"Moretti Vineyards began with my great-great-grandfather, Salvatore Moretti, who immigrated to America in the early 1900s. He came from a small village outside of Florence in the Tuscany region of Italy. Not one for books, Grandpa

Sal spent most of his youth working in the vineyards near his home. Over the years, he saved every lira he could, keeping his savings stored in a small box his father had made."

A movement out of my peripheral caught my attention.

Everyone followed my gaze.

All eyes watched as Michael made his way over. He was wearing a T-shirt and jeans. And that same damned baseball cap I had met him in. He looked so damn cute in it, and I couldn't resist his sexy boyish appeal. He could probably wear anything and look delicious. In a baseball cap, though, I wondered if he didn't have some kind of hidden agenda like I thought he had that day in the tasting room. When he tricked me.

He shook hands with Pops and smiled at Vickie and her friends. They were mesmerized. I knew the look. The same stupid look I constantly tried to hide on my own face.

"Sorry for the interruption, folks. Don't mind me. I'm just the friendly neighbor coming over to enjoy some fresh air and beautiful scenery. You don't mind if I join you, do you?" His gaze landed on me. I tried my best for a neutral, unaffected look.

I heard Vickie and her gal pals giggle in amusement as they agreed. They clearly weren't immune to the physical beauty of Michael either. Everyone was looking at me again.

And I was at a loss for words.

"Sorry, Siena. Please, continue," Michael prompted.

I had to clear my throat to get my voice back. "Yes. So, Salvatore Moretti immigrated to America in the early 1900s. He came here from a small village outside of Florence—"

"Honey, you already told us that," Joanna, Vickie's friend, said, a knowing laugh in her voice.

Michael rocked back and forth on his feet, what I had already come to know as his cockiest, self-satisfied smile in place.

"Oh, right." My cheeks heated, and I swore they were

flushed bright red. *Get a grip. Him being here isn't a big deal.* "Sorry. Where was I?"

"At the part about how he saved all his lira," Vickie reminded me.

"Yes, right. So, he was in love with the daughter of the man he worked for, a wealthy and prominent Tuscan winemaker. Knowing his beloved was already betrothed to another and that he could never offer her the kind of life she deserved, he tried to break things off. But Giuliana was determined to marry for love, not obligation. And so, she convinced him to elope with her and start over in America. For weeks she saved seeds and protected them inside homemade envelopes or stored them in glass jars. She spent the last week at home, secretly meeting her husband-to-be in the vines, late at night, cutting and pruning branches they would bring to America. Salvatore and Giuliana finally left Italy *together*, determined to develop wines that reflected and honored their Italian heritage and their love. Two things they always held near and dear to their hearts."

The women swooned, dabbing at their eyes as I turned toward the vines. "Let's head out to the vineyard and look at the original vines Salvatore and Giuliana planted." I led the group, quickly turning away from Michael's stare. He was watching me a little too intently, looking through me. But I didn't know if it was me overreacting to him being here or if I was just insecure.

I took the group through the most historic portion of our tour first, explaining how my great-great-grandfather had planted the first vines in the north. "Grapevines are incredibly vigorous, so cutting and transplanting from his original plants resulted in the expansion of more live grapevines. As you can see, he started here with these first plants, and then expanded bit by bit over time toward the edges of the property lines." I let my arms direct our group's attention to the flow of vines.

"It's so beautiful," Vickie sighed.

A throat cleared. "Yes, beautiful. Over there is where the vineyard connects to my property." Michael pointed to the divide. All heads turned and followed his gaze.

"What's your property?" Clara asked, confusion evident in her question.

I snorted a bit too loudly. Michael turned to look at me. His eyes narrowed under his baseball cap. "Well, right now, it's just a lot of dirt and debris. The original building burned down."

"Oh no, what happened?" Georgie asked, genuinely concerned. She had no idea it wasn't his property that had been destroyed.

"Oh, he's building a huge, massive hotel," I butted in.

"I'm going to be building a *new* hotel. We just bought the land a few months ago and have been in negotiations with developers, contractors, etcetera."

"So, what burned down?" Georgie asked.

"The former hotel," I said.

"Inn," Michael amended. "It burned down in the wildfires. We purchased the land with plans to renovate it and transform what was there into a spacious and luxurious hotel," he explained as he produced his business cards from his pocket and handed one to each lady. "Blaire Enterprises will be happy to welcome you on a future visit. Please feel free to contact me, and I will upgrade you to one of our exclusive suites."

The women giggled enthusiastically, taking the proffered cards.

"That would be amazing," Vickie said.

"It's gonna be something," I added sarcastically, quickly covering my snide tone with a cough, so my guests wouldn't detect my bitterness.

Michael chuckled, picking up on it. "Yes, it is," he agreed. And something about the way he said those words made my skin heat.

Feeling flushed with excitement again, I turned my focus back to the group. I began walking, telling them, "When the vines were strong enough to be transplanted without damaging them, Salvatore and Giuliana cut and transferred the larger ones to different areas, which enabled them to grow more grapes. And over his years of developing the land, he added more varieties. Year after year, our friends, family, and employees, worked hard to cultivate our vineyard into what you see today." I extended my arms, gesturing to the expanse of land in front of them. From this vantage point, they could see almost every acre we occupied.

Michael was walking a little too close for comfort, and I was nervous he'd be able to feel the heat emanating from my skin. When we stopped again, his arm brushed up against mine, and I could feel the wispy hairs on his arm tickle me. His dropped hand brushed against mine as he maneuvered to the side of the group. "Sorry," he said as our eyes met and held for a moment longer than necessary.

I was both excited and irritated by his flirtation. Something about him triggered the woman in me. I tried reminding myself that I should be turned off by him because, technically, he was the enemy. Or something akin to it. Even though I had sworn off men, and even though this man infuriated me, I couldn't help the flutter of butterflies stirring inside me. My feelings were at war, and I didn't know what I should do about them. Roll over and surrender, or stand up, fight, and never back down? I stole a glance at him.

And the look he was giving me was so deliciously enticing.

Fuck it, I finally decided. *What's so bad about a little harmless flirtation?*

♥ ♥ ♥

WE MADE OUR WAY TO THE FINAL PORTION OF THE TOUR, showing everyone our facilities and the overall process of cultivating the grapes to the delectable liquid they would enjoy shortly. I stood next to a set of original barrels that we had preserved and put on display, then turned and addressed the group. "Here at Moretti Vineyards, we believe that our land is a continuation of our family's legacy. Our wine holds a powerful connection to our past, our present, and our future. Moretti Vineyards is firmly rooted in the connection to our heritage, and it is with pride and love that we share our traditions with you. Wherever you are, and wherever you go, make time to enjoy a bottle of great wine with people who fill your life and your heart with happiness. Every one of our bottles is created with family in mind. And we hope you come to love Moretti as part of your own family."

The friends chatted and asked a few questions on our way back. I smiled as I overheard Vickie say, "I never knew so much patience went into making wine. I thought you just had to stomp and smash the grapes like on *I Love Lucy*." She giggled, "I knew there was more to it, but wow!" She turned, looking around at everything. "This is all so incredible. Such a great experience." She joined hands with her best girlfriends and pulled them in for a hug.

"We hope you enjoy your time here with us." I stopped at a table reserved for them when we arrived back at the tasting room. "*La nostra famiglia è la tua famiglia*. Our family is your family." Everyone smiled, looking at one another. "And here, where we will bid farewell for now, I'll leave you with our philosophy. Our wine is everything life is supposed to be—exhilarating, wild, and fulfilling. We hope you find pleasure when you drink with us. *Salute*."

I caught Michael's gaze as I turned to go. He raised his glass. "*Salute*."

I handed each guest tickets for complimentary tastings. "I always like to suggest our sangiovese for red lovers and the pinot grigio for white enthusiasts, but please feel free to peruse through our lists and select whatever tickles your fancy. I will be available if you have any questions or need recommendations. And Jenny and my grandmother, Sophia, the Moretti family's matriarch, are available as well. We will be more than happy to assist you should you need anything. I'll have a complimentary appetizer sent to your table." I bid them farewell and started walking back to the bar when Michael sauntered up to my side.

"That was very nice," he said, joining me.

I stopped at an empty table. "What was?"

"Free wine and appetizers."

"Just part of the service. But I liked them, so I gave them something extra on the house."

"Well, I just might have to come and get a *private tour*."

His suggestion made my stomach flutter, and I was silently listing all the places on my body he might want to start his journey. I tried to control my nerves, telling myself not to blush. I grinned. "Notice I said I liked *them*."

"Ha ha. Although, for some reason, I don't think you're joking."

"You know, you could always just buy some wine and appetizers."

"But I enjoyed the tour. And I like the way you talk."

My eyebrow rose in speculation.

He groaned with annoyance. "I meant how you talk about the winery. You come alive. And everything was really interesting."

I kept silent, playing with him. Just to see if I could make him squirm.

"Really. I was genuinely impressed and enjoyed myself. How is it you got to know everybody on the tour in such a short amount of time?"

I smiled, feeling a teensy bit of satisfaction that he seemed affected by me too. "Pops passed down the teachings of my great-great-grandfather who said, 'If we treat our customers like family, we will create a lasting relationship with them. Just like paying attention to every detail in the vineyard, we pay close attention to our guests. So they feel the essence of Moretti Vineyards. So they feel a familial connection to us.'" I lifted my hand. "Thus, we produce what you just witnessed—an immediate connection—an everlasting link. They feel like part of our family, a part of us, and they become loyal to our name, just like it was their own."

"Impressive." He tucked his hands in his pockets, rocking back and forth on his toes. "You just might make a fan out of me yet."

"How's that?"

"I like wine, but I've always been more of a beer man. But you? You could definitely persuade me to the dark side." I felt a flurry of excitement rush through me.

"The dark side, huh?" The butterflies danced in my stomach. All these sexy remarks and innuendos were getting to me.

His eyes sparkled with mischief. "Yep. Definitely."

Pops sidled up to us. "What are you two jibber-jabbering about over here?"

"Michael was just complimenting us on the tour."

"Well, you are more than welcome to stay awhile. Order whatever you like. On the house," Pops said as he walked off.

"At least your grandpa likes me. He invited me to stay and eat."

"Yeah." I touched his upper arm in a friendly manner. "Just let one of us know what you want." His arm felt rock solid and had me wondering what he did to work out.

"Unfortunately, I need to get back to work. I've spent longer taking a break than I planned."

"Okay. Then I guess I'll see you." I stopped to think. "Whenever I see you."

"Hopefully sooner rather than later." The butterflies took flight again. "Oh, and Siena?"

"Yeah?"

He took a step toward me and leaned in close. "There's plenty I want."

I could *feel* his words. His breath was minty fresh and warm.

"And I will definitely let you know." He winked and strolled away.

♥ ♥ ♥

"What'd tall, dark, and handsome want?" Jenny purred, waggling her brows.

"Huh?" I asked, grabbing a towel and wiping down absolutely nothing on the counter.

"Don't play coy with me." She snatched it out of my hands.

"He's just flirting with me."

"Mm-hmm."

"What?" I squeaked.

"*What?*" she mocked.

"I have absolutely no interest in him," I retorted, desperately trying to get the damn shriek out of my voice.

She scoffed. "Yeah, right!"

"Seriously! After my most recent debacle, I have sworn off men. But it's still fun to flirt."

"What do you mean *you've sworn off men*? We all need a little somethin' somethin' from time to time," she crooned.

"The last thing I need is another man fucking up my life. Again."

"But he's a really *hot* man!"

"Regardless of his hotness, I do not need to start something with a guy who's just going to leave."

"That's the perfect way to get over an ex! Get under a new one. Or on top." She waved her hands. "Whichever." She winked. "Any kind of way with *that* man would suffice."

I rolled my eyes at her.

"What better way to get over Tim? You get revenge and a cathartic release. Not to mention a couple of hot romps in the hay with that delicious slice of man." She dusted her hands together. "Problem solved!"

"He probably doesn't even look at me that way. Bet he's got a string of girls he's already doing that with."

"So?" *She has a point.* "So? You know, rubbers?" she asked again, waiting for a logical answer, to which I had none.

"I just need to focus on myself right now."

"And how is getting some action from that hot piece *not* focusing on you?"

I laughed. "True. But I need to work on getting my crap back on track too."

She slapped me with the towel and shook it at me. "You are hopeless."

"I know. I'm pathetic."

"What you need is someone to help you get over Tim. Some no-strings-attached seriously intense sex."

"What I really need is a night with my friends."

"Done. Monday night, girls' night!"

"Perfect." I grabbed her in a hug and kissed her cheek.

I laughed as she danced her happy dance, unladylike movements on her tiptoes, jumping back and forth and wiggling her ass as she texted Lauren and Audrey in our group chat.

♥ ♥ ♥

I hadn't talked to Nev much since I'd arrived. Her job kept her busy, and lately, she'd had to work extra hours. Not to mention she was seeing some new guy, and she was a teensy bit obsessed with him. It gave me something to tease her about. I wasn't prepared for what she told me.

"Tim tried getting ahold of you again. He showed up at my place yesterday. I told him you weren't available."

"I blocked him, so he can't call or text me."

"He said as much. I told him you obviously didn't want to talk to him. Said if you ever wanted to get in touch with him, he'd know."

"Thanks. I don't need his shit right now."

"I didn't mention you'd left. I know you didn't want him to know."

"Thanks."

"So . . ." she began, knowing I didn't want to focus on Tim, "how's everything going in Monarch?"

After my quick chat with Nev, I grabbed a jacket and told Pops and Grams I was going for a walk. Talking to Nev stirred up my emotions, reignited my anger, and if I was honest, a little bit of sadness. I knew I had to get in touch with Tim. I just wasn't quite ready to yet. Getting ahold of him was the only way to take care of the one thing still tying me to him. Nev was a true friend. She was my best friend in San Francisco, and again, she proved just how awesome a friend she was by protecting me from my shitbag of an ex.

Even though I shivered as tiny goosebumps dotted my arms, it was such a nice evening. It was cool, but not freezing. I tilted my head up, taking in the beauty of the brilliant full moon. Its light cast a brilliant glow, a candescent light that illuminated the winery and bathed the hillsides in white-silver luminance. It was a cloudless night, and, being so far away from the city, I could hear nothing but the chirp of crickets, the rustling of leaves, and the beating of my own heart. The trees in the distance were silhouetted against a deep velvety sky. Sometimes the nights were so dark the blackness almost swallowed you whole. But tonight? Tonight was a gorgeous splendor, and I hoped a walk under the moonlight would help clear my mind.

Fresh air was what I needed. Fresh air and no one to distract me. I loved my grandparents and my friends—my extended family. But right now, I just needed to be alone with my thoughts. I could smell the night-blooming jasmine. Its flowers opened, perfuming the air with its sweet musky scent. As a child, Pops had taught me great-great-grandpa Moretti's tradition of strategically planting trees, flowers, and herbs near the vines to enhance the flavors and aromas of our beautiful bouquets. Cherry, lavender, currant, black pepper, rosemary, raspberry could be recognized in the undertones with just one sniff or taste.

I knew in my heart that breaking up with Tim was the right thing to do, but I still felt a deep sense of loss. Although nothing as intensely romantic or as beautiful as what my grandparents shared, we'd had a decent relationship. Maybe that was the problem. I never felt connected to him in a deep way, the way my grandparents seemed to be. They had always been the shining example of what a true and loving relationship was and should be. Tim and I'd had great sex. At least in the beginning. We'd had great communication. Again, in the beginning. We'd made plans for the future. Plans of opening our own restaurant. It had all seemed normal and exciting. Until he ruined everything.

I wondered now, even if he hadn't cheated, would I have stayed?

"I don't know," I said aloud to myself. "I just don't know."

"Don't know what?" a deep voice asked.

CHAPTER Ten

MICHAEL

SIENA SCREAMED, CLASPING HER HAND over her heart. Her chest heaved up and down as she took deep breaths. I grabbed her by the elbow, and she moved to lash out like I was a predator.

I held her at arm's length, trying to avoid her strikes. "It's just me. It's Michael."

"Jesus H. Christ! What the hell?!" She pulled out of my grasp. "You scared me! Fucking A," she gasped, still trying to catch her breath. I patted her on the back and rubbed gentle circles.

"I'm sorry, I thought you heard me." I took a deep breath, trying to keep myself under control. But I couldn't keep it together. I started laughing hysterically.

She punched my shoulder. "What's so damn funny?"

"Ow!" I pretended to be in pain as I rubbed the spot where she'd hit me. Siena rose to full height and stood with her hands on her hips, waiting for me to explain myself.

"Okay." I took a breath. "Okay." I took another. "Oh, man. That was some funny shit. Here you are talking to yourself. I come up thinking you're talking to me and I scare the living shit out of you. And all because I was trying to be nice and bring back your dishes." I held them up as proof. "See? All nice and clean."

She looked confused. "You walked over here to bring back a dish?"

"Mm-hmm."

"In the dark?"

"Yep." I patted my jacket pocket. "But I do have that trusty flashlight button on my phone. You know, just in case it gets dark. Or I get scared," I teased.

"Yeah. Like someone jumping out of the bushes at you?"

"I didn't jump. And I wasn't in the bushes."

"You were totally lurking."

"No, I like, *totally* wasn't." I imitated a Valley Girl.

"Then what *do* you call what you were doing?"

"Taking a delightful walk in the moonlight. Bringing back your dishes."

"Oh, you mean from the brownies you *hate*," she mocked in a deep voice. Clearly, she was still a little bent out of shape about me insulting her. I was surprised she hadn't brought them up before.

She had every right to confront me. If she'd only known the truth. "I didn't hate them," I confessed.

"Probably threw them in the trash." She pouted as she kicked at a pebble on the ground. "And they are *delicious*, by the way."

She didn't have to tell me twice. "Were," I corrected her.

"Were what?"

"Delicious." Her head cocked, confused. "Your brownies were delicious," I added.

"I thought you *hated brownies*." She mocked me again in a burly, snotty voice, screwing up her face.

"I lied . . . And I'm sorry."

That shut her up. It appeared she didn't know what to say to my admission.

"I wanted to make you mad."

She scoffed, "Well, you did a good job."

"Good."

"Wait, what? Why'd you want to make me mad? I was trying to apologize."

"Like I told you before, I was still a little irritated with you. Then you were there in my trailer, pissing me off again. So . . ." I shrugged. What else could I say?

She rolled her eyes. "So, you thought you'd insult me? Real mature."

I grinned. "It worked, didn't it?"

"Yeah," she sneered. "No."

I laughed at her words, how she contradicted herself. "Which one is it? Yeah or no?"

Her lips fought to suppress a smile. "No," she said, but the corners of her mouth said otherwise.

"You're lying. Of course, it did. I've already learned that much about you, darlin'. But we've already made a truce. Let's not fuck it up again by arguing."

She raised her hands in agreement. "All right." Her quick acquiescence surprised me.

I quickly regrouped. "Good. Because you and me? We agreed to start over. We're gonna be friends, the two of us."

"Seriously, what kind of person doesn't like brownies?" she asked me. "A crazy person," she answered herself, twirling her hand next to her head with her finger extended. "Cuckoo, cuckoo," she added, imitating a bird.

I chuckled, rolling my eyes. "Well, I promise you I'm not crazy."

"Yeah, right," she scoffed, tucking a flyaway hair behind her ear, "that's what all the crazies say."

This chick cracked me up, ticked me off, made me smile, made me cringe. One minute I wanted to smother her with a pillow, the next, I wanted to smother her with kisses. Everywhere.

Her skin glowed in the moonlight. My god, she was fucking lovely.

"Hey? Where'd you go?" Her velvety-sweet voice brought me out of my reverie.

"Huh? Oh, sorry. What were you saying?"

"That you're crazy."

My Cheshire-cat grin widened across my face. "Right." I was so mesmerized by her I didn't have a wiseass comeback.

"Well, I guess I'll just take those from you."

I held them out, close enough that she'd have to take a step forward. A mouse lured to the trap with the promise of a tasty treat if she'd just take one teeny, tiny step.

She took it. And then I grabbed her by the waist and pulled her into me. Damn, she smelled good. "I think we should stop fighting this thing between us." I looked down at her, waiting. Begging silently for her to reply. I lowered my head, ready to get a taste.

"Siena?" her grandmother called out for her from the house.

Impeccable timing.

She blinked, looking into my eyes. "Yeah?" she called, not for a moment breaking eye contact. Our lips were almost touching.

"You coming back inside soon?" Sophia asked.

I knew she couldn't see us, but suddenly I felt like a teenager trying to sneak my girl into the house without my parents finding out.

"Yeah," she answered. She smiled guiltily and immediately broke out of my hold. I heard her giggle as she pulled my hand and dragged me with her.

"What are you doing?" I groaned, linking my free hand with hers.

"You wanted to bring our stuff back. Well, you're bringing it back."

I squeezed her hand. "We're not through with this yet."

"Yeah, yeah," she sniggered.

"Now who's being insufferable?" I taunted.

She snorted. "Now you know how it feels."

"Did you just snort?"

"Don't make fun of me. Snorting is one of my more endearing qualities."

I walked through the door and into the kitchen, following Siena. Her grandparents were sitting at the table enjoying a nightcap.

"Grams, Pops. Look who I caught lurking in our bushes."

I shot her a look of mock irritation.

"Oh, what a nice surprise."

Siena rolled her eyes at her grandmother.

"Michael." Sal half stood, outstretching his hand to me. "What brings you by?"

"Well, besides playing hide-and-seek with Siena here, I was actually just bringing your dishes back, Mrs. Moretti."

"Now, now. We've been through this already, Michael. Call me Sophia."

"Sophia. Sorry."

"Sit, sit." She patted the seat next to her. "No formalities needed in this house."

I placed the dishes on the table. "Sorry. Just the ingrained training of my mother." I immediately felt at home with them as I took a seat.

"No need to be sorry. Unless you call me Mrs. Moretti again." She wagged her finger at me, a sparkle in her eye. "Can we get you anything? Coffee? A nightcap?"

"Coffee'd be great."

I topped off my mug with a massive amount of cream. Siena smiled at me and gave a nod of approval. "Just like Pops and me," she said, bringing her mug to her perfectly pink, pouty lips.

My eyes were glued to hers. I couldn't tell what she was thinking. But like me, she also didn't have the strength to look away. *Good. Keep your eyes on me, beautiful.*

Ever so slowly, the corners of her delicious lips creased

into a smile. I felt the quirk of my lips, and the look that passed between us was heavy and sensual. The suggestiveness of her expression shot a bolt of heat right through me. *Thank god I'm sitting at the table,* I thought, wondering how in the hell I'd explain my current awkward physical situation to the woman's grandparents.

Sal cleared his throat, and I immediately felt sheepish. "How are things going over at Grayson's?"

I begrudgingly tore my eyes away from his gorgeous granddaughter. "Fine, for now." *Jesus Christ, Blaire, keep your fuckin' head in the game. You're in their house, for fuck's sake.* I shifted in my chair, trying to alleviate the ache in my balls. "There's still a lot to do. Still a lot up in the air."

"You're not done yet?" Siena asked me.

I laughed. "Not even close. There's a lot of balls being juggled. Lots of decisions to be finalized." My mind jumped to my father and the wrath I had endured during our latest conversation.

A schoolgirl giggle escaped her, and she covered her mouth.

"Siena, really now? Do you have to be so crass?" I laughed, feeling the immediate need to poke fun at her. I couldn't help but tease her. Plus, I needed to lighten my own thoughts and forget about my father's ultimatum.

"You're the one talking about balls."

Sophia and Sal exchanged a look and erupted in laughter.

"See?" She jerked her thumb at them. "They're just as bad as I am."

They didn't stop laughing, which made Siena and me laugh harder. They were so easy to talk to, so easy to get along with. So easy to just sit with and be *me*.

"Where do you think I get it from?" She shook her head mockingly.

"Keeps us young at heart, Michael," Sal said, a twinkle in his eyes.

"I bet," I agreed. Who could argue with that logic? "I've been on the phone all day talking with planners, contractors. Everyone and their mother." I didn't dare mention my father. I knew where that might lead and was willing to do anything to avoid that cataclysmic disaster.

"Sounds like quite the feat," Sophia chimed in.

"When do you think you'll break ground?" Sal asked as he took Sophia's hand.

I looked at their joined hands. "We still have a couple of weeks yet, maybe a month or so. But hopefully, soon."

My stomach flipped as my nerves shot into overdrive. I wanted to tell them more, but things were going so smoothly right now between Siena and me. I didn't want to rock the boat.

"Well, is it a big secret, or do we get to see your plans?" Sal asked the question I knew Siena wanted to know. If I knew her at all, and I thought I had gotten a rather good read on her thus far, she'd probably been dying to ask it herself.

"I'd be happy to as soon as they arrive. Everything's still in the works, but my father never disappoints." This statement was true, I could confidently admit. I just had to find a way to get him to back off about the winery.

Siena scoffed, rolling her eyes.

"Siena!" Sophia admonished her.

"What?"

"I'm sure we'll all be very impressed with what you've created," Sal interjected, trying to circumvent another impending battle between the two of us.

"I'd be more than happy to show you once Mosby sends them."

"Mosby?" he asked.

"Yes. Our architect. She's brilliant."

Siena opened her mouth to retort, but Sophia cut her off, "That'd be wonderful. Wouldn't it, Siena?"

Siena gave her a sideways glare. "Yeah." She plastered on one of the fakest smiles I'd ever seen. "Just dandy."

"Great," I copied her tone and insincere smile. I knew it'd get to her.

"Can't wait." Her voice was laced with sarcasm. But I didn't mind. It turned up the heat just a little more. Moth to flame. Even though she seemed annoyed, I was certain part of her annoyance was because of her attraction to me. I felt the same way regarding her.

I cocked my head and switched tactics. "We should go for another run tomorrow morning." I smiled my most charming of smiles—The Panty Dropper. It worked like a charm. Every. Single. Time.

I could see the immediate change in her eyes. "Huh?" Confusion rippled across her face. I could see the wheels turning in that brain of hers as her pupils dilated. The slight twinge of annoyance and angst evaporated and was replaced with a softer, more relaxed look.

It was my job to read people. I made a living at it. And the change in her eyes told me I could ask her to run a marathon tomorrow morning, and she'd consent. She'd probably agree to almost anything in this moment.

"Siena?" I asked, claiming her hand.

"Hmm?" She looked at our entwined fingers.

"A run? Tomorrow morning?"

Siena shook her head, probably trying to clear her thoughts. "Sure. That's fine."

"Can't wait," I copied her earlier choice of words and winked. "I'll be here at, what?" I checked my watch. "Seven? That work for you?"

"Seven is fine," she said nodding.

"Gotta find a way to release all this energy I seem to have found out here." I winked at Siena. I knew she got my innuendo when her cheeks flushed a bit.

I bid the Morettis good night, making sure to thank

Sophia again for her wonderful hospitality. I genuinely liked them. The fact I was attracted to Siena had nothing to do with her grandparents, and me liking her grandparents had absolutely nothing to do with her.

I looked forward, a little bit more than I had initially, to the time I'd be spending out here. It wasn't as awful as I thought it was going to be. The fact I had a particular interest in Siena shouldn't affect things if we both knew upfront that this was not a long-term thing. We had our own lives and our own careers to focus on. And, if I were completely honest with her, and if we agreed on terms, physically speaking, things would be fine. If she didn't have any interest in me, no skin off my nose.

But if she felt anything close to what I was feeling, why not mix a little business with pleasure?

It'd be a win-win situation.

CHAPTER Eleven

SIENA

GIRLS' NIGHT OUT—OR RATHER, *In*.
Jenny's place was a cute two-bedroom house she'd bought years ago. She'd gutted the entire place, renovating it from floor to ceiling with her father and brothers. Her dad had taught her everything she knew about construction, and she worked for him at their family hardware store when she wasn't at the winery.

She had torn down the dividing wall between the living and dining rooms, creating an open concept. The large room had light cornflower blue walls with a navy accent wall. A brick fireplace, which she'd painted white, glowed with pillar candles of various sizes instead of logs.

A huge cream-colored couch big enough to seat five people sat in the center of the room, along with two navy club chairs. And pillows galore in bright colors from every hue of the rainbow added pops of color and a cheery brightness that matched Jenny's personality. The sofa was so cushy and soft, you almost wanted to take a nap every time you sat on it.

With four bottles of Moretti wine and my overnight bag in tow, I walked up the front steps and through the screen door. "I'm here," I called out, setting my bag down, "and I come bearing gifts." I walked through to the kitchen and placed the bag of wine on the counter. "Something smells good." Two pots rested on the stove—one simmering with sauce and one with water for pasta.

Jenny's hair was braided, silver studs in her ears. A white eyelet apron was tied around her waist. She had jeans and a deep purple top on, her feet clad in fuzzy slippers.

"Ooh." She rubbed her hands together. "Wine, wine, wine, and more wine," she counted out as she retrieved the bottles one by one. She smiled broadly, full of excitement. "You're in charge of the garlic bread," she instructed as she slid a loaf of French bread to me. "I'll do the salad."

She watched as I minced several cloves of garlic. "That's an awful lot of garlic."

"You planning on kissing anyone tonight?" I teased. "'Cause I'm not."

She thought for a moment, contemplating. "Nope."

"Didn't think so." I laughed.

I grated a cup of parmesan and added half of it to the butter mixture. Combining everything into a delicious buttery spread and slathering the bread halves, I sprinkled the top with a little more parmesan. It would crisp up nicely in the oven. "You can never have too much cheese," I said with a flair of my wrist.

"And wine." She motioned to the wine. "Speaking of which"—she topped the salad with avocado and seasoning—"I don't know why we're sitting here talking and cooking without any vino in our hands."

"Done." I grabbed the wine opener off the counter.

"Normally, I'd let the wine breathe for a bit, but fuck it. Just pour." She held out her glass to me.

"Cheers!" I clinked my glass with hers, and we both sipped.

"Ding dong!" Audrey and Lauren sang together as they came through the screen door. It slammed behind them as they hurried through to us.

They screamed, dropping their bags to run to me and embraced me in a tight hug.

♥ ♥ ♥

WE SAT AT JENNY'S TABLE, SUFFICIENTLY BUZZED, AND DONE with the small talk. I knew it was just a matter of time before the Timothy topic came up, and I'd have to fill them all in on the clusterfuck that had become my life.

"So, I'm sure you've caught Jenny up. But tell us everything," Audrey said, starting the ball rolling.

"Actually, we haven't had much time to talk. Between work and her flirting with the new hot piece of ass next door."

"Oh god," I groaned.

"What? Who?" Audrey asked, eyes going wide. "Do tell! Details. Details."

"First, King Fucktard. Then, Mr. Fuck-Me-Hard. Leave the good stuff for last," Jenny instructed, rubbing her hands together.

"Yes! Yes! Yes!" Audrey and Lauren yelled in unison like they were having an orgasm.

I refilled everyone's glasses. We were going to need it. My friends knew bits and pieces of my debacle, but they didn't know everything. They didn't know the one piece of the puzzle that I was still hiding from everyone. And they were going to freak out when they heard what I did. I had lived through a complete shitstorm and just wasn't too excited about rehashing everything—even for my best friends. It wasn't just heartbreaking. It was fucking embarrassing.

Still, if you couldn't share the most embarrassing moments of your life with your closest friends, who could you share them with? I took a deep breath and another sip of liquid courage. "Okay, so you know about the cheating part."

Jenny and Lauren nodded, but Audrey raised a quizzical

yet accusatory eyebrow. "Was this the one and only time he cheated?" she questioned, skepticism dripping off every word.

"Yes. Well, technically, since we committed."

"But there was the other girl when you were first dating, right?" Did I need her to remind me there was *another* technicality on his record?

"I can't fault him for that though, can I?" I met each of their eyes in turn. "Since we weren't 'exclusive'?" I asked, using air quotes. Silence followed as they exchanged glances. "I was exclusive. And I thought he was too. But as he reminded me, 'We never discussed exclusivity,'" I mocked, using a low voice. I took a deep breath and another sip of wine. "So, can I really count that?"

They all exploded one after the other, their answers blurring into one another.

"Um, yes," said Jenny.

"Yes!" shouted Lauren.

"Fuck yes, you can!" Audrey yelled.

I winced from the sheer volume of their rebuttals. "Okay, okay. I get it."

An uncomfortable silence ensued as they waited for me to admit the ugly truth. "Then twice, I guess."

"Twice that you know of," Audrey sneered.

I nodded, feeling ashamed and stupid. I twisted my glass around in a circle on the table. "Twice. That I know of," I agreed.

"Slimy, fucking asshole!" she said.

"And you know my motto. 'Fool me once, shame on you. Fool me twice, shame on me.'" Jenny's words were slurred as she raised her glass in another salute.

Lauren teased her, "Jenny, that's *everybody's* motto."

"It gets worse," I told them.

They looked at me, waiting, it seemed, with bated breath.

"Well, are you gonna tell us? Or are you gonna make us guess?" Audrey asked, her dark eyes narrowing.

I took a deep breath, preparing to rip off my invisible bandage. "He knocked somebody up." My words came out so fast I wasn't even sure they had heard me.

Three pairs of blinking eyes.

Then another explosion of noise as their mouths began moving in unison.

"What the fuck?"

"You've gotta be fucking kidding me!"

"That piece of shit!"

I grimaced, folding in on myself. At least I wasn't the target of their venomous wrath—and part of me hoped wherever Tim was now, he was experiencing a pain akin to someone viscously stabbing a voodoo doll.

"Yep." I slapped my hands on my thighs, stood up, and started pacing. "That's about the reaction I had. At first, I got angry. Then I got sad. Then I just got angry all over again. So, I packed my stuff and left. I stayed with Nev for a few weeks to figure out what to do. But I just needed to get away from everything. The job. Him. The memories. And, *voila*." I lifted my hand. "Here I am."

"Oh, babe. I'm so sorry," Aud said, reaching out for my hand. "I'm so sorry." She looked at the others, who nodded in agreement.

I sat down, surrounded by my closest friends in the world.

"At least you had Nev to go to, though. She's been a good friend," Audrey said.

"Yeah. She's my best friend up there."

Lauren's perfectly sculpted eyebrow raised.

I held up my arms like someone under arrest. "Not like you guys. You're my best, best friends. For fucking ever."

"Damn straight!" Audrey wagged her finger in my face.

"You bet your sweet ass," Lauren resounded. "And don't you forget it!"

"I won't. Promise." I crossed my heart, just like we all had done since we were kids. "I don't know what I would've done without her." They nodded, thankful I had someone in San Francisco to help me when I needed it most. Especially when I was so far away from my home and my family.

"But . . ." I cringed. I had stalled, trying to put off this last part for as long as I could. "That's still not even the worst part." I opened one eye to look at them, afraid.

"What'd you do?" Lauren asked, accusation in her voice. She knew me too well. She knew if there was an "even worse part," it most definitely had to have come from my own doing. Her bug-eyed stare was starting to scare me.

I didn't know how to admit my stupidity to my best friends. "Before I found out . . . before I knew . . . I gave him . . ."

"Gonorrhea," Audrey answered for me, a grin splitting her face.

"No!" I scorned.

"Damn! The bastard would at least deserve it!" She hiccupped at her own joke.

"Jesus, Aud!" Lauren elbowed her.

"What? He does!" She rolled her eyes. "That or crabs. I'm surprised he didn't give anything to you. Fuckin' sleaze!"

"He didn't give me anything. Thank god! But . . . I gave him . . ." Their eyes were like steel knives cutting into me. I swallowed the hard lump in my throat. "Thirtythousanddollars," I said in one quick breath, no break between the words.

Blank stares.

No words emanated from their lips.

We all sat staring at one another, not saying a word.

"Fuck," Audrey whispered. She was the first one to speak.

Jenny and Lauren remained dumbfounded and silent.

"Yep." I held up my glass again. "Cheers to me and my fucking stupidity."

"Well, shit . . ." Lauren began, "I don't know . . ." She stood up and paced. "You have to get it back!" she yelled at me. She was thoroughly pissed off and ready to fight.

"I know." My voice was barely a whisper.

"Why'd you give him that much money?" Jenny asked, touching my arm. I could see the concern in her eyes—motherly love exuding from her.

"Because. Well . . . because we were planning on opening a restaurant together."

A moment's silence passed between us as we exchanged looks. I knew they weren't judging me but rather trying to help me figure out a solution. I could tell they were treading lightly not to make me feel like a fool or let me fall apart.

"So, he still has it?" Jenny asked. "Right?"

"Yeah. As far as I know."

"Jesus. Fuck. Jesus." Lauren paced back and forth, thinking.

This was the biggest challenge to my situation. While it totally blew balls to lose the guy I thought I was going to marry, especially to another woman carrying his child, what was even worse for me was that I had handed over thirty thousand dollars without even blinking. I hadn't even given it a second thought.

I had followed my goddamned heart. And look what it got me. Not only had I lost the guy, the job, and my dignity, but I had lost almost every penny I had saved.

I felt like I had just been steamrolled all over again. "I don't know about you, but I could use some actual food now. Something apart from liquefied grapes to wash out this terrible taste in my mouth." My eyes suddenly filled with tears and overflowed. The girls all scooted in and embraced me.

"Let it out," Jenny whispered as she rubbed my back.

"It's gonna be fine," Lauren said, joining her. "We'll figure it out."

"Yeah. We'll get your money back. We'll figure something out," Jenny soothed.

"Even if we have to hogtie him and take him to the bank," Audrey threatened.

I laughed, wiping my eyes. "Thanks. I needed a good laugh."

"Who said I was joking?" Audrey countered, hand on hip.

"I got rope and duct tape," Jenny offered.

"Of course, you do," I said. "I'm not sure if it's for your other job or just 'cause you're kinky as fuck."

She stuck out her tongue. "Maybe it's both."

"I've got a truck," Lauren proposed.

"And I've got—" Audrey thought a second. "Well, I don't know what I got. What do I got?" she asked, looking at each of us one at a time. "What else do we need?"

We busted up laughing.

"Well, regardless, I'm in," Audrey began again. "I'll do whatever I can to nail that bastard, and his balls, to the wall!"

"We all will," Jenny said.

"Yeah," Lauren agreed.

"Seriously, you guys are the best." I hugged them all again. "All right, enough of this. Let's eat. I'm starving."

♥ ♥ ♥

Lauren smacked her lips together. "Can I just say, *best* fucking garlic bread. *Ever!*" She leaned over and tore off another huge piece and shoved it into her mouth.

"And I have the crème de la crème of desserts!" Jenny added.

Five minutes later, Lauren, Audrey, and I sat on the couch, music playing in the background. Jenny rolled in a dessert cart, on top of which sat one of the best cheesecakes in the world. Audrey and Lauren clapped their hands like two elementary schoolgirls. "Compliments of Sophia—aka best adopted grandma ever."

"When'd you sneak that in behind my back?" I asked.

Jenny winked. "I might have bribed her the other day."

Lauren grabbed the large carafe of coffee and poured us each a mug.

"Quite a setup," Audrey said, eyeing everything. "So glamorous, dahling," she drawled, using her best hoity-toity impersonation, touching her imaginary pearl necklace.

"Anything for my best bitches," Jenny answered in a crass county hick accent as she cut into the cake. "And to top it off"—she held a glass bowl up in display—"raspberry purée."

"This is pure sin." Audrey handed her plate over to be topped off.

"And pure delight," Lauren concurred.

"Speaking of sin and delight. Fill us in on Mr.—what'd you call him?" Audrey asked.

Jenny laughed, a mouthful of cheesecake temporarily prohibiting her from speaking. "Mr. Fuck-Me-Hard," she finally said with a laugh. All three of them began gyrating in fake throes of passion.

"You guys are so dumb. His name is Michael."

They cleared their throats. "Mr. Fuck-Me-Hard," they corrected me in unison.

"Please." Lauren held up her hand. "You must play by the rules, Siena."

"That's right," Audrey said. "When we assign a code name to a guy, said guy must be referred to as his code name."

"Fine," I grumbled. "Okay, so Michael, aka Mr. Fuck-Me-Hard . . ." They all burst into fits of giggles again. "Fuck you guys." I laughed, throwing a pillow at them.

I told them how we met at the winery, which made them laugh even more hysterically, at my expense, of course. Then about our flirtation and the sexual tension that seemed to emanate from both of us. How his deep throaty laugh made my toes curl. How his perfect smile and sexy smirk made me want to slap him and kiss him all in the same instant. How Grams interrupted us when we almost kissed, and how I had thought she had saved me in that moment from making a huge fool of myself. "And after that, he tricked me into going for a run with him this morning."

"Ooh," Jenny hummed.

"Yeah. Part of me didn't want to go because I'm still annoyed with him over this whole hotel thing. But . . . it was actually good. A little weird, though. I thought he'd try to put a move on me again. But he didn't. He was just, I don't know. *Normal.*"

"Ugh. Stoo-pid," Audrey dragged out the word.

I laughed. "I know, right? I was expecting him to try to dazzle me with his smile and good looks, and I had prepared exactly how to deny him. But he acted like any regular guy. Like a friend, for fuck's sake."

"Hmm," Lauren wondered. "Sounds like he's playing your game."

"I'm not playing any game," I insisted, indignantly.

"You're totally playing hard to get."

"Am not."

"Don't get defensive. You gotta play the game. At least a little." She shrugged and swiped her finger through the raspberry puree on my plate. "It seems like he's into you. Maybe he's just reading your vibes, ya know?"

"Yeah, you need to be a little more open. Unless you want to turn him off," Jenny said.

This was something to consider. Maybe I was putting off a bitchy vibe without being aware. I didn't want to come across as a complete and total bitch, even though I had every right to feel the way I did. I was hesitant and entirely against him building a typical E Hotel, but like Michael had said, it wasn't him making the decisions.

My mind drifted to our run. His perfect smile made my insides melt. And beneath the morning sun, his luminous skin made me want to grab him and kiss him.

Get it together, Moretti. Your head's in the clouds. He's the enemy, remember? Keep him at bay.

But, I argued with myself, *I should keep my enemies closer,* reiterating the last half of the well-known adage.

Hmm, my wayward thoughts disputed, *how much closer?*

"So," Audrey said, breaking into my rambling thoughts, "what are you going to do about him?"

"Nothing yet."

"Why not?"

"Right now, he's the enemy."

"He's not your enemy," Lauren chided.

"Okay. Enemy might not be the best word. But I have to be careful. I need to protect my grandparents. I can't let Michael, or his father, screw them over. Like, what if he does something sketchy, and I'm not around to defend them?"

"Hey, we're family," Jenny said, touching my knee. "I will look out for them."

"Me too," Audrey said.

"Me, three," Lauren agreed.

"You guys are the best." I wiped a pretend tear from my eye.

Lauren jumped in. "Yes, we are. And don't you forget it!"

"To my best bitches," I toasted them with my coffee cup.

"Best bitches," they all resonated.

"Okay, but seriously, when are you gonna fuck him?" Jenny prodded.

"What?" I feigned shock, bringing my hand to my heart. "Why?"

"'Cause I'm living vicariously through you right now!"

"Soon," I promised without thinking. And my stomach flipped at my admission. "And it has to be soon." I looked down at my empty plate and wondered if Michael might taste just as good as my dessert. "I got two callbacks for head chef positions in San Francisco."

Their words overran one other as they congratulated me and asked questions about the jobs I'd be interviewing for in a couple of days.

"It sucks you might be leaving again so soon, but I get it," Audrey said.

"We all do," Jenny agreed. "This is great news." She grabbed me in a tight hug.

"I know. I didn't think I'd hear back from any of them so soon. If I can get back up there ASAP, *and* get the money from Tim, then I can finally put that chapter of my life behind me and pick up right where I left off. I'm overwhelmed at the moment with everything going on here, but I'm excited."

"You'll get the job you want, and everything will work out. I just know it!"

I looked at my three best friends in the world. The girls who always had my back no matter what. They had seen me through the thick and thin, the ups and downs. And they never faltered. I knew I could always count on them.

ALWAYS.

CHAPTER Twelve

SIENA

THE NEXT MORNING, WE SAT outside Stella's, donning our sunglasses to shade our sensitive eyes from the bright morning sunshine. The air was cool and crisp, the perfect weather to nurse our hangovers.

"Cell phone," Lauren said, holding out her hand, her ebony hair back in a sleek ponytail. She pulled her mustard-colored cardigan tighter to her, her black and white plaid scarf still hugging her neck. I begrudgingly dug it out of my abyss of a bag, hoping to avoid this moment as long as possible. It was, as Lauren put it, time to "shit or get off the pot." Avoiding the inevitable was only going to prolong this. The fact of the matter was, I not only needed my money back, but I also needed closure. I didn't want—couldn't have—this connection with Tim, and the money was the final thing I needed to handle so I could cut ties once and for all. I turned my phone over and over in my hands, nervous about contacting him.

Lauren drummed her amethyst lacquered fingertips on the table, thinking out loud. "What should we say?"

"We?" I tucked my hair behind me. "It's just me, not *we*. I don't have multiple personalities."

"This is a group effort," Audrey corrected me. "*We* have

your back, and *we* are with you all the way on this. So, '*we.*'" She quoted the invisible word in the air.

"How about 'Hey, dickwad, I need my money back'?" Lauren suggested, leaning forward, elbows on the table.

"Ooh, I like the dickwad part. Or asshat." Audrey laughed loudly, then cringed, pressing her temples, her dark auburn hair a messy knot on her head. "I hate hangovers!" she groaned, unbuttoning her bulky camel-colored coat. "Jesus fuck, it's hot. I'm sweating balls in this jacket."

"Yeah, we can smell the alcohol seeping out of your pores," Lauren teased.

"Look who's talking," she snapped. It was uncharacteristic of Audrey to go off like that, to yell at any of us. We looked at her, wondering what the hell was going on. She waved her hand. "Sorry," she grumbled, taking a sip of her coffee. That was all she said.

We collectively blew it off, figuring it was just the hangover talking, but something nagged at me about her quick, bitchy response and then her nonchalant attitude when she dismissed it.

"Drink more water." I filled up her glass and slid it to her. "You need to hydrate." Digging back into my bag, I produced a bottle of pills. "Everybody take some aspirin. And hydrate, for god's sake." I unlocked my phone, held it out for Lauren. "Can we get back to this? I want to get it over with."

Lauren pulled her ponytail tighter against her scalp, getting into serious thinker mode. "Right, okay." She took the phone and started typing. "Hey, asshole, I need my money. Send it to my grandparents' address." She looked up with an arched eyebrow and a cunning smirk.

"No, absolutely not."

"Ah, why not?" She pouted, crossing her arms.

"One, I don't want name-calling. Two, I don't want to be demanding or bitchy. Three, I don't want him to know where I am."

"Why the fuck not? After what he did?" Audrey scoffed. "He should know you escaped as far away from him as you could."

"I don't want him thinking I ran to my grandparents because of him. I didn't. I just wanted some distance and space to clear my head. And I don't want any hassle or fighting. Hence, the no name-calling. He doesn't know where I am, and I don't want him to."

"Don't you think he has some idea?" Jenny asked.

"He thinks I'm still at Nev's." I sighed. "How about . . ." I suggested, taking my phone back and typing, "I need the money I gave you. Can you do a wire transfer to my account? Thanks."

I could imagine the eye-rolls behind their shaded lenses. But like Grams always said, *You catch more flies with honey than with vinegar.*

"I guess. Sounds kinda weak with the 'thanks.' But it gets the point across."

"That's all I need it to do. Well, that and convince him to give the money back." My finger hovered over the send button. "What do you guys think? Is it okay?"

"Send it," they conceded. I exhaled loudly, a huge huff of air, and with it, the weight of the world finally lifted off my shoulders.

"Okay." I clicked the button closing the screen. "That's done."

Audrey's lip curled up. "Fucking bastard."

"Cheers to that!" I held up my mug for them to clink.

DJ, our favorite waitress, brought our breakfasts over. I ordered biscuits and gravy, my go-to after a heavy night of drinking. Lemon ricotta pancakes, crème brûlée French toast, and a Spanish omelet were the gals' other favored dishes. You'd think four girls ordering breakfast would be simple. But with us, as per usual, the table was covered with dishes galore —entrees, sides, and huge cups of coffee.

We sat, enjoying a last cup of coffee after we cleaned our plates. My phone chimed, indicating an incoming text message.

"Oh, gimme, gimme. Took the asshole long enough." Audrey snatched the phone to read Tim's response. "*Hey, Siena. It's Michael . . . Ooh,*" she read, raising her eyebrows. "*Just wanted to let you know I'm bringing the plans over Friday night. Sophia said that'd be a good time,*" she finished, a sultry cadence in her voice.

"How'd he get my number?"

"*How'd you get my number?*" Audrey typed, then smiled gleefully as she pressed send.

"What the hell, Aud? Why'd you text that?" I screeched.

"I thought you were dictating," she giggled, brushing me off with a wave of her hand. "Ooh, he's texting back." She danced in her seat as we all scooted closer, watching the dots move on the screen. "*Sophia gave me your number since she didn't know when you'd be back,*" she recited aloud. She wiggled her eyebrows. "Oh! Another one." We watched in anticipation as the dots blinked again. "*You'll be there, right?*" she read.

"Sounds like someone wants to see you," Lauren crooned in a singsong lilt.

"Oh! Shut up!" I snatched the phone away as they all laughed.

"Yes, I should be there," I read aloud as I texted back.

"*Should?*" Jenny scoffed. "Like you have something better to do?"

"Um, maybe I'll be out doing something." They rolled their eyes. "Or maybe I'll be washing my hair." I rolled my eyes back at them.

"You wouldn't dare!" Jenny shouted.

"Oh, wouldn't I? It'd serve him right."

"You can't!" Lauren insisted.

"And why not?"

"Because we need more juicy details!" Audrey added.

"And I'm living vicariously through you, remember?" Jenny exclaimed.

"Yeah, the suspense is killing us!" Lauren agreed.

"And I know it's killing you!" Audrey slapped me on the arm. They all joined in laughing at me. Could I blame them? They were absolutely right.

"We'll just have to see what happens. Stay tuned." I smiled a minxy smile, arching my eyebrows over my mug as I took another sip of my hangover killing coffee.

♥ ♥ ♥

The sound of my grandparents' laughter brought a smile to my face. I peeked in to watch them as they sat together. They were adorable. Smiling at each other, hands clasped, Pops gently caressing Grams's palm with his thumb. He leaned forward, puckering his lips. She didn't hesitate for one second.

What the two of them had was what I genuinely wanted, what I was looking for. I thought I'd had that with Tim. But some things just didn't work out the way you thought, or hoped they would. "Should I give you two some privacy?" I teased from the doorway.

"Siena!" Grams pressed a hand to her heart. Her cheeks flamed pink, caught in the act. "Why are you trying to sneak up on us old folks?" She immediately began fluffing her hair, making sure there wasn't a strand out of place.

I laughed. "You guys are not old. Stop that. And it's almost eleven. According to your timetable, you're running late, mister. Why are you guys still in your pajamas?"

Grams's cheeks flushed red once more as she avoided eye contact. *A little morning hanky-panky,* I mused to myself. *Good for you two!* Pops took her hand again, placing a chaste kiss upon it. "We're allowed to sleep in once in a while, smartass." He chuckled, a twinkle in his eye.

"Mm-hmm. It sounds like you two enjoyed having the house to yourselves last night."

"And this morning," he whispered.

"Oh, for heaven's sake," Grams admonished, getting up from the table.

Pops erupted in laughter, deep from the belly laughter, and I couldn't help but join in. Seeing Grams flustered like this just made my day. Again, I knew that this—what was going on between the two of them after all their years together—was what I wanted. Someday.

"In all the times I've seen you blush, Grams, this one takes the cake."

"You two are just a barrel of laughs," she said, scolding us.

"You can cuss and say the dirtiest words, but the mention of sex gets you all riled up?" I shook my head, a huge grin plastered on my face.

"Well, it's a private thing."

"I'll say," I snorted. Pops laughed so hard he almost knocked himself out of his chair.

"Siena Giuliana Moretti!" Grams yelled.

"What?" I questioned innocently. "At least you guys still got it! I'd be high fiving each other if I were you! Like, 'Yeah, we still got it!'" I pantomimed a self-high five.

Pops held his hand up for my grandmother. She chuckled, hesitating for a moment before raising her hand to slap against his, and again blushing like a second-grade girl.

"So, did you girls have fun last night?" Grams asked, changing the subject.

"We had a blast. Thanks again for making your cheesecake. We devoured it!"

"Anytime," Grams answered.

"Okay, girls. Time to get our asses to work. It's a beautiful day." Pops looked at us with a smile. "Beautiful women," he added with a wink. He whistled a sweet tune as we cleared the table.

♥ ♥ ♥

IT WAS INDEED A BEAUTIFUL DAY. THE SUN WAS SHINING; THE birds were chirping. There was a slight breeze blowing through the vines. The air was warm, but not hot. Cool, but not cold. It was almost *the* perfect day. I was strolling down the aisle, looking over the plants, as I did almost every day, just as Pops was doing a couple rows over.

Out in the vines, Grams sidled up to me, donning sunglasses, a hat, and a huge smile.

"Seems someone's in a mighty good mood," I said.

"Yes, I am. It's a gorgeous day, I'm with my favorite granddaughter, and I have an amazing husband."

I laughed at our inside joke. "I'm your only granddaughter, so I better be your favorite."

"Well, I do have three adopted granddaughters." She shrugged with a mischievous laugh. "I guess you never really know, do you?"

Jenny, Lauren, and Audrey were considered family. My grandparents had seen us through every stage of our lives—middle school and high school, dances, college, and boyfriends. They had witnessed us fight and had helped us to make up when we were too stubborn to admit our faults or apologize on our own. My grandparents were everything to me: mom, dad, friend, confidant, supporter, encourager, and, well, just everything. I couldn't imagine my life without them. And while there remained a hole in my heart from never really knowing my parents, they had done their best to make sure I felt every bit of the love that a child should.

I nudged her playfully. "You're a riot, Grandmother."

She wrinkled her nose. "Don't try to age me with that heinous word. *Grandmother!*" She shuddered.

"Only because I know how much it bothers you."

"Smartass."

"You're smarter," I jabbed playfully.

She crossed her arms over her chest. "I notice you're in a cheerful mood too, young lady."

"Must be the gorgeous day and being with my favorite grandma," I copied her.

"Hmm," she wondered aloud and removed her glasses. She took a step closer so she was inches from me and looked me directly in the eyes. "You sure it doesn't have to do with a man?"

"No," I said, turning away, fiddling with a stem.

"Mm-hmm. I think you're full of shit, Siena Giuliana Moretti."

"And what man would I be swooning over, Grams?" I didn't dare look at her.

"Gee, I just don't know."

I couldn't help it. I turned back toward her.

She tapped her finger on her chin. "Hmm . . . Maybe, Michael?" She grinned cunningly as she stepped around me to inspect another vine. She waited a few seconds, then turned back to register my reaction.

"No, Grams," I replied, trying to keep her at bay. "Michael is just our neighbor. The only interest I have in him is in regard to business."

"Uh-huh," she mumbled. I knew this tactic: a lioness stalking her prey.

"What?"

She remained silent, inspecting the vines, not looking up. I wasn't going to let her beat me at her own damn game. She was the master of holding out until her prey finally gave in, giving her what she wanted. She always won silly arguments like this with us. She was a frustrating woman. But I would not cave. I would not!

I sighed, moving around her and down the row, leaving several feet between us. I would not let her words get to me.

She was humming to herself, a sweet sound breaking the

silence. It was calming, soothing. A gentle tune I had heard countless times over the years.

"So," she began as we arrived at the end of the row and turned down to the next set of vines, "did he call you?"

"Who?" I pretended like I'd forgotten what we'd been talking about.

"You know who. Michael. Did he call you?"

"No." It wasn't a lie. Michael hadn't *called*. He'd texted, but I wasn't giving her free information. "Why would he call me?"

"He said he was going to."

I rounded on her, narrowed eyes, pointing my finger. "Ah-ha! What are you up to, woman?" I wanted to laugh, knowing she most certainly had something to do with him contacting me.

"Nothing." She waited a beat for me to say something. When I didn't, she asked, "But, really, he didn't call you?" She sounded so dejected and confused.

"Nope, he didn't call."

"Then why all the fuss about making sure you'd be available?"

I didn't know if she wanted me to answer. Hell if I knew what Michael's play was, but I guessed he was trying to figure out a way to sway us to his side so we wouldn't fight him on the hotel's development.

I decided to put Grams out of her misery. The look on her face was so sad. She had looked so bright and cheerful a few moments ago. Now she looked like someone had run over her prized garden. "Grams?"

"Hmm?"

"He texted me."

"But you said he didn't."

"No. I said he didn't *call*. Which technically, he didn't." I laughed when she realized her error.

"Of all the games to play!"

"*Me*? What about you?"

"I'm not playing any games."

"The hell you're not." I chuckled. "Trying to be some damn matchmaker!"

"I just gave him your number so he could get ahold of you about the designs."

"Mm-hmm. Sure you did."

"I did." She couldn't look me straight in the eye, and I knew her trying to play Cupid was not even remotely innocent.

"And?"

"And, you seem mighty interested in them," she deflected. "Just figured you'd want to see them for yourself. I know you'll put your two-cents in, even if it is unwanted."

"Well, don't you care about what they build there?"

"Of course, I care, Siena. Don't be foolish."

"I'd think we have some kind of say-so, seeing as it's right next to us. Don't you? Shouldn't our opinion matter a little?"

"Well. We might not have any right or say-so, but remember, you—"

"Catch more flies with honey than with vinegar," I finished with her.

"*Si*." She beamed, patting my cheek.

"I know, Grams. I'm just anxious it will overpower us and take away from the beauty of what we have here. What we see when we look out across this valley."

"Are you sure it's not more than that?"

"What are you getting at?"

"Just that . . . I see the way he looks at you."

"Yeah, right!" I scoffed.

"And the way you look at him."

"I look at him with annoyance."

"Well, you may not see it, but I do. I know that look."

"Grams, I'm not even done with this whole Tim thing yet."

"Maybe not yet. But you're getting there."

I sighed, leaning into her, "Why do guys suck so bad?"

"Oh, *Cara*. They only suck if they're not the right one. The right man won't make you feel that way."

"How would you know? You've been with Pops forever."

"Yes. But I've seen my fair share of the boys all you girls have dated. Trust me, that's enough to teach a handful of women about finding Mr. Right. I may have gotten lucky with the first boy I fell in love with, but I've been there to wipe your tears. And Lauren's. And Jenny's and Audrey's. Not to mention my friends too." Her words reminded me just how lucky I was to not only have her as my grandma but as my friend.

Life wasn't always easy. Not having my parents around to watch me grow up and help mold me was a hard fact of my life. But, in all honesty, I completely lucked out with my grandparents. They stepped in when needed and filled those gaps over time. While I could still feel a hole in my heart, I knew that over the years, that hole had shrunk as my life filled with their love, devotion, and support. They were the ones who taught me what family truly was, what true love really looked like, and what friendship really meant.

"Just remain open-minded. You don't have to accept or agree with everything he says or does." She cupped my hand in hers.

"It's just so hard. On the one hand, their buildings are amazing. Gorgeous, in fact. But I just don't think that one belongs here in Monarch."

"We have no idea what they have planned. And we can't control it. So why stress over something that is out of our hands? Hmm?" She cocked her head to the side.

"I know you're one hundred percent right. It's just so damn hard."

"Let's just wait and see what's what when he comes over."

I agreed, feeling a mixture of relief and defeat.

♥ ♥ ♥

Twenty texts were waiting for me when I went to my room after dinner. The girls were going crazy in our group chat over my impending meeting with Michael. *I'm back*, I sent as I considered the four outfits on my bed.

Lauren: What are you going to wear?

Me: Idk. I have a few ideas in mind.

I switched the black and red sweaters to see how they paired with the jeans I had chosen.

Audrey: Are you going for sexy or comfy-casual?

Jenny: Don't overdo the makeup.

Lauren: Go for SEXY!!!

Audrey: Wear your hair pulled back and the black sweater.

Me: I had that as one of my top choices.

Jenny: Love it!!!

Heart and thumbs-up emojis followed from all of them.

Jenny: Send pics!

Their excitement was rubbing off on me. I wiggled into my favorite dark denim jeans and checked myself out. Damn, these jeans made my ass look awesome! I pivoted from side to side. Yep! Definitely needed to go with these.

I slid the soft fabric over my head, made sure my hair was in place, took a selfie, and sent it so the girls could see: Black sweater—not too revealing, but a touch suggestive with my skin showing. Tight dark denim jeans that showed off my derriere.

"Eat your heart out, Michael!" I sent, as I checked my reflection in the mirror one last time. I'd worn some sexy lingerie underneath, too, just to give me an extra boost of confidence. I smiled, imagining just how I would take Michael and his stupid building down as I hung up my clothes and got ready for bed.

A text alert startled me out of my sleep. I opened one eye and glanced at the bedside clock. 10:33 p.m. One glance at the name, and I popped straight up.

A text from Tim, aka *Dickwad*, illuminated my screen.

CHAPTER Thirteen

SIENA

I HADN'T BEEN ASLEEP LONG, but I was still irked he texted me this late. *Like he couldn't have texted earlier in the day? What the fuck?*

Tim: Siena, I'd really like an opportunity to talk with you. The money is yours. I'll get it back to you. Can we please talk?

Was he freaking kidding me?
I waited a moment to reply.

Me: I don't think that's a good idea.

Tim: Why? Really? I'm sorry. I don't know what else to do to prove to you how sorry I am.

I didn't respond. What the hell was I even going to say to that? He hadn't even done shit to prove he was sorry except profusely apologize. Too little, too late. Nothing he could say or do would matter to me in the least. My screen lit up again.

Tim: There are some things I need to tell you and talk to you about. Things I need to say. Please.

I still had nothing to say. I didn't know what to say. Or think. Or feel.

Five minutes later, another text came through.

Tim: PLEASE.

Oh, for fuck's sake!

I finally texted, *I'll think about it.*

He immediately responded, *Thank you! I know I don't deserve it. But thank you.*

I couldn't help but roll my eyes as I slammed the phone down. I didn't know if I'd actually think about it or not. The bottom line was I needed the money. It was mine. He knew it. I knew it. But was I up to seeing him? Would I be able to see him in person and not punch the living daylights out of him? Would I be able to hold myself back from exploding like a grenade? I didn't know what to do.

I didn't want to see him because it still hurt too much to admit I'd been too fucking naïve, too fucking blind, to see what was going on right under my goddamned nose. But, maybe I *should* meet up with him and get everything off my chest. Say the things I didn't when I was still in shock.

Didn't I owe it to myself to get some closure? I knew I didn't owe Tim a damn thing, but didn't I deserve to tell him everything he had made me feel? And since I'd be there anyway, hopefully accepting a new job as head chef, why not just get it out of the way and be done with it? A simple meeting: get the money, let him say what he had to say, say everything I needed to say that I had been holding in and holding back. Then walk away knowing I had done the right thing and could finally move on.

Was I right to think this way? Should I avoid him or meet him? Should I be the bigger person or just say *screw you*? I needed to talk to the girls.

Sleep came surprisingly easy, and so did dreams about a

sexy beast of a man with unruly dark brown hair, chocolate eyes, and a devilishly delectable smile.

I was cranky when I woke up. I knew why. Not only did I have Tim to deal with, but I dreamt about Michael. Again. Why couldn't I get that fucker out of my head?

I had woken up wet between the legs and sweaty all over. I didn't remember much of my dream, but the part I remembered was how he was grabbing my ass and grinding into me. I was frustrated, both emotionally and sexually. Maybe I needed to do what the girls suggested and just bang his head against the headboard a few times. I decided what I needed right this moment was a hot shower.

The shower helped ease some of my tension. I was ready to talk to my three besties.

Me: 911. Tim text. He wants to see me. Can we meet tonight?

Audrey: FUCK him!

Lauren: Yes! I'm down for Happy Hour!

Jenny: No way! What'd he say?

Audrey sent an eyeroll emoji quickly followed by a middle finger.

Me: He said he has some things to "talk to me about." Can everyone meet tonight? Let's get some drinks.

Lauren: Some DRANKS! LOL!

Jenny: YES! We're gonna need them!

Audrey: MEXICAN???

Thumbs-up emojis all around.

Me: Kay! 5 o'clock. Whoever gets there first grab a table.

More thumbs-up emojis pinged through.

♥ ♥ ♥

The girls were all waiting when I arrived at Tres Hermanas, one of our favorite spots. Lauren had ordered a couple of pitchers of margaritas.

"Time for you to catch up." Lauren pushed a drink into my hands.

I clinked glasses with them all and took a long sip. "Ah, that's the stuff," I said, licking salt from the rim.

"Mm-hmm," Lauren moaned as she finished hers and refilled the glass.

Audrey twirled her index finger in the air, signaling me to finish mine as well, so I gulped it down. "Ick." I wiped my mouth with the back of my hand.

"Oh, they're delicious, and you know it," Lauren said as she poured me another.

"All right." Audrey rubbed her hands together. "Hand it over." She held out her hand for my phone. "We've got a few drinks in us. It's go-time."

We were three rounds in as I munched on chips and guacamole, and my friends huddled over my phone. They were intensely focused as they read through Tim's texts.

"Okay, so what do you think?" I exhaled through my pursed vibrating lips, sounding like a frustrated horse.

"I don't know, Mrs. Ed." Audrey erupted in laughter, copying me.

"Ha ha." I screwed up my face but laughed anyway. "Cut it out." I took a sip of my margarita. "I need you to be serious. What I need is some sage, sound advice."

"What you need is a big ole dick!" Jenny nudged me, winking. Our waitress giggled at us as she brought more salsa. We were officially tipsy.

"Yep! That'll make you forget all about Tiny Tim." Audrey wiggled her little finger and erupted again. I snorted, laughing along with her.

"Look . . . I don't need to forget about him."

"Yes, you do." Audrey looked at me with one eye closed, trying to keep my face in focus. "And the perfect way to get over him is to get underneath someone else."

"He's already outta my mind."

"Yeah, 'cause of that hunk next door." She closed her eyes and fanned herself like a verklempt southern belle.

I brushed her off with a flick of my wrist. "Michael has nothing to do with any of this."

"Yeah, right!" Jenny burst out.

"Don't lie!" Lauren said. "Jenny showed us his pictures!"

"I'm not lying. I never said he wasn't attractive. I only meant that I want to get my money back from Tim. Period. I don't want to cause any waves or give him any reason to hold *my* money over *my* head."

"You think he would?" Jenny hiccupped.

"No. I don't think he'd be like that." I popped another chip into my mouth. "Of course"—I swallowed—"I didn't think he'd be a lying, dumb-fuck cheater who'd knock somebody else up, either." I took another hefty sip of my drink. "So, there's that."

My girls all nodded in agreement.

"I thought he was *it*. You know. I thought I had finally found Mr. Right."

"Pshh—" Audrey's eyes were glazed, and her speech a little slurred. For some unknown reason, she was pounding the margaritas back tonight with fervor. "He wasn't Mr. Right. He was Mr. Left, Mr. Wrong. He's every opposite you can think of for Mr. Right." She shook the contents of her glass, lifted it to her lips, and slurped the rest of the liquid down. "Men suck!"

"Ignore her," Jenny instructed, brushing Audrey off. "Look"—she waved her hand nonchalantly—"okay, so you *thought* he was Mr. Right. Clearly, he wasn't. Mr. Right wouldn't do you dirty like that. Maybe you could get over the cheating." She shrugged. "But a baby? Yeah, hell no!"

"Ah, *hells no*!" Audrey hiccupped, her head bouncing from side to side like a Bobblehead.

"I think you should just see what he has to say. Hear him out. Be the bigger person," Jenny said.

"But don't fall for his bullshit excuses or lies," Lauren warned.

"Yeah. None of"—Audrey hiccupped—"what she said."

"I just want closure."

"I get it," Lauren said. "Just use your head, not your heart. Bastard doesn't deserve it."

Jenny placed her hand on my arm. "You need me to come with?"

"No. I think I'll be okay." I swirled the straw around in my margarita.

They stared back at me, and I could tell they weren't entirely convinced. "I'll be fine. I'll only be gone a few days." I watched my cocktail swirl in my glass, the ice cubes riding around in the liquid like little kids in a jacuzzi.

"It'll be fine." Audrey touched my hand, hiccupping again. She reminded me of the little mouse in *Dumbo*.

I squared my shoulders. "I'll go on my interviews and meet up with him afterward if he's free. If not, oh well. That's his problem."

"Damn straight!"

I shrugged. "I can be the bigger person and hear him out. As long as I get my money I don't care."

"But, remember, we are only a phone call away." Jenny swiveled her head, making eye contact with the others. "And seriously, if you need me, I can come up with you," Jenny reminded me.

I squeezed her hand. "I know."

♥ ♥ ♥

Later that night, I broke the news to Grams and Pops that I'd be heading to San Francisco for some interviews.

It was a mixture of happiness and sadness. Happy because it was what I wanted, and I was following my dream. Sad because it meant I'd be leaving again.

"We were just hoping you'd be able to stay a little longer."

"I know, Grams." I fiddled with my cup.

"It's not that I don't want you to go back, but . . ." She sighed. "Actually, I'm selfish, and I want you here." She smiled, grabbing my hand and holding it between hers. "But I know owning your own restaurant is a dream of yours." She kissed the back of my hand. "And"—she shrugged—"who knows. Maybe you'll open up a restaurant down here someday." Her support eased the guilt I was feeling.

"You never know what the future holds," Pops said with a smile at Grams.

"Nope. I've certainly been surprised a few times lately, that's for sure." The idea of leaving them again broke my heart, but I needed to follow my own. Sure, it'd be nice to stay with them for a couple of months, help out, and just be with them. My grandparents were by no means old, but they were the only family I had, and I knew they wouldn't be around forever.

"I just wish you could find a way to settle here. I love you, *Cara*," she said with a sniffle. "She's grown up on us, Sal." She turned to my grandfather, circling her arms around him and nuzzling into his chest.

"She sure has," he said as he embraced her tightly. He looked at me and smiled. "We are so very proud of you."

"Thanks, guys." I felt the threat of tears coming. My grandparents were my best friends. My avid supporters. They were the people I knew I could always count on when shit hit the fan, or whenever I needed some advice . . . or a kick in the ass. And looking at them now, united as a team, they reminded me that a partnership was what I was missing. Leaving them would be much, much harder this time around.

CHAPTER Fourteen

Michael

Thursday morning, and it was early as fuck. Again. The sun was rising. I could tell from the bright light glowing around the edges of the curtains. Why couldn't these tin boxes come with blackout curtains? Who the hell wanted to be woken up by bright-ass morning sunlight?

I sat up, the covers dropping to my lap. I was naked underneath, as usual. I rubbed my face and felt the hint of my beard coming back in. I liked not shaving every once in a while. Having to do it every damn day was a chore. Some men liked it. I was not "some" men. I liked having the freedom of letting the stubble do its thing. Out here, I had the luxury of not going into the office every day so I could relax on the grooming.

I checked the time. It was early, but not too early. I didn't know what kind of response I'd get, but decided to chance it.

Hey, you up? I texted.

I knew she'd be up. She was an early riser, just like me. But unlike me, she probably relished waking up at the ass crack of dawn. Texting her first thing in the morning might make her kind of grouchy. Good. The idea made me laugh out loud.

Part of me was just messing with her, pushing her buttons, and trying to get a reaction. Harmless flirting to see just what made Siena Moretti tick. Another part of me wanted to know how she'd react to me contacting her first thing in the morning.

I checked my phone. No response yet. I sent another one, *I know you're awake!!! Get up!* I could picture her cursing my name. Something about that image made me smile. I fluffed the pillows and sat back as my phone vibrated on the bed.

Siena: Ugh! Yeah. I'm awake!

Me: You wake up on the wrong side of the bed this morning, Sunshine?

Siena: No. Just laying here . . . hating tequila.

Me: Ah. Fun times last night? Do tell.

Siena: What do you want? You're annoying me! I'm trying to sleep.

Me: Poor baby. Wanna go for a run?

Siena: Not really.

Me: Too bad. Join me anyway.

Siena: I'm hungover.

Me: And? Lame excuse. Put your big girl panties on. Or don't . . .

I waited, thinking about her without underwear on.

She knew a hangover was a weak-ass excuse, the same as I did. I was ready with another comeback just in case. I knew which levers to pull to get her to react the way I wanted. This knowledge made me want her even more. I itched to see her any way I could.

A friendly morning run was as good a reason as any. And I was hoping the panties comment intrigued her enough to make her want me. Or at least want to run with me. I didn't want to wait to see her and couldn't wait until Friday.

Me: Get your ass up, or I'll come over there and drag you out of bed. LOL

I laughed to myself when she replied with an eyeroll emoji.

Me: I'll be there in five minutes, Ms. Moretti.

Siena: All right, all right. Fucker!

Me: I'll meet you at your place.

I whistled a tune as I grabbed some waters on my way out the door. It was a quick drive to the Moretti house. I did some light stretching as I waited for the girl with the almond eyes. For some reason, I pictured her bouncing out of the door, a cheerful smile on her face.

Instead, she emerged, scowling, eyes narrowed as she zipped her jacket. "You've got a lot of nerve, Blaire." Siena was apparently not as chipper in the morning as I pictured her to be.

"Eh." I shrugged her off as I passed her a water. "You were up anyway."

"What if I had been sleeping in?"

"You weren't though."

"But what if I had?" She tucked the water between her knees and pulled her hair back into a ponytail.

I started walking. I knew she'd follow out of a sheer desire not to be one-upped by me. "Ms. Moretti, part of my job is to be able to read people. In your case, you're a creature of habit. You wake up before eight every day. Probably before seven on most days. You like to get an early start to your day. And you don't like being rushed. Therefore, you wake up early, so you have time to relax and enjoy a morning cup of coffee at your leisure. You might read, but you're probably more of a sit and enjoy the silence type of girl. Here, it's the sounds of nature. In San Francisco, you probably sat and looked out the window and watched the world below . . ." I trailed off, stopping, letting my gaze move to the rows of vines.

She was right behind me. I could feel her, a kind of magnetic pull.

I turned, tilted my head. "Tell me I'm wrong?"

Her eyes narrowed. "Okay. That's creepy." I laughed at her shocked expression. "Did you run a background check? Hire a private investigator to spy on me or something?"

I laughed again. "No, Siena. I didn't spy on you. Although I do have a really good PI. You know"—I bopped her nose—"just in case." I winked.

"Seriously spooky," she said as she pulled her heel up to her ass.

I copied her movements as she went through her series of stretches. "Yeah, well. Creepy, or not, it's what I do. I read people for a living in order to run the business. Something I've honed over the years. Psych one-oh-one, babe."

"Yeah. In addition to constructing massive hotels. That's got nothing to do with psychology, *babe*."

She bent over, giving me a wicked view of her backside. Tight. Plump. Glorious. *Fuck me sideways*. She had a spectacular ass.

She shot upright so quickly I thought I might get whiplash. *Did I say that out loud?* She turned back with a mischievous smile. She reminded me of a cat. A glorious specimen, a tigress with hazel eyes. Greens, golds, and browns all swirling together in a perfect sphere. Her sphinxlike grin, almost wicked, held a hint of delight and a promise of pleasure. She licked her lips, and in that moment, I felt more like the prey than the hunter. "Ready?" Her eyes gleamed as she smiled seductively, I hoped, at me.

Words would not form. I couldn't even think of anything clever to say. A simple yes would've sufficed. But the tiny word eluded me. And for the life of me, all I could do was nod like some lovestruck dumbass.

She shot off like a horse out of the gate. My vision cleared, and I was determined to make her the prey again. I sprinted after her, swearing not only would I *not* let her beat me, but I would also *not* let her get away. She was my quarry, and she had started me on what felt like the race of my life. And, while we were both stubborn and headstrong—both unyielding and unwilling to give up what we believed in, both certain we were right—only one of us would emerge victorious.

My feet kissed the earth. I loved running. Feeling the cool morning air, the wind kissing my cheeks, running so fast, it felt as if I might be able to travel at the speed of light. I watched Siena, keeping her in my sights, allowing her to lead the chase, and relished the view before me as her feet, the paws of a tigress, propelled her forward.

She led me up a hill, past the same path we had run the other morning. I followed willingly, not knowing where exactly she was leading me. I didn't care. This creature could lead me straight to the gates of hell, and I would happily follow.

I caught up, her breathing steady. This girl was born to run. She was born to lead the chase. And I was born to pursue her.

We were standing at the top of a hill overlooking the valley. I hadn't realized we'd climbed as high as we did. But it was truly a sight to behold.

In the distance, surrounding the farm fields, orange groves, and rolling hills of grapes were majestic ranges of mountains, shades of purple in the morning haze, their peaks rising into the sun-kissed sky. Other wineries, orchards, and ranches could be seen on several adjacent hills and down other roads. Patches of trees dotted the hills, much like the ones on the hill where we were witnessing the glory of Monarch. *Wow. Why hadn't I noticed all this before?*

"I thought you said you were hungover," I said, trying to catch my breath.

She unzipped her jacket and dropped it at her feet. "I am. Or was, a little."

I peeked at her through the hair hanging over my eyes. "Could have fooled me." I blew out a breath and stood up, swiping my hair back.

"It's beautiful up here, isn't it?" She stood on her tiptoes and held her hands as high as she could in a full-body stretch. Her shirt lifted just enough for me to see the skin underneath. She turned around and caught me looking at her.

"You talking about the view or *the view*?" I looked her up and down.

She shrugged, turning back. "Maybe both."

I walked to where she stood, at the precipice of the hill, and looked out. We stood in companionable silence. It really was magnificent. We could see everything from up here, high enough for this view to have a profound impact.

I took a pull from my water and passed it to her. She smiled up at me, took a sip, and passed it back. She leaned slightly into me, and I hugged her close to my body. It felt good, just standing there with her, enjoying the view.

"You've probably seen this a thousand times, but it is really awesome."

She let out a long breath. "It's one of my favorite places. We don't get the seasons like you do in New York, but we still have some great scenery."

I kissed the side of her head absentmindedly. It wasn't

what I was planning to do, but it just felt natural. She peeked up, a smile tugging at her lips, and said nothing. She didn't turn away.

It was the perfect moment.

I bent down, holding her gaze in mine. Our lips had barely met when a scurrying sound rustled in the bushes under a nearby tree.

I jumped back. "Jesus, what the fuck was that?"

"Just a—"

"I think it was a mountain lion. I've heard they roam these parts." My eyes darted back and forth, trying to locate the vicious beast about to spring.

Siena started laughing. She bent over and giggled mercilessly.

"Seriously, what the fuck was that?" I waited for her answer. "Stop laughing!"

"Okay . . . okay . . . whew." She stood up, catching her breath. "It was just a fox."

"A fox? How do you know what it was?"

"Well, it certainly wasn't a mountain lion."

"How do you know?"

"Well, for one, they rarely come around here. They're more standoffish and like to keep to themselves. However, you could still see one. So, if you ever come out here by yourself, you need to be careful. But it was a fox. I saw it as it ran away when you scared it off."

"When I scared it off?"

"Yeah, when you jumped and yelled."

"Whatever. How was I supposed to know what it was? It sounded huge!"

"That's because it's so quiet up here." She paused. "Anyway, scaredy-cat." She walked past me, a sassy smile in place. "Don't worry, I'll protect you."

I grabbed her around the waist, stealing a squeal as I tickled her.

"I'll hold you to that," I whispered in her ear from behind.

Her giggles turned to a contented sigh as she leaned back into me.

We enjoyed the view for a few more minutes before she said, "All right, time to get back." She grabbed my hand, pulling me with her.

We were more than halfway back, enjoying the walk together, when she asked, "Speaking of big cats, have you heard the story about the city-slicker who came out here and was attacked and eaten by a mountain lion?"

I turned around, looking for some crazed animal to jump out at us. "What the fuck? No."

She erupted in laughter as she kept walking backward, a little hop in her step. "God, you're so easy!" She snorted with her finger pointed. "Gotcha."

"Oh, I'm gonna get you for that."

She squealed and started running. I took off after her. The chase was back on.

She stopped at the bottom of the driveway with me hot on her tail.

"You are a little shit, Ms. Moretti."

"Oh, come now, Mr. Blaire. Surely you're not surprised." Her cheeks were flushed.

I grinned. "No. I'm not, Siena," I said, my voice deep and serious.

She cocked her head. "So how come you call me by my name sometimes and Ms. Moretti at others?"

"I don't know. Guess it's the business side of me. Why, do you not like it?"

"It's just kind of formal. I don't know how to take it when you call me Ms. Moretti. It's like you're mad at me or something."

"No, it doesn't mean that." I liked calling her by her last name. I found it kind of sexy. But I didn't want to sound creepy, so I kept it to myself.

"You want to come in for some coffee?" she asked, looking back at the house.

"Thanks, but actually, I'm going to have to take a raincheck."

"Oh. Okay." I could hear the disappointment in her voice. Encouraging.

"I'd like to, but I have a lot to take care of today." I smiled, hoping she wouldn't take my decline personally. I really had a ton of stuff to do, and I was already behind on my work. But I just had to see her this morning.

"It's okay. I get it."

"I'll see you later?" My statement was more of a question, and I hoped she'd accept.

"Okay."

I walked to her, taking her hands in mine. "Thanks for joining me."

"No problem."

"I'm glad you came."

"Me too."

I leaned into her. So close, I could smell a mix of sweat and lavender. Her breath hitched. I knew she was willing as I ran my hands up her sides and up to her neck, where I could feel her pulse under my thumb at the base of her throat. It was wild, fluttering erratically. I looked into her eyes and brought my lips to each cheek, the way she and her grandmother did.

I wanted more; I really did. I wanted so badly to grab her in my arms, pull her into me, and cover that sweet mouth. I knew I'd regret not taking the chance right then and there. But this wasn't the time . . . or the place.

CHAPTER Fifteen

Siena

I WAS FEELING CONFIDENT AS I sashayed downstairs. I hadn't seen or heard from Michael since our run yesterday morning. He clearly got too busy with work, hadn't come by like I thought he would. I was hyperaware of the clashing emotions coursing through me. Exhilaration. Suspicion. Anticipation. Anxiety. I couldn't deny I was excited to see him, but I was not looking forward to another fight about the hotel. And something told me a fight was inevitable. I'd have to remain calm, keep a neutral demeanor. I just didn't know if I had it in me when my grandparents' livelihood might be at stake.

My hair was pulled back into a low ponytail, draped over my bare shoulder. I wore silver hoops in my ears, a dusting of brown eyeshadow, mascara, rosy blush, and pink lips. And a matching set of red lace lingerie.

Michael was bringing the plans for the hotel. I was bringing my A-game.

Grams had fresh coffee brewing and was working a crossword puzzle. "Seven letter word for a scoundrel," she mumbled.

"Michael," I said as I looked out the window.

"Siena!" The sheer pitch made me cringe.

"No, Grams." I stuck my finger in my ear, wiggling it to

quiet the ringing, "Michael is *here*." I walked to the door, shaking my head. "Although, who knows. It might turn out to be quite apropos," I added as Michael followed me in.

"You need to dial your feistiness back a few notches." Grams's laughter warmed the room as she rose to greet him. She kissed each side of his face, her hands framing his chiseled jawline. "So nice to see you, Michael. Can I get you some coffee?"

"Yes. Thank you." He set his plans and bag against the wall. "Why didn't you greet me like she did?" he whispered as he passed me.

The hairs on my neck rose in excitement, my arms broke out in goosebumps, and I had to clear my throat to get my words back. *Damn it.* Why did he have this kind of effect on me? Not even two minutes in his presence, and I was a pile of mush.

As I moved to get a coffee for myself, I felt his eyes on me. A heat rose from my toes and spread through my body. I knew I wasn't coming down with something. This heat wasn't a fever of sickness—it was a fever of lust. And my loins were on fire.

Grams slid his coffee to me. *One, two, three, four, five.* I felt myself counting through deep breaths. *Act natural!* I avoided eye contact with Michael as I took a seat. I stirred my coffee, not looking up, hoping Grams would hurry and get her butt back in her chair. *My god, woman, what are you doing over there?* I smiled meekly, stealing a peek at Michael before turning away to see what the hell was taking her so damn long.

His eyebrow jutted up, and his lips formed into a smirk. He winked and took a slow sip of his coffee, watching me over the rim. I couldn't help but feel my cheeks warm from his sensuality. He leaned on one elbow as he set his mug down. "You look beautiful, by the way." And there was that grin again. That smug, self-satisfied smile showing off his perfect teeth. My eyes moved to focus on his sumptuous lips, then up to his rich, chocolate eyes. God, he had a delicious face. The things I'd like to do on that face.

I shook my head, clearing my insane fantasy. "Thanks." I tried to keep him at a safe distance so his sexual energy didn't make me waver in my stance. I needed to remain strong and not let his prowess unnerve me.

I had to remember to keep my head in the game, make sure he wasn't taking advantage of my grandparents. They were nice people, and while they could be skeptical and shrewd, people like the Blaires were much more cunning and clever than they ever could be. Especially when it came to business. The Blaires had years of practice at takeovers and conniving business ventures. Manipulation and persuasion were the names of their games. And I had to do everything I could to make sure my grandparents didn't become their next victims.

Michael's eyes were still fixed on me. I heard Grams rummaging around in the pantry and prayed for her to hurry. I felt like a doe caught in the crosshairs of a hunter's rifle. The scope was zeroed in on my skull, and Michael was about to pull the trigger. He bit his lip seductively as he pushed himself up from his seat. He walked a little too close as he asked Grams, "Can I help you with anything?"

"Oh, no. You just sit and make yourself comfortable, hon."

Hon? I rolled my eyes.

"I'm gonna go find Sal," she announced, leaving us alone.

Shit!

Michael sat back down, grinning from ear to ear.

I rolled my eyes again. This time he saw.

Oops!

Michael's haughty, purely masculine chuckle annoyed me. I exhaled an exaggerated breath and shook my head. "Stop being so smug."

"Who, me?"

"Yes, you." My tone mimed his. "Wipe that smile off your face. You know exactly what you're doing. And I'm not playing your silly game."

"I can't help that you find my smile, or me, devilishly handsome."

"More like *just the devil*."

"Admit it. You find me charming. And funny." He leaned in closer.

I could feel my heart beating in my chest. I swallowed, hoping the sound wasn't audible to him the way it was to me. "Maybe funny *looking*."

"Jesus, Siena." He laughed. "You are a brat, you know that?" He smiled that darkly charismatic smile he'd just been boasting about. And he was right . . . it made my toes curl.

"And?"

"And I like you. I just hope we can mix some business with pleasure."

"I don't think that's a good idea."

"And"—he leaned closer, his musky scent invading my nostrils—"why not?"

"Because . . . I just don't."

"It was worth a shot." He laughed, pulling back. "I just wanted to get you riled up. I know what you mean. But still—" My grandparents' entrance cut him off. "Could be fun," he added as he turned to greet Pops.

How could this obnoxious man get to me the way he did? A few seconds ago, I wanted to deny him any possibility of the two of us. But now? Now I craved the need to prove to him that I was *exactly* what he wanted.

"Michael!" My grandfather's voice boomed as they clasped both hands. "How's it going?" I didn't like that he was so friendly with Michael. It wasn't fake or over the top, but the fact he seemed to have no reservations about this man, his father, or their intentions with the property right next to us was frustrating. I got that my grandparents were trying to stay impartial about everything, but just once, I wished they'd be a little more wary and aloof.

"Doing great, Sal. Siena and I were just starting to talk business." He sent me another wink and a smile.

Michael wasn't a complete asshole. If I was honest, he had a likable personality. I found myself laughing in his presence and enjoying his company. Our banter and flirting were fun. I just wasn't sure if he had any sneaky tricks stored up his sleeve. And if he did, how would they affect us? Was winning me over all part of his strategy? My stomach dropped at the thought.

I was sure whatever plans and proposals he had were going to be gorgeous. E Hotels were known for their beautiful and magnificent buildings. But, as I'd mentioned to Grams, I couldn't see how their hotel was going to fit into Monarch. I was skeptical—skeptical it might take away from the natural beauty we had. That it would be akin to a woman getting a horrible facelift and ending up looking like a circus freak. Would the new hotel add to Monarch? Or would it be like the Maryland hotel, where people in the area thought it was a complete eyesore? Like how some Parisians considered the light show at the Eiffel Tower an abomination.

I lifted my chin. "And I was about to remind Michael that Monarch is not a huge city. We're humble and value our quiet space and modest luxuries."

Michael barked out a laugh. "You act like you live in the middle of Timbuktu. Siena, you live in an up-and-coming city. Sure, it's not *San Diego*, but it's not Benbow either."

What was he doing, making up cities now? "Benbow?"

"Yes, Benbow. It's a super small city in northern California. Quaint little town. Humboldt County, if I'm not mistaken."

"Are you making this shit up?" I had no idea what the hell Michael was talking about.

He chuckled. "Nope. Scout's honor." He saluted me with a wink.

"I don't believe you. You're making it up. I can tell."

Pops and Grams were watching our tennis match across the table.

"I'm not. I swear. I'm telling you the god's honest truth. But you can google it if you want." He crossed his arms across his chest with a smirk. "You know all about doing a Google search . . . if I'm not mistaken."

Pops erupted into laughter. Grams and Michael joined in. I turned beet red. My cheeks became hot. My pits were sweating like nobody's business. "You all suck. Seriously suck." My outburst just made them laugh harder.

"Okay, okay." Michael clutched his stomach, trying to catch his breath.

I was so utterly embarrassed. Why'd he have to go and bring up old shit like me googling him?

"Whatever!" I huffed my way out of the room, making a dramatic exit. I'd barely escaped to the hallway when an arm came around me.

"Siena, I was just teasing you. Don't be mad." He tugged me closer.

"Ugh. You're insufferable!" I wiggled in his grasp. I could imagine the looks my grandparents were exchanging in the other room. I didn't need him adding more fuel to their fire. "Let me go," I demanded, trying to sound angry. Instead, I sounded husky and breathless, and I felt my cheeks heat again.

"Only if you promise not to be mad." I felt his breath against the back of my ear and down my neck, his heart was beating in his chest against my back. And was that—was he hard? I swear I could feel him against my backside. Holy crap!

"Why?" I squeaked out. I wiggled again, shamelessly trying to feel him.

"Promise you're not mad," he exclaimed, more for my grandparents' benefit than mine.

"Fine!" I said in defeat. "I promise."

I felt him grind into me as he released me, turning me so I could return to the kitchen.

When I looked back, he smiled smugly as he readjusted himself. He stayed a moment more, trying to control the bulge in his pants.

"All right, Michael, let's see these plans of yours," Pops said when we'd walked back in.

Michael, calm, cool, composed—back in control. It gave me a glimpse into how he'd act in a real meeting. "They're not my plans though. They're Mosby's. My architect."

"Ah. *Your* architect." My words were clipped as I drummed my fingers on the table.

"Well, our architect," he corrected. "She's one of my best friends." He grabbed the tube and slid out a massive collection of blueprints. I watched as he unrolled them, securing them with our coffee mugs as paperweights. "Welcome to Monarch—an E Hotel." His proud smile illuminated his face.

My hackles rose in immediate defense as I looked at the top sheet. It was an enormous structure. This building was gorgeous, no doubt about it. A luxury resort hotel that rose over twenty-five stories high. While it'd be great in another city, it was way too big for Monarch. It would tower over the winery and distract from our own picturesque and panoramic views.

Pops whistled loud and long. "That's quite a building."

"It's beautiful. And big," Grams added. She ran her fingers along the bottom of the sheet as if touching the paper might bring it to life for her. "Wow." She plucked at the bottom edge of her shirt, pulling it down and smoothing it out. "That's certainly quite a building," she echoed Pops.

"Siena?"

"Hmm?" I looked up. His chocolate eyes stared into mine. "Thoughts?"

"Oh . . . mmm . . . I don't know exactly what to say," I lied.

The room erupted in laughter again.

"That'll be the day. You at a loss for words." Pops's laughter made his eyes crinkle around the edges.

"Sure as the sky is blue, this one"—Grams's thumb shot out at me—"never has nothing to say. You can always count on my Siena to have an opinion."

"Never been the silent type. Since the day she was born, she's always made herself heard. I hope you know what you're asking for." Pops clapped Michael on his back in camaraderie.

"Siena?" Michael said, forcing my eyes back to his.

"Um." I faltered. Could I be honest with him? How would he react if I told him I absolutely hated it? It would take away from everything my family had built. Blood, sweat, and tears—all for nothing. I didn't want to create a divide between us, and I didn't want to jeopardize anything for my grandparents. But I had to protect them at all costs.

"Stop pussyfooting, Siena," Grams said. "Just be honest."

"What are you afraid of, Siena?" Michael asked.

"I just don't—" *Feel safe . . . Trust you . . . Want to piss you off and have you take it out on my grandparents . . .* How did I explain my feelings without seeming conniving or even petty? "I don't know." I waved my hands, not knowing what else to do.

"Just tell me what you think."

"I can't."

"Yes, you can," Grams said. Pops nodded.

"I . . . I . . ."

"Well, this is a first," Grams said, chuckling.

"Stop it, Grams. I'm serious. I can't deal with all this right now."

"All what?" Pops asked.

"This!" I slapped my hands down on the paper. "You!" I pointed to Michael. "And this!" I gestured to all of us. "This is all just too much. It's too fucked up," I finished breathlessly.

"I don't get it. It's just a building, Siena. We're not talking about global warming or ending world poverty. It's just a hotel," Michael said.

"No, it's not." My eyes filled with tears. "It's not *just a hotel*. You don't get it." I swiped at the tears. I didn't know how to explain it to him. How would he understand the history and the meaning of this place? He was a stranger, an outsider. He wasn't one of us. Michael didn't get that this hotel would probably be the end of our winery. His father would most likely find a way to buy my grandparents out if he wasn't already scheming to do so.

"What don't I get? This is business, Siena. It's nothing personal."

"That's exactly right. It's not personal. *That's* the problem."

"I don't see how that's a problem."

"Of course you wouldn't!" I raised my voice.

His head jerked back in shock. "I know you're not shouting at me right now. Right?"

"Yes! Yes, I'm shouting at you!" My chest heaved up and down.

He put a hand on my shoulder and remained the image of calm, cool, and collected. "Siena, calm down." I angrily shrugged him off. I would not let him touch me right now.

How could he be so relaxed? It infuriated me. "Calm down? Calm down? *Idiota.*" I began shouting in Italian. I talked with my hands, my words guiding my gestures, as my feelings and frustrations all came bubbling up inside me. I pointed an accusatory finger, appealed to the heavens above, and shook my fist at him. I was cursing him, his father, and his entire family. I stomped around the kitchen, raising my hands, going on and on about the winery and all our work, our family, our history, our legacy. How we weren't going to just bend over and take it, no matter what.

I heard Grams yelling. "Siena Giuliana Moretti! You stop it. Stop it right now! Now, you just calm down."

I turned, ready to lay into her too if need be. I needed to talk some sense into them. But the look in her eyes, so loving and warm, full of concern, broke me. I inhaled through my nose and let my breath out slowly the same way.

I knew I had gone overboard, but I just couldn't take it. I raised my arms, let them fall. "All right." I took a deep breath. "Okay. I'm okay." Calmer now, but still angry, I turned to glare at Michael.

But the shocked expression on his face—eyes wide and bugging out of his head—like I had just slapped him, stopped me.

"What?" I clasped my hands in front of me.

His eyes softened as he seemed to consider what exactly had just happened.

What was this?

Did Michael Blaire actually have a heart?

CHAPTER Sixteen

SIENA

"Damn," Michael said, his face twisting and contorting, as if he was trying to recover from a physical blow, from intense pain. "I don't even know what you said. But I can feel the animosity." His voice sounded wounded, strained, and full of anguish.

His words struck me. I hadn't intended to make him feel like I hated him. I was upset and frustrated at his lack of empathy, especially after our run together. "I got a little carried away. I'm . . . I'm sorry." It was so damn hard for me to say those words. I realized I was lucky he hadn't been able to understand me.

Pops sat quietly, like he always did when he was in deep contemplation. Having a hotel with a name like Blaire attached could be of great financial benefit to them. It could generate more business without a ton of extra work. Maybe they'd have to hire more employees, but that was a good thing if it meant an increase in revenue. We'd discussed this at length several times. I knew they weren't jumping up and down doing celebratory dances over the elaborate designs though. They were keeping their mouths politely shut, perhaps hoping for a better outcome, but ready to accept whatever Blaire was planning. After all, it wasn't their money.

But it *was* their future.

Grams's face was unreadable to Michael. But the link she and I shared made it easy for me to read. She appeared relaxed, but her face was etched with worry. She needed me to keep the peace with the Blaires. There was no room for error here. We had to work together to keep the winery and our legacy intact. I knew we didn't have the money to outmaneuver someone of Allan Blaire's business prowess, so we would do best to partner with him rather than turn him against us. But this hotel sucked. It was wrong. All wrong.

"Siena's being overprotective, Michael. It's in her nature to defend those she loves," Grams explained with a small smile, trying to smooth the waters.

"I have no idea what you were going on and on about. I could barely understand a single word," Michael said, addressing me. "But I could feel your passion. And . . ." He took a breath and held up his hands in surrender, probably to make sure I wasn't going to jump down his throat again. "I get the gist that you're . . . angry?" The last word was a question, and he was waiting for me to reply.

"I don't know what I'm feeling exactly." My arms flailed up again in frustration. How did I put into words what I was feeling so he would understand?

He reached out and tentatively put his hand on my arm. "Why don't we start over? In English this time, so I can understand what it is you're saying."

"Oh, I don't think that's necessary," Grams piped in, knowing precisely what had come out of my mouth. And for all intents and purposes, she didn't want me repeating verbatim what I had said or what I had called him and his entire family.

"You can tell me whatever it is you feel I need to hear." He cocked his head, his words sincere. "Okay?"

"I think maybe I should just leave this to them." I jerked my head to my grandparents.

Pops turned his mug in circles on the table. "Siena, this is a family decision."

"And we have to work together as a team," Grams agreed.

"I should just butt out. Or at least take a breather. I'm obviously too worked up about this to think straight."

"Siena, your grandparents are right. We all need to work together. Just tell me what you think. What you *really* think." Michael's words pulled at me.

"You are not part of *we*."

He flinched at my words. "Okay, let me rephrase. I care what each of you thinks. So, I want you to be one hundred percent honest."

I lifted my chin. "And you'll listen to what I have to say?" My challenging stance dared him to say anything different.

"Yes."

"Without judgment?" I cocked my eyebrow.

He cocked his in response, his mouth lifting into that damn sexy smile. "I'll try my best."

"And you won't take it out on them?"

"What?" Confusion rippled across his face.

"Is that what this is all about?" Grams asked.

"Siena, is that what you're afraid of?" Genuine shock registered in Michael's voice. "That I'd punish *them* in some way?"

I looked from Michael, to Pops, to Grams. "Yes." I finally admitted my biggest insecurity. I was on the verge of tears. I couldn't help but be protective of Pops and Grams. They were all the family I had. I had my friends, sure, but once my grandparents were both gone—hopefully, a day long, long, long in the future—it would be just me. And then, what would I have? What would I do without them?

"I wouldn't do that." Michael insisted.

"How do I know? How am I supposed to believe you?" *How am I supposed to trust you?* He didn't answer. "How can I be sure you won't do something to hurt them if I piss you off? Because let's be real, I piss you off, Michael."

He took a moment to answer, a slightly defeated look on his face. "Yes, you piss me off. And, no, I guess you don't know that you can trust me."

I didn't intend to show him how surprised I was at his candor. "Exactly."

"All I can do is give you my word. I wouldn't, and I couldn't take anything out on Sophia or Sal." He looked from me to them and back. "For any reason," he concluded. "Okay?"

"I need you to promise."

"Siena, this is business, not kindergarten."

"Ha ha. You're so funny," I screwed up my face. "I know it's business. But I still need you to promise," I said. "Or no deal."

"Okay, fine." He looked me dead in the eyes. My heart jumped. "I promise."

"Okay. Now"—I crossed my heart in demonstration—"cross your heart and hope to die."

"No way. Uh-uh." He shook his head furiously. I couldn't help but laugh at him.

"I'm joking. A promise from your lips is good enough for me."

His eyebrow cocked up. And that sexy grin slowly spread across his face once more. Damn.

I stood facing the firing squad. Time for the truth. Time for me to say what I was feeling. "I hate it." Silence, complete and unnerving silence from all three of them. "Okay, hate might be too strong of a word." I thought for a moment. "Nope. Hate pretty much covers it."

His brows furrowed together as he looked at the designs. "What exactly do you hate?"

"It's too big. With too many floors."

"It's a hotel, Siena. What do you expect?"

"I don't know. I just thought maybe you'd have looked around the area, done some research, maybe felt the place out, come up with something a little less . . . audacious."

"Audacious?"

"Yeah. It's too much. All the glass at the front. It's too . . . what's the word?"

"Ostentatious?" Grams suggested. She smiled meekly at Michael.

"Yes," I flipped my hand. "Exactly."

"I'm sorry, Michael. I don't mean to offend you." Grams explained.

"No, no. It's quite all right, Sophia." He stood looking down at the designs, hands on the table. "It's a great design. I just . . . I don't know. Ostentatious? Really?"

"Oh! It's a beautiful building," Grams said. "Don't get me wrong. You agree, don't you, Sal?" Grams bumped him, trying to force him to say something.

"I don't mind it. I certainly don't hate it. But I'm not paying for it, so I say let 'em build what they want."

"Pops! How can you say that?"

"Siena, look . . . regardless of what they build, having a hotel here will bring in more clientele to the area. And that's good for business. It's good for all of us."

"Yes, Sal. That's the point. A name like Blaire—an E Hotel—will generate more business for you, for us, for the entire community. We hope to put this city on the map, so to speak. From what our research and development team has studied, Monarch is proposed to be the new up-and-coming city just north of San Diego." His smile was broad and genuine as he finished his spiel.

I was still not buying it. Not with all his well-rehearsed lines. "I get your point, Michael. I do. I just think you should try for a more natural look. A different feel."

"It's not up to me."

"How is it *not* up to you?"

"Again, these aren't *my* designs. They're Mosby's and were designed with other Blaire hotels in mind. Her designs are based on my father's request. He wants to move forward with them."

"He won't consider other options?"

"Not that I've ever witnessed. Once he's made up his mind, there's no changing it." Michael's shoulders seemed to sag with resignation.

"Why not? People change designs all the time. That's why they're called 'plans.'" I air quoted the word for effect. "It's not set in stone yet."

"Maybe not for you, but for Allan Blaire, his decisions are pretty much final."

"Ah-ha!" I shook my finger at him, grinning. "See, you just said *pretty much*."

A smile slowly crept across his beautiful face. "I just don't think he'd reconsider."

"Well, I think you should try. There must be something you can do. I can't imagine you became the successful businessman you are by doing what everyone else tells you." I aimed to boost his ego a little. I needed Michael to talk to his father. For Grams and Pops. For me.

He gasped and clutched his hand to his heart. "A compliment? From you? I'm speechless."

"I'm serious."

He chuckled. "So am I. I don't think there's anything I can do."

On some level, I felt sorry for him, laying all this out like this. But he had asked for my opinion. I couldn't help that he didn't like my answer, and I couldn't help it if his father didn't want to hear it either. I needed to try to do something, though. If Michael understood my feelings, why couldn't he try?

Grams interrupted my thoughts. "Maybe we should call it a night. Get some sleep. Think about things. Siena, you've got a lot to figure out and plan for San Francisco. You've got enough on your plate right now. And it sounds like there's not a lot any of us can do about this," she pointed to the sheets on the table, "tonight."

"Did I hear something about San Francisco?" He had been bent over the plans, rifling through them, obviously lost in his thoughts.

"A new job. Just a couple of interviews," I told him.

"In San Francisco? I thought you were staying here." What was that shift in his voice?

"I am. Well, for right now, anyway. Until I can fix things and get everything back on track up there."

Michael didn't say a word, just stood looking down at the plans, fiddling with one of the corners of the paper in between his fingers. "What does that mean?" he whispered.

"It's kind of a long story."

"Huh? Oh, I didn't realize I'd said that out loud?" He looked around the room at us in turn. "Well, I've got all night." He walked over and dumped his cold coffee out and poured a fresh mug. "Refill, anyone?" We shook our heads. "So, what's the story?" he asked, taking a sip, leaning back against the counter.

I don't know why I felt compelled to answer him, but I did. Was that how he got business done? Was this why he was so successful? He just waited out his opponent until they caved. "I'm down here until . . . well, until I get a new job up there." Michael's eyes bored into mine, waiting for answers he seemed to know I was evading. I did *not* want to bring up Tim. Not only was it none of his business, but I didn't want my grandparents to ask why I was planning on meeting up with him. I certainly didn't want them to find out about the money. "I came down here temporarily. I got a call back from two places back home."

"Wait." He shook his head. "I thought *this* was your home."

"Yes. This is my *home*, home. It's always been home." I

shrugged my shoulders. "But I've lived in San Francisco for the past six years. I created a life there. My job, my future . . . are all up there. Everything."

"Oh. I see. All righty then."

"Siena's leaving on Monday," Grams said, jumping in. Why'd she tell him that?

"Grams, Michael doesn't need a play-by-play."

"Actually, this is really quite convenient."

My interest was piqued. "How so?"

"Potential business opportunity. Something you might be interested in."

I shook my head with a snort. "Doubt it."

"Don't be a brat, Siena," Michael said. "I actually forgot all about it. You know, wrapped up in these plans." He tapped the papers still spread across the table. "When I heard San Francisco, I thought that's what you were talking about and realized I still hadn't discussed it with you guys. So how would you even know?"

I rolled my eyes in jest. "Get to the point already."

"Siena," Grams admonished me.

The corners of my mouth turned up. "What? I mean, jeez, what's with this long-winded dissertation?" I baited, loving the sound of his voice but antagonizing him just for fun.

"Anyway," Michael said and cleared his throat. "San Francisco."

"What about it?"

"Well, it kind of involves all of you." He took his seat. "I was talking to a friend of mine"—he started rolling the papers back up—"in Carmel."

"What are you doing?"

"New item of business. We don't need these anymore."

"Wait." I grabbed my phone from the counter. "Let me take some pictures."

"I thought you *hated* them," he mocked me.

"I do. But I want to show Jenny."

"Why?"

"She might have some ideas on how to fix this big ole mess."

"Siena. You need to be more open-minded."

"Agree to disagree." I took a picture of the first page and instructed him to flip through as I took a few more. "Let's get an unbiased opinion."

"Unbiased? She's your best friend. Of course, she's going to side with you."

"She will." I laughed. "But she'll also take these into consideration and be objective. She's got an eye for design."

He shook his head. "Whatever you say."

"Who knows, maybe she'll be able to change my mind." I smiled sweetly.

"Your heels are already dug in. I think"—Michael felt his back—"I can still feel them," he remarked, playfully.

"I'm just going to ask her to take a look. She might have some ideas you'll like."

"Sure, whatever." He waved his hands in defeat. "You done?"

"Yep." I put my phone away. "Thank god I don't have to look at those again any time soon," I said sarcastically.

"Well, the next time you see them, it'll be in person. Good thing for you, it's within walking distance." I could tell by his tone that he was teasing me right back.

"Not if I have any say so."

He leaned back, smug and confident. "You don't."

"We'll see." I crossed my arms across my chest.

He shook his head and laughed. "Back to the next item on our agenda. My friend up north runs a small hotel, and he's interested in selling your wine."

"We always welcome new clients," Pops said.

"I was hoping you'd say that. I told him I'd bring a couple of bottles next time I go up."

"You could just ship them," I said.

"Well, since you're already heading that direction, maybe I'll join you. Mix a little business with pleasure." The words he chose sent a delicious shiver up my spine.

"Yeah," Pops said. "It's always best to meet a client face-to-face."

"There's no need to have you go out of your way," I told him. I wasn't sure about taking a trip with Michael when I had personal stuff to focus on—a new job and meeting up with Tim. I also didn't trust him enough to be alone with him overnight. Or was it that I didn't trust myself?

"Honestly, I don't mind," Michael countered. "I insist. Really. I have a couple of days to spare right now since there's nothing pressing I need to deal with."

"That's not necessary. Really, Michael. I can handle a meeting with a prospective client. Just give me his info, and I'll set it up."

"Just let him go with you, Siena," Grams said. I glared at her.

"Yeah," Pops agreed. Him, too? "It'll be good for Michael to help introduce you, seeing as it's his friend. You did say he's a friend, right, Michael?"

Why were they taking his side in all this?

"Yes," he answered Pops. "Plus"—he looked at me—"I think having me there will help seal the deal." The arrogant smile on his face irked me. Was he smug because he thought I couldn't handle it on my own or because he was wheedling his way into going with me? Was his intent purely based on business? Or *pleasure*?

My eyebrow shot up in question. "Oh, really? You don't think I can handle business myself? I will have you know I am a *sure thing* when it comes to sealing the deal, pal."

Did he just blush?

"I have no doubt. But you don't know my friend. Just trust me. You'll thank me for coming with you."

"Doubt it." But I was intrigued, so I reluctantly agreed to let him come along.

I gave Michael the details of my itinerary, where I needed to be and when. He said he'd take care of the travel arrangements, emphasizing that we'd have separate rooms. His statement made me question whether he was trying to relieve me or my grandparents. Either way, I didn't care. I wasn't going to let anything, or anyone, come between me and my dreams.

CHAPTER Seventeen

Michael

"Walk Me Out?" I asked Siena.

"Sure."

"Thank you again," I said to Sal and Sophia. I shook his hand, and Sophia kissed me goodbye on the cheeks.

I followed Siena out. "Wow, look at all the stars." The night sky was glittering.

"I know. Isn't it gorgeous? Probably don't get much of this in the *big* city."

"Not like this."

"It's the same way in San Francisco. Too much artificial light. It's one of the things I love about Monarch. All the natural beauty."

Her words reached me on a level I hadn't considered before.

We stood, our necks craned back, taking in the blanket of stars above.

The sky was velvety dark, glittering with starlight, like jewels, promising hope and possibility. The stillness of the air made me feel like we were creatures in the night searching for a place to seek refuge from hunting predators. It was a spooky and unnerving feeling to be out here in the dark, not knowing what might be hiding in wait. My mind was running away with itself, imagination taking over and creating a terrifying tale in my head.

I felt something touch my hand and jumped back at the unexpected contact. My reaction sent Siena into a fit of giggles as I turned around looking for the beast that had touched me, crawled on me. Like a spider or a snake. Had I not been lost in my thoughts, I wouldn't have freaked out. But my imagination had run away with itself, and with it, all semblance of reality.

"Sorry, I was trying to get your attention," she said between snorts.

Her laughter and the memory of her words from the other night, about her endearing quality, made me laugh despite my embarrassment.

"Come on," I said, heading to my car. I stowed my things, shut my door, and turned to look at the beautiful girl with the mesmerizing hazel eyes. I couldn't see their color in the dark, but I could if I closed my eyes and imagined. A dangerous thing considering everything that had transpired tonight. *Stay on her good side*, my subconscious warned.

I leaned against my car, trying to find the words I wanted to say. "Look," I began, my hands coming together, clasped in front of me, "I know we have our differences. And I know we don't see eye to eye on some things."

"Some things?"

God, this woman was infuriating. "Yes. *Some things*. What else do we argue about besides this fucking hotel?"

Her shoulders rose. "I don't know. I might sound foolish, maybe even like a child, Michael, but I don't care. You have to understand where I'm coming from." She looked past me into the vast darkness.

I sighed. "I get it. I do. I don't have any more control over this than you do. And I do understand your perspective." I gently lifted her face, forcing her to look into my eyes. "I do, Siena. But I also don't have a lot of say so."

"Why not?" she whispered.

"I don't know." I dropped my hand from her lovely face. I didn't know how to put things into words she'd understand. And I didn't know if I wanted to let her in on what was going on with me and work. Now or ever.

"Yes, you do." She framed my face in her petite hands. "Yes. You do," she mimicked me. I knew she was perceptive. Damn it. I knew she'd be able to feel me holding back.

"Look . . ." I paused, trying to evade the question. Or evade having to give her an answer. "My dad's my dad. For better or worse, you know? I don't have another one."

She flinched. "At least you have one."

I didn't know she didn't have a dad. I knew he wasn't around but didn't know any of the story behind why. "I'm sorry, I didn't mean to be insensitive."

"I've learned to deal with it." She dropped her hands and looked at the ground, but I could have sworn there were tears in her eyes. My face missed her touch immediately.

"Do you want to talk about it?"

"That'd be a hard no."

"Well, if you want to talk, my door's always open."

"Thanks, but I don't want to open up that can of worms right now."

"I get it. I don't know what happened with your dad, but you've got your grandparents, and from what I can see, you have a great relationship with them." I shook my head. "Things with my dad aren't anything close to what you have with them. It's different, and it's complicated." I ran a hand through my hair. "I don't know how to explain it."

"Well, maybe if you tried, I might understand better."

We were standing in the shadows, but the night sky illuminated her face. "I just can't. That's *my* can of worms I just can't open right now. But trust me on this."

"It's hard to trust someone who . . ."

"Who what?"

"I don't want to start another fight, Michael. I'll just say your father has a reputation that doesn't bode well for you. I'm trying to give you the benefit of the doubt, but it's kind of hard knowing your father is the one calling the shots, and you're basically just his little errand boy."

Not this shit again! If she only knew how much I was trying to avoid being exactly that. "I'm *not* his errand boy." My voice was hard, harder than I meant it to sound. But I was pissed she saw me this way. Despite not giving a shit how most people saw me, I didn't want it from her. "Can we please stop talking about my dad? Obviously, fathers are a touchy subject for both of us. The point is, I'm doing my job. Period. Let me do mine. And you do yours. Okay?"

"Fine."

"I will do the best I can. But for right now, I just need you to trust me." I caught myself. "To try to trust me." I needed her to meet my eyes. "Let's just try to get along. Deal?"

She looked at me. "Fine, whatever."

I stuck out my hand and waited. When she hesitated, I reached for it myself, held it a moment longer than necessary. As she stared at me with those magnificent eyes, I couldn't help myself. I pulled her to me. I could feel the heat of her body as I told her, "You need to say *deal* first." Was she as seduced by me as I was by her?

She grinned seductively, her mouth full and sultry. I loved the way she was looking at me.

My throat was suddenly dry.

Our eyes locked.

I smiled down at her, knowing exactly what I needed to do.

And then her mouth crashed into mine.

Shocked and thrilled by her boldness, I let her start, slowly easing into her, gauging her reaction to my lips against hers.

I heard a soft moan as she moved into me.

And that was all I needed.

My hands were around her waist, pulling her close, deepening the kiss. She needed to know, needed to feel, how much I wanted her.

Her tongue slid across my lips as her passion became emboldened by my response. I slid my hands up her sides, gently grazing her breasts.

She gasped, then her hands slipped inside my coat, her fingers dancing over my chest. We moaned together as she brought her hands over my abs, then slid under my shirt, where she scraped her nails against my skin. She pushed me back. I might have fallen to my knees in front of her if not for the pressure of the car behind me.

She was already driving me crazy. I was rock hard and straining against the fabric of my pants. She must have noticed because she moved closer, pressing her thigh into me as her legs straddled mine.

Every muscle in my body tensed as she rubbed herself against me. My insides felt like liquid heat as I dove into her mouth, tasting that sweet tongue laced with a hint of coffee. I plunged into her mouth the way I wished I could into her tight, sweet heat.

Our tongues danced with each other's, slowly, intensely. Erotic. I was desperate to give her just a little glimpse of how I could use my tongue on other parts of her.

She moved beneath me as she kissed me back and pulled my tongue deeper into her mouth, sucking, her hips rocking against my leg. She gently nipped my bottom lip, her fervor giving me an idea about how she might use those lips on my cock. I groaned as she ran her hand against my dick and cupped me, squeezing tenderly.

My gasp turned into a growl as I grabbed her ass and ground into her. She felt so fucking good. I wrapped my other hand around the base of her neck, moved my mouth to the sensitive zone at the base of her throat, and ran my tongue along her collarbone before biting, nipping at the tender spot pulsing under my lips. I reached my other hand around to cup and squeeze her breast, rubbing my thumb over her hardened nipple. "God, you taste good, Siena," I said in between kisses.

"Mmm," she moaned, my mouth against her. Her fingers squeezed my balls with just the right amount of pressure to make me go weak.

I bit and nibbled, running my thumbs across the tightness of her top.

"We have to stop," she whispered.

"Not yet." I claimed her mouth again, biting her lower lip.

"Please," she whimpered.

I broke contact and looked into her eyes. "Please what?"

"Please—don't stop." She collided into me again and dove deep.

I couldn't get enough of her. Her sexy curves. That sweet mouth. Her pouty lips. Her perky tits. I cupped them again and squeezed, eliciting another delicious and sultry moan.

She ran her hand up my chest and squeezed me back with a desire that held the promise of what it would feel like to have her naked body in my bed.

But I knew I couldn't. Yet I didn't want to stop.

I moved my hand to her lower back, down over the glorious, perky mound of her ass. I squeezed, hard, and ground into her again.

And then I heard it. "Michael."

My name on her lips sent my heart racing faster. I pulled away and looked into her eyes. I slowly moved my hands, caressing, massaging the curves of her ass. I lifted an eyebrow and asked huskily, "Yeah?"

I was feeling the need to take her on the ground right there under the stars. Now. I couldn't fight this off much longer. I was going to explode if I didn't find release soon. But

I didn't think it would be very neighborly of me to take Siena on her grandparents' driveway.

Reluctantly, I gave her three sweet kisses on her lips as I broke away from the heat of her body.

My heartbeat was erratic. Her chest was rising and falling, her breath shaky with the intensity of our encounter. Even though those beautiful eyes of hers were shadowed in the darkness, I knew what they looked like, dilated with pleasure and excitement.

A muscle in my jaw twitched, and my mouth curved into a satiated smile. I bent toward her lips again, took her face in my hands, and kissed her sweetly.

She leaned into me, and I could sense, just like me, that she didn't really want this moment to end.

I pulled away with a grin. Her face split into a self-satisfied smile. Mirror images.

She tilted her head and took my hand in hers.

Speechless, I chastely kissed the top of her hand.

She shook my hand, sent me a wink. "Deal."

CHAPTER Eighteen

SIENA

WHAT THE HOLY HELL? That kiss was mind-blowing. Quite possibly the best kiss of my life. My lips were still stung and swollen from where Michael had deliciously abused them. As I brought my fingertips to them, a huge, kid-in-a-candy-store grin popped into place. I couldn't help it, couldn't stop it. Jesus Christ, I was glad I had made my move.

I opened the group chat. *OMG! Holy shit!!! Conference call. NOW!!!!*

Thumbs-up emojis lit up my screen right before Lauren's face popped up. "I got Jenny on the line. You're on speaker with Audrey and me," she said breathlessly, her words coming out on one quick stream of syllables. "What's wrong?"

"Nothing's wrong." I giggled. I couldn't help it.

"She's gone bonkers," I heard Audrey say.

"Oh. My. God. You guys!" I squealed.

"What?" they all shouted.

"I just totally put the moves on Michael!"

Loud, shrill screams echoed through the phone as I held it away from my ear.

"Tell us everything," Jenny instructed.

"And don't leave out a single detail!" Lauren said.

"Well, he came over to show us the designs," I began.

"Not that shit. Who cares!" Audrey shouted. "Skip to the good part!"

"Okay, but first, Jenny? Can you look at them and give me your honest opinion?"

"Yeah, yeah. Sure. Whatever you want. Details!"

"I could seriously use your expertise and unbiased opinion."

"Yes, fine. What the fuck? Why are you stalling?" She was breathless, on edge, waiting for me to regale them with all the dirty details.

"Thanks," I laughed at her outburst. "I just had to get that out of the way. Shit kind of hit the fan. But it seems we cleared things up before he left."

"Ugh. Quit jibber-jabbering!" Lauren squealed.

"So, he asked me to walk him out when he left and hot damn!"

I took them through everything, not leaving out one single detail. They were my best friends, and they deserved the best rendition of tonight's main event.

I sat on top of my bed, holding my pillow and twirling my hair, feeling like a giddy teenager. It reminded me of when we used to have slumber parties and would talk about the boys we had crushes on. "He is the perfect kisser. Omigod, that mouth. Fuck me!" I swooned. "And now, it appears, we're going to San Francisco together."

"What?" they all shrieked through the line.

"I know! Right?" I filled them in about his friend. "I don't know how much I believe him that this just worked out perfectly, timing-wise. It all seems a bit too coincidental to me."

"Who cares!" Lauren said! "You're gonna get laid! You're gonna get laid!"

Audrey and Jenny joined in with her teasing.

"Shut up!" I started giggling again, feeling like I did when I lost my virginity. I had been the last one of our group to lose my V-card.

The girls started talking over each other in excitement and anticipation. "Where are you gonna do it? Where are you staying? Oh, hopefully he books the penthouse or some fancy suite! What are you gonna wear? Don't forget to wax!"

A trio of laughter broke through on the last one.

"I'll book you an appointment with my girl," Audrey said.

I groaned. "Fine. I don't know where we're staying, but he said he'd take care of all the details."

"Ooh-wee," Lauren whistled.

"But he did say he'd get us separate rooms."

"What the hell? Why?" Jenny asked.

I laughed. "Pretty sure it had something to do with the fact my grandparents were sitting right there. That and the fact I hadn't thrown myself at him yet."

"Right. Right," she said. I could tell she was trying to figure out if that was the reason behind Michael's decision.

"That's just semantics. Don't you worry your pretty face," Audrey chimed in. "You're gonna get laid," she sang again.

"What about Tim?" Lauren asked.

My heart sank. "Ugh!" I buried my head in my pillow. "I forgot about him. Not really forgot. But you know . . . just forgot. Shit." I said. "Shit! Shit! Shit! I don't know how that major detail slipped my mind." Perhaps it was Michael's thumbs scraping over my nipples.

"He's *not* the major detail of this trip," Jenny chastised.

"Yeah, the major detail is Mr. Fuck-Me-Hard." Audrey's bark of laughter filled the line.

"He's the *second* major detail. The priority detail is the interviews," Jenny said. "Focus on those. Then you can focus on Mr. Fuck-Me-Hard." She snort laughed.

"I agree with them," Lauren said. "Tim is a tertiary focus."

I rolled my eyes heavenward. "I wish I didn't have to deal with him at all."

"I know," Lauren said. "But you need to get your money back. Then you can move on to the next chapter of your life free from drama and your shitty ex."

She was right. They all were. And I knew they understood all the frustrating pieces I was trying to deal with. With Michael on my brain, and on my lips, and fighting with him about his stupid hotel, I'd managed to put this Tim crap out of my mind, even if for only a moment.

"Yeah," Jenny sniggered. "He kissed you senseless."

"Yep," Audrey said. "Kissed that smart little brain of yours stupid."

"Oh my god!" Lauren yelled.

"What?" I asked, frightened at what she was going to say.

"If he kisses as good as you say, just imagine how good he fucks."

We all burst into laughter.

🖤 🖤 🖤

I looked in the mirror after washing my face and brushing my teeth. My lips were still tingly from Michael's assault on them. I smiled as I remembered how worth every tingle it was to have kissed him.

God! Good kissing fucking rocked. I didn't realize until I felt Michael's mouth on mine how much I had missed the sensation.

I couldn't help but wonder if he would still feel the same in the morning. Would his feelings for me change because of our kiss? Would he still be interested or was this some sort of cheap thrill for him, and he'd lose interest because now he knew I was interested?

I didn't know how I would look him in the eye without my physical need for him showing. Maybe a few days' reprieve would do us both some good. It would give us time to think about how we wanted to handle things. He jokingly mentioned mixing business with pleasure. But what about friends with benefits? I didn't even know if I could do that, but I was more willing to try now that I'd gotten a sample of him. I'd just have to make a conscious effort to keep my feelings in check and take a page out of Audrey's playbook on this one. Safe and simple. No strings attached.

With a couple of days to go before San Francisco, several thoughts still ran through my mind.

How was I going to make it clear to him that I just wanted something casual?

Did I?

How was I going to keep business and personal things separate for both of our sakes?

Could I?

How was I going to go the next three days before I could have him under my hands again?

I closed my eyes and brought our kiss, and his lips, to the forefront of my mind. Thinking of his touch, his scent, how big he felt made my skin feel like it was going to ignite. I might self-combust with all the sensations I could still feel, even though his hands were no longer touching me. The pulsating sensation between my legs returned, and I knew there was no way I'd be able to sleep with Michael and his wicked mouth consuming my mind.

I trailed my hand slowly down my body, imagining it was Michael's, not my own. I couldn't wait to kiss him again, taste him again. To finally savor *all* of him. I couldn't stop imagining how he'd feel buried deep inside me. Deep, deep inside. Igniting my skin with the delicious pleasure of his mouth while he filled me to the hilt.

My fingers glided over my own wetness, deliciously pleasuring myself as I thought of my ravenous hunger for him. It seemed my body craved him just as much as my mouth did, and it didn't matter that, for right now, I'd have to take care of myself so I could fall asleep.

CHAPTER Nineteen

MICHAEL

I JERKED OFF THREE TIMES last night.

And again this morning.

My dick would be raw if I kept this shit up. But I didn't care.

I couldn't get Siena out of my head. Her lips. Her tongue. The feel of her in my arms. The weight of her against me. What the hell was happening to me?

I hadn't seen her in a day and a half, but it felt like forever, and it was getting to me. How long had it been? I looked at my watch, calculated the hours—34 to be exact. I had to see her. If only for a couple of minutes. Jesus Christ! Who was I? Some lovestruck fifteen-year-old?

I called Jax, filled him in on my impromptu trip up to see him again. I needed him to have my back. His laughter riled me up, but he got the gist. He needed to save my ass. I'd need him to play along and just go with it.

After getting him to agree, and after a shitload of crude comments about "this pussy must be some serious kryptonite," I dialed the one person I knew could help center me. Mosby.

"Hey. I was just thinking about you. I just sent—"

"I'm fucked," I interrupted her.

"Why?"

"I'm royally fucked, Mos." I leaned into my hand and pulled at my hair.

"Okay, calm down. What'd you do?"

"I didn't do anything."

She laughed. "Of course, you didn't." She was probably rolling her eyes at me like she always did. "Is this about work? Or a chick?"

I dragged my hands over my face. "What do you think?"

She laughed again. "Knowing you, a chick."

"Not a chick. A woman."

"Ooh, okay. I'm gonna need my coffee. Keep talking."

"So, it's Moretti. Siena Moretti."

"Uh-huh."

"I told you about her the other day."

"Mm-hmm." I heard her keys clacking on her keyboard. Fucking multitasking like usual.

"Something happened."

"What the hell, Michael? I told you not to go there!" She was right. She had warned me to stay away. She had advised me not to get mixed up with her. The winery situation was super sticky, and my father's obsession with getting it had not subsided.

I got up and paced back and forth in the small space. "I know, I know. I couldn't help it. There's just something about her."

"She has a pussy and a pulse." I heard Mosby's throaty laugh come through.

"Stop it. Jesus. You sound like Jax." I was going to run this carpet through to the floor if I didn't sit down. I turned my work chair around and sat.

"Tell me I'm wrong."

"You're not wrong," I admitted guiltily. "She does have a pussy. And a pulse. But it's not as crass as that. It's more than that."

"Isn't it always? You're sick and twisted, a glutton for punishment."

"Don't be like that. I need you."

She sighed through the line.

"Help me, Mos. I need your brain. Mine has gone to shit since meeting her."

"Ugh."

"Come on. Be a pal. I always have your back when you need it."

"Fine. All right. What happened?" I heard her chair squeak through the line, and I could imagine her leaning back now with her feet propped up on the desk.

I started at the beginning, taking her back through how I had met Siena. How her gorgeous, earthy eyes had struck me down. How I'd been surprised she was the granddaughter of the winery owner next to our new property. And how we'd spoken, sparred, and flirted every single time we'd seen one another since. And finally, to the kiss. The kiss that had my head turned around ass-backward.

"Okay, so let me get this straight. You keep figuring out ways to get ahold of her. Not, vice versa."

"Yeah. I know. I'm a pussy, aren't I?"

"And she vehemently hates my designs and wasn't afraid to let you know?"

"She doesn't *completely* hate your design. There have been some tears over it, and I did have to convince her to trust me about it, but yeah, sounds about right. She's not afraid to stand up for herself or tell me what she thinks, that's for sure." I rubbed my face, feeling tense and anxious.

"Sounds like a real ballbuster."

I looked at the ceiling. "She is. You'd like her."

"But what the fuck? She doesn't like my designs? That hurts."

"Mos, don't take it personally. She didn't hate it overall.

She just hates it for Monarch and for next to her family's winery."

"Still. It's a bit of a knife in the heart."

"Don't be melodramatic. She said, and I quote, 'It is a beautiful building.' But she just feels that it belongs in downtown San Diego or along the water, not here in Monarch."

"Are you going to tell your father?"

"Yeah, right. You know him. He's a hard-headed fucker."

She sighed. "Yes, he is."

"I don't know which one's worse, Siena or Allan." I looked toward the ceiling, praying silently for some sort of divine intervention.

"I could design something else. Even though I did pour my heart and soul into this one. Bitch." She laughed loudly.

I bristled. I knew what she meant though. "She's not a bitch."

"I know. If she were, you wouldn't be so sprung on her."

"I'm not sprung on her."

"Right. You just can't stop thinking about her. Or talking about her. Or contriving ways to see her again." She laughed at me from the other end of the line.

"Pretty much. What the hell am I going to do?"

"You can go with the old tried and true 'No Care, Blaire' maneuver."

"I can't do that. Not with her. And besides, I haven't done that shit since college."

"I beg to differ. Do you not remember . . . oh, what was her name? The cute redhead with the nose ring."

"I have no idea." I quickly sifted through the mental list of faces from my past. But I couldn't, for the life of me, remember who the hell she was referring to.

"Couple of years ago. Down in Miami. Or Memphis."

"Nope! It was—"

"Milwaukee!" we finished together with a laugh.

"Still don't remember her name."

Mosby laughed. "Figures."

"I don't want to pull that old trick. Not with Siena, anyway. It's not like I'm trying to commit to her, but there's more to her than just banging for a couple of nights."

"Why, Michael Aiden Blaire, I do believe you've met your match."

"Get the fuck outta here. No way." I shook my head, although I felt some truth in her words that I didn't want to admit.

"Yes, way!"

"I don't think so, Mosby."

"And why not?"

"Well, for one, she's got her own goals and dreams."

"And?"

"And she's going back to San Francisco soon. Two, she's not the type to let a man get in her way or let someone else call the shots on her future."

"Okay, so she knows what she wants."

"Exactly."

"And she's not going to let any man, no matter how charming he may be, stop her."

"Precisely."

"Yep. Sorry to break it to you, but you've definitely more than met your match."

I realized she was right. "Fuck me." I let my head fall onto the back of the chair.

"Pretty much. I can't wait to meet her." Mosby's warm chuckle vibrated through the phone.

"Don't get ahead of yourself. I'm not sure where things will even go. And the thing is, I'm not sure where I want them to."

"That's something you'd better figure out. You can't screw things up for the business, so you'd better be careful. Not to mention, you don't want to get hurt."

"I'm not going to get hurt."

"Okay, Mr. Macho. Nothing gets through that hard heart of yours. Do you want to hurt *her*?"

"No! Christ. Why would I want that?"

"I'm not saying you do. But the fact you're so passionate in your response . . . Well, you'd better make sure you're upfront with her and do everything in your power not to hurt her."

"Fuck. This is too much to deal with."

"It's called, being in a—"

"Don't even say it!" I warned her. I knew what she was going to say. *Relationship*. But I wasn't in one. I wasn't even looking to be in one. I just wanted cool and casual. A no strings attached kind of thing. *Really, Michael?*

"Whatever, Michael. *Now* you're a pussy."

"Bite me."

"Um, hard pass. But, regardless, you better figure it out before you take her to San Francisco."

"I'm not taking her. It's business."

Mosby laughed. "Call it whatever the hell you want. You finagled a way to get her alone, away from the winery, away from her comfort zone. You're taking a woman you've got feelings for on a trip. The only difference is, there is a bit of business to deal with now that you've brought Jax on board. Man, he's gonna bust your balls about this for years to come."

"Don't remind me."

"You're gonna owe him so big. I just hope she's worth it."

I sighed. "She is." Mos was right. I was captivated by everything about Siena. I had cunningly maneuvered all of this to get her alone. The only thing to figure out now was where she stood and how she felt about me.

If I was gauging anything off our encounter the other night . . . well, Siena and I were both royally screwed. Now I just had to figure out how to get us through this in one piece. With my heart intact.

♥ ♥ ♥

I checked my teeth in the mirror, thinking of the other night when I'd gotten the kiss of my fucking life.

I was looking forward to another round.

I needed to talk with her about our itinerary anyway. This was the perfect excuse. I knew I could text or call, but I didn't want to give her a chance to evade me. At least this way—going to see her face to face—I'd be able to gauge her reaction.

There she was. The sight of her took my breath away. What was it about her that could make me feel like a freaking teenager?

I watched as she talked to customers, smiling and laughing. She was in her element. Her dark brown hair was pulled into a messy knot on top of her head, loose strands hanging down, framing her beautiful olive skin. Even in a work shirt, she looked phenomenal.

Yep, I definitely met my match.

"Can I get you a glass of our Guilty Pleasures?" Jenny was staring at me with a smirk on her face.

"I'm sorry? What?" I asked, thinking about Jax and how guilty I should feel for setting this whole charade up. But I didn't care. I had to have her.

"Guilty Pleasures," she said as she looked from me to Siena. My gaze followed hers. I felt even more guilty as my thoughts turned seductive. "Guilty Pleasures is one of our best sellers, dark ruby-colored wine with flavors of black plum, raspberry, jasmine, and black pepper. It's a syrah, pairs well with meat dishes like lamb and beefcake . . . I mean beef," she said with a giggle.

"That's a powerful sell. How can I resist?"

"You can't," she said with a laugh. "Anything else?"

I shook my head and watched as she sauntered past Siena, whispering something as she grabbed a bottle and a glass. Jenny had a mischievous grin on her face. Siena looked at me, a hint of a smile on her lips.

Jenny filled my glass. "Enjoy," she said with a wink, a playful cadence in her voice.

Twenty-five minutes later, two glasses of Guilty Pleasures in my system, alone with my thoughts, my mind was still fixated on one thing—the stunning Italian who was only a mere eight feet from me. I did my damnedest to play it cool like I was enjoying wine like everyone else.

A slight turn of her head and I couldn't help but smile as our eyes met. She said something to her customers, laughed at their replies, then turned and walked straight to me.

"Hey stranger," she said. Her voice was sultry. It wasn't intentional, but her voice just had that sound of sex and seduction. I felt a wave of relief wash over me. We were good. The other night hadn't changed anything, except for the better.

"Hi." I cleared my throat. I had a slight buzz from the wine. "How's everything going?"

"Been busy."

"Busy is good."

"Yeah. So, um,"—she examined my glass—"Guilty Pleasures, huh? You like it?"

I tilted my head, leaned in, turned up my smile. "Are you flirting with me? Trying to seduce me?"

She laughed, cheeks turning pink. "Very cute. But not while I'm on the clock."

I sat back, held her gaze, swirling the rich red wine in my glass by its stem. "What time do you get off then?"

A laugh lit up her face, her eyes flashing the same way they did right before she kissed me the other night. "You know what time I get off," she said, holding my gaze.

"That I do. What are your plans after work?"

"Dinner, packing, getting ready for San Francisco," she replied, a bit too casual for my taste.

I couldn't tell if she was blowing me off or just playing the game. Either way, I could play too. "Speaking of which, I brought you a copy of the itinerary." I reached into my back pocket, pulled out the papers, and sent a silent thanks to Jax. "Everything's there," I said, sliding them to her.

She skimmed over the pages. "You got separate rooms?"

I huffed out a breath, feeling frustrated that's what she noticed. "Yes, Siena. I got us separate rooms."

She looked at me. Was that regret or relief I saw in her eyes?

"Okay," she said. But I noted a faint hint of disappointment as she stuck them in her back pocket. Right on top of her ass, where I wished my hands were.

"But they are adjoining." I raised my eyebrows. "You know, just in case."

A snort of laugher escaped, and she covered her mouth. "Don't get ahead of yourself, Romeo."

The familiar ache in my balls returned. "As I've learned, Ms. Moretti, in business and in pleasure, it's always best to be prepared."

"Yes, it certainly is."

"Anyway, I wanted to come by and say hi. Let you know everything's been taken care of. I'll pick you up at eight."

"I can drive us."

"In that tin can of yours?" I shook my head. "No, thanks."

Her eyes rolled back in derision. "Just 'cause it's not a Benz doesn't make it a tin can."

"I know. But still."

"Good, then I'll pick you up at eight."

"Nope. Sophia warned me about your lead foot. I'll pick *you* up at eight." I held up my hand as she opened her mouth. "End of discussion, Ms. Moretti. You're not going to win this argument, so just accept it."

She blew out a frustrated breath. "Fine. You win."

"Thank you. The last thing we need to do is fight about who's driving."

She shook her head and laughed. "Exactly. Do you want anything else?"

The sides of my mouth perked up at her words. I leaned on my elbows. "What might you suggest?"

She leaned toward me, just a few inches out of reach. I could feel her breath as she held my stare. I could see my reflection in those greenish-brown orbs, she was so close. She blinked once, twice. Held my gaze and leaned even closer, the tip of her tongue caressing her upper lip.

I returned the gesture, wishing I could lean in for a quick kiss.

She pulled her bottom lip in between her teeth.

I swallowed and could hear the echo of the sound in my head.

She let go of her lip, and a sexy smile pulled at the corners of her mouth. She cleared her throat. "I might recommend . . . a cold shower."

I blinked twice before the words registered in my brain.

Siena laughed and smacked the back of my hand. "God, you're so easy."

"Only when it comes to you." I hadn't meant to admit that out loud.

It caught her off guard. "I-I-I," she stuttered. "I mean . . . you know what I mean."

"I sure hope I do." I smiled. "I'll see you tomorrow at eight."

Mosby's last words rang through my ears as I made my way back to the trailer—*Good luck, Michael, you're gonna need it.* She was right. I was going to need all the luck I could get. I was completely screwed.

CHAPTER Twenty

Michael

Siena seemed nervous as we took our seats. She was a little stunned that I'd booked us first-class seats but commented, "Figures," as she stowed her carryon. She was fidgety in her seat, kept looking out the window even though we were still on the tarmac.

Something was up. "You scared of flying?"

"No." She pulled the shade down.

"Don't worry. It's a quick flight."

She settled back into her seat. "I'm not scared of flying."

I didn't believe her. No one was this restless if they weren't nervous. "We'll be there before you know it."

She peeked out of one eye. "I'm not scared of flying, Michael."

"What is it then?" I sucked in a surprised breath and brought my hand to my heart. "Is it *me*? Wink-wink." She didn't laugh like I expected her to.

"No," she scoffed. "Get over yourself."

"Oh. It *is* me then?" I feigned a lightheartedness I didn't really feel. I knew I had to ask before we got too far into this trip. "Do you regret what happened between us the other night?" I reminded myself that her flirtations at the winery couldn't have been just in my imagination.

She sat up, looked me in the eye and said, "It's nothing regarding you. In a bad way, I mean." The flecks of gold in her eyes melted away any sense of doubt I'd let creep into my head.

"Okay." My body sighed with relief. I brushed my finger across her forehead and tucked a lock of hair behind her ear. "I don't know about you, but I haven't been able to stop thinking about what happened the other night."

"Oh, hmm." She tapped her chin with the sunglasses she was still holding. "The other night?" She stifled a giggle, trying in vain to appear oblivious to what I was talking about.

"Oh, really! Do I need to demonstrate it for you?" I looked around at the other seats nearby. Still empty, I noted. "There's no one around yet." I slid my finger down her neck to the base of her throat.

She laughed again, smacking my hand away, then sat back in her seat with a sigh.

"What are you acting so tense about then?" I asked, relieved it wasn't me.

"Just a lot on my mind."

"Your interviews?"

"Those, and . . ." She stopped.

"And what?"

"I don't know." She fiddled with her sunglasses. "It's stupid."

I shook my head. "Who cares. If it's bothering you, might as well talk about it." She didn't answer, but I could tell she wanted to. "Spill it, Siena. What's up?"

"It's about my ex."

"Oh." *Oh.*

"He's up there. And you and I are going up there. And—"

I cut her off. "Look, don't worry about him. If he's there, he's there. There's nothing you can do about it, right?"

"I guess so."

"And you're going for a potential job, not for him. Right?"

She twisted her fingers together. "Right." She nodded. There was something about her answer that left me uneasy.

My heart raced. "Unless you're planning on getting back together with him?"

"God, no! It's just I'm nervous about seeing him."

"You don't have to see him unless you want to. You should know how to avoid him if you need to."

"That's true. It's just, well . . . he knows I'm coming up there."

"What? How?"

"Well, for one, we used to work together at his family's restaurant. I had to put them down as a reference, even though I didn't want to. But it wouldn't look good if I didn't, you know?"

"Makes sense. He's not going to give you a bad recommendation, is he?"

"No. It'd be his mother they'd talk to anyway, so I'm not too worried about it."

"Then I wouldn't stress about it. Unless he's harassing you or

something." I looked at her, dead serious. "He's not, is he?" I wasn't trying to be possessive. Call it protective. Okay, call it possessive, if need be. But I didn't want anybody messing with her.

"No. He's not harassing me. He's harmless."

"Okay, then. Don't stress about him. Focus on your interviews. Don't let him creep back into your head and psyche you out."

Her plump, pouty lips turned up into a half-smile.

"You got this, Siena." I watched her chest rise with a deep breath.

"It's just . . . he really fucked me up. Fucked me over bad."

"You want to talk about it?"

"Nope."

"Are you still hung up on him?" I tried to sound more casual than I felt.

"No!" she answered quickly. "No." She touched my arm. Sparks. "It's nothing like that." She looked at me directly in the eye. "I started thinking about what happened the last time I was up there. And I guess it just kind of all came rushing back to me."

"Well, if you want to talk, I'm here. But don't sweat it. You're good. Everything will be all right."

"I think you mean 'all righty.'" She poked me in the thigh, laughing.

I chuckled at what had now become our own inside joke. What in the actual fuck made me say *all righty*? Didn't matter. Saying it made her smile. And I was becoming addicted to that smile.

Siena began rifling through the in-flight magazine. I wasn't going to let the energy between us dissipate. "I've kissed a lot of people. *A lot*. But damn. That kiss." I whistled my amazement, shaking my head in disbelief, hoping to egg her into a replay of the other night.

She barely gave me a sideways glance, but I could see the corner of her mouth turn up. Got her.

"I'm not trying to brag. I'm sure you've kissed a lot of people too."

The familiar exasperated look which told me I was starting to get her riled up crossed her face as she rolled her eyes. Perfect.

"What I'm trying to say is that we've *both* kissed a lot of people—"

"It's not a competition, Michael."

"I'm just merely pointing out that . . ."

"What? You're a man whore?" She laughed.

"No. That *our* kiss was different. Amazing."

"Such a smooth talker."

Damn it, she was getting the upper hand. "Let me try this

again." I lowered my voice and edged my mouth close to her ear as another couple took their seats directly behind us. "Our kiss was electric, Siena. You felt it too, right?"

Silence.

"Don't deny what happened when I kissed you," I whispered.

She quirked up an eyebrow. "*You* didn't kiss me. *I* kissed *you.*"

"Same diff. I know you felt it. *You* know you felt it. I felt it too." Was I babbling? I was babbling. It seemed like I was totally babbling. *For fuck's sake, Blaire. Get your shit together. You can do better than this.*

"I'm not going to be another notch on your belt, Michael. Clearly, you have enough of those already."

Michael Blaire, badass in the boardroom and in the bedroom, became a blathering idiot in the presence of Siena Moretti. I had to try to come back from this. "You're not a notch, Siena. Jesus, c'mon. You know there's something between us."

"Like what?" She tilted her head. "Friendship?"

"There's something more between us than being *just* friends."

"Yeah, but I feel like every time we turn around, we're starting over again. We're finally in a good place. Let's not make a mess out of things. I don't need any more complications right now. The other night was fun. But let's just focus on dealing with the hotel, at least for the sake of my grandparents."

"I agree. I don't want to screw things up with you." I was a bit disappointed, but I didn't want to fuck this up by being more demanding or persistent than she seemed to want right now.

"We need to set some boundaries."

"You really are a ballbuster, aren't you?"

She laughed. "I can be."

"Can be?" I needed to get us on the same page. I didn't want her thinking I was just trying to use her for sex. It was more than that. I genuinely liked her. I respected her even. "Look"—I tried focusing—"you're a headstrong woman. You're not a pushover. You're smart, dedicated. I—"

She cut me off. "Michael, I'm going to be honest. I'm attracted to you. But I have too much going on for me to think about things too deeply. I don't want or need complicated right now."

"I understand."

"Good." She looked at me directly in the eye. I could feel her sales pitch coming. "Let's just deal with things as they come. Keep things casual and friendly. I can't risk getting hurt, or starting something new right now, especially with someone like you."

"What do you mean *someone like me?*"

"Someone I'm in business with. Been there, done that. And learned my fucking lesson."

I took a moment considering what she'd said. "All righty." *Fuck, not again!*

She chuckled. "So, I think a no-strings-attached approach would work best. For me, at least. All righty?" she mocked, tilting her head playfully.

Wow. This was different. I was used to women trying to lock me down. Siena was turning the tables on me, using a page out of my own playbook. "So, you're saying if we can agree on things—"

"Yes. Exactly."

"Okay, you're the boss. You set the rules."

"It's simple. No strings attached. Let's just enjoy things as they come. But no confusing business with *us*. I won't back down about the hotel."

"I wouldn't expect you to."

"Good. I don't want you to think that just because I'm attracted to you, I will stop fighting you about the designs. I still believe in what I said and what I want. What I think is best for Monarch. For my family." Despite all of her *keep this casual* talk, I could still feel her pull to me.

"You can trust me, Siena. I hope you know that. And if you don't know it yet, then I'll prove it to you. I want the best things for you. I hope you believe me when I say that." I leaned into her, a breath away. Her chest was rising and falling, her pupils dilated. I could see the temptation in her eyes. I wondered if she could feel mine. "But just know, I won't back down either."

"You're distracting me," she whispered.

"Am I?" I asked softly.

"Yes."

"Good," I said smugly and sat back into my seat.

"Whatever, tease."

"I never said any different, did I?"

She shook her head. "Leave me be. I need to concentrate on my interviews and what I plan to say and cook, in case they ask for a demonstration."

That perked me right up. "You want to role play?"

She snorted and covered her mouth.

"'Cause I'm really good. And you know, practice makes perfect." I wiggled my brows.

She smacked me on the chest, a smile plastered on her face. "Stop."

I laughed and grabbed her in a quick kiss.

Shocked surprise crossed her face as the flecks of gold in her eyes shimmered. She touched her lips, dumbfounded as I eased back.

I was surprised myself and surprised at how easy it was for me to just kiss her out of the blue. "I'm sorry. I didn't mean to . . ." I didn't finish the sentence. This woman got me so tangled up sometimes that I couldn't think straight.

"It's okay." She smiled shyly at me. This interaction was weird, even for us.

I wasn't sure why I was even apologizing, only that I did so because this certainly wasn't a "no strings attached" kind of reaction. *Fuck me. Was Mosby right? Relationship?* I tried to play it cool, keep the thoughts whizzing through my mind at bay. Remember what Siena had just said about keeping things light. "I was serious. Even though I wouldn't mind the alternative." I winked at her, grinning from ear to ear. "But really, I'd be more than happy to go over questions or strategies for your interview if you want. And I'm certainly down to be your guinea pig on some good food."

"I think I'm okay. I just need to keep my head in the game and stay focused."

"Absolutely. Focus on business for now." I smirked, taking her hand and rubbing tiny circles over her knuckles. I licked my lips. "Besides, there will be plenty of time for *pleasure* later."

She playfully shoved me. "Shut up and buckle your damn seatbelt."

I followed her instructions with a smile. "Satisfied?"

"Not yet. But there's still tonight."

Holy shit, woman. Light? Casual? Jesus Christ, she knew exactly how to get me going. "Being this close to you with nowhere to escape"—I looked at the other passengers—"really does put a damper on things." I chuckled at her groan of annoyance. I knew by her smile that she was more frustrated with our current situation, being surrounded by people, than she was with my lusty playfulness and innuendoes.

"Keep it in your pants, Romeo."

"Tsk-tsk. No strings attached, right?" I winked.

She winked back. "Exactly. I'm glad we see eye to eye on at least one thing."

She giggled as I readjusted myself, sat back in my seat, and closed my eyes.

Perfect timing. The flight crew was just starting their preflight safety briefings and preparations.

CHAPTER
Twenty-One

SIENA

I WAS FLOATING ON A cloud.
I was back in San Francisco. Michael and I had shared some good conversation on the flight. He had brought up the winery, telling me again that he was looking forward to the meeting with his friend, Jax. He'd asked questions about Grams and Pops and appeared genuinely interested in helping us. I asked about his interest in wanting the land for development, and he reassured me that it just seemed like a win-win for both of our businesses. When I suggested that his father better not try to schmooze my grandparents, he brushed me off, stating, "I've already told him it's not for sale." For some odd reason, this was the first time I felt like he had no ulterior motives.

My interviews had gone extremely well, and I was confident I'd receive an offer from at least one of them. One was a popular upscale steak and seafood restaurant, the other a fancy French bistro. I had eaten at both over the years and liked each one for different reasons. Mostly, I liked that they weren't Italian restaurants, especially considering what I had gone through at the last one.

I'd loved working at Scarcella's and felt right at home from the first day. I had flourished there. The owner, Tim's mother, had been willing to let me experiment with various items. Her traditional family recipes were off-limits, but other than those, I brought my own authentic flair to the dishes. I respected her commitment to her legacy and her willingness to help me grow as a chef.

It sucked that, because of Tim, Scarcella's was no longer my haven, and I had to start over. Prove myself all over to a new owner and manager, new crew, and clientele. "It is what it is, though," I said out loud. While I dreaded starting over, I did what Grams advised me to do when an obstacle got in my way. Use this new opportunity to build the future I wanted.

I texted Nev to let her know that I'd finished my second interview. I was hoping I'd be able to see her while I was here, but her schedule was jam-packed, and she was on a deadline. *So excited for you! I can't wait for you to be back up here for good!* she sent back.

Next, I texted the girls to let them know I finished my interviews. And within moments, Jenny's face popped up on the screen.

"How are things going?" she asked.

"Just got out of the second interview. They both went really well, and I can see myself working in either location."

"Awesome!" The happiness my best friend felt for me flew through the line.

"Yeah." I looked up at the blue sky. Not a cloud could be seen. "I'm glad it's over. Now all I have to do is wait and see."

"Someone's gonna snatch you up. If they know what's good for them."

"I have a really good feeling. I'd kill to work for one of them. And I know I'd be happy at either place. So that's a relief."

"Good. I'm happy for you."

"I know you are. You're my biggest fan."

"Well, the second biggest. Grams is the first." She was right. No matter what happened, I knew Grams was rooting for me. I was lucky. I seriously had the best support system. Grams, Pops, the girls. "So, when do you meet up with Tim?" I could tell Jenny was trying to be blasé about it. One, she didn't want to upset me. Two, she wasn't Tim's biggest fan. And although she was biased toward me, she tried to be Switzerland and remain neutral for my benefit.

"Uh," I glanced at my watch to check the time. "In about an hour or so. I am so not ready for this."

"So, don't go."

"That's not very Swiss of you," I joked.

"Right, right. Switzerland. I am Switzerland," she reminded herself.

"Yes, you are."

"Let me try again. Ahem." I imagined her smoothing her long, sandy blond hair away from her face in an attempt to get into character. "It's okay that you don't want to go. That's a natural reaction to what you've experienced. But just remember, you want closure. And the best way to get it is to be the bigger person and hear him out."

I looked at the time again. "Still, this is going to suck major balls."

"Closure. Just remember closure. And balls. Balls are nice too." Classic Jenny. God, I loved her.

"Thanks, babe. I needed a little pep talk. I've been dreading this all morning."

"No problem."

"All right," I said, trying to get my own balls back. "I got this."

"You got this."

"Yep." I plastered my smile in place and set off on my mission.

"Oh, one more thing."

"Yeah?"

"Don't stop yourself from throwing a drink in his face." I

heard her laughter as she hung up on me before I could remind her that she was supposed to be Switzerland.

♥ ♥ ♥

I got to the restaurant early. I wanted to be in control of the situation. I didn't want Tim picking a table or ordering me anything before I arrived. I needed to be in charge of this conversation—this goodbye.

He'd already tried to get me to meet him at one of our "favorite" places. But that was just not going to happen. I didn't want to be somewhere familiar and comfortable with him. Not that anywhere would be comfortable right now. I was going out of my mind and just wanted this done and over.

I pulled out my phone. I still had a couple of minutes to spare. I sent the girls a message letting them know I was seated and waiting—impatiently.

Audrey: Don't be stupid and fall for any of his bullshit lies or excuses!

She was always straight and no games.

Lauren: Don't be a total bitch, but definitely be a bitch. LOL

She was the funny one.

Jenny: Be nice, but not too nice. You can forgive. But don't ever forget! NEVER forget what he did!!! Remember . . . you want CLOSURE!!!!

She was the solid, sound voice of reason.

A text from Michael popped up. *Hey! I hope everything went great today! Call me when you're on your way back.*

I felt a slight twinge of guilt that I hadn't been upfront with Michael about my plans to meet up with Tim. I didn't know if it was shame, embarrassment, or apprehension that kept me from saying something. I didn't want him to know what an idiot I had been by giving Tim the money, and I didn't want him to see my decision as a sign of weakness. I already felt stupid enough as it was. I didn't need him making me feel worse. Best to keep everything to myself and go through with my plan. Once that was done, surely, I'd feel better about keeping him in the dark. At least about this one small detail.

I was a Nervous Nellie waiting for Tim. I knew he'd be right on time. That was one of his more annoying habits. He was a schedule keeper and follower. He was a planner—never spontaneous or adventurous. It killed him to be late to anything, and he knew it drove me crazy. But it was a quality I secretly admired. If you needed something, you could count on Tim. Well, unless that something was *to be faithful!*

I froze when I saw him. Seeing him in the flesh gave me a shock I wasn't expecting. Everything I felt that fateful day come rolling back to the surface. Anger. Nausea. Emptiness. Rage. Even sadness, which pissed me off. I felt like someone had sucker punched me.

He bent down and kissed my forehead when I didn't stand. "Thank you for coming," he said, more casually than he deserved to feel. I thought I was going to throw up.

The waitress came over, saving me from having to answer, and asked what he wanted to drink.

"Black coffee for now, please."

She smiled awkwardly, obviously aware of the tension between us. It was palpable. He was rigid. I was avoiding eye contact.

"Siena?" My name as a question forced my eyes to his. He had dark circles under his eyes, looked tired and ragged. Still handsome, but it seemed he had aged since the last time I saw him. "I know how much you hate me, and I don't blame you." He reached for my hand. I grabbed my water, avoiding his touch. "Please. Say something."

"You wanted to meet, not me." I had a speech prepared, but now, looking him in the eyes, seeing his distress, and secretly reveling in it, I couldn't say what I'd planned.

"Please talk to me."

"You're the one who had something to say. I came here for closure."

"I don't want closure, Siena. I don't want to lose you."

I was dumbfounded. "What the hell kind of thing is that to say? What does that even mean?" I was trying to keep my cool. *Be Switzerland. Be Switzerland.* But already, I could feel my blood pressure rising, my heart rate increasing, perspiration breaking out.

"I don't want closure. Siena, I want another chance."

"What?" I screeched. I took a breath, trying not to draw attention. I lowered my voice back to normal. "How the fuck can you even say that to me? How can you even ask something like that?"

"I can't lose you, baby."

"You already lost me, remember?" I made a bump gesture against my stomach. "And don't call me *baby*."

"Please, baby—"

"The only one you should be calling baby is your unborn child." I could feel the bile creeping up my stomach and into my throat. "You make me sick." Tears formed in my eyes. I had loved this man so much once upon a time. Did I still? How could you tell the difference between love and hate? After all, they say the opposite of love is hate. So, if you truly hate someone, you're not that far off from loving them.

"Siena. Please—"

"What?" My face turned up into an ugly version of someone about to projectile vomit, I knew, but I just couldn't take it.

"There are things I need to tell you. Things we need to talk about."

"I don't want to talk about *things*. I just want my money." I was thoroughly pissed off. I wasn't Switzerland anymore. I was an atomic bomb about to explode.

He looked like I told him his puppy just died. Tears glistened in his eyes. He cleared his throat. "I never meant to hurt you. I never meant—"

"To be a piece of shit," I finished for him.

"Yeah, pretty much."

"Understatement of the fucking year."

"I know." He looked at me, deep into my eyes, and chanced another grab at my hand. He raked his hand through his hair when I pulled away again, repulsion covering my face. *Jesus, was his hair thinning too?* "Please let me explain. I promise, if you still feel the same after I'm done, you never have to speak to me again."

"Did you bring the money? I don't have time to play games with you." I raised my eyebrow, questioning him.

"It's not a game." He reached into his left coat pocket and retrieved an envelope. He placed it next to his napkin, just far enough out of reach.

"Fine." Regardless of what he said or didn't say, I figured at least I'd get my money in the end. Breathe. Let him finish. Let this finally be the end. "I don't know what you could possibly explain or what you could possibly say to make me change my mind about you. But, whatever." I flipped my hand. "Go ahead." I sat holding my glass on the table, not daring to make my hands available for him to reach out and touch.

He released his breath. I could tell he was nervous, which satisfied me. I was secretly jumping for joy that he was more worried than I was at this point. It was obvious that he had been stressing out about seeing me, the dark circles, a slight pallor to his complexion, his receding hairline. *How had I never noticed that before?*

"When I told you about Adriana—"

"Don't you dare say that slut's name to me," I warned, cutting him off.

"Right." He cleared his throat and started again. "When I told you about . . . what I did, I told you because she was pregnant." He waited a beat for any reaction, but my face was stone cold and blank. "I didn't want you finding out from her, which she threatened if I didn't tell you myself."

"Well, that's a huge relief." Sarcasm dripped from my tongue. "She's both a slut and a conniving bitch."

"You can say that again," he scoffed. He smiled, trying to make amends of some sort. Like the fact he agreed with me was going to make me run back into his open arms. When I didn't react, he continued, "I felt awful about everything. I didn't know what to do. So, I did the only thing I could. I came clean and told you what you needed to know."

"What I needed to know?" I shrunk back like he had just struck me.

"I needed to be honest with you and figure out what we should do?"

"What we should do? What *we* should do? No, no. What *I* should do is walk away knowing I gave you the best of me, and you . . . Well, you . . . *you* knocked somebody up."

He ran his hands back through his hair. "I know I fucked up. Royally fucked up."

"Yes, you did. And I don't feel sorry for you. But just like I need to get closure and move on, you need to do everything you can for your baby."

"There is no baby, Siena. That's what I've been trying to get to."

"What do you mean there's no baby?"

"Well, there is a baby. But it's like you said, she's a conniving little slut."

"I'm confused, Tim. Is there, or isn't there, a baby?"

"Yes. There is a baby. But it's not mine."

I felt the breath leave my body.

"What do you mean the baby's not yours? She lied?"

"Kind of."

"What the hell does that mean?"

"Well, she is pregnant. But it's not mine."

"Uh-huh." Everything was happening in slow motion. Like my body was floating above us watching all of this unfold.

"She said I was the father. But the more I thought about it after you left . . ." He looked down at his lap, then back up to me. "I just couldn't shake the feeling that it didn't add up."

"What didn't?"

"The timing. It just didn't make sense."

"And why not?" I sneered.

"I don't want to get into all that right now. But, eventually, I figured things out and confronted her about it."

"You confronted her? Jesus, you're a jackass sometimes, you know that?"

"Clearly. I royally fucked things up with you. Jackass"—he pointed back toward himself—"in the flesh."

I laughed in spite of myself.

"God, it's good to see you smile, to hear you laugh." I could tell he was trying. But what good was that in this moment? It couldn't erase everything bad between us. "Anyway," he continued. "When I brought it up to her and asked for an explanation, shit kind of just hit the fan."

"I can only imagine."

"Turns out she knew she was pregnant with some other dude's baby. But when she told him, he freaked out and ghosted her. And that's when she came to me, hoping that I'd help her out."

"Help her out? She ruined our relationship. No. Correction. *You* ruined our relationship. But she lied her way into trying to get a baby daddy. Who does that?"

"Someone desperate."

"Ya think?"

"So, she came clean. I blew up and fired her and told her to go to hell. But she cried, and I didn't know what to do. But I was pissed."

"So, what'd you do?"

"I told her that I wasn't going to be strung along into this charade and that she definitely needed to figure out what the hell she was going to do about the real father."

"I see." Did I though? This all sounded like an awful soap opera. What the fuck was I caught in the middle of?

"When I finally calmed her down, I got her to see that she needed to think about things and stop lying because she was ruining other people's lives."

"You told her that?"

"Absolutely. I told her she couldn't play games like this and needed to act like a grownup."

"Then what happened?" I couldn't believe I wanted to know what happened after that.

"Well, she apologized, said thank you, and left."

"Huh." I sat back into my chair. "That's a doozy. Bitch is cuckoo." I twirled my finger in the air.

"Pretty much. But shit—" He dropped his head into his hands on the table. I could hear him sniffling, and somewhere, way down deep, my heart broke a little for him.

"Hey." I reached out, touching his arm.

He looked at me, his tear-soaked eyes blinking. "I'm sorry. I didn't want to break down like this. But you just don't know what I've been going through."

"You? What about *me*?"

"No. I know. Everything is just so fucked up right now. You just don't know how much you mean to me."

"You're right. I don't."

"Siena, I'm so . . . so fucking unbelievably sorry."

"I know."

"Siena?"

"Tim, I just don't know what to say right now."

He looked at me from across the table. "It's a lot to process. I understand. I do. But I want you back. I'm not afraid to say it. And I will do anything"—he grabbed my hand—"anything to make it up to you."

I shook free of his hold. "Tim, she may not be pregnant with your baby, but you still fucked her. The reason you *thought* it was your baby was that *you fucked her while we were together.* I seriously can't do this now."

"We had something. We were planning on building a life together. A home. A restaurant. I know you're mad and hurt, but I can see your hesitation. There's something there, Siena. I know there's still something there."

"It's more than that, Tim. So much more." My mind shot back to Michael.

"Siena? Look at me." I looked back into his eyes. "All I care about is you. About us. You and me." His smile was genuine and full of hope. I remembered that same smile after we'd made love. *Damn it!*

I stood up, almost knocking the table over. "I have to go. I can't do this right now."

"Will you promise me that you'll think about things? Really think?"

"Sure."

"Promise." He sounded a bit desperate. I remembered the kiss with Michael against the car. When we made our deal. Damn this whole fucking mess to hell.

"I will think about things," I promised futilely, feeling like an idiot because I didn't know what the hell I was going to do. There was so much going on in my mind, too many factors. My future. My life. My hopes and dreams. Tim. Michael. *Shit. Shit. Shit.*

He stood up then, came around the table, and pulled me to his chest. For a moment, everything felt like it used to. "Here," he said, smiling softly, handing me the envelope. "As promised."

I took the money and tapped it against my palm. "Thanks." I started to lift my hand to his face then stopped myself as he went to lean into it.

He opened his eyes, realizing I'd pulled my hand away. "Call me later?" he asked tentatively.

"Sure," I said, stuffing the envelope into my bag. I walked to the front entrance and turned around a last time before exiting. He was still standing, watching me with his hand on his heart.

For Christ's sake, what was I going to do? I had not intended to come here and have *any* of my old feelings for Tim rise to the surface.

On the one hand, I had Tim professing his love and commitment to me—something I had longed for and wanted the whole time we were together. On the other, I had Michael, with whom I had an insane connection, both physically and, as much as I didn't want to admit it, even emotionally. Sure, we disagreed about one major thing between us, but I realized now, deep down, that he was loyal and trustworthy.

Why couldn't things just be easy for once?

CHAPTER Twenty-Two

SIENA

I WALKED AROUND THE CITY for the next hour. I took in the sounds and smells, letting them soak into my soul, making me feel like I belonged. Unfortunately, *my city* wasn't enough to shake the turmoil I felt over what happened with Tim. How I felt about Michael.

Sitting down on a bench in my favorite park, I texted the girls and told them I needed a conference call. He had asked me to, but I didn't call Michael yet because I didn't know what I was going to do, and hearing his voice would only complicate things.

Jenny already had Audrey and Lauren on the line. "Let the conference call commence," Lauren said.

"Wait. First, did you get the money?" Jenny asked.

"Yes. Got it in my bag right now."

"That's a relief," she said, down to business and always looking out for me.

"Okay, so what'd the slimeball have to say?" Audrey asked.

I could visualize all their minds exploding before their mouths finally caught up when I told them he wanted another chance. When the cacophony calmed down so I could get a word in, I said, "You guys gotta talk one at a time. All I heard was a few 'fuck him' and a 'you gotta be kidding me?' I couldn't make out any of the rest of it."

"I said fuck him," Audrey spat.

"Me too."

"Me three."

"Okay, so, you're all in agreement there." They were loyal to the last.

"I'm going first," Audrey declared. "What does he mean he wants you back? How's that supposed to work in his deluded, fucked up, little world?"

"Let me finish the rest of the story, and that will make sense."

"Fine, proceed," Lauren instructed.

"Please don't interrupt until I'm done. Okay?" They all agreed halfheartedly. I finished without any more interruptions. "Okay. Now, I'm done," I said.

"Don't do it," Audrey warned. "Once a cheater, always a cheater."

"That's not true," Lauren countered. I wasn't sure if she was defending Tim or trying to console me.

"I agree," Jenny said.

"With whom?"

"With Lauren. Some people cheat once and never do again. They learn their lesson. Some people just keep on cheating. Who knows why?"

"This is so not helping me." I held my head in my hand.

"What you need to do is find out if it was one time or not," Jenny suggested.

"And how am I going to do that?"

"You just gotta bite the bullet and ask him flat out."

"Yep," Lauren agreed.

"Audrey?" I asked. "What do you think?"

"I don't give a fuck what he says. I say you forget about him and ditch his sorry ass like the fuckwad he is. Michael's hot. He's into you. You're into him. And what does Tim have?

Nothing. Nothing but baggage and bad memories." Her words were harsh but true.

I hung up with the girls and dialed Tim's number before I lost my nerve.

"Hi, you." I could hear his smile through the phone. "I'm glad you called. I can't stop thinking about you, about us. I wasn't expecting to hear from you so soon, but I'm glad you did."

I cleared my throat. "Look, Tim—"

"Oh, no. I don't like the sound of this." I heard him sigh.

"I need to ask you something."

"You can ask me anything."

"And you'll be completely honest?" I was irritated even to have to ask him this. Honesty shouldn't have to be asked or begged for. Ever.

"Yes." A simple reply. A simple one-syllable word that held the fate of my future in its teeny tiny little hands.

"Did you sleep with Adriana more than once?"

I heard another sigh. I didn't like that he was taking more than a moment to answer. Time was moving in slow motion as I waited. Why was he hesitating?

"Yes," he finally answered.

My stomach was in knots, twisted and turned up around itself. I was in physical and emotional pain all over again.

"Siena?"

The tears pooled in my eyes.

"I can't say I'm sorry enough—"

"For how long?" I cut him off, knowing in my gut that I wasn't going to like the answer.

"How long what?"

"How long were you sleeping with her?"

"Siena—"

"Just answer the goddamn question!"

He hesitated. I heard him inhale as he approached the

firing squad. And I was the one holding the gun. "Two months."

Tears spilled over as I realized that I had been lied to over and over and over again. "Goodbye, Tim." I heard him call my name as I disconnected the call. I felt my phone buzzing as I walked to the hotel, completely mortified, utterly devastated. I knew it was Tim. I pulled the phone out and looked at the screen. His profile ID picture of us from my birthday last year popped up. We looked sublimely happy and in love. But as I stared at our faces, faces from what seemed like a lifetime ago, I realized those days were long gone. I didn't see any way to get past that kind of betrayal, that kind of deceit. *Could I? Could I ever trust him again?*

I needed to call Audrey back. She would give me the swift kick in the ass that I needed. She didn't take shit from anyone, especially men. Audrey was a grab 'em by the balls and twist *hard* kind of girl. And right now, I needed that strength and no holds barred reasoning.

Tim was calling again. Fuck this guy. I threw off my clothes, changed into sweats and a tank, then threw myself across my bed. Another call from Tim. I declined it and pulled up Audrey's number.

"'Lo," she answered.

"Can you talk?" My voice hitched as tears I'd been trying to hold back fell around my neck and onto the pillow under my aching head.

"Yeah. Hold on a sec." I heard her mumbled speech as she talked to someone else on her end. "'Kay. I'm here. Just put my client under the dryer. So, perfect timing. What's up?"

"I hate him. I really fucking hate him," I sobbed out.

"Take a breath. Take a breath, Siena."

I took a deep inhale and exhaled as instructed, calming myself.

"Better?" she asked.

"Yeah. No, but yeah."

"What happened?"

"I called him back."

"What'd he say?"

"He'd been sleeping with her for over two months, Aud. It wasn't a one-night fling. He fucked her more than once."

"Uh-huh. Typical."

"Don't patronize me, Audrey. Go ahead. Say it. Say, 'I told you so. Once a cheater always a cheater.'"

"I'm not going to say that. I'm not that petty. This is your heart we're talking about."

Tears filled my eyes again. "But you were right."

"Well, yes. And no."

"What does that mean?"

"Well, yes, I do believe that once a cheater, always a cheater. But maybe he only cheated this one time, and he won't again. I don't know."

"There's no way for me to ever trust him again, is there?"

"That's something only you can decide."

"He cheated on me for at least two months. Even if it was with the same girl, it was a long-time thing." I lifted myself off the pillow and sat cross-legged on the bed. "I don't know if that makes it better or worse."

Her silence was unnerving me.

"What do you think, Aud?"

"Honestly?"

"Duh?"

"And you promise you won't get mad?"

I knew she wasn't going to hold back and that sometimes her truth could be blunt and a little ruthless. But I needed to hear it. I pulled up my imaginary big girl panties. "I promise I won't get mad. Cross my heart." And I crossed my heart to seal the deal, even though I knew she couldn't see me.

"You just crossed your heart, didn't you?"

I groaned. Sometimes I hated the way she totally and completely knew me. "Sure did." Images of us as young girls, making each other cross our hearts or pinky swear whenever we promised anything to each other, flashed through my mind.

"You're so dorky. But so adorable."

"I know," I snorted. "Anyway, tell me the truth. The honest truth."

"In this case, I think it's worse. It wasn't just once. He knew what he did, what he was doing. And kept doing it anyway. He's a selfish, self-absorbed asshole. He'll never change."

Her words didn't sting as they hit me, and that surprised me. In that moment, I couldn't help agreeing with her words.

"Sleeping with someone once could just be a total lapse in judgment. Like 'Hey, I'm an asshole, I totally screwed up, but I swear it won't happen again.' But repeatedly? Especially for that long? That shit's intentional."

She was one hundred percent right. "I knew that deep inside before you even said so. But I just needed to hear it from someone else."

"I know you loved him. But seriously, this is beyond fucked up."

"Hearing those words sealed the coffin for him. The last nail kind of a thing."

"I just know you. And I know you're not going to be able to forgive or forget this kind of betrayal. I know I can't either."

"What?" Her words brought me to a halt. "What do you mean *you* can't *either*?"

"Couldn't. I meant couldn't. Or wouldn't." I heard her shuffling some papers on the other end. "Sorry. I'm multitasking. I'm totally listening to you though."

"You sure nothing else is going on?"

She hesitated again. "With me? Nope. Nothing I can think of. Just work, work, work." Her words came out hurried.

I wasn't buying it. "You're sure?"

"Yep." *She was lying!*

Audrey was hiding something, although I wasn't sure what it was. Or what it could be about. Clearly, she didn't want to talk about it right now. I promised myself that I'd talk with her when I got back and make sure she knew I had her back just as much as she had mine. Everything lately seemed to be revolving around me and my messed-up life. I didn't want to be the kind of friend who got all the attention and support but didn't reciprocate when it was needed in return. My friendships with Audrey, Jenny, and Lauren were everything to me. They were my lifeline. Without them, I'd be completely and utterly lost. "Thanks, Aud. For everything."

"Shit, I didn't do anything."

"You listened. And you said everything that I needed to hear."

"Yeah, yeah." Audrey wasn't a big softy and hated any display of emotions. She hated seeming weak, even if it was warranted. "So, you good?"

"Not good. But better. At least I'm not crying anymore, right? I'll be okay. I just need to face the facts and realize I wasn't meant to end up with him. I pretty much realized that the first go around. Now I just need to accept it for what it is and put it behind me. Thankfully, I got my money back."

"'Atta girl! Now, what you need to do is freshen up and have a few drinks. Where's Michael? Have him take you out. He'll make you forget all about lame ole what's his name."

"Oh shit! I forgot I was supposed to call him on my way back."

"Well, text him when you get off, you know, the phone with me. Wink, wink." A snort of laughter escaped her.

"Oh my god." I smacked my forehead at her too obvious of a joke.

"Just tell him to meet up with you at the bar. Have some drinks, flirt with that hot piece of ass. And get yourself back in the game."

"Oh god," I groaned.

"Better yet, get your ass in his bed and revenge fuck the shit out of him."

I groaned again at her apparent sex on the brain.

"What? You know he wants you. And you definitely can't deny that you want him." I didn't respond, so she jumped right back in. "Can you? Can you seriously say to me—straight-faced, dead in the eye—that you don't want to bang his brains out?"

"You are so crude. And, PS, you can't see my face. We're on the phone!"

"I may be crude, but how often have you seen me down and out over a guy?"

"Not since the tenth grade."

"Bobby fucking Fletcher. That asshole."

"Sounds like someone's still holding a grudge." Oh, high school.

"Not me. That fucker can kiss my pretty, perky, perfect sweet ass."

"Uh-huh. Sure. Liar."

"Am not."

"Whatever you say, sweetie."

"Shut up. Go fix your face and bang a headboard." I could hear Audrey banging on something in the salon, exaggerating the sounds of sex.

"Get your mind out of the gutter, perv."

"I may be a perv, but I have mind-blowing sex. Can you say the same?" She was laughing, and I couldn't help but join in.

"Bitch," I teased.

"Whatever. You know you love it."

"I do. I love you and your pervy mind."

"Yeah, yeah." A timer sounded on her end. "That's my cue. Gotta go check my girl's color."

"Okie dokie."

"You sure you're okay?"

"Yeah." And I meant it.

"Positive?"

"Yes," I assured her, rolling my eyes.

"Cross your heart?"

"And hope to die," I swore, crossing my heart again. "I'm going to freshen up and head down to the bar."

"Good girl." I smiled at her silliness. "Tell Michael I said hello," she sang.

"Yeah, yeah, yeah." I brushed her off, finally smiling. I checked myself in the mirror: smeared mascara, raggedy top, old sweats. *Get your ass in the shower. The night's not over, and neither are you!*

After a reinvigorating shower that helped erase the last few hours, I texted Michael, *Drinks? Downstairs?*

Michael: Hey there. Glad to hear from you. I thought I might have to send out a search party.

Me: LOL. It was a long day. I could use a drink . . . or 20.

Michael: LOL

Me: I'll be down in the bar in 15.

Michael: Am I invited?

Me: Scroll back. I already did.

Michael: Hmm, so you did. Can't wait to come . . .

Me: Me too. See you there.

I looked at myself from every angle in the floor-length

mirror. I loved this mirror. And this room. Everything about it made me feel glamorous. I felt fantastic despite everything that had happened that afternoon and didn't know if it was finally getting the closure I needed or the anticipation that I was about to see Michael. The more I got to know him, the more he made me feel sexy. And wanted. Maybe Audrey was right, and I should just bang his head into the headboard. Or maybe I should let him do that to me and fuck any residual feelings about Tim right out of my system. Either way, I popped a mint in my mouth, applied a little more gloss to my lips, and fluffed my hair as I left my room.

CHAPTER Twenty-Three

Michael

I COULD FEEL HER BEFORE I even saw her. It was like my body had a sixth sense when it came to Siena Moretti.

I had been in the bar for the past ten minutes, like a damned schoolboy waiting for his crush to show up. I turned and watched in silence as the gorgeous brunette that consumed almost every waking thought glided over to me. Every head in the room seemed to watch as she moved across the floor. And she was walking straight to me.

Fuck me. Her legs. Those heels. And that dress. *Holy shit!* I'd never seen someone so mouthwatering.

I stood and held out my hand. When she placed hers in mine, I pulled her closer, placing a chaste kiss upon her lips. The sultry scent of her perfume was an intoxicating, heady scent of vanilla and honey that assaulted my senses. She smelled like heaven and looked like temptation personified in a purple dress that hugged every one of her delicious curves and dipped almost to her navel in front, hinting at the softness of the glory that lay below that plunging *V*. "You look beautiful. As always."

"My, aren't you being a gentleman." I watched as the skirt of her dress hitched up higher, showing off her tanned, toned thighs that led straight down to a pair of five-inch stilettos.

"Sometimes, I can be quite gallant, Ms. Moretti." I winked, taking her in from head to toe one more time.

She shook her head, her hair swaying with the movement. Those dark locks rested like feathers over her natural firm tits. I watched as she slowly tucked her hair behind her ear, never taking her eyes off mine as she leaned closer, her glorious breasts rising with her breath. I looked, taking in the tops of that beautiful flesh, willing myself not to reach out and touch her. Right there. In front of everyone.

"You are smooth. I have no doubt about that, Mr. Blaire."

Jesus. It was fucking hot in here. *She* was fucking hot in here. "A glass of your sangiovese," I told the bartender. "They don't have Moretti wines here," I scoffed as the beautiful woman before me perused the wine menu. "I already checked." She looked at me, and I flashed her a hungry grin.

My heated flirtation and obvious interest in her family's label earned a heartfelt laugh. She leaned closer, whispering conspiratorially, "Yeah, this place is kind of a dive. Right?" I inhaled her scent again, honey and woman. I wanted her to be my woman, and I had to get a nibble of her. Tonight.

I appreciated her trying to turn down the heat. If she didn't, I was going to lift her off that barstool and carry her to my bed. "I know. Sheesh. Who decided on this dump, anyway?"

"I believe"—she ran her finger down my tie, back up, circled her hand, and tapped me on the nose—"that was you."

We leaned into one another and shared a laugh. She and I both knew I'd take her to only the best hotel. It's the least she deserved.

"To a bright and beautiful beginning," I said, raising my glass to hers when her wine arrived.

"Cheers." She smiled at me over the rim of her glass and sipped the rich red liquid.

"How'd your interviews go?" I asked, genuinely curious,

although still a bit disconcerted that a job might take her away from Monarch. Away from me.

"Good." She took another sip and smiled. "This is nice. Excellent choice."

"I've been doing my research. Plus, I've had a good teacher who's offered a little one-on-one attention."

"Oh." She licked her lips. "Sounds like Jenny's been quite the help."

I clinked my glass to hers again. "And you."

Her eyes sparkled as she brought her glass to her lips again. "Yes. You're a quick study, Mr. Blaire."

"When it comes to something I want, absolutely." I held her gaze. I didn't know how long we'd be able to keep up this charade. But it was fun playing.

Our conversation stayed on the light and flirty side for several minutes while she talked about her interviews. Until her phone rang. "Sorry," she said, reaching into her bag and pulling it out. I detected a scowl cross her face.

"What's wrong?"

"Nothing." She turned her phone to silent and tossed it back into her purse.

"You sure?"

"Yeah." She touched her hand to mine, her smile less full than a moment ago.

"Is it about work?"

"No." Her smile seemed fake, but I didn't want to pry. "I think I'm going to need another glass."

I could tell something was bothering her. I raised my hand, gesturing to the bartender that we'd both take another round. "So, do you have a preference?"

"For what?" she asked, blinking. She seemed to have lost all train of thought.

"The restaurants. Any preference over which place you'd rather work?"

She took a moment to think. "They're both great options.

Different vibes, different cuisines. But I think I'd be happy at either of them."

"That's good." *Not really. Not for me.* "I'm sure you'll have your choice. From what I've heard, you're amazing in the kitchen. And from what I've tasted so far, you're quite delicious. Your cooking and baking, that is," I added with a laugh.

Her eyes shimmered, the golden specks flickering with the candlelight from the bar. "You have quite the way with words, Michael."

She was still flirting, but she was also going through this second glass a lot faster than she had the first. Yep, something was definitely up. But I figured it would be best if I didn't pry.

Only ten minutes had passed before she downed her second glass of wine and asked for another.

"Okay, someone's a little thirsty," I said as she took a large gulp.

"I'm in the mood to celebrate. Aren't you?" Her eyes twinkled with the rheum of intoxication from the sangiovese. She giggled.

"And what, pray tell, are we celebrating?"

"I don't know." She giggled again. "A successful day, I suppose. Two great interviews. Closure"—she peered at me with one eye—"friendship?" She smirked. I didn't know how sarcastic she was being.

Just go with it, I told myself. "Those are all good things." I pushed a bowl of bar mix to her. She needed to eat something.

She grabbed a handful and started munching away, a little chipmunk who'd found her hoard of nuts.

I grabbed another bowl a few seats down and slyly slid it toward her. I grabbed a handful too, not touching my third drink.

While Siena was distracted with her snacks, I closed our tab. I grabbed her hand and gently pulled her with me. She was tipsy already, and I didn't want her completely drunk or incapacitated. Not tonight.

"I like you, Michael, you know that?" she admitted, a slight titter in her words.

"I like you too, Siena." I looked at her, captivated by the way she moved in those heels, that dress.

We rode the elevator up to our floor, neither of us saying a word. I held her hand. She gave me her keycard, and I slid it into the slot, unlocking the door.

"You're coming in, right?"

Fuck yes, I was. There was no way I'd be able to sleep tonight without touching her. I nodded and let her pull me into the room.

She left me in the entryway and plucked off her shoes, letting them drop to the floor. I tossed my jacket onto a nearby table. Undid my tie, tossed it onto my jacket. Not for a moment did I let my eyes slip from her luscious form.

I opened the patio door, letting in the cool night air. We needed to breathe. She grabbed a bottle of water on her way and followed me out onto the balcony.

"I fucking love this city."

"It's a good city," I agreed, popping a couple of buttons free from my shirt, then from my wrists.

"It's a *great* city." She raised the bottle to her lips and took two huge sips.

"You think this is great? Nah. New York. Now *that's* a great city."

"Haven't been there much. But it's definitely a close second."

I laughed. "I'll take you there sometime." *What? Where the fuck had that come from.*

"Hmm," she wondered. "Maybe." Her smile let me know that my offer wasn't completely off the table.

"How you feeling?" I came closer and wrapped my arm around her.

"A-okay."

"Good." I was rubbing circles against her back. She leaned into me and sighed. I kissed her head, enjoying her smell and the warmth of her body.

She shivered against me. "Cold?"

"A little." She snuggled into me.

I took her hand, kissed it, and led her back inside where it was warm. I didn't want this night to end. In fact, I had a completely different idea of how things were going to go tonight. But I didn't want to take advantage of her if she was drunk.

I was an idiot frozen in confusion, trying to figure out what my next step should be. One part of me told me to leave and let her get some sleep. Another part reminded me I wouldn't be able to sleep unless I made her body mine.

She broke into my thoughts. "Why are you holding back?" It appeared she was reading my mind, that she was attuned to my internal dilemma.

"I'm trying to be a gentleman." A guilty chuckle escaped me. "For tonight, at least. You've been drinking. And—"

She quirked up an eyebrow.

"We've been drinking," I amended.

"And?"

"I don't want the first time we're together to be when we're drunk."

She looked at me, blinking, trying to maintain focus. "I'm not drunk. Are you?"

"I've had more drinks than I'd like to have in me for this" —I gestured in between us—"to happen tonight."

"All righty," she giggled out. "Whatever you say." She tossed her hair back and gave me a suggestive look. "But just so you know, you're missing out."

It was my turn to raise my eyebrow. "I bet I am."

She stepped closer. "I am too."

Her words quashed my internal struggle. I was done

fighting this need inside me. I looked into her stunning eyes and whispered seductively: "I'm not going to let you sleep tonight until I have completely satisfied you."

She sucked in a breath, obviously dumbfounded by my words and my confidence. I pulled her against me, kissing her deeply.

"Come with me," she said, pulling me to the bed.

I kissed her mouth, once, twice, before pulling back and looking at her face, into those magnificent hazel eyes.

Her eyes flashed her utter willingness.

I plunged into her again, sucking her tongue into my mouth, assaulting both of our senses.

She broke away, peeking up at me. "That was no gentleman's kiss."

"I'm not feeling very gentlemanly right now."

Her laugh was deep and husky. "Good."

I grazed my hands down her waist, caressing her body as I traveled back up, gently squeezing the sides of her breasts.

Siena emitted a carnal growl and took me in for another deep kiss. She tasted like mint and smelled like honey—a mixture of sugar and spice.

I lowered my hands and brushed my fingers over her hips, inching up the hem of her purple dress. I ran my hand up her exposed thigh, teasing her with the tips of my fingers along the edges of her underwear, feeling the soft fabric and her even softer skin.

I dipped my fingers underneath the lace that held her warmth. My finger traced the slit of her lips, and I sucked in my breath. I could barely get out the words: "Fuck, you're wet."

She pushed into my hand until my fingers disappeared inside her. Whimpering, she hungrily grabbed the back of my head and pulled me to her for another kiss. When she had captured my mouth, she moved her hands to my belt and yanked my shirt out of my pants, working furiously to unbutton it. Her hands felt like velvet as she ran them over the ridges of my abs, across my pecs, and up around my shoulders. The feel of her caused my dick to strain even harder against the fabric of my pants.

She pushed my shirt off, stroking and massaging my arms all the way down. She grabbed my hand, helping me plunge it deeper into her hot, wet center. Our hands worked together as she rocked against my fingers, teaching me exactly how she liked to be touched.

I loved how she knew her body and wasn't afraid to show me how she wanted to be pleasured. It was such a fucking turn on, both of our hands working her simultaneously. Tonight, despite my own need, I intended to focus solely on her pleasure, to learn her body and to watch how she reacted to my touch, what she liked, what she needed.

I pulled one side of her dress off her shoulder, her breast popping free. I leaned down and took her pert nipple into my mouth and sucked. She groaned as she fisted her other hand in my hair. Then she let go, pulled the other side of her dress down, squeezing her breast to my lips, enticing me so I could savor more of her.

Her tits were in my face, and I moved back and forth over them, sucking, biting, squeezing them in my hands and rubbing them against my face as she rocked against me.

I knew she was mine. I palmed her in my hand, letting her grind against my fingers, rubbing herself over me, bringing herself pleasure as I tasted the honeyed flesh of her succulent breasts.

Her movements sped up, and her breath became more hitched and erratic. I knew she was on the verge of coming.

"I'm gonna come," she panted, her voice raspy and on the edge of climax.

I slowed my movements, removed my hand, brought my fingers slicked with her wetness, up over her body. I used both hands to grab her tits, suck her nipples into my mouth, flicking delicate licks and nips over their silky surface.

"I'm so close. I don't want you to stop. I need to feel you," she moaned, grasping my head in her hands. Her mouth was hot as she plunged into me, sliding her tongue over mine.

I pushed her dress over her hips, pulled myself away from her heat, her warmth, and looked at her body clad only in her underwear and the light moisture of our lust. I moved my hands behind her, feeling her plump ass in my hands, and squeezed while I trailed my fingers up her crack and traced the line of string. Then up, over her hips, following the lace down both sides of her front.

She moaned, uninhibited and animalistic. "Touch me," she instructed. I slid my fingertips underneath the elastic down both sides of her *V*, bringing them to her center, not quite touching her where I knew she wanted me to.

Her gasp was almost a cry, and I gently pushed her back into the mattress, the comforter a feathery pillow beneath her. Her smile was loaded with mischief and want as she laid back. She swept her hair from underneath her neck, tipped her chin up, plunged her finger into her mouth, then skimmed along her collarbone and down between her breasts. She slowly circled each nipple, never taking her eyes from me. My god, this woman captivated me with every move she made. I moved over her, straddling her slight frame, kissing her neck. She moaned and shifted her head so I'd have better access. I lost myself in the sounds she made as I lapped at her and reveled in her scent.

I moved down her body, starting with her legs, using my tongue and lips, slowly making my way up until I reached her hips, where I pulled at the edge of her thong with my teeth. I nipped tiny bites along the inside crevice between her thigh and her pelvis, where the material met her skin. She squirmed, arching closer to my face, begging for more.

I lifted myself, moved down toward the edge of the bed,

and kneeled in front of her—a beggar to his queen. The floor lamp in the corner of the room provided just enough light to see her glistening body. I ran my hands slowly up her legs and back down, watching my fingers move over her, using her sounds to gauge her desire, what she liked and what she wanted. I couldn't tear my eyes away from watching me touch her, urged on by her tiny gasps and shudders.

Her legs were opened slightly as I ran the backs of my hands up the insides of her thighs, flipped them, and brought my fingertips back down. "Let me see you. All of you." I pulled off her thong, and she spread her legs open before me. I met her eyes one more time to make sure she wanted this as much as I did. She bit her lip and nodded. Needing no further invitation, I slid my fingers along the folds of her pulsing lips. I massaged tiny circles over her, turning them into figure eights as I relished in her wetness under my fingertips.

I kneeled closer, inhaled deeply, loving her scent. I peered up at her, my mouth still close enough for her to feel my breath on her sensitive skin. "I've wanted you for so long. I can't wait to taste you."

A lascivious groan from this gorgeous woman spurred me on.

I took a lick, just a quick flick of my tongue. I raised my head, smiled wickedly at her, knowing I would take my time pleasuring her tonight. She groaned helplessly.

"Please," she begged, closing her eyes, grabbing my head.

I shook loose, pinned her hands. I wanted her stupidly satisfied and gloriously fulfilled when I was done. But I would take my time.

I dipped my head, nipped at the crease where her thigh met her sweet center. Her skin was warm as I licked over her. She was bare beneath me except for a teeny tiny strip of hair. I ran my nose along the edges, letting my lips follow as I traced the pattern.

Her breath hitched, and her hands yanked from beneath

my hold. She pushed her fingers into my hair, pulling at the strands. "Michael, please." Her words stole my breath.

I groaned against her as my fingers spread her lips to expose her most sensitive part. I blew against it and licked lightly before I drew it into my mouth and tugged gently. I slipped one finger inside her while my tongue ran circles around her clit. She rose to meet my mouth.

"Faster. More," she groaned.

I slipped another finger inside, speeding up my movements as she rocked against my hand, just enough to elicit another throaty moan from her.

I worked my tongue and fingers as she pushed herself up to meet every move I made.

She tasted like nothing I'd imagined. She was better than anything I'd ever had, more than anyone I'd ever wanted. I could suck on her for hours and not tire of her salty perfection. She was warm, heady. I swirled my tongue up, over, back, and forth. My fingers moved in her, my fingertips massaging that most sensitive point deep inside.

"Yes, yes, yes," she moaned out in succession. "I'm gonna come."

I pressed the tip of my tongue harder onto her clit, finger fucking her with all the abandon she elicited underneath my hands and my mouth. I felt her explode from deep within. She cried out as she came in my mouth, her muscles contracting against my fingers. "Michael!"

When the waves dissipated, her breath uneven and ragged from the sensation, I slowed my pace, removed my fingers, took one last luscious lick, and placed tender kisses on her inner thighs.

I crawled up her body, trailing kisses and bites over her beautiful form until I was face to face with her. Supporting myself on my forearms above her, I brushed a few stray strands of hair away from her face, kissed her jawline. "You are fucking perfect."

She pulled at my belt.

I pushed her hand away.

She tried again in vain.

She tilted her head, evidently confused.

"Just let me focus on you tonight." Her eyes widened, and she smiled.

I could die in that smile. I was so intoxicated by her. I felt a tingling sensation roll through me just from the gratification that exuded from her. Her scent was an aphrodisiac for me. I was high off her smell, and, yes, of course, I wanted to be inside her. But more than that, I wanted to make her say my name again while I savored the sweetness of her.

"That doesn't seem fair," she pouted, still slightly breathless.

"Well, now, if there's one lesson I've learned, it's that life's not always fair, is it?"

She shook her head, a hint of sadness coming into her eyes. "No, it isn't."

I touched her face. "Baby, smile. I've got you. Right here, with me."

The sadness disappeared as I moved down between her breasts, kissed each hard nipple, then lifted her legs over my shoulders as I lowered back down. "I can't get enough of you," I whispered against her hot flesh.

Taking my time, I brought her to another series of orgasms, and after the fourth one, her legs shaking convulsively around my head, she begged me to stop, told me she couldn't take any more.

"Oh my god, Michael," she whispered, and I couldn't stop myself from smiling in between her legs. There it was again. My name on her lips.

I slid up, licked her belly, nipped at the soft smoothness of the side of her breast, then kissed her neck. She was limp and almost lifeless beneath me.

I moved to her side and leaned on my elbow.

She turned her head to face me, and in the dim light from the other room, I saw her smile. "That is one incredible mouth you've got, mister."

I chuckled, then kissed her again. She teased my lips with her tongue ever so lightly.

"I knew I enjoyed looking at that mouth. But damn," she hummed, touching my lips with her velvety fingertips. "That was amazing."

"The pleasure was all mine, Ms. Moretti."

She sighed, absentmindedly content.

I kissed her again softly. "We have a bit of a drive tomorrow. And we're meeting with Jax." I kissed the side of her head, the sweet, tender part of her temple.

"I know." She sounded relaxed and sleepy.

"Better get some rest."

She put her lips to my chest, kissed me on my heart. "Okay."

"Sleep well, baby," I whispered.

She nestled closer and closed her eyes.

I knew I should go back to my room, but lying here felt right with her in my arms. I decided I'd stay until I knew she was sound asleep. Then I'd go back to my own bed. I was playing with fire staying here and her words about "keeping things casual and friendly" repeated through my head. Still, I couldn't bring myself to leave.

I played with her silky tendrils, drawing them through my fingers while mentally reviewing my notes for tomorrow. It'd take a couple of hours to get to Jax's. We'd stop for lunch on our way. Get there, settle in, and go over her presentation and her sales pitch. I knew she'd be able to sell him on Moretti's—their reputation spoke for itself. I couldn't wait to hear Siena talk about the wines again. She had a certain flair, and listening to her talk about things she loved made me itch to touch her and get her alone. There was just something about watching her—her voice, how she spoke, how she smiled and seemed to come alive—it was such a turn on.

My eyes sagged with fatigue. Siena was breathing deeply, her head nestled into me, my arm tucked beneath her. Moving would surely wake her. My eyes strained as I tried to stay awake. I'd wait until she turned over, then leave. Her soft breathing settled me, my eyes fluttered closed, and a quiet hum from her was the last sound I heard before I fell fast asleep.

♥♥♥

What the hell was wrong with me?

I slept. In her bed. All night.

Fuck me.

Why didn't I go back to my own room?

It was right fucking next door!

I was breaking her rules. Shit, I was breaking *my* rules.

No strings attached did not look like this: me spending the night in her bed, holding her, and waking up before she did so that I could watch her.

What the fuck was happening to me?

I needed to get my shit in check before I scared her off . . . or did something even more stupid.

CHAPTER Twenty-Four

Siena

THE SHRILLNESS OF MY ALARM woke us out of a dead sleep.

We shot straight up in bed like we'd been caught doing something illicit and forbidden.

I laughed as Michael leaped out of bed, covering himself like someone had just walked in on us. "Good morning to you too. Whatcha hiding there?" I made a playful grab for the pillow, giggling as I silenced my phone.

"Jesus. That thing is fucking loud." He scrubbed his face, dropping the pillow.

I swallowed as I took him in—all of him. He was wearing a pair of boxer briefs, and the massive bulge in his pants had me choking on my tongue. Sometime in the night, he must have shed his pants and gone back to sleep. I flashed back to when I had awoken around two and found him still there, his arm loosely wrapped around me. The memory made me smile.

"Sorry. I forgot I'd set it."

"No"—he raked a hand through his come-fuck-me hair—"I've been awake a while. I didn't want to wake you by getting up."

"Well," I said, letting the sheet fall lower, my breasts full out, as I arched my back in a dramatic stretch, "since we're up, I guess I'll just hop in the shower." I pulled my hair through my hands, draped it over my shoulder. "Care to join me?"

He walked to me, rested his hands on the bed, kissed the corner of my mouth. "Ms. Moretti, if I take you up on your invitation, we might never leave this room today."

I laughed, sweeping his wild bedhead hair back. "Is that such a bad thing?"

"Not at all. But we do have an appointment to keep. So, as much as I'd love to join you, I think it's best to raincheck that shower."

"Suit yourself."

He groaned, pushing off the bed. He stuck his hand in his boxers, readjusting himself. "Trust me. It does not suit me at all right now."

I groaned myself, planting a pout on my lips. "Fine. But you owe me."

"I believe I paid up four times last night."

I felt my nipples harden and my clit tingle. "Five, if we're counting. But don't let it go to your head." I hopped out of bed, completely and gloriously naked. I danced my fingertips from his shoulders to his cock and palmed him. "I'm going to take a shower." I placed a chaste kiss at the corner of his mouth. "You know where it is if you change your mind."

I turned, knowing he'd watch every step I took. I walked through to the bathroom, grabbed the door jam, and turned back to look at him. As suspected, he was still standing there watching me, hard-on fully raging. I licked my lips, appreciating his rippled body.

"Bitch," he teased, tossing a pillow at me.

I giggled, ducking out of its way.

I was already under the warm water when the shower door opened. He didn't say a word, just came behind me, wrapped his arms around me, and let one hand tickle down my stomach. He wrapped his other around my hair, moved it over my shoulder, and placed kisses upon the bare skin of my back as the water drenched us. He moved his hands slowly up my waist, cupped my tits, then moved back down my belly, in between my legs. I had to slam my hand against the wall not to fall to the shower floor when he slipped his fingers in between my folds.

He growled in my ear, taking my lobe between his teeth. "You're so fucking wet already."

I dropped my head to the side as he drew his fingers in circles over me. I ground back into him, feeling his full length in between our bodies, ready and willing, just like me. The tip of his cock strained against me, his fingers still moving inside of me.

He pushed in deeper, drawing a low groan from my throat. I rolled my eyes back, relishing his touch and the feel of his cock against my bare ass, and how his fingers filled me up.

I reached back and fisted my hand into his hair, guiding his mouth to my neck to where I wanted it. He nipped at my skin, sucked, nipped again. I arched my back, pushing into him, moaning as he kissed me from behind.

I turned my head, met his mouth. His tongue glided over mine, mirroring the way his fingers were sliding into me. I rocked into his hand, my movements jagged and wild.

"You feel so fucking good," he growled.

"Oh god," I whispered. "Michael, please."

"Like this?" He circled and rubbed, doing that figure eight thing again.

"Just like that." I moved against him, trying desperately to get closer.

Our bodies were slick from the water, and it felt heavenly as the warmth ran down me, hot and steamy, my insides burning up from the pleasure Michael was bringing me.

"Faster. Harder," I instructed as he slid his fingers in and out, circled his thumb over my clit. "So close," I groaned, wanting his dick inside me. It was a torturous dilemma—wanting his cock so I could feel him deep inside but loving how he pleased me with his hands. His arm tightened around me, supporting me as I thrust myself against his hand, shuddering against him as I came undone.

I felt myself convulse and throb around his fingers. He retreated slowly, biting then kissing the sensitive skin of my neck. Turning, I grabbed him in a kiss that stole the last of my breath.

I ran my mouth along his chest, biting and licking, feeling the sinuous muscle under my tongue and between my teeth. I moved down his center, a trail of kisses in my wake as I lowered myself, kneeling before him.

I looked up, the water sluicing over my head. He smiled, brushing my hair back from my face. I pushed him back a step, against the wall, took his long length in my hand, stroked down and back up, rubbed my thumb over the tip, and slightly squeezed. He growled like an animal. I relished the sound.

With my eyes fixed on his, I opened my mouth and started at the base, flattening my tongue against him as I moved up his long shaft. I watched him as he watched me. I swirled my tongue around the top and cupped my lips to trace my mouth down and back up, repeating the swirling of my tongue over the tip of his dick.

He moaned deeply, and I thought I heard him whisper my name. He shoved his hands through my hair, holding my head. I peered up at him again. He looked lost. Lost in pleasure, lost in the feeling of himself against my lips. I lost myself in his eyes. He held my gaze, his fingers flexing against my scalp. I felt a tug deep within as I held him in my hands, my lower lip against the tip of his manhood. I was getting wet all over again, turned on by his eyes on me, watching as I was about to bring him glorious pleasure. A wicked gleam flashed in my eyes, an even more wicked grin crossed my lips, then I broke eye contact and swallowed him.

He cried out. I bobbed my head up and down, his hands still tangled in my hair. I heard his head hit the back of the shower wall, and another moan escape him. The sound was glorious.

Using my hand and lips to guide, suckle, and stroke his smooth cock, I worked my mouth over him, following the rhythm and sound of his breathing.

I reached around, taking his firm ass in my hands. I squeezed, massaged his cheeks, feeling him flex in my grasp as he moved back and forth into my mouth. My lips and tongue moved freely over him, suctioning him smoothly as I helped guide him back and forth with me.

"Damn, woman, that mouth of yours," he rasped out with heavy breaths.

I grinned at his words, brought my hands back, cupping his balls, squeezing, rubbing him as I moved faster over the length of him.

His breathing was intensifying. He was close. His movements sped up, his fingers digging into my head, trying to keep hold.

"You don't know what you're doing to me," he groaned out, lost in pleasure.

His balls still in my hand, I moved my index finger around the back of them, my thumb in the front. I pulled just the slightest bit to create tension and pleasure. His groan of approval, gruff and guttural, spurred me on. I was getting off from the sounds he was making above me. I moved faster, relishing the feeling of him hitting the back of my throat. His hands left my hair, and I heard them slap against the shower walls.

"Siena, I'm gonna come," he warned me.

"Mm-hmm," I gurgled around him, not taking my mouth off him.

"Fuck, so close, baby." One hand came back to my hair, his fingers pulling at it now. Hard. And the slight pain of it, mingled with my own gratification from pleasuring him, was an exquisite, hedonistic combination.

His body began to jerk. He pulled again on my hair and held my head still as he plunged back and forth into my mouth. He came, yelling my name as he spilled into my mouth, down my throat. I felt his vein pulsing with his release, my tongue pressed against him. I swallowed every bit as I slid my mouth back up his shaft one last time. He relaxed under my hands as I slid them along his hips, my fingertips tracing up that sexy *V*, over his abs, across his muscles. He took my hands in his as he helped me stand. As I rose, I licked his stomach, kissed his chest, then looked into his beautiful face, smiling with selfish satisfaction.

He smoothed my hair off my face, still pressed against the wall. He closed his eyes, hands splayed over my hips, still maintaining physical contact. He peeked one eye open, looked at me, and grinned.

I couldn't resist grinning back. His innocently relaxed boyish charm seized me, mesmerized me. He tugged on my hips, forcing me to him, our bodies touching, gloriously naked. His arms wrapped around me, enveloping me in the warmth of him, the water running down my back. "Holy crap, Siena." He sighed as I lay my head on his chest, listening to the beating of his heart. "You. Those lips. Amazing."

I smiled at his words, glad I could finally reciprocate the insane pleasure he had given me last night and just minutes ago.

His fingers moved to my chin. I opened my eyes, his own studying my face as he looked at me. "I think . . . I can finally move." He chuckled, making me laugh. He bent down, claimed my mouth, and kissed me sensually.

I circled my arms around his neck. "If we don't get moving, we'll never leave."

"I don't see a problem with that right now."

"Except for the meeting we have with Jax."

"Oh, right," he said, popping off the wall, standing up. "Completely forgot about that. Wonder why?" he said with a smirk.

I couldn't help the shit-eating grin that covered my face as his eyes roamed my body.

He leaned down again, covering my lips with his as he guided me back under the water for another orgasm.

♥ ♥ ♥

It was a little after eleven when we finally left, our shower rendezvous consuming much of our morning. We drove along, listening to music, talking, and getting to know each other as friends do. I told him how Audrey, Jenny, Lauren, and I met and some of the fun and silly adventures we had been through growing up. We exchanged stories, talked about college, traveling, and our careers.

I found Michael incredibly easy to talk to when we weren't bickering about the hotel. I already found him charming, charismatic, and sexy. But now, spending one-on-one time together, I was getting to see the funny, silly, lighthearted side of him. His genuine interest in me, my work, and my life made it surprisingly easy for me to open up.

There were two things he seemed to avoid talking about: the hotel and his father. He shared stories from his childhood, about growing up with his mother while his brother stayed with his father, how their relationship was a bit strained and dysfunctional.

We reminisced about our first crush, our first kiss, and the first time we had sex. I told him a little more about Tim, our working relationship, and his infidelity. I was one hundred and ten percent open and honest about everything that I had been through, even finally admitting that I had stupidly given him the money and how I had successfully gotten it back. I left out the details of him asking for another chance when we met up yesterday. His ploy to get me back didn't matter in the least to me, and it didn't hold any significance regarding my future. Or to Michael.

"Sounds like the fucker didn't deserve you," he said without hesitation. He was so matter of fact about his conclusion, and it left me a little confused. Even though Tim didn't deserve me, I still felt lost because I didn't yet know or believe in what I did deserve.

It came out of nowhere when he asked about my parents. What could I really tell him? There wasn't much to the story.

Swallowing the lump in my throat, I started, "My dad died in a plane crash when I was five years old. My mother left shortly afterward because she 'never intended on being a single mom.' I'm not sure she ever wanted me to begin with." I shrugged. "She gave up her rights, signed me over to my grandparents. I don't remember much, other than being devastated about my father's death. I was too young to really grasp what it meant to lose my dad," I sighed. "But I still get sad about it every now and then."

He reached over and took my hand. "That's understandable," he said and sent me a kind smile. "What about your mom?"

"What about her?"

"Do you ever—"

"Wonder about her?" I finished for him.

"Yeah." His thumb ran in small circles over the back of my hand.

"I did for a while when I was younger. But"—a heavy sigh left me—"I just accepted it for what it was. Audrey helped me a lot with that. She had a similar situation with her mother."

He nodded, and we both became quiet for a moment.

"I've never been in love," he admitted out of the blue, breaking into my thoughts.

My head whipped around. "Seriously?" I wasn't entirely shocked to hear this, but his confession left me in a state of confusion. Should this come as a relief or a warning?

"With my parents' divorce, I have just always been a little put off by the whole *true love* thing. Plus, I've been too busy focusing on my work, my career. I haven't had a whole lot of time for serious relationships." His shoulders rose in a shrug. "I don't know."

"I guess that makes sense. But don't you get lonely?"

He shot me an arrogant look.

"Right. You're never lonely." I shook my head. "Figures."

"I'm not a complete shmuck, Siena. I've always been honest with the women I've been with. I don't have time for games. Or lies. Even if I haven't been serious about my relationships, I don't think my partners deserve dishonesty." His fingers absentmindedly tapped the steering wheel in time with the music. "I've just always found it's best for me to keep things simple, uncomplicated."

"Yeah. No strings attached." My eyes were glued to the road in front of us. "I get it. Simple. Uncomplicated. Seems to work for you." I chanced a glance.

"So far, so good. For you, too, right? Your rules?"

An incoming call halted our conversation. "Allan fucking Blaire," Michael muttered, pressing the ignore button, sending his father to voicemail. I didn't know whether to be relieved or insulted.

I stared out the window, our conversation not picking up again. It seemed Michael's father still had the power to come between us, even if we weren't talking about him.

I relaxed into my seat, trying to enjoy the drive. Michael turned up the radio, humming along with the music, neither of us saying a word.

The silence offered me some time with my own thoughts.

Talking about Tim, the slimy, conniving, two-timing jerk

brought back everything I had put aside yesterday. And it plagued me.

I was happy to be putting some physical space between us again. I couldn't stand to be up there right now and have him roaming the streets, reminding me of him. It was incredibly important for me to put all of this in the past officially. I had my money in hand, a gorgeous man beside me, and the promise of a new career right in front of me.

Michael was a much welcome distraction to the turmoil I was experiencing and the upheaval to my life that I was trying to forget. I had allowed him to help me get rid of the awful memory of my ex. And I had done it without any question.

I wanted and accepted Michael's advances for all the right reasons. I had *really* wanted him, craved him. But I still felt a sense of guilt that I hadn't told him the complete tale of what had happened with Tim after my interviews and at least given him the opportunity to make up his own mind about what would happen next between us. Instead, I kept him in the dark. I was surprised and irritated at my guilt. The girls assured me that I didn't need to tell Michael anything. Tim and I weren't together. That was all that mattered. But something was nagging at me. I honestly didn't know how I'd feel if our roles were reversed.

I had used Michael, at least a little bit. But wasn't he using me too? We both had been clear about keeping things light. No commitments, no hassles. Should I feel guilty that he was there, ripe for the picking, exactly when I needed him? My eyes shifted to him for a quick glance. God, he dazzled me. Perfect hair, impeccable smile, stunning looks. And awesome personality to boot. Not to mention his skillful tongue and mouth and flawless body.

Think about it, Siena. Really, really think about it. He's been with countless women, according to the tabloids and the internet searches I did. So what if he was one of only ten guys

I'd slept with? Were we really in a competition? He wanted me—that was obvious. I wanted him too.

I knew we agreed to no strings attached. It seemed he accepted my rules: keep things between us uncomplicated. But now that I had gotten to know him and had gotten my hands on him, I wondered, *How long could things stay uncomplicated?*

All I knew now was that last night and this morning, holy fuck-a-moly!

I already wanted more.

How long could I keep up this façade?

CHAPTER
Twenty-Five

SIENA

Jax O'Halloran's Place was a chic, boutique hotel. And it was stunningly gorgeous. The driveway was lined with immaculately shaped shrubs and dotted with planters that housed palm trees and birds of paradise. A few rounded turrets stood atop the ends of the pristine cream stucco façade and Spanish tiled roof.

Located along the coast, the azure blue backdrop added to the already picturesque scenery. The fact the hotel was near the water was a definite plus. I sucked in a breath at the magnificent view, inhaled the salty air laced with freshly mowed grass and fragrant flowers. Trees swayed in the breeze and overflowing planters of bright flowers bordered the entrance in a rainbow of colors. It was an oasis of posh luxury right from the driveway.

"You know the owner of this place?" I couldn't hide the awe in my voice.

Michael chuckled. "Not the owner. The manager. It's one of the perks of having him as a friend. Impressed?"

"Maybe"—I held my fingers an inch apart—"just a little."

He chuckled, patting my knee, lingering just slightly before returning his hand to the steering wheel. "He's one of my best friends from college. We were both business majors, same frat, brothers, you know?"

"I'll say. I wish I had a friend with a hotel like this."

"You do."

"I do?" My mind sifted through all the people I knew. "Who?"

"*Me*. You can stay at any of the E Hotels whenever you like." His eyebrow rose, a twinkle of playfulness in his gorgeous eyes. "I know they're a little *audacious*, I think is the word you used, if memory serves." He shrugged his shoulders, smile still tactfully in place. "But, as my *friend*, you always have an open invitation. Any time."

"What's the catch?"

"This is a *no strings attached* arrangement, Siena. There is no catch." Something about the gleam in his eyes told me there had to be a catch, some kind of strings, something required as payment. My breasts tingled thinking about the delicious possibilities.

"Jax is a real lady's man. He's a dog, but he's my bro." He shrugged nonchalantly, chancing a look in my direction. "Just so you're forewarned."

I sensed some trepidation in his voice, so I cocked a brow and smirked. "I think I can handle him. You haven't been too difficult so far."

His roar of laughter filled the car. "I may be a lady's man, but I'm not a dog."

"Walks like a dog. Barks like a dog—"

"Oh, come on. I think I've proven, at least a little, that I'm not like that." He grinned broadly, flashing those perfect pearly whites at me, twitching his brows suggestively. "After all, last night was all about *you*," he said as he pulled to a stop.

The memories flashed, and I shivered with delight. I wasn't about to let him know the effect he had on me though. "One night does not cancel out all the stuff I found on Google."

"You and your infamous Google searches. You can't always believe everything you read online or in the tabloids, Ms. Moretti. Most of it's just fodder to boost sales."

I crossed my eyes and stuck out my tongue. "Mm-hmm."

Michael took my hand in his as he led me under a row of curved archways. This simple gesture made my insides flutter with anticipation.

I was just as impressed with the hotel's interior as I had been with the exterior. The enormous foyer was lined with white marble floors upon which sat huge black and gold planters filled with leafy parlor palms, lady palms, spiky yucca trees, and fiddle leaf figs. Other smaller decorative containers filled with orchids, bromeliads, and hibiscus stood atop large glass tables.

"Mr. Blaire! So nice to see you again. And so soon," the front desk girl, her name tag reading *Nicole*, said, flashing a toothy smile, her face lighting up at Michael's arrival.

"Will you let Mr. O'Halloran know we're here?"

"We?" she asked, a hint of surprise in her voice as she looked at me and realized he wasn't alone. "Oh, yes. Right away." Recovering from her obvious shock, she smiled meekly at me. Nicole may have regained her composure, but I sensed some disappointment. I couldn't help the twinge of irritation as she eye-fucked Michael, pushing a line on the phone.

"He'll be right out, Mr. Blaire," she said a little too cheerfully. I liked neither her tone nor the seductive glances she was sending Michael.

"Thanks." He seemed unaffected by her flirtation.

"Thank you, Nicole," I said, ready to link my arm through Michael's. Instead, he grabbed my hand and placed a sweet kiss on it before turning us around and guiding me to a sitting area full of plush couches and wing-backed chairs in dark grey fabrics.

"Thanks," he said as we sat down and I dug into my purse, retrieving a small makeup bag. "You saved me."

"I did? From what?"

"From the receptionist."

"Oh?" I was trying to hide my reaction to Nicole's obvious interest. My chest felt tight and hot. I didn't like the fact that some flirty bimbo could trigger these feelings in me. I didn't like it even more that I couldn't deny that I was, in fact, just the teensiest bit jealous.

"Yeah, she's a little too . . . What's the word?" He raked a hand through his hair.

I swiped my lips with candy pink gloss. "Obvious?" I smacked my lips together. "Eager? Desperate?"

"Desperate," he said a little too loudly, his word echoing in the wide-open space. I laughed at his bug-eyed expression. "Her. Not you."

I patted his knee.

"She's a nuisance. Has been since I first met her. I've politely declined her previous invitations. And still . . ."

I leaned in, eyes wide. "Ah, don't tell me Mr. Popular is surprised." *Damn, he smells good.* I wanted to lick up one side and down the other. "You're used to it. Don't play."

"Good thing I have you here as my *beard*."

I smacked him on his arm. "I am not your *beard*!"

"Well, for all she knows, you and I are quite serious." He wrapped his arm around me, leaned in to kiss me. "Come on, let's show her how serious we are." He waggled his eyebrows, smiled that panty-dropper smile.

"Get outta here!" I playfully shoved him, then silently begged him to take me right then and there in a passionate and unquestionable *Hands-off, bitch!* kind of kiss.

"Suit yourself," he said smugly. "You know you want it."

"You're ludicrous." I tried shrugging off my true feelings. I needed something to occupy my thoughts. I turned in my chair, looking around the space, noting how luxurious and gorgeous it all was.

Michael cleared his throat and tapped my knee, bringing

my attention back. He stood, holding his hand out to me, as a tall, impeccably dressed man made his way over.

"Michael!" he hailed, clasping Michael's hand in his before clapping him on the back. "Brother! So glad to see you again." He turned his head toward me meeting my eyes. "Ms. Moretti, I presume. I'm Jax," he said, holding his hand out to me.

"Siena, please," I said, awestruck by his dazzling dark blue eyes and undeniable attractiveness. His hand was soft and warm, his shake firm. He was gorgeous. Not gorgeous like Michael, but, *Oh my!* I could see now why Michael was so adamant about coming up here with me. Jax O'Halloran was tall, a few inches shorter than Michael, but he still stood inches above me. His shoulders were broad like he lifted weights or played football or maybe swam the 200-meter butterfly. He filled out the lines of his suit like it was tailor-made for him. His shirt brought out the blue of his eyes. His skin was tanned, making his eyes seem even brighter. He clearly took exceptionally good care of himself—his skin and his body were flawless.

"It truly is a pleasure," he said, placing a kiss atop my hand.

"Thank you. Michael's told me a lot about you." I kept the "dog" part out, feeling that particular comment was probably best left between Michael and me.

He laughed. "I'm sure he has. They're all lies, of course."

I smiled, immediately taken with him. "Of course." His voice was deep and smooth, like pure velvet. I could see why, according to Michael, he had so much luck with the ladies. I twisted a strand of hair around my finger and felt immediate embarrassment at the schoolgirl reaction he drew from me.

"I've booked two rooms, as per your request, Michael. But I can always upgrade to one of the larger suites if you'd like." He looked back and forth between us.

"Oh, no," I blurted a little too quickly. "That won't be necessary."

"Right," Michael butted in. "We're here on business."

"A gorgeous woman like Ms. Moretti in your company, and there's nothing more? I'm disappointed." His eyes twinkled with a bit of mischievousness, gauging our reactions.

"Siena. And we are here for business, Mr. O'Halloran." I wasn't going to let him goad Michael or me into anything personal here in the hotel foyer.

"Please, call me Jax. *Mr. O'Halloran* is too formal and has too many syllables. We'll reserve that for the employees." He winked.

I laughed. "Yes, of course, Jax. Like I said, we're here strictly on business. But Michael and I have formed a friendship. Right?" I turned to get his approval.

A small smile curled on Michael's lips. "I'd like to think so," he agreed.

Jax's eyes twinkled, and I wondered if he could feel the vibe between us. "Nothing wrong with mixing a little business with pleasure," he said with another wink.

I laughed. "So I've been told."

"Let me show you to your rooms. Then Michael can take you on a tour." He paused, smiling between us, keeping the thoughts that flashed across his face to himself. I followed, Michael right behind me, as Jax led the way to the main building's elevator.

"Your rooms are right next to each other," he informed us as the elevator took us to the sixth floor. My room was exquisite. The bed looked like a cloud: king-sized, puffy white comforter, pillows galore. The little girl in me wanted to run and take a flying leap onto it.

A smile tugged at one corner of Michael's mouth as he watched me walk around the room, running my hand over freshly polished furniture and crisp linens. "This is beautiful," I said, popping my head into the bathroom.

"Thank you, Siena. We aim to bring our guests the best of

the best, luxurious and stylish accommodations in a most spectacular setting."

"You're telling me." I felt like my eyes might pop out of their sockets. The bathroom was three times the size of mine and housed a gorgeous jacuzzi tub and walk-in shower. Marble countertops and inlaid tile floors. Gold hardware accentuated the cabinets and faucets. It was breathtaking.

"I don't think we hold a candle to Blaire hotels," Jax stated from behind me, "but we do just fine."

Michael choked on his laugh at the look in my eyes.

Jax ignored Michael's teasing. "Please enjoy any of our amenities—on the house. Michael, as you requested, I've scheduled massages for three o'clock."

Michael cleared his throat as I raised my eyebrow at him. He reached his hand out to Jax and clapped him on the back in another brotherly hug. "Thanks, Jax. We'll see you at eight."

Jax's eyes darted to me, a sly smile on his lips. He took my hand in his, placed a kiss on it. "A pleasure to finally meet you, Siena. Enjoy your massages," he added, sending *another* wink to me.

I shoved a finger in Michael's chest as the door closed. "You are very sly, Mr. Blaire. If I didn't know better, I'd think you were trying to bribe me."

"Bribe you? *Never!*" There was the faintest smile behind his eyes. "I just thought it might be nice for us to indulge a little. Might as well enjoy ourselves while we're here."

I went to the slider, moved the curtains aside, and looked out at the property below. A large pool glittered in the sunlight as several guests sat enjoying their lunch and lay on lounge chairs, appreciating the sunshiny spring day.

I felt Michael come up behind me. His proximity started my heart beating faster. I turned to him, breathing in his intoxicating scent. He tucked my hair behind my ear, a featherlight tickle as his fingers skimmed my cheek. "I'm glad you are quite taken with your room and with Mr. O'Halloran. I mean Jax," he crooned, fluttering his eyelashes, swooning in jest.

"Oh, shut up." I pushed at him. "I was being polite."

"If only our first meeting had been that polite." He leaned against the doorjamb, a smart-ass smirk covering his face. "Let's grab something to eat."

"Okay." My hand itched to reach out and pull him in for a kiss. *No strings attached,* I reminded myself. Begrudgingly, I obeyed my subconscious.

"Remember, my room is right next door if you need anything in the next five minutes." His words sounded suggestive, and my skin tingled from the excitement they brought.

♥ ♥ ♥

AFTER A DELICIOUS LUNCH OF CRAB LOUIE SALADS AND A ninety-minute hot stone massage, we made our way around the property. I couldn't deny the fact that I was so relaxed from the massage. Rick, my masseur, had done a splendid job melting all the hidden tension right out of me. Standing with the salty ocean breeze blowing through my hair and whispering through the trees made me feel like I could fall fast asleep. I felt Michael's hand as he traced figure eights on my back. What was it about him and his touch that made my toes curl and my skin tingle?

As for the property, there were three buildings that housed half of the rooms available at the hotel. These formed a box around the center of the grounds. The main building, which we were staying in, was three times the size of the others and made up the fourth side of the boxed arrangement. It was its own private oasis: a gorgeous oceanic atmosphere outside the walls, a private and intimate escape for its visitors inside. Every room had a balcony that overlooked the pool and a charming courtyard furnished with several tables and chairs.

There was a gigantic two-way fireplace, perfect for cozying up with someone at night, a twelve-foot water wall surrounded by rocks and café style seating, and a spacious gazebo that housed more tables and chairs. It was indeed a perfect location to enjoy a meal or cocktails with someone or to just enjoy some solitude in the sumptuous and stunning ambiance. The pool was large and heated, the hot tub steaming in the cool March air.

"I don't think I'd ever get sick of staying here." I sighed as Michael's arm came around me. His body was warm against mine.

"It really is a gorgeous space."

I sucked in a breath. "This is it!"

I felt Michael's laugh before I heard it. "This is what?"

"This is what you need to create." I turned facing him, my eyes dancing as inspiration hit. "Scratch your original designs and create something like this. The buildings are perfect, and the design is intimate and unique."

Michael rubbed at his chin in consideration.

"You could still do it bigger. *Not* too much bigger, even though you have the space. But this hotel is awesome. It should be your muse. I could totally see something just like this in Monarch."

His eyes followed mine as I turned back, looking at everything, checking it out again. "Interesting insight, Ms. Moretti."

"Is that a yes?" I was about to jump out of my skin and do a happy dance. I was bursting with glee, a smile spreading over my lips, taking over my entire face.

"It's an *I'll think about it*. It's a sensitive time for development and construction. But"—he took my hand and kissed my palm—"it's something to consider." He planted a soft kiss at my temple, then said, "Let's go get ready for dinner." He kept his arm around me as we made our way back to our building.

♥ ♥ ♥

My temper was steaming even more than the hot shower I'd just taken. After we had briefly discussed my presentation, I told Michael I was going to take a nap before dinner. Complete and total lie. Instead, I called the girls to fill them in on the last day and a half. They'd really wanted to talk more about Michael, but I needed their help to devise a plan of attack.

I couldn't believe he had just shut me down like that with his parental and noncommittal tone—"*I'll think about it*"—the words every placating parent uses when they mean "No." I was bristling, knowing that his reaction was because of his father. But if I'd learned anything recently about Michael, it was that I'd have to play it smart, and *nice*, to work him over to my side. Being irritated or argumentative would not cut it. The girls devised a perfect plan for getting him to see exactly how *right* I was.

I felt sexy and confident in the dress I had chosen. Red, one-shouldered, and sexier than anything I'd ever wear to a meeting.

A brisk knock at my door had me hustling. I'd been mentally playing everything out in my head, and I'd lost track of time. Allan Blaire was going to be the demise of me. "Be right there," I called.

I felt my breath leave my body. There he stood, clean-shaven, dressed to the nines in charcoal gray slacks and a black dress shirt. A sweet aromatic scent mixed with woody notes of cardamom, orange, and fir gave him a wild smell and captured his desire to rule and to conquer. If only he could get out from beneath the shackles his father kept him in. He smelled like a *man* and looked like sex. Everything about him made my mouth water.

"C-come in. I'm sorry, I'm just running a smidge behind."

"You look sensational," he practically growled.

I felt him walk past me, the energy coming off him almost like his hands feathered all over my body even though he hadn't laid a finger on me. I already felt the pulsating between my legs. My body was hungry for his touch, for his taste, to hear the sounds he made as he pleasured me, to hear his groans as I pleasured him.

"Thank you." *Play it cool. Don't let him know how much he gets to you.*

I felt his eyes on me as I sashayed barefoot to the dresser, put my earrings in, and fastened the clasp of my bracelet—a simple chain of gold with a dangling heart. The charm, with the initials *AJLS* engraved on it, a gift to each of us from my grandparents at our high school graduation. I always wore it for good luck, and tonight I needed all the luck I could get. Swaying Michael over to my vision for the hotel was going to be quite the battle. Especially when that meant him fighting his father. Hopefully, he could figure a way to convince his boss when I finally found a way to convince him.

Nude heels sat like obedient little soldiers awaiting their orders. I tossed my hair over my shoulder, stealing a look at him. He held my eyes as I slid my dress open, exposing my leg, showing off the contour of my calf as I raised my foot and slipped it on. His eyes roamed over my body as I shifted my weight and raised the other side of my dress higher than necessary to slip my left foot into the next one. My four-inch fuck-me heels accentuating my legs, my dress hugging every curve of my body, offered me the perfect mix of sensual and sexual. I licked my lips as Michael's eyes traveled back up my body to my face. "I'm ready."

His Adam's apple bobbed.

"Yes. Yes, you are."

♥ ♥ ♥

"Ms. Moretti, you look exquisite this evening," Jax said. "Michael said you were a phenomenal chef and a savvy businesswoman all rolled into one. But he didn't say you were gorgeous on top of it. Well done, brother," he said as he clapped Michael on the back.

"Siena, please?" I asked with a smile, trying to keep my glee at a minimum. "I'd like to think that since Michael is a friend, that perhaps that makes us more than just potential business associates."

"Of course, of course. Your beauty must have struck my brain cells momentarily. I lost all train of thought."

I laughed, reaching out to place my napkin in my lap as the waiter popped a bottle of champagne. The smooth sound of jazz carried lightly through the speakers.

"Your label, Siena," Jax said as the waiter poured.

He lifted his glass. Michael and I followed suit. "To business and friendship," he said, clinking his glass against ours. "Michael has told me quite a bit about your family's winery. You work with your grandparents, right?"

"Yes, that's right." I told him about my great-great-grandfather and our legacy, essentially taking him through a tour of the winery like I would if he was visiting.

The waiter rolled over a tray containing other bottles and additional glasses. "Which should we try first?" Jax asked.

I tapped three of our best sellers, telling him about the flavors, notes, and pairings that would go best with each. Jax ordered according to my suggestions—a salad made of spring greens, feta cheese, pomegranate seeds, avocado, and a champagne vinaigrette and freshly baked French bread to start. We chatted companionably, and the conversation focused on business and family. We discussed Moretti Vineyards, our wines, and what we would provide as a partner.

I asked Jax about the hotel and his history running it. He amused me with some funny stories about Michael, how they had become friends during rush week of their freshman year, and how they'd been inseparable since. He was easy to talk to, and the fact that he was so open and honest made it easy for me to just be myself. He was unintimidating and laid-back. I hadn't been worried about meeting him, but I had told myself to be cautious since he was a friend of Michael's.

I poured glasses of Guilty Pleasures, sending Michael a flirtatious wink.

"Mmm, I taste raspberry, I think," Jax said.

"That's right. Plum and raspberry to sweeten it. It goes perfectly with the steaks we're having tonight."

Our dinner of filet mignon and giant prawns served with fingerling potatoes and broccolini was divine. Jax complimented the Moretti wines again. Business was going extremely well, and I was proud of the job I had done. Michael seemed satisfied, as well.

"I'm sorry to interrupt your dinner, Mr. O'Halloran. A call for you," the maître d' said.

"I'll just be a minute." He wiped his mouth, excusing himself.

"This is going really well. Thank you. For everything," I said, sitting back in my chair, sufficiently full.

"You're most welcome. It is going extremely well. But I see what you're doing."

"What?" I played coy.

"Talking up the hotel. Asking questions about the customers and reviews."

"I don't know what you're talking about," I lied, a smile creeping up.

He scooched closer to me, just a whisper away from me as he leaned in. "I think you know exactly what you're doing." His voice was husky and hungry. "Doing everything you can to make me agree to change hotel plans."

"So what if I'm taking an interest in this hotel, Michael? It's not fake. I'm genuinely taken with this place. If you opened your mind enough to see what I do, then you would realize that I'm right."

"When did I say you were wrong?" he challenged. I could feel his hand on his knee, right next to mine.

I swallowed, feeling a sense of shame. And a tinge of desire. "You didn't."

"Exactly. So why the incessant need to ask these inane questions, flirt with Jax, inflate his already huge ego, and try to make me jealous?"

"My questions aren't inane. They're legitimate . . ."—my eyes grew wide with shock—"Jealous? You're *jealous*?"

Michael cleared his throat as his hand snuck over to the soft spot under my knee. "I said *trying*. I'm not jealous, Siena." He stared into my eyes.

I swallowed, suddenly feeling parched. "Oh."

"I know how you feel about me." His hand slid up the inside of my thigh, under my skirt, and right between my legs where I was already hot and wet. "I can *feel* how you feel about me." I squirmed under his touch, my eyes boring into his, begging him to slip underneath my panty line and touch me, please me.

I tilted my hips closer, and he inched back. A carnal chuckle vibrated in his throat. I couldn't tear my eyes away from his. I licked my lips as his finger crept underneath the elastic. "You are wet for *me*." His eyebrow lifted. "*Right?*"

I looked down at my lap, where his hand was resting, his fingers twitching against me. I squirmed, trying to get closer.

"Uh-uh," he chastised, pulling away. "Answer the question."

It was shameful how wet I was. Just being in his presence, seeing him, the true him, interacting with his best friend, watching him conduct business in the easiest of ways turned me on so much. He was powerful, commanding, and arrogant, but equally charismatic, charming, and delectable. "Yes," I whispered, looking down, wishing I could see through my dress to his hand on me. "Yes, Michael." My words sounded more like a plea than an admission.

"I thought so," he answered. As hot as I found his arrogance, I wanted to reach for that face. Kiss his lips, swallow him whole, savor him until the only thing I could taste was him.

I felt the briefest flicker against my clit before he pulled his hand away and squeezed my knee. I wanted to scream in frustration.

"Sorry about that," Jax addressed us as he returned to the table and took his seat.

I tried to calm my racing heart, my pulsing loins, as Michael shifted ever so slightly to adjust himself. He was just as turned on as I was.

"Any big fires needing to be put out?" Michael asked as he made eye contact with me again, letting me know the question was really for me and not Jax.

I squirmed, wishing his hand was still on me so I could rub myself against it.

"No."

Michael brought his hand to his face, in an innocent gesture, but I knew what he was doing, knew he could smell me on his fingers. He inhaled deeply, his nostrils flaring, a smile kissing the corners of his mouth.

I took a sip of wine, trying to quench my thirst.

I decided to switch to water for the remainder of our meeting. Jax opened a bottle of our merlot, commenting on the flavor.

"Its aromatic taste comes from black cherry, plum, and even chocolate. The fruits and easy tannins give it that smooth, soft velvety finish."

As we wrapped up, Jax said, "Please draw up the contracts. I'm looking forward to working with you. As you know, I pride myself on offering our customers the best of the best."

I felt my chest swell. Grams and Pops were going to be so pleased. Another substantial account for Moretti Vineyards in the books.

"I knew you'd see what I saw, Jax. Great wine, great people. You'll be very happy with the decision." Michael seemed as happy as I was.

"I expected nothing less. Thank you for bringing Siena to meet me. So much better than having to deal with just you." He laughed, clapping Michael on his arm.

Michael's laugh warmed my heart. I loved the sound and seeing him genuinely happy. "It was a pleasure meeting you, Jax. Thank you for dinner. I'm so glad we could do this."

"Me too, Siena." He brought my hand to his mouth, gently placing a kiss upon it.

"We'll come to see you tomorrow before we head out," Michael said.

"See you then. Enjoy the rest of your evening," he bid us. And I swear I saw a twinkle in his eye as he looked between Michael and me.

Michael took me by the elbow and led me out before anything more was said. My heels on the marble floors were the only sound as we made our way across the lobby. He hurried me into the open elevator. I could feel the warmth emanating from him, the soft fabric of his shirt tickling my arm, causing goosebumps to break out on my skin.

He was stoically still next to me, but I would not touch him no matter how much I wanted to. I would not give in. Not yet. The heat he'd generated at the table continued to rise. My lips begged for him to kiss me. My body ached for his touch, but the only hint of his reciprocal feelings was the slight twitch of his hand next to mine. I desperately wanted to wrap myself around him, kiss him, but I needed to draw this out. To let him know, no matter how wet he'd made me earlier, he didn't always have the upper hand.

"Sixth floor," the automated voice announced. The

elevator slid open, and Michael held his arm across the door as I stepped past him, brushing my body against his. I turned to look at him, waited for him to lower his arm, and fully exit the elevator before I crashed into him and pushed him against the wall as the steel doors slid closed next to us.

My hands immediately jumped to his head, fingers pushing through his hair as I held onto him, our tongues tangling. His hands ran over my body, from my shoulders, over my breasts, down to my waist.

"I want you," I said breathlessly.

His mouth found mine again, his lips soft, his kiss rough. "You fucking torment me," he growled.

"I want you inside me. I need you inside me. Now," I said as I pulled him with me toward my room, my hand trailing his body, grabbing his hard length.

He groaned, then pushed me against the wall, pulled my lips with his teeth. I grabbed his hand harder and led him quickly down to my door. I felt as he swept my hair to the side, kissing my neck as I dug in my bag for the key.

"I'm gonna kick this fucking thing in if you don't hurry." He dug his hard-on into my backside.

I groaned, my excitement building between my legs, my anticipation making me quiver. "Ah! Finally." I swiped the key, opened the door, and dragged him with me.

CHAPTER
Twenty-Six

Siena

He had my hands clasped in each of his, holding me as his willing prisoner against the closed door. His mouth was hard, desperate for my taste. I kissed him back with equal fervor, felt him shift and pull back the slightest bit. His mouth softened, and the kiss grew seductive, his tongue moving into my mouth sensually, softly. He loosened his grip, testing me. For a moment, I looked into his eyes and saw his vulnerability. Would I pull away, out of his reach? Did I really want him?

My answer was obvious as he dropped my wrists and my hands moved into his hair again. I yanked slightly, just enough to pull his face away from mine. I looked into his eyes and dove again. My mouth claimed his, and I took over once more. I slipped my tongue into his mouth, tasting him, the spicy tang of wine on his tongue.

His hands came to my breasts, and I moaned into his mouth. More, I wanted more. His hands drifted down my sides until he found the hem of my dress. He lifted it slowly, feeling his way up my thighs, my waist, lingering over my skin with a light touch, a tease. He pulled the fabric up and over my head, breaking our kiss. It fell to the floor with a whoosh, and he stepped back and stood looking down at me.

"Fuck. You are beautiful."

I reached for him, unbuttoning his shirt. His eyes locked onto mine as I undid the buttons one by one and slid his shirt open and off his shoulders. He made to remove his shirt all the way but found his hands imprisoned by the buttons at his wrists. He laughed huskily, "Looks like I'm trapped."

"Maybe I want you trapped."

"Help me with these, would you?" He offered his wrist. I pulled it to my mouth, my tongue flicking over his pulse as I undid the button. He pulled his hand through, grabbed me, bringing me back to him.

"You want me to get the other one?" I asked, both of us breathing heavily.

"Fuck it. I only need one free hand to do what I want." He claimed my mouth again.

I laughed against his lips, finding his other hand, then freeing the button and pushing it off his perfect body. He wrapped his arms around me, enveloping me in his embrace.

I could feel the heat of his breath against me. I heard him inhale, taking in my scent. He looked at me with longing. "I've been waiting to have you all day. Fuck, more like forever, it seems."

He kissed me again until I was breathless. Clad in only my bra and panties, he trailed kisses down my décolletage. He nipped at the fabric as he reached around and undid the clasp. I shrugged out of it, his lips claiming one nipple, his fingers the other, tugging it. He moved to the other one, kissing and biting the tender flesh before circling my nipple and covering it with his lips. I felt his teeth bite down, causing me to moan with exquisite pleasure and pain. He continued his torturous assault down my body as I quivered under his touch, his decadent mouth.

He kneeled before me, a mirror image of last night. God, this man made me heady with desire. I lusted for him. Craved him.

He smiled up at me, reverently. "You smell divine," he said as he kissed my hip.

He rubbed me with his nose and brought his mouth to my inner thigh, brushing my skin with kisses. He nibbled the delicate flesh of the inside of my leg, right next to my panty line, and ran his tongue up and over to my hip where he nipped again. My legs were shaking, and I felt they would buckle beneath me at any second. He ran his hands up my legs, squeezing my ass, holding me firm. I felt his fingers slip under the hem of my underwear as his mouth pressed against my heat. He pulled his head back fractionally and looked up into my eyes again. I gripped his shoulders, steadying myself. All I could do was watch him watching me. His eyes burned with lust as he slowly slipped the last of my clothing from my body. It seemed to take forever, him peeling this minuscule fraction of material down my legs.

I stepped from them, my hands on his shoulders for support, his eyes still locked onto mine. I felt his touch at my ankle, felt him slowly caress his way up my calf and squeeze. Up the back of my knee where he grazed my skin with his nails, tickling me, causing me to shiver as goose bumps prickled my skin. He chuckled to himself and kissed the inside of my knee. "Steady," was all he said before he lifted my leg over his shoulder and dove in.

I gripped his head, my hands tugging his hair, moaning loudly at the onslaught of his tongue against my bare flesh. Tasting me. Licking, nibbling, sucking. His hands grasped my ass, pulling my cheeks apart, bringing me closer to his mouth. He kneaded my cheeks as he worked his tongue over me.

He growled into me, moaning while he lapped me up.

"I need you. I. Need. You," I moaned while he sucked.

He broke away and looked up at me. "Fuck. I need you too." He pulled his lower lip into his mouth, sucking my taste from it. My chest was heaving up and down. He stood up, kissed me, and held me as he moved me back toward the bed.

I felt the back of my legs hit the mattress. He held my face in his hands, kissing me. I scooted up the bed to the pillows. He followed. I wrapped my arms around him and fell back down upon them, pulling him with me.

I moved my hands to his shoulders, over his arms, feeling his muscles tense from supporting himself. My fingers slid across his back, down his torso, and in between us, where I started unbuttoning his pants. I moved my hand lower, pressed it flat against him, and palmed him through the soft fabric. His cock was rock hard, and he leaned further into my touch, moaning into my mouth.

He lifted his ass to give me better access. I got the message he was sending. *Pants off. Now.* I shoved them down his hips and used my feet to push them the rest of the way. He reached behind himself and pulled free of them, now completely naked. This motherfucker went commando tonight. Nothing turned me on more.

I stroked him a few times, his cock thick and heavy in my hand. It was smooth and slid easily in my hold. I twisted and pulled him through my grip, his tip slippery with just a drop of silky liquid. I moved my thumb over it, spreading it in a circle, massaging and squeezing a little to pump him. I could feel him watching me as I watched my hand work him. I looked up, and a faint smile crossed his face right before he brought his mouth to mine.

His hand slid between us, down to my pussy. I was already so wet from the combination of my own juices and his mouth. He began by rubbing my clit, running circles over it again and again. I groaned loudly into his ear, moaning his name, and biting his earlobe.

"Fuck, yes," he growled. "Keep doing that." I moved down his neck, nibbling along the way and then back up again, this time a little harder. I pulled his earlobe into my mouth, sucking it hard and biting it. "Argh," he moaned, shoving two fingers into my tight hole.

"Michael," I panted. I moved against his hand, feeling his fingers move in and out of me. He stayed deep in me while he pulsated and rocked his fingers back and forth, rubbing them against me, deep inside, pushing and gliding. He pulled back, teasing, testing me, then continued as I ground against his hand, feeling the friction and the heat he was creating. I could feel the warmth spreading deep within me, all the way down to my stomach. My pussy was clenching. I was moving against his hand with frantic speed. "Yes!" I urged into his neck. "I'm gonna come."

He moved down my body so quickly, and it felt like he had never been there to begin with. It was such a sudden movement. And then . . . then I felt his mouth on me, sucking and pulling at my clit. He was using his fingers to drive me while his tongue bathed me. My hands gripped the linens, pulling at them while my legs were bent, and he was lying between them.

"Fucking give it to me," he growled. "I want to taste you when you come." And his tongue was back inside me. Fucking me, licking me, guiding me up and over that glorious crest.

I called out incoherently, fireworks bursting inside. Hot sparkling shots pulsed down and out of me, making me shudder again and again. I could feel my insides flexing around him as he moved in me and over me with his fingers and tongue. I came again. "Fuck yes," I called as my insides seemed to turn to liquid.

My raging subsided, and he could feel the calmness run over my body. My hands released the fabric I was clinging to, my chest rising and falling so rapidly I could have sworn I had just finished running a marathon. "Holy shit." It was all I could utter as I tried to catch my breath.

"Holy shit is right," he said from below. "You taste so fucking good I could eat you forever."

I laughed. "Too bad you'd wither away and die if you only dined on me."

"Then I'd die a very happy and contented man." He climbed back up to me, hovering over me. "Besides, who wouldn't want to die in between a sexy pair of legs and a delicious pussy?"

"You're disgusting," I joked.

"Disgusting?" he gestured with mockery. "I think it was pretty clear that you were totally into what I was doing."

"God, you're a dirty bastard."

"Dirty?" He clicked his tongue and winked. "And what about you, Ms. Tackle Me in the Hotel Hallway? Besides, you loved every second." He bent toward me in challenge.

I grabbed his head between my hands. "Yes, Mr. Blaire. Yes, I did." I pulled him back down, kissing him hard.

I felt his length heavy against me.

I was hot.

He was hard.

He moved away, digging into his pocket frantically. He returned, looking victorious, ripping the foil packet open with his teeth. He moved the condom down his length, lowered himself, moved his cock against my wetness, slick and velvety. His tip grazed my hood, and I shuddered at the instantaneous thrill it brought. He thrust his hips a couple of times, sliding his big dick across me, teasing both of us. He pulled his hips back a fraction, and then I felt him at my entrance, just the tip. That awesome sensation right before being spread apart, right before being filled up. He locked eyes with me as he entered slowly, ever so slowly, until he was as deep as he could get.

Propped on his forearms, he pulled back, then slowly pushed back in. Once. Twice. Three times. He let go of a groan that made my nipples harden. It was hot. Animalistic. His breath was ragged, and his eyes burned into mine with a heat so intense it seemed to beg me to touch him.

"I'm trying to maintain some sort of semblance of sanity here, but fuck, Siena."

"I know," I said, keeping my eyes fixed on his, "you feel so good."

He kissed me chastely, then stayed with his lips against mine, his forehead pressed to mine. He picked up the pace as I raised upward into him, urging him to move. I wanted him faster and harder. He felt so insanely amazing. I just wanted him to swallow me whole.

I wrapped my legs around him, squeezing him between my thighs. With my legs pulled back and him riding me, we created friction between us, rubbing me in the most delicious ways. I was getting close, and I could tell he was too. He was holding back, waiting for me to come again.

The tingling sensation wound through me, and I could feel the tiny pulses starting inside me where he was grinding and thrusting. "Yes, Michael. Just like that," I coaxed. Our murmurs of urgency, ecstasy, and desire rolled off our tongues until we were both panting out our demands.

The familiar tremble returned, and Michael could feel my muscles clamping around him. I cried out as he moaned his release. I milked him for every ounce of his desire.

Spent, we lay there, our breath coming out fast and hard, his face buried in my neck, the weight of his body on top of me making me feel like a sumptuous cake covered in chocolate. He kissed the side of my throat before rolling to the side. He clasped my hand, cupped it to his chest, both of us resting in the stillness of the room.

"Holy shit," he said after some time, mimicking the same words tumbling in my brain. I felt the bed dip as he got up to dispose of the condom.

My body felt cool now that he wasn't on top of me with his warmth, a chilled sheen of sweat covering me. He climbed back into bed and we resumed our positions—him on his back, me curled next to him with my hand over his heart. I shivered beside him, then leaned down to grab the sheet.

He helped pull it up over us, kicked a leg out from under

it. "Oomph." He exhaled, tucking his arm behind him. I didn't want him to leave, but wasn't sure if he wanted to stay again. Keeping things "uncomplicated" meant he should go, but thinking about being without him in the bed made me feel that I'd be lonely. Minutes passed while we lay there, my hand on his heart, his hand caressing up and down my arm.

"Do you want me to go?" he broke the silence in such a low whisper that I thought I might have misheard him.

"Do you want you to go?" I asked.

The bed dipped as he shifted, turned on his side toward me. "Siena?"

"Hmm?" I kept my eyes closed. I couldn't look at him without my eyes betraying me.

"Open your eyes." I felt his fingers under my chin.

Reluctantly obeying, I opened my eyes and prayed he wouldn't be able to read into the depths of them or into my heart.

"I'll go if you tell me to. But—"

"But what?"

He remained quiet, just staring into my eyes. And I saw what I needed to see.

"Don't go," I said, touching his face.

His smile was all the reassurance I needed. While I couldn't know exactly what he was feeling, his eyes told me he felt something close to what I was. He brought his lips to mine. I felt him harden again. I reached down, wrapped my hand around him. He flexed himself in my hand. "Find something you like?" He smirked, looking down at himself, then back up at me.

"It'll do. I mean, I've had bigger, but it'll do."

His hearty belly laugh filled the room as he nipped my lips, then pulled me on top of him.

CHAPTER Twenty-Seven

Michael

I needed a gallon of Gatorade, an oxygen tank, and perhaps a lobotomy.

Four times in the span of six hours.

We'd had sex three times before falling into a comatose sleep. A few hours later, when I felt her ass brush up against me, I got rock hard again. She'd felt me and wiggled against me some more before finally turning to me, climbing on top, and taking both of us through another mind-blowing climax. If she kept up this pace, we'd need to buy an economy size box of condoms. I smiled at the idea.

It was eight-thirty in the morning by indications of the bedside clock. But I was nowhere in the mood to get out of this damn bed. I kept still as Siena slept beside me, curled on her side, softly breathing.

Another night. Another amazing night spent next to this woman who captured me, who seemed destined to have her life entwined with mine.

A change in her breathing caught my attention. It wasn't by sound that I noticed but by feel. As if by some phenomenon, my mind could feel her awaken next to me. She hadn't even moved, but as I shifted my head, my eyes moving over to her face, those newly awakened orbs, seemingly a darker shade of hazel, peered up at me.

Silence. Who would be the first to speak? Who was going to break first? Certainly, it wasn't going to be me. And I knew her stubborn ass was probably thinking the same thing I was, *Don't speak first!*

She moved her hand up my body, feeling her way, her hand tracing my form like a vine crawling up a trellis. She stopped at my shoulder, moved a strand of hair back from my forehead, smiled, and bit her lower lip like the naughty minx I knew she was.

She trailed her hand back down, nails scraping at my flesh on her way to my stomach. Her tongue darted out, moistening her lips with a delicious sheen. I watched as she licked again, an invitation. My dick twitched, getting hard. And then her hand was wrapped around me, a vice holding me in place. I couldn't move. I was transfixed by this woman who had a hold of my cock in one hand, my heart in the other. *Fuck. Where the hell did that come from?* I kept my face neutral, watching as she covered me, my eyes steadily locked on hers as she lifted herself and straddled me.

Cock still firm in hand, she moaned and bit her lip as she stroked herself with it before bending down, pressing her forehead to mine. She slid her lips over mine, then around my jaw, over to my ear. "What do you want?" she whispered coyly before sucking my lobe back into her mouth. I could hear as her breathing increased, that faint flutter of excitement as her pelvis ground against me. She was already slick, sliding over me and down to my balls.

"I want you on my dick," I said, gripping her hip in one hand and pulling her hair so her head moved back, exposing that long neck.

She moaned as she moved over me until the head of my dick was at her hot, wet entrance. Her eyes came to mine, and I felt as she took me in, slowly sliding down my length at such a deliberately gradual pace I knew she could feel every inch of me as I filled her up.

It felt so delicious inside her, it almost hurt. "Damn, you feel so good," I told her as I looked down and watched my cock slide in and out of her. The sight of her pussy lips wrapped around me, taking me in all the way before she rose back up to do it all over again, would be engrained in my mind for eternity. There were some things you wanted to forget and some things you wanted to remember forever. She was something I wanted to remember. Her scent, her taste, the image of me sliding into her over and over. These were things I never wanted to be erased from my memory.

She continued to grind her hips over me, back and forth, up and down, again and again. "I'm gonna come if you keep working me like that," I said.

A sly smile covered her mouth, and carnal conviction flickered in her eyes. Her tits bounced as she rode me. I held her hips, guiding her. *Fuck, I'm gonna blow. She knows exactly how I like her to ride my cock.*

It was like she could read my mind. Like all my dirty, nasty thoughts turned her on. She was clenched around me. So tight, so perfect. She screamed my name as she came undone, digging her nails into my shoulders, throwing her head back, eyes closed in complete bliss.

"Yes, baby, give me that cum," I said, as she rode me hard, making me bust deep inside her. We bucked together, each finishing the other off.

She collapsed on top of me, still holding me deep inside her. I could feel the tiny pulsating beats throb around my dick, the aftershocks of her orgasm. I couldn't resist pulling her hair to the side so I could kiss the tender part of her neck.

My heart pounded in my chest, my skin covered with sweat, my body limp. *What the hell kind of hold did this woman have on me?*

Vibration from the bedside table broke me out of the

thoughts that were skittering through my mind. Relieved to be distracted from the emotions I was feeling. I didn't know if I was even ready to handle things this fast, this soon, I grabbed the cell phone on the nightstand, clicked to disengage the call, and saw the name on the screen.

An incoming call from Tim.

Siena's head was still nestled into my neck, my free hand stroking her hair.

Who the hell?

Shit. This wasn't even my phone. Put it back, put it back.

The vibration stopped, and notifications started popping up. I couldn't help but look.

Three missed calls from Tim.

Two text messages.

I didn't mean to invade her privacy, but the words, *I KNOW WE CAN WORK THINGS OUT. PLEASE GIVE ME ANOTHER CHANCE!* had me doing a double take.

What in the actual fuck?

She rolled off me, curled up, and ran a hand through my hair, none the wiser.

I dropped the phone next to me on the bed. It immediately began ringing again. *Are you fucking kidding me? This jackhole had some fucking nerve.*

"I think someone's trying to get ahold of you," I said as I climbed out of bed. The bed that now felt cold and empty even though she was still right there, freshly fucked, beautiful, and warm.

♥ ♥ ♥

"Jesus Christ," I said to myself as my forehead rested against the cold tile of the shower. I didn't know what I was going to do. What was I supposed to do? Was there a simple explanation to all of this, or was this some gut-wrenching, knife turning, pour some more salt on that open wound bullshit that I'd have to work through? Another wild and turbulent test to prove my own worth, my desire to succeed, and my will to survive?

Images of yesterday replayed in my mind. Siena down on her knees in front of me, mouth wrapped around my cock, swallowing me, my hands tangled in her hair. I rubbed a circle on the steam covered mirror, stared at my reflection. "Come on, Blaire, get a grip."

I turned the water off, wrapped a towel around my waist, and stepped out of the shower. A wail of crying came through the closed door. She was sobbing. *What the hell?* The hero in me had me running to her aide.

"What's wrong?" I tucked her hair behind her ear, lifted her chin so I could look her in the eyes. *Moment of truth.*

Her cries softened. "Siena. Say something. What happened? I can take it."

"It's my . . . It's Pops. He had a heart attack. Late last night."

"Oh my god," I said, taking a seat next to her on the bed.

She wrapped her arms around me, cuddling into me, warming me. Her skin against mine was like a cloak of warmth, a shield of heat.

I sat with her as she calmed down, taking me through the phone call that I never, in a million years, thought would be the call that we'd receive this morning.

WE?

Knock it the hell off, Michael. Her ex is texting her about getting back together, for fuck's sake.

Don't let yourself get in too deep.

Too late.

♥ ♥ ♥

A quick text to Jax: *Emergency in Monarch. Must leave ASAP. Text you later.*

A phone call from the car to book two seats on an emergency flight back to San Diego.

Siena like a ghost beside me. Hands clasped in her lap, head against the headrest, staring out the window.

Everything in fast forward, but feeling like I was moving in slow motion.

Siena remained mute and curled up in her seat on the flight home, cocooned in an oversized sweater and black leggings. I think she fell asleep for a while. She hadn't stirred, not even when I covered her with a blanket. She had been a walking ghost following my orders, not fighting me, or suggesting another "better" way to handle things. She had become subservient, doing what I said when I said it. A few times, over the course of knowing her, I would have given my left nut to shut her up. But now, with her sitting stone cold and silent beside me, I didn't like it, couldn't stand it. I'd give just about anything right now for one of her verbal lashings. I'd relish her anger, welcome her yelling at me. Just to see some color in her cheeks, some feeling or emotion. *This* Siena scared me.

A short flight and a speedy drive got us to the hospital where Sophia was waiting. I broke every law known to man as I raced to get her to her grandfather.

Sal was sleeping. The meds were still working through his system. Sophia was sitting next to his bed, holding his hand, the monitors rhythmically beeping, displaying his vitals. She seemed frail seated in the large chair, her petite frame barely taking up any space. Such a contrast to the strong, independent woman her granddaughter so beautifully took after.

Siena broke down again when Sophia looked up. Sal's coloring was drastically different compared to his natural olive complexion. The white sheet, draped with a blue blanket, was barely a contrast next to his still form.

"Oh, Pops," Siena cried, leaning down to kiss Sal's cheek. She straightened his dressing gown a little before taking his hand, placing a kiss on it, linking her free hand with her grandmother's.

"He's going to be fine, *Cara*." Her hand moved in circles over her back. "The doctors have a very optimistic outlook and say he'll be back to normal in no time."

Siena sat in the empty chair, still holding her grandfather's hand.

"He's gotta make some changes and take things easy. But he'll be just fine."

"That's good news," I said. Siena looked up at me, her eyes empty and far away. I didn't know what to do to comfort her. I wanted to reach out and hold her, but I didn't want to intrude on this family moment. I also, selfishly, didn't want to be turned away.

Sophia smiled, then reached out for my hand, making me feel less like an intruder and more like family. "Thank you for helping get her back home so fast, Michael. I don't know what we would've done without your help."

"Of course, Sophia. Anything for you guys." She squeezed my hand before letting go.

Siena's lips lifted, acknowledging her thanks, her eyes glimmering with tears. And even though it was a silent gesture, it relieved me to see her smile.

"I'm going to get us some coffee," I said as Siena turned back to her grandfather.

The atmosphere of the hospital was getting to me. All this sterile white and heartless gray. Colorful pictures and artwork lined the walls, but it did little to shake the sense of dread I felt. Doctors and nurses were milling about, running here and there, walking purposefully with something to do.

I felt helpless as I headed to the cafeteria. After the intensity of last night, the image of Tim's name on Siena's phone, and the emotions of hearing about Sal, I needed caffeine, and I knew Siena did too.

"I think it's pretty close to what you like," I said, handing Siena her coffee. "Plenty of sugar and cream. Black for Sophia." Sal was awake and looking better, the color having returned to his face. Maybe it had all been in my head, me thinking he looked pale and weak. Having Siena here seemed to perk him up, get him back to looking like his normal self.

"What about me?" he asked, clearly disappointed and jonesing for some caffeine.

"None for you, Pops," Siena scolded, fluffing his pillow. She bent down, looking him squarely in the eyes. "Strict orders. And we're gonna follow them to the letter. I'll let you smell mine if you want."

"That's just cruel and unusual punishment. Do you see what they're doing to me, Michael? They're ganging up on me," he said, looking to me for sympathy.

"I can see that." I sent Siena a wink. "But it's for your own good. We're all here to help you, Sal."

Thank you, Siena mouthed to me. I sent her a nod back.

"Okay, tell me what you know," I addressed them. "What's the next step?"

Sal settled back onto the pillows with a grunt, frustrated and annoyed. But I knew deep down that even though he was trying to be strong for Siena and Sophia, he was scared. This quick brush with death had been a wake-up call for all of them.

Sophia flipped the pages back on her notepad, tucked her dark hair behind her ear, and slipped on some reading glasses. "He had what's called a coronary artery spasm. The *silent heart attack*. Scary little fucker." She looked at Sal, a small smile of love. "Thank God I rushed him over here. He thought it was just some indigestion. But he was having muscle pain, so I shoved his ass in the car."

Sal shrugged. "How was I to know?"

Sophia looked at us. "They went over his medical history, did a physical exam and an EKG, blood tests, and meds. They asked a lot of questions. Luckily, there was no permanent damage. But he's at risk for another heart attack, so he has to be extra careful."

"When does he get to come home?" Siena asked.

"He'll stay here in the ICU for now so they can monitor his heart, keep an eye on him after the"—Sophia looked back down at her pad of paper—"electrocardiograms and any other tests they need to do."

The doctor and two nurses came in, checked the monitors, made notes on their charts, asked Sal more questions about how he was feeling. He seemed tired and overwhelmed.

"I think we can move you to a different room tomorrow," the doctor said. He turned to Sophia. "He'll have to continue being monitored, but as long as nothing suspicious pops up and he keeps improving, he'll be able to come home in another day or two. Depending"—he looked back at Sal—"on how he does."

"I'm already feeling better. I just want to go home," Sal said, eyes heavy and sad.

"I know, Pops. We want you back home too." Siena's smile was hopeful, even though it was laced with worry.

"Keep making positive improvements, and we'll get you home ASAP," the doctor assured him with a nod.

"He has to follow every instruction to the letter, take all the medications they prescribe. We'll have to follow up with his primary doctor and the cardiologist to determine when he can resume normal activities," Sophia told us.

"Seems simple enough," I said.

All eyes were on Sal, making sure he understood the severity of his situation. It was a bit of doom and gloom, but everything seemed very promising.

Moments later, he fell back asleep, breathing softly as the machines monitored his vitals and beeped rhythmically.

We sat in the quiet of the room. "Michael, thank you again, so much, for everything you've done," Sophia whispered, mindful of Sal's sleeping.

I cleared my throat. "I'm just sorry we were out of town. If I had known—"

"Oh, honey. No." She got up, coming straight to me, took my face in her hands. "Don't apologize. None of us could have foreseen this."

I didn't know what to say. I felt guilty that we had been away from home. That my own selfish wants and needs took Siena away.

"Michael," Siena said. "Thank you." Her simple words were a lifeline, bringing me a little peace in my inner turmoil.

"We're going to be here all day. Michael, why don't you go on back. I'm sure you have work to do," Siena said, getting up.

I tried to read the emotions in her eyes, tried to find any semblance of feeling or connection. I had to give her credit for what she was going through, being tired, dealing with everything going on. She gave me a friendly hug, but her eyes were empty, and it made me feel the same way inside. Empty and devastated. I thought back to the messages on her phone before the call about Sal came through. Her ex. *Fuck. So much for casual, dumbass.*

I left after saying goodbye, still feeling a bit like an outsider. Sophia had promised they'd keep me updated. What was I supposed to do? They were both right. I had work to do. And even though they hadn't said it out loud, I wasn't one of them.

The trailer seemed even more desolate and in the middle of nowhere than it did when I first arrived. Back then, I had a stick up my ass, full of myself and my plans. After meeting the Morettis, I began to feel a sense of belonging, a sense of family. Then Siena and I got together, and I felt even more like I was needed. Like I mattered to her. Now no one was here. I was alone again.

And the man who had fucked Siena over wanted her back.
Thursday.
Friday.
Saturday.
Sunday.

Chapter Twenty-Eight

Michael

Sunday afternoon, still alone. Barely any communication from Siena in the last four days. Just quick updates about Sal. Every time her ringtone pinged on my phone, my heart just about stopped. I cautioned myself to take it down a notch. The last thing she needed was me adding to an already stressful situation.

Sal would be okay. But would I? I couldn't keep pretending, like I did that day in that hospital, that everything was okay. I was churned up over her prick of an ex. When the smoke cleared with Sal, I had some questions that needed answering.

I didn't know what Siena was thinking.

Was she seriously considering going back to Tim? My hands balled into fists at the thought. What in the actual fuck? Cheat on a girl, knock the other girl up, and still want to be with the one you completely fucked over? Lots of people make mistakes only to realize what they had after the fact. But this guy? *Tim.* My lips curled up into a sneer. *This* guy took it to a whole other level.

And what was really pissing me off was the fact that I was freaking out this much. When she had broken down on the phone, I hadn't hesitated at all. I pulled her to me and held on. She fit in my lap perfectly, and when she nuzzled into me, I didn't go into autopilot or freeze up. That was a first. She was the first woman to just feel natural—normal. Like home.

Fuck.

I'm fucked.

Completely and royally fucked.

I realized in that instant it wasn't just her body I missed, but her. I missed *her*. Her smile, her laugh, her smart-ass mouth, her witty intellect. I'd only been with her a couple of nights—several times in those couple of nights, sure—but our brief time together solidified the feelings that had already slowly been creeping up over the last several weeks.

Not to mention her family and friends. I'd called Sophia and asked if there was anything I could do to help. She instructed me to get in touch with Jenny, who was taking charge with everything going on. From there, I'd been invited to help at the winery for the next few days. Audrey and Lauren would be there too, but she'd said she'd appreciate any extra help she could get.

So, for the next couple of days, I'd worked with them, learning about the ins and outs of the Moretti vineyard and getting to know them. I could see how these four girls had remained best friends. They were all welcoming, all dedicated to Siena and her grandparents. The winery had been hard work, not knowing what the heck I was doing, and they all got a good laugh at my expense when they caught me fumbling and completely confused.

Friday night, I left the winery completely exhausted and dead to the world after working a full day there and then late into the night with hotel stuff. Saturday, I'd shown up midafternoon and worked with the girls until closing. I'd felt a little odd joining them for dinner afterward, but they'd insisted I come along, telling me, "A successful team effort needed to be commemorated." I felt a connection to Siena being with her three best friends. They made me feel like a part of a team, like part of their family.

It was a strange feeling, and I wasn't sure exactly how I felt about it. I was torn. Building these new relationships in Monarch felt like a betrayal. A betrayal to Siena, to her grandparents, and even to the girls because I knew my father was still insistent that he get the winery at any cost, by any means necessary.

And it felt like a betrayal to my father because I just didn't know if I was still willing to try to get it for him.

My phone vibrated, indicating an incoming call. *Siena*, I thought, my heart skipping a beat as I turned it over.

"Shit." Deflated, I waited a second before answering, remembering the other missed calls from him that I still hadn't returned. "Hi, Dad. What's up?"

"You've been a difficult man to get ahold of." His curt tone made me cringe like a child being scolded.

"Sorry." I rolled my head back and forth to release the immediate tension he brought. "Things have been crazy around here, but they're still on schedule."

"Good. I was calling to let you know that I sent Walter out. He spoke to Mr. Moretti, but—"

"What?" I yelled. "You had no right to do that." I didn't know why I didn't foresee this move. I should've known he'd send Walter, his bulldog, out when I didn't immediately close the deal.

"I beg to differ. I am the owner of the company. I do as I see fit. And since you weren't getting anywhere, I sent Walter out to sweeten the deal."

"I told you they wouldn't sell. I got you the best deal I could—"

"No, Michael," he cut me off. "You got the best deal you thought you could. There's always a way. You know better."

"Their whole world is that winery. You don't know these people. I do."

"I see." I could hear his fingers drumming on his desktop. He was annoyed. Now, so was I. "Regardless, there are a couple of things I need you to handle."

I didn't like the sound in his voice.

"Walter didn't get any further than you did. Mr. Moretti dug in his heels and said he wouldn't deal with anyone but you."

"I told you, Dad. I've been working on building a cohesive relationship with them." I didn't dare tell him more than that. If he knew about Siena and me, he'd blow a gasket.

"Well, that's all well and good. Doesn't seem to have helped with getting the winery, Son. I told you before: *I want it.* And I will do whatever I have to do to get it."

"I don't know how—"

"It sounds like there might be a conflict of interest," he stopped me, interrupting.

"There isn't, Dad. I'm just saying—"

He cut me off again. "Maybe I need to bring Matthew in on it, see if he can get things done." I was used to this kind of exchange—Allan Blaire making demands, silencing me when he didn't like what I had to say.

"Do whatever you have to do. But I'm warning you—"

"*Warning me?*"

"Sal's had some heart trouble. Steer clear of him."

"I'm not trying to cause problems, Michael. I'm simply doing business. I hope I don't need to remind you: *My business.*"

And with that, he hung up—getting the last word in like he always did.

"Goddamn it!" I yelled, pulling my hair. "Mother fucker!" My eyes landed on the plans rolled out on my desk. I stared at them, slapped my hands on the table. "Fuck!" I roared, my voice echoing in the empty space. I flung the papers to the floor and slammed my fists down onto the bare tabletop.

My phone vibrated again.

"What?" I bellowed into it.

"Michael, it's Sophia. Am I calling at a bad time?" Her voice sounded surprised.

"Sorry, Sophia. I thought you were some idiot from the office calling me back." I took a breath to calm myself.

"I'm sorry. I don't want to cause you more of a headache. But I need a favor."

"Anything. How's Sal?"

"He's doing better. We finally got him settled in his own bed. Thank god for you and the girls. You all totally stepped up. They've done nothing but rave about you and how amazing you are."

"It was nothing. Just friends helping friends." I didn't think I could still blush, but Sophia Moretti's words made my cheeks feel hot.

"No. You're not a friend."

My heart stopped.

"You're family, Michael. You've proven that time and again."

"Sophia . . . I . . . Thank you."

"For what?"

"For making me feel appreciated and welcome. I'm an outsider. I know that. Things between us may have started out a little tense, with the focus on both of our businesses. But I know our lives have begun to merge."

"Entwined."

"Yes, exactly. And I'm thankful for that. I'm glad Sal's home."

"Me too." I heard her sigh through the line, a sense of relief. "You have no idea."

"So, what's this favor you have?"

A few minutes later, our phone call ended. I had tried to sound nonchalant when I asked about Siena, but I could feel Sophia had some inkling about us. My thoughts drifted back to the hospital: Sal in the hospital bed, Siena looking lost, and Sophia looking worried and tired.

I took a few deep breaths, thinking about everything that had transpired, trying to figure out what I needed to do. Tim contacting Siena. Sal's heart attack. My dad's phone call. Sophia's favor. Siena.

I didn't want to betray my family. But I didn't want to betray the Morettis either.

"Fuck it," I said, grabbing my phone from where I'd dropped it just moments before. I texted Jenny, made contact, and got what I needed from her. *What the hell am I doing?*

"Exactly what you need to do," I told myself as I pulled up Mosby's number and dialed.

"I need you to do something for me, no questions asked," I told her when she answered.

"Okay." She seemed slightly hesitant, but her trust in me, as well as my tone, told her to do exactly as instructed.

CHAPTER Twenty-Nine

Siena

THE OVERCAST MORNING SKY WAS blanketed in pewter nimbus clouds. It was beautiful, except for the threat of rain, the earthy aroma of an approaching downpour in the air. The showers should hold off for a couple of hours, but I grabbed my jacket and umbrella just in case.

Michael's back was to me as he leaned against Pops's truck, our name and company logo, a cluster of dark purple grapes, on it. His jaw was taut, covered in several day's stubble as his finger scrolled over his phone. His jeans showed off the impeccable curve of his ass, and a flannel shirt with its sleeves rolled to right below the elbow accentuated the muscles in his forearms. His dark hair was windblown and unruly, his skin a golden tan, his beautiful eyes hidden behind a pair of sleek and sophisticated Ray-Bans.

My heart skipped a beat. His beauty took my breath away. I didn't know how he knew I was there, but he did. His head lifted in acute awareness. When he didn't turn around, I cleared my throat, announcing my presence. Why was he purposefully ignoring me?

He worked his fingers over his phone a few more seconds before finally lifting his head to acknowledge me. He removed his glasses, slipped them into his shirt pocket, and eyed me from head to toe and back again. "Ms. Moretti." The simple utterance of my name made my skin heat. "I offered to help Sal and Sophia any way I could. Lucky me, I get to chauffeur you around for deliveries."

My heart stopped and my breath hitched. What the fuck was wrong with me? *Get ahold of yourself.* "Yeah, hi." I aimed for an amiable tone, hoping he couldn't see the war raging inside me. I wanted to slap him across the face for being such a pompous ass. But I also wanted to grab him and hold him tightly against my body, never letting go.

"Shall we?" He tilted his head toward the crates of wine stacked next to the truck.

We bumped heads, both bending to grab a crate at the same time.

"Ow. What the fuck?" I shouted, grabbing the side of my head.

"Yeah, what the fuck is right. Be careful!"

"Me?" I hollered, almost dropping the entire case of bottles. I hefted it onto the bed.

"Yeah. Throwing that hard head of yours around. Not watching what you're doing." He grabbed another crate of wine. His brute strength was forceful as he shoved it in alongside mine. I could hear the bottles clinking together. "That it?" he asked as he rubbed his head where we had banged into each other.

"Careful," I criticized. He sent me an exasperated look as I loaded the last crate and secured it into place. Something was off, and I didn't know what it was, what I had done.

"Sal said I should drive"—he slammed the bed closed—"so you could work on the orders."

"Fine," I snapped. Despite my irritation, I realized he was doing us a favor and added, "Thanks."

"Yep," was all he muttered in return.

As I double-checked our packing, making sure nothing would slide around, he walked to the passenger side and opened my door. He could be a brute, but at least this brute had deep-rooted manners. I climbed in, and he promptly shut the door, sealing me inside. I pulled my seatbelt on while he rounded the hood to the driver's side.

A loud rumble erupted as he started the truck. "Where to first?"

Still unsure why he was so distant, but not wanting to ask, I gave him the address. He typed it into his cell and started the route guidance. I didn't have the heart to bicker with Michael. All my worry, all my concern and fear for Pops had taken the fight out of me. I should have known better that my grandparents wouldn't be around forever. And now, it appeared, Michael was going to be next.

"I can tell you where to go," I suggested, trying one last time to get him to open up.

"I'll use the GPS." He didn't even look at me, just kept his eyes glued on the road.

I sighed in defeat. Why the distance, the coldness? Everything, including him, had done a complete one-eighty, and I felt like we were right back to where we first started. Enemies.

"I appreciate your help," I said while simultaneously pretending to type on my phone. I couldn't look at him. My insides were churned up between a mix of love and hate. *Love?* I silently questioned myself. *Lust! It's just lust . . . and infatuation*, I corrected my subconscious.

Besides, nothing remotely like love was coming from Michael.

His silence gave me time to think. While Pops's heart attack had kept me too busy to think about Tim, when the smoke finally cleared, so had my head. Watching Grams care so deeply for the man she loved, seeing the worry mixed with relief in her eyes, made me realize that I could never feel that way about Tim. Even if I could love him the way I thought I had before he betrayed me, I needed someone to love me, to need me. I also needed someone I could love and need. And, when things got tough, I needed someone who would stick by me no matter how hard our lives got. Tim's infidelity proved without a shadow of a doubt that he was not *the one*. He never could be because I deserved more.

Could Michael be the one?

"We're here," Michael's voice shocked me out of my private thoughts.

Clearing my throat in order to clear my head, I read the order as he grabbed the crate, hefting it from the bed and carrying it like it weighed next to nothing. I walked beside him, hoping we'd get to talking with the presence of a buffer between us. The buffer being our customer. But, sure as shit, he didn't make a peep. He simply made the delivery and headed out. As I finished getting the signatures and securing the next order, Michael had already gotten back into the driver's seat and started the engine. He was checking messages on his phone when I climbed in.

"Where to next?" he asked, not looking up.

I read the address. He plugged it in and started the navigation guidance all over again. No words. No eye contact. All right, fucker. Two can play this game. I kept my eyes glued straight ahead too. I checked my phone for anything to take my mind off the silence. It was deafening.

Frustrated and disheartened, I looked at the darkening sky, the threat of rain imminent. As if hearing my thoughts, the sky opened, and I listened to the faint sounds of raindrops hitting the windshield. I watched the sprinkling of rain as it covered the glass. It wasn't falling too hard right now, but it was coming. I could feel it. Tonight, there was going to be a huge storm.

He pulled up to our next delivery. I waited for him to turn off the engine. "Order?" he asked. One word. Two syllables. That was all he was going to give me. He took the dolly from the bed of the truck, loaded the crates, and wheeled them inside. This time, he exchanged greetings with the customers but had little more to say as he maneuvered the wine to the designated space. I swear I could hear him whistling something on his way out. Who would be whistling in the rain? Surely, I had to be mistaken. Probably the wind or something.

He was sitting again, looking surly behind the wheel. Two more deliveries continued like this: "Where to?" Give him the address. He plugs it in and drives. We deliver the goods without speaking. It was driving me bananas. And the whistling? I knew I didn't imagine it as I purposefully listened for it during our latest stop and received a head nod confirmation from our customer, Mr. Simons, that yes, he was indeed whistling. *This motherfucker was doing this on purpose.* He knew he was driving me crazy and was relishing in the fact that I was miserable. His version of payback. Goddamn him! I ran to the truck, trying to dodge the rain, which was falling heavily now. I ducked my head, opening the door.

I knew the charade would start all over again when I climbed back in the truck. So, I already had the address pulled up and ready to read to him. But when I pulled my phone out of my back pocket and unlocked my screen, it went black and turned off. "What the fuck?" I yelled, shaking my phone. Tiny splashes of rain on the screen. I wiped them off, shook the phone again.

"What?" he said, glancing up.

"My phone just turned off," I pushed the buttons, trying to bring it back to life.

"Give it here," he reached out. Our hands touched as he made to grab the phone. He didn't pull away. I looked up and our eyes locked. Time seemed to pass in slow motion. I saw him swallow, his Adam's apple bobbing up and down. Without letting go, he lowered his eyes, bringing the phone into focus. I watched as he pressed and held the button down, waiting for it to turn back on. "There you go," he said as the screen switched on. He let go. I purposely brushed my fingers over the back of his hand.

All he said was, "Okay, where to?"

What? "Um . . ." I pulled up the address and reluctantly read it off.

He put the truck in reverse, but as he turned to look over his shoulder, our eyes met again. He cleared his throat and struggled to put it in drive.

"Look, Michael—" I tried to implore him to talk to me.

"Not now, Siena," he said as he took off down the open road.

"But—"

"I said not now!" he yelled.

The sheer ferocity in his voice shocked me back into the seat. I couldn't believe it. His venom stung and hurt. And although I hated myself for it, I couldn't help the tears that formed. I wiped them away quickly, hoping he wouldn't notice. A sniffle escaped me.

I felt him look at me. I guess he could indeed tell. He turned back and slammed his fists into the steering wheel.

"Fuck!" he roared. "Goddamn it, Siena."

"What the hell did I do?" I shouted back, glaring at him, tears straining my words.

"You know exactly what the fuck I'm talking about."

"No, actually, I don't. You haven't said but ten words to me all day." I was literally dying inside.

"I'm fucking mad, but I don't want to talk about it right now."

"Why not?" I asked.

"Because I'm too pissed off."

"Then, when *are* we going to talk about whatever it is that pissed you off?"

"I don't know . . ."

"You don't know. You. Don't. Know." My voice was swelling with anger and dripping with sarcasm. "Well, maybe we should schedule something. We're all business, right? So, let's pencil something in," I snapped, then opened the calendar on my phone.

"Don't be stupid," he chided.

"What date works for you?" I asked, ignoring his insult. I was being stupid, childish. *But so was he*, and I didn't give two flying fucks. "Let's see. I have tomorrow, noon to two available, and Wednesday, any time before four. But after that, and I'm just going to have to get back to you."

"Goddamn it! You're being ridiculous," he said as he jerked to the side of the road and slammed the truck into park.

"Oh, *I'm* being ridiculous?" I could feel my temper rising, feel the blood boiling through my veins. My voice became low, calm, and I hissed my words at him like a poisonous snake, "I think you are, Mr. Blaire. In fact, I think you're being a total—"

He lunged across the seat, his lips crashing into mine, shutting me up immediately. His tongue assaulted my mouth, the heat from him seeping into me. His hands grabbed my ponytail, yanking my head back, and his lips were on my throat.

My breath was coming out in gasps, but my hands clawed at his arms, pushing him away.

"Fuck," he growled as I shoved him back. He looked at me quizzically, trying to put his lips back on mine.

"Michael! Stop it! What the fuck are you doing? You can't scream at me one minute then expect me to just fall into your arms the second you change your mind."

"Siena," he moaned, trying to take my face in his hands.

"What the fuck is wrong with you?" I pushed at him, trying to make him look at me.

He gasped, something in his eyes breaking as he looked at me, a desperation I had never seen on his face before.

He lowered his forehead to mine. I could feel his heart beating, bursting inside his chest. "I need you to want me. I need you to need me." Even though his voice was low, his words echoed in the small space.

My heart stopped. All the anger was gone from his voice. He sat there, vulnerable in front of me. I could feel him shaking. Everything cool and collected about him disappeared in front of my eyes.

I put my hand on his chest. "Michael."

Nothing.

"Michael, look at me."

His eyes slowly raised to mine. I could see a hint of shame in them, but also a hint of something else. *No, Siena. Don't go there.*

"Michael."

"Yes?" he whispered.

"Take me," I whispered, pulling his shirt from his waistband, my hands sliding up his sides as I felt his obliques quiver under my touch.

His eyes lit up, looking straight into mine.

I smiled then, coaxing him. In our silence, with nothing between us but the pounding of the rain against the truck, I willed him to take me—to take me roughly and without surrender.

His lips curved into a gentle but heated smile as he looked deeper into me. He grinned wickedly, right before I ripped his shirt open, buttons popping off and flying around us. Then we lost ourselves in each other.

CHAPTER Thirty

Siena

I couldn't tear my gaze away from Michael's as I slowly slid down the seat until he was hovering over me. Time seemed to stop as he looked at me.

He unbuttoned my shirt, keeping his eyes on me, watching me. I hummed as he moved his hand over my bare flesh. His nostrils flared with a deep inhalation. He shut his eyes as I brought my hands to his chest, running them over his impeccable pecs and down his rigid stomach. I pulled on his belt, jerking him closer to me, then undid it and the buttons on his jeans. I pushed at the waistband, shoving his pants down his legs. I moaned as soon as I realized I touched his smooth flesh because he wasn't wearing anything underneath.

I struggled to get my own pants off and was happy when I could get one leg free.

He looked down between our bodies and chuckled. "You need some help there?"

"No. It's fine." I smirked at the coincidence of our situation. "I only need one leg free to do what I want."

Michael grinned, then laughed as he put two and two together. He teased me with his kisses, and I lost myself to him, his lips moving from my mouth then down my neck. I could feel his warm breath against my skin. He pulled the cups of my bra down, freeing my breasts, and took one nipple into his mouth as he palmed the other one, pinching with his finger and thumb. I arched up, my head hitting the door behind me. I ignored the slight pain as I relished in his mouth roaming over my skin, then back up to my lips.

I opened my eyes, whispering against his mouth, "I need to feel you."

He stared right into me as his hand moved over my waist and slowly down my leg. My muscles clenched in anticipation of where he was headed. He took my lip roughly between his and pulled me to him. He deepened the kiss, his tongue invading my mouth, his finger moving under the soft fabric of my underwear to massage my clit. I groaned out as he slipped one digit inside me and began to move.

His free hand fisted into my hair, and his other pleasured me with his rough, sensuous touch. Our tongues slid against one another's, mirroring what he was doing with his fingers. I gasped as his hand left me and he bent toward me, grinding his cock against me. "Yes," I moaned as I wrapped my leg around him.

He cupped my breast roughly in his hand. But he didn't take me like I thought he was going to. Instead, he looked at me as if trying to memorize this moment.

I slid my tongue up the length of his neck, tasting the saltiness of his glistening skin. I groaned out as he pressed his hardness against me. He kissed me, urgently touching, tasting every inch of skin he could get his mouth on.

Wanting to tease him the way he was teasing me, I palmed him and stroked my hand up and down.

He quickly sheathed himself. The sheer exhilaration of being caught was a turn on, and I wanted to take my time reveling in these sensations, but I knew we needed to hurry. We were on the side of the road, and anyone could pull up behind us at any moment.

I pulled my panties to the side and moved his hard length

over me, letting my wetness slick him. "Tell me you want me," I said, using his words from just moments before, urging him to claim me, to make me his.

He kept his forehead pressed against mine as he whispered, "I want you, Siena." Then he slammed into me, owning me.

He pulled out all the way, rotated his hips, pressing against me. That delicious sensation of him being so close to being inside of me made my insides pulsate. He stilled at my entrance, blinked once, making sure he had my full attention. He pushed into me, just light enough to make my eyes roll back in ecstasy. He moaned and bit his lip as he seemed to relish in the feeling of being just barely inside me. "I need you," he said, slamming into me again.

I moaned out as the sensation of him filling me made me ache for even more. He set the pace, the necessity of speed at the forefront of both of our minds. I met him thrust for thrust, lifting my hips for him, each time more intense than the last.

He pushed my leg back up toward me with his arm. He moved back into me, rocking his hips, forcing his cock deep inside me, the angle allowing him to fill me to the hilt. "Come on, baby. I need to hear you." His biting kisses radiated pleasure all the way to my toes. I felt his hands gripping my hips to the point of delicious pain. But his smooth strokes in and out of me were the perfect combination—glorious pleasure entwined with delectable pain. I looked down to where he was pressing, digging into me, and moved my hands to cover his as he rammed into me over and over.

The pain of his fingers digging into my flesh added to the intensity of the moment. "Harder," I moaned out as he gripped me, his grunts fierce and loud. This raw animalistic passion between us drove me to a place I had never been with any other man.

It was as if he elicited something wickedly and wildly wonderful. His body called to mine, and only he could make me feel whole. Even when he was fucking me like a wild beast, a torrid romp on the side of the road . . . even like this, I felt complete when he was inside me. This realization made me quiver, gush with wetness.

Michael hissed when he saw the change in my eyes, felt the heat building in me, about to erupt. "Let me hear you come when I'm buried this deep inside you."

"Oh god, yes," I screamed, exploding from the deepest parts within me.

He closed his eyes as he came, his dick throbbing, his hips bucking. He stilled with a shudder, then collapsed on top of me.

Minutes seemed to pass as his forehead rested against mine. The windows were steamed up, our breathing creating a heavy haze on the glass.

He was still in me when I asked, "Are we going to talk about why you've been so crabby?"

He grunted. I nudged him. "Maybe. When the blood finally returns to my brain," he said.

I continued to play with his hair, twirling it in my fingertips. I pulled, tugging his head up. "Michael, we need to talk about—"

"Ugh. The infamous words of a woman."

My eyebrow shot up. "What are you implying?" I pulled his hair harder.

"Ow. Okay, okay." He kneeled back, pulled on his pants, wrapped the condom in a napkin I'd retrieved from the glove compartment, and sat back against the seat.

I wiggled back into my own pants, tucked myself into my bra, and pulled my shirt closed.

"That was hot," he said.

I chuckled at his boyish perversion. "So, what's going on?" I asked, silently begging him to open up and be honest.

"Fuck, Siena. I don't know. There's so much going on."

I rolled down the window, letting in some fresh air. "Okay, well, let's take it one item at a time."

He eyeballed me, speculatively. I remained silent, waiting for him to start. I didn't want to push, even though I did. But a man like Michael, sometimes you just had to sit quietly and wait for him to take the initial step.

"I guess, part of it is Sal. That shit was . . . unexpected. And I know it was even scarier for you. But I guess, I just felt—"

"I'm sorry." I interrupted him. "I should've been more communicative." My hands lifted of their own accord and fell back into my lap. "I just got consumed with him and didn't consider your feelings. I should have said thank you. I should have called . . . but, I didn't. I was selfish. I'm sorry."

"I'm glad he's okay. That you're . . . that you're all okay. That's all that matters." He shrugged.

"We would have been lost without you."

"Don't forget the girls."

"Yes, all of you. I've been a shitty friend. I haven't even thanked them either."

"They understand what you're dealing with. Don't worry about them." He grabbed my hand, pulling my eyes to him. "You've got really amazing friends. You're lucky."

"Funny. They said the same thing about you." I thought that'd get a smile or a chuckle at least, but Michael seemed to be occupied with whatever else was bothering him. "Okay, what else?" I gently prodded.

He leaned his head back against the headrest and sighed, eyes closed. "Work. But what's new?"

"Meaning?"

"My father."

"Ah. Okay, let's skip that one for now."

He chuckled, opened one eye. "Agreed."

The windows were cleared up now. The span of land covered in a blanket of wild grass dotted with scattered trees looked inviting. My eyes danced across the speckles of purple, yellow, and orange wildflowers battered by the rain.

The quiet between us was deafening. Michael and I both exhaled a breath through our lips at the same moment, sounding like Mr. Ed. The laugh rippled through me, remembering Audrey's mockery. Michael was laughing too, both of us taken over from the ridiculousness of the sound and the situation.

He took my hand, kissed the inside of my wrist, then rested it against his thigh. I looked at him, beaming. His face was alight with a smile that spread to his eyes, but the one thing he hadn't brought up was still nagging at me. I had to come clean about Tim.

Michael deserved that.

So did I.

"I can't thank you enough, Michael." I squeezed his leg. "I just couldn't deal with everything going on while I was worried about Pops. I know you know about Tim. About him calling and texting me. And I have to be honest with you. He wants me back."

"I know." His voice was low, almost inaudible.

I let a quiet breath out, shook my head. "After everything he did, he *still* wants me back. I had a lot to think about."

His jaw tightened. His eyes flashed.

I knew, after what Michael said—*want me, need me*—this wasn't easy for him to hear. But I was speaking honestly, trying to help him understand where I was coming from.

"Siena, I won't play this game with you. I won't be someone you keep on the side while you figure out if you're getting back with your ex or not. Despite everything you think you know about me from those goddamned Google searches of yours, I'm just not that fucking shallow."

His intensity surprised me. "I know that."

"Do you?"

"Yes, Michael. I do. And I need you to know I didn't

respond to him. There's nothing he can say or do that would make me change my mind."

"I see."

"And"—I peeked up at him—"ever since you and me . . . that night you unselfishly focused on *my* pleasure . . . Then when I found out about Pops's heart attack and your only concern was *me* and getting me home . . . I realized that, because of you, I could never be with him again. I haven't thought about him—he hasn't even crossed my mind. Until now." I could feel my cheeks beginning to burn.

"Really?" He cleared his throat.

"Honestly." I crossed my heart. He turned to me, stared into my eyes for a long moment, then pulled me to him, and kissed me deeply.

Gently pulling away, he kissed my nose, touched his forehead to mine. I could feel his body sigh with relief. "I have to admit. It's been eating at me. The thought of him having a better hold on you than I do . . . it's been killing me."

"Michael—"

"I know it's all happening so fast. But can you deny this thing between us?"

I bit my lip, trying to fight the emotions welling up in me. To hear these words, to hear these feelings. Were they true?

"Can you?" His words stuttered my heart as he looked into my eyes, beseeching me to deny it. "C'mon, Siena. You know how it is between us. I haven't ever felt this way before."

I couldn't speak. My chest felt tight.

"If you don't feel the same, it's okay. But I just couldn't let you go right now without saying something. Tell me, what do you feel?"

I didn't know what to say. So, I answered him the only way I could. I grabbed his face and kissed him.

CHAPTER Thirty-One

Siena

THE CLOUDS, AN OMINOUS SHADE of gray, continued to build after the initial rain. They were dark and promised a crazy storm. But nothing could dampen the feeling inside me.

Michael brought me home after we finished the rest of our deliveries. A tender kiss goodbye and a promise to see him later. My feet were light as I bounded up the steps, a feeling that I could take on the world flowing through my veins.

The air smelled of onion, garlic, and spices, a rich aroma that made my stomach grumble. I walked to the stove, lifted the lid, steam rising in the air. Minestrone made with fire-roasted tomatoes, carrots, zucchini, cannellini beans, kale, and fusilli pasta simmered in the pot. "Smells delicious." I inhaled another deep whiff before pulling out a spoon to get a quick taste.

Grams's eyes landed on Pops. "I thought it'd be a good night for a hearty, healthy soup."

"More like keeping me filled with rabbit food," Pops complained.

"You'll eat it, and you'll like it," she admonished. "It's not only your favorite, but it's good for you."

He grumbled into his water. "No coffee, no wine. No nothin'."

"C'mon, don't be like that. We just want to make sure you're okay. Can't wait to eat," I said, going to my grandfather, kissing his cheek.

"We have to follow doctor's orders. Things will get back to normal soon," Grams said.

"I know. I just don't like feeling like every move I make is being monitored. It is. I know it's for the best. But it just—"

"Sucks," I finished for him.

"Yeah."

"I'm sorry, Pops. I know it does. Will you hate me if I make a coffee?"

"No." He scowled at the machine, his now sworn enemy.

"Let me make you some tea," Grams said.

"Blech." He stuck out his tongue.

"If you have some tea, I'll have some tea," I said, trying to persuade him.

"Herbal tea. Nothing with caffeine," Grams warned.

"I'll just suffer in silence."

Grams and I burst out in laughter together. "Yeah, right," I said as Grams shook her head.

Thunder rumbled, loud and mighty.

"Exactly," Pops said, looking skyward like the weather was agreeing with him.

I glanced out at the darkened horizon. "It's gonna be gnarly. Sky will open up any minute now."

"Wonder how Michael will be," Grams said.

My eyes drifting toward his place. I longed for him with every part of me. My stomach fluttered at the passionate and emotional memories of earlier.

"You want to make a salad for dinner?" Grams asked.

"How about a steak?" Pops chirped in.

"Ha ha, Pops. Sure, Grams. I'll make one in a few." I

squeezed Pops's shoulder as I passed him and headed to my room for a quick shower.

Twenty minutes later, hair thrown into a bun, sporting yoga pants and an oversized sweatshirt, I threw together a salad to accompany our minestrone as I told them about my day.

"Thank goodness for Michael," Grams said.

"That boy has really stepped up," Pops agreed.

"He might be asking for a raise soon," I joked, squeezing lemon juice over the lettuce. "The girls all texted saying how wonderful he is and how much they like him."

"And what about you?" Pops asked.

"I guess he's okay." A slight smirk kissed my mouth as I turned. They sat staring at me, waiting for something more. "Okay, okay. There have been some recent developments in that area."

"And?" Grams asked.

"I don't kiss and tell, Grams."

"I knew it! I knew it!" She clapped her hands together. "I told you so," she said, leaning over and grabbing Pops's hand.

"That you did, Soph."

"You guys are a couple of gossips!" I teased. "Nosy, meddlesome—"

"And completely right!" Grams stopped me.

She was grinning from ear to ear. It was infectious.

"Don't get ahead of yourselves. We've both agreed to take things slow. See what happens."

"What about San Francisco?" Pops asked.

"I don't know. We need to figure things out around here."

"We've been talking," Grams said, meeting Pops's eyes. "And you need to follow your heart. Follow your dreams. If San Francisco's what you want, then you need to go. Don't worry about us."

"I appreciate that, Grams. I just have a lot to think about." Their complete understanding and unfaltering support meant the world to me. But leaving meant worrying about them, especially Pops. Leaving meant starting over and beginning something new.

Sitting with my grandparents, eating dinner, and enjoying each other's company left a knot in my stomach. I would give this up again if I left. I'd come down here, knowing that I would go back as soon as I could. But after Pops's heart attack, I didn't know if I could leave without feeling guilty.

Something was up with them. They weren't saying much, their lack of words resounding and thunderous, even in the storm. We chatted, but the elephant in the room wasn't being addressed. Their superficial and surface-level conversation, pushing just a little too much about San Francisco, didn't sit well with me. I didn't like the feeling I was getting.

Grams and I had just finished cleaning up when the sky erupted, thunder roaring and lightning flashing. The lights flickered and went off.

Immediately grabbing some flashlights out of the drawer, I took one to Pops and handed another to Grams. "Sit, Grams. I'll get some candles." The last thing I needed was for her to fall or hurt herself in the dark. Imagining something happening, even something small, made my mouth dry, made my stomach clench with worry.

"Don't you think you should go check on Michael?" Grams asked as I scattered candles around.

"Why?"

"I know he's a grown man, but maybe you should go on out there just to be sure."

"He has a generator, Grams. He's fine."

"Well, maybe just go anyway."

"I don't feel right leaving you here by yourselves in the dark."

"Oh, posh! We've been in worse circumstances than this. We'll be fine, honey." Grams was right, but I got the feeling she was trying to get rid of me. "Go," she said again.

"Fine. If it makes you feel better, I'll go check on him."

Even in the candlelight, I could see the smile of self-satisfaction covering her face. What was she really up to? And was Pops in on these plans too?

I shoved myself into a jacket. "Are you sure you guys are okay?"

"Yes. We're fine. I'm tired anyway, so I'm going to go to bed." Pops's voice, still strong, sounded weary.

"The power will be back on soon. I'll go check on the breakers after I get your grandpa up to bed and settled. Don't worry about us. We've got flashlights."

"Oh posh," I imitated her, bending to kiss her cheek.

"Just be careful," she said, kissing me back.

"Night, Pops," I said, wrapping my arms around his shoulders, kissing him on his head. I grabbed the leftover soup for Michael. "You're sure you guys are okay?"

"Oh, for Pete's sake. You're worse than your grandma," Pops teased.

"Should I wait up for you, dear?" Grams asked me, a humorous inflection in her question.

"Good night, Grams." Laughing, I opened the door and dashed out into the rain.

As I drove toward Michael's, I glanced in the rearview mirror. "I'll be damned," I said as I saw the lights flicker back on.

As expected, Michael's electricity was working just fine. I ducked under the hood of my jacket and ran to him, knocking rapidly on the door, wanting in. Not just in from the rain, but into his warm embrace.

He opened the door. "Hey there," he invited me in with a sweep of his arm.

He hung my jacket next to his. He smelled good—freshly showered, the familiar citrusy woodland fragrance clinging to him. He looked even better. His hair was damp and disheveled, like he had just raked his fingers through it, letting it air dry. It was almost black when wet and gave his bronzed, chiseled face a villainous appearance. This was exactly what his doppelgänger would look like: slicked-back black hair, dark eyes, bronzed skin, chiseled features but with tattoos running up his muscled arms and across his perfectly sculpted chest. My mouth watered at the bad boy image.

Michael looked mouthwateringly scrumptious, even in a T-shirt and sweats. His feet were bare, trimmed toenails and little tufts of hair on his toes. "What? No leftovers?"

I shivered. "Shit, I forgot your soup in the car."

He shrugged, pushing me back toward the closed door.

"I can run out and get it," I said as his mouth traveled over my skin.

"No. That's not necessary." His voice was low and rumbly. "I already had a bite earlier." He licked his lips as my back met the wall.

I leaned forward, already hungry for him. He pulled away with that cocky smirk in place. "Not yet," he whispered as he pulled my sweatshirt over my head. I was naked underneath. His eyes darkened with appreciation as he took his bottom lip between his teeth.

He placed his hands on my shoulders, brushed his thumbs across my collarbone, and dipped his head closer. His tongue glided across his lips as he drank me in. Chills raced through my body as anticipation rolled through me. His fingers danced over my neck, barely touching my skin. His eyes, full of emotion and hunger, captivated me, and I wondered briefly if he felt what I was feeling.

He shifted his body forward an inch. My body began to vibrate in response. Before I could say anything, his mouth was on mine and the slow burn that had been building on the inside flamed to an inferno, the torrid passion raging between us, all-consuming.

I couldn't stop myself as I entwined myself with him. Even as my hands dove into his hair and I pulled him to me, I couldn't get close enough. He ran his hands down my body, lifting me slightly, then slipped into my yoga pants and cupped my naked ass.

"Fuck," he dragged the word out against my neck as he slid his palms over my bare flesh. I wrapped my legs around his waist as he pressed me further into the wall, holding me up. He took my nipple into his mouth and sucked, his tongue circling lazily around the hardened peak. My head hit the wall as I let it fall back. The scruff of his stubble scraped deliciously against my skin as he moved to the other side. His cock pressed even harder against my already heated and pulsating center.

My noises were strangled and shallow as I dug my fingers into his shoulders. He kissed me harder, claiming my sounds, my lips, our tongues swirling together.

"I need you. Give me all of you. Please, Siena."

I silently implored him to take whatever he wanted. I nodded, and his lips crashed to me again, rough and unyielding.

He held me in his arms as he carried me, wrapped around him, to the bed. His hands moved over my body, tearing off my pants in a frenzy and throwing them and my shoes to the floor behind him. He traced his finger from my sternum to my belly button, watched as I shivered from the slight touch. I groaned in frustration as he broke contact.

"Tell me what you want." His voice was impatient with want as he pulled his shirt over his head, slid his pants down, and kneeled between my legs, spreading me open before him. He traced his finger down the middle of my body as he instructed me, "Tell me, Siena, what do you want me to do to you?"

I loved him like this, in absolute and total control, but still asking how I wanted him to pleasure me. "Touch me," I told him, watching as his hand hovered over me. He slowly brought his hand back up my body. I arched off the mattress into his touch.

"I want to take my time with you tonight. Tell me more."

"Lower," I whispered.

"No rushing," he said, moving his hand to my bared apex.

I tried to get closer. To feel the friction of his fingers against me.

He smiled wickedly. "We have all night, and I'm going to spend it with you . . . in this bed . . . filling you up, pounding into you until you scream my name." He traced his finger up, pressed onto my clit, dominating me not only with his touch but with his words.

Needing more of him, I coaxed him. "Put your mouth on me."

"Is that what you want, Siena?"

I moaned out, pleading. Damn, this man and his words and his wicked mouth were going to be my undoing.

"You are so beautiful," he said, pushing his finger into me. My body bucked at the feeling of him finally inside me. His Adam's apple bobbed as he swallowed, bringing his other hand upward, over my stomach, and finally to my nipple.

He placed soft biting kisses across my skin as he trailed his mouth up my body. Then he took his time traveling back down. His breath was featherlight against my skin, his kisses torturously intoxicating.

His nose traced the crease of the inside of my leg as his finger moved in and out. "I'm going to watch you come. Again and again." I nearly shattered from his promise, his voice low and primal. He looked up at me, and I met his eyes. The hunger in them knocked the air out of my lungs. In that moment, I'd never felt sexier.

I closed my eyes at the bliss about to come.

"Keep your eyes on me," I heard him say as he withdrew his finger.

I opened my eyes and picked my head up. He placed both hands on either leg.

"That's right. I want you to watch me as I eat you. As I bury my tongue deep inside you and suck you off."

I gulped at his hedonistic words.

He leaned into me, and I heard him inhale my scent. His tongue swiped at my center, feeling like heaven. He continued to lick and suck at the bundle of nerves. I clutched at the sheets, rocking up into his face, moaning out, telling him yes, and not to stop. His tongue moved over me, licking, sucking. It wasn't going to take long at all. "Fuck, yes. I'm so close. Almost there."

"You taste so good. Give it to me."

"Michael." His name was a prayer on my lips. And just like that, as if he knew that was the exact moment, I felt his fingers enter me again, filling me, curling upward as he pressed harder with his tongue.

My back bowed off the bed as I exploded, his face buried between my legs, his tongue lapping me up, groaning out, muffled moans of pleasure from him as his lips stayed on me.

My head dropped back, my eyes fluttering with the aftershocks that rippled through me. I felt as he shifted and moved up to me.

He kissed me deeply, his tongue sliding against mine. I wrapped my arms around his neck, tasting myself on his lips.

Enfolding me in his arms, wrapping me in his hold, I groaned into his mouth as his chest grazed my hard nipples.

He grabbed a foil and handed it to me. As I slid it down, he said, "I want to bury myself in you over and over again."

I rocked my hips up, his cock sliding against my soaking heat. I moaned with each pass along my crease. With one quick move, he'd be buried deep inside me.

"I am fucking dying to be inside you," he whispered as he slid up and down.

My breath caught, and I whimpered from his teasing, rocking higher off the bed in search of him.

"Is that what you want?" he asked. His tip grazed my entrance.

"Yes," I begged as I turned my head, barely able to contain myself. "Please. Now." I ran my heels up and down his legs, locked them around his waist. I wanted to prolong this provocative pleasure, but I couldn't stand it anymore.

He took each of my hands and placed them above my head, entwining our fingers.

"Please," I whimpered out. "I'm going to lose my fucking mind if you don't let me feel you."

He lowered his head to mine, touched my lips with his, and pulled my bottom lip into his mouth as he slowly pushed deep inside me. I was so lost in him and how he made me feel.

"Oh, fuck," I moaned into his mouth when he finally filled me.

Time seemed to stop for a few magical moments as he looked deep into my eyes. He smiled, kissed my nose, and pulled out to repeat the movement again.

We began moving together, our bodies sliding against each other.

"Say my name." His eyes were on me, watching. His breathing intensifying, becoming breathless as he moved faster in and out of me.

"Michael—" With every thrust he made, I raised my hips to meet him, my legs around his waist, trying to pull him even deeper into me.

"Yes. Say it again," he growled as he pulled himself up to his knees, hooking my legs over his arms, and ramming mercilessly into me while he still entwined my hands with his.

I happily complied as I said his name again. "Michael."

"I can't get enough of you," he growled. "Of how fucking good you feel," he said, his lips kissing my leg.

"I can't get enough of you."

"Give it to me." His voice was ragged and desperate as he continued to beg. "Let me feel when you come all over me again."

"Michael. Oh god," I moaned.

"You want more?"

"Fuck yes," I growled, loving his dominance, the way he said dirty things to me.

He smiled that cocksure smile. "I've wanted you every single day. Every time I look at you, I want you. I want everything."

"Like what?"

"Your mouth on my cock. Your perfect fucking lips, especially when they're wrapped around my dick and you moan. Fuck, you sound so good. My tongue in your sweet pussy."

My eyes snapped open, then down to where I could watch as he filled me over and over. I moaned, coaxing him to say more.

"Like right now," he told me, "I can tell you're close. Just by the way you sound. There's nothing better than being buried deep in you, watching you, hearing you come for me."

I felt myself coiling up from within. Our hands still tightly clasped above my head, keeping me in his control, drove me harder. I squeezed harder with my legs, forcing him to push harder into me as he drove me to the point of no return.

"More," I begged.

His head lowered, his eyes meeting mine. "Tell me how you like it. Tell me how good this is. How you want me to fuck you harder, deeper."

That was it—the precipice. And he pushed me there. "Harder! Fuck me harder!" I cried out, his name on my lips, repeating it over and over. "Michael. Michael. Oh god . . . I'm coming."

He deepened his strokes, lifting me off the bed with every thrust. "Oh, fuck. I'm coming again," I yelled out for him.

He was relentless. I tried to pull my hand out of his to

stifle my screams as he continued to pump inside me, feeling the onslaught build again. But he grabbed my hand and held it above me again. "Uh-uh. Tonight, I want you to break the fucking windows with your screams. Come for me again."

His words spurred me on, and I kept my eyes locked to his as I nodded and he continued, "I love how you sound when you let yourself just feel. How you cry out for me. Nothing in the world feels as good as this. Right here. You feel this?" He made sure I felt each and every pump of him.

I pleaded for more. My body seemed to be addicted to his words, his dirty talk. I was ready to fall again.

"You feel me, buried deep inside you? You're so fucking hot inside. Come with me, Siena. Let me feel you come again. With me. Together."

"Yes! Now!" I roared. And with that, I let go, screaming his name as I came again. Exploding around him as he finally let go and emptied himself inside me.

Our breaths heavy, Michael loosened his grip on my hands. They were tight and sore as I flexed them open and closed. He rolled to the side, tossed the condom into a trash can, and pulled me into his body. His heart hammered against my hand. I couldn't help but trail my fingers up and down his chest as we both lay there.

"You're staying the night, right?"

And with that one simple question, I felt blissfully complete. I hooked my leg over his and snuggled closer. Placing a kiss against his chest, I laid my hand over his heart and closed my eyes.

CHAPTER Thirty-Two

MICHAEL

THE BED WAS EMPTY. I touched the space where she had been, trying to feel any warmth leftover from her body. Had I overplayed things? Moved too fast, too soon? My heart dropped as I realized Siena must have left in the middle of the night. I grabbed the pillow she had slept on, inhaling her fragrance, trying to glean any trace left of her. What was that scent?

I buried my face trying to determine what I was smelling. Weird, but it smelled like a combination of vanilla and . . . coffee?

I held the pillow away and inhaled the empty air. Coffee.

Faint footsteps stopped my heart.

She was still here. She had stayed.

The sight of her, wearing my shirt over her tiny frame, took my breath away. It was baggy but showed off those lean legs, the hem stopping mid-thigh.

"I made coffee," she said, handing me a mug. "Your brand sucks, by the way. But I did the best I could." Only those bright hazel orbs could be seen as she took a sip. "And I brought the soup inside. It's in the fridge."

I shifted, propping myself up with the pillows, and held out my hand, gently tugging her close when she put hers in mine. "Good morning." I lifted the hem of the shirt, featherlight touches to her flesh. She shivered at the gentleness of my fingers moving over her skin to that sweet spot where her leg joined her smooth, bare center.

As her breath hitched, I took her mug and set it next to mine. She bent, framing my body with her hands and brought her lips to mine, warm from the coffee, soft and full. I pulled her lip into my mouth, suckled gently.

As she stood up straighter, the quirk of her eyebrow made me smirk. She realized my intention. I lowered the sheet slowly from my waist, her eyes on my hands. Her small gasp when I uncovered my rock-hard cock made me twitch with desire. I pumped myself, my dick jumping with the flexing.

"I suppose you have something in mind for that?" She watched as I put a condom on, stroked myself again.

"Oh, Ms. Moretti. I have something in mind that you'll appreciate."

She laughed as I pulled her down on top of me. She wasn't wearing a stitch other than my T-shirt, which I promptly pulled up and over her head. I cupped her perky mounds, squeezed, and kept my hands tight against her skin as I slid them down her body. She rocked up when I reached her hips. I slid into her inch by inch. She leaned forward, pressing herself into my chest, and started moving. Our lips locked, our hips drove into one another, and I couldn't think of anything more perfect than an early morning quickie in bed with this beautiful woman.

Sated, exhausted, and full of her, I walked Siena to the door an hour later. I wrapped my arms around her waist, grabbed her ass, and pulled her to me. "Thank you again for coming last night," I said, kissing her softly.

"I think you mean coming over," she said, her lips against mine.

"Nope, I meant *coming*," I laughed, squeezing her ass.

"You're quite welcome." She splayed her hand on my face,

then ruffled my hair. "Go do something productive. It's a workday."

Inappropriate thoughts came quickly. "Yeah, but I wouldn't object to playing hooky."

She scrunched her face, contemplating the option. "Maybe later. I need to check on Pops. Maybe I'll come back later and check on you."

"If you don't, don't blame me for what happens."

"You don't scare me, Mr. Blaire." She jutted her chin out, stubborn, obstinate little thing.

I leaned against the doorjamb, scratched at an itch I didn't have, pushing at the waistband of my sweats. I watched her eyes follow my movement as her tongue traced her plump lips. "On the contrary, I'm trying to entice you."

"You are a greedy man."

"I'm not the only one who's greedy. Exhibit A—" I flicked my finger over her hard nipple.

"Oh, shut up!" She pushed at me. I grabbed her wrist, pulled her to me. Her chest was already rising and falling with excited breaths. I covered her mouth again, her arms laced up behind me, holding me close to her. "I'll see you later," she said, pulling away. "If I don't leave now, I'll be late."

"I'll be waiting," I said, reaching down, adjusting myself. I couldn't help feeling smug when she groaned in frustration and turned to walk to her car.

A knock at my door a couple of hours later made me smile. I knew she'd be back. I smiled my sexiest smile as I opened the door to welcome my greedy little vixen.

The face in front of me was not the one I was expecting.

Matthew Allan Blaire. My little brother. In the flesh.

He stood there casually, not a care in the world, with hands in his pockets, looking around at the vast property that was now part of our empire.

"What the hell?" My arm shot up to the doorframe, blocking his entrance, refusing him an invitation inside.

"Hello to you too, big brother." He tried to peer inside, scope the place out. My fingertips gripped the back of the frame, clamped down harder for leverage. "So, this is your humble abode?"

I narrowed my eyes. "What are you doing here?"

"Business, man. Dad called me the day before yesterday. Told me to get my ass out here. Help you close this deal."

"What deal?" I asked, already knowing what he meant.

"The winery."

I took a step forward, forcing him back down a step. "Not gonna happen."

"What?" His shocked expression was laughable.

I moved forward another step. "I said, Not. Gonna. Happen." I trailed him down the steps, pushing at his chest.

"What the fuck, Mikey. Why all the hostility?"

"You have the nerve to ask me that?"

"I don't get you. All I'm trying to do is help."

"Stay out of it. I don't need your help." My voice dripped with contempt.

"That's not what I heard." His childish words reminded me of when we'd fight as kids, squabbling over action figures or who was going to get the last of the chocolate ice cream.

Siena's words were like a boomerang, thrown out and coming back to smack me in my face. "You're just a fuckin' little errand boy," I told him. I was taunting him, poking him where I knew it would hurt.

"Fuck you," he snarled.

"Fuck yourself," I snapped back.

"Jesus. What the hell is your problem?" He took a step closer.

"Back off," I warned him.

"Or what?" He took another step, eyes narrowed. I saw that same gleam I'd seen countless times when we were younger flash in them, challenging me.

"Or else." My words were childish, and I knew they were weak, but at the moment, I didn't give two shits.

"Dad said—"

That one syllable—*Dad*—and I lost it. My fist came out, an automatic reflex, connecting with his jaw.

His fist flew back. I ducked my head, avoiding the initial blow, but he came back with a left hook, catching me squarely in my eye.

"Mother fucker!" I yelled, swinging back.

He grabbed my wrist, knowing my moves, learning from past scuffles we'd had over the years. Another punch caught me on the side of my head.

As I leaned down, he jumped on my back, grabbing me in a chokehold. I couldn't swing him off. I was turning wildly, trying to shake him off like a rabid monkey. I shifted my weight back, making us fall to the ground. He lost his grip and we were wresting in the dirt. Scrapping, swinging, tearing, punching blindly.

I heard faint yelling. The screams and shouts were muted in my ringing ears.

"Stop it! Stop it! Get off him!" A pair of hands pulled at me, ripping me off Matthew. "Hey! Break it up! Michael, what the fuck?"

Matthew and I finally stopped and just sat there on the ground, covered in dust, huffing, trying to catch our breath.

"What the hell is going on?" Siena asked in a tone I had never heard from her before. A demanding tone that oozed authority.

I looked up. She stood, hands on her hips, face red, chest heaving from pulling at me with all her might.

"I asked you, *what the hell is going on*? Answer me." She looked between the two of us, her face solemn, her words direct and tolerating no nonsense. This new side added to her already spectacular magnificence.

"Nothing," I said, my words trite and immature. It was like being scolded by our mother.

"Doesn't look like nothing." She held my eyes, not backing down. "Why are you beating up a complete stranger?"

"A stranger?" I grunted, my thumb jutted out, pointing at Matthew. "This douchebag? He's not a stranger. Although, he'd have been better off if he were." I sniggered, looking at my brother, who was dabbing at his puffy lip.

"And he wasn't beating me up," Matthew said, an arrogant smile in place. "I was beating him up."

She rolled her eyes and huffed. "Jesus."

I grunted, "He's my brother."

"Brother? I thought your brother lived in Florida."

"He does. Fucker's here now, though. Matthew, Siena. Siena, Matthew." I swiped at my mouth, wiped the dirt away, and spat.

"Asshole," he grumbled, then cleared his throat and smiled. "Nice to meet you, Siena." He brushed his hand off, stuck it out. She leaned down and shook it tentatively.

"I was coming to see if you wanted to go for a run"—she looked back and forth between us—"but I can see you're busy."

"Matthew was just leaving," I said, shooting him a death stare.

He didn't back down. "I just got here. *And* we have things we need to discuss."

"Uh, not now. It's not a good time. I already have plans. See?" I jerked my thumb at Siena.

Her hands fluttered, dismissing me. "We can reschedule. What were you guys fighting about anyway?"

"I'm out here to check on—"

"Nothing," I cut Matthew off. "It's family shit. Nothing that concerns you."

"I see." A combination of hurt and irritation flashed in her eyes as she nodded. "Well, I'll just—"

Shit. "I didn't mean—"

"No, no. I understand." The flick of her hand stopped me. "No need for me to get in the middle of *family shit*." She shot me a look that made my balls shrivel up into my groin. Then she plastered on a smile. The one I knew all too well. The smile that could freeze water. "Nice meeting you, Matthew," she said, not even bothering to look at me.

I knew I should chase after her. Apologize. Explain. But I also knew her well enough by now to know that she wouldn't be easy to talk to right this minute. I'd give her some time to cool off. Then I'd grovel. "Jesus. Fuck, man. Perfect fucking timing," I sneered at Matthew, standing up.

He shook his head and laughed. "Who was that?" he said, jutting out his hand so I could help him to his feet. I pulled harder than I needed, but I was proving my point.

I huffed. "Siena. Siena Moretti."

"Hmm," he considered with a nod, looking to where she'd disappeared. "Quite a woman."

"Don't even think about it," I warned.

He did a double take. "Wait. Moretti? As in Moretti Vineyards?"

"Don't go there, bro."

He chuckled, cupping his chin in his hand, massaging his jaw. "This is all starting to make a lot more sense." His shit-eating grin was pissing me off.

"Fuck off."

He laughed. "A little touchy, are we, big brother?"

"Shut up. Come on," I said, leading him up the steps. I walked to the fridge, grabbed two beers.

"Man, this thing sucks," he said from the couch, trying to get comfortable.

"Tell me about it." I handed him a bottle. "Cheers."

He clinked his bottle to mine. "Yeah. Thanks for the heartwarming welcome."

I held the cold bottle to my throbbing eye. "No problem."

His face was expressionless, waiting.

"I guess I should apologize. I just . . . well, you know how I get about Dad."

"I thought you'd worked through all that shit. You keep everything to yourself, bottled up. But you said you were in a better place. Guess you're not."

"No, I am. It's just this place . . . this situation . . . there's more to it than just a simple purchase. And he doesn't get it."

"What doesn't he get?"

It took over two hours to tell Matthew everything that had happened since coming here. About Sophia and Sal, meeting Siena, forging a relationship with them that wasn't superficial and full of shit. About Pops's heart attack. "I swear to God, if Walter had anything to do with it, I'll fucking kill him. When I saw you, I thought maybe *you* had something to do with it too. Then you mentioned Dad. It just set me off."

"I got in yesterday. If you'd bothered calling me back, you'd know that."

"Why didn't you text me to let me know?"

"I don't know." His shoulders rose and fell, making me remember that he was my little brother. That I was the older, supposed to be more mature, brother. "I guess I was just looking forward to seeing you."

I immediately felt guilty. "Shit. I'm sorry."

He shrugged, not replying.

The weight of everything came crashing down. How was I going to fix this clusterfuck of a mess? "Listen. There's something I've been thinking about. I was thinking about . . . hoping to bring you on board . . . when I had them more refined. But, seeing as you're here, now . . . might as well show you."

"What is it?"

"Here. See what you think. It's what we talked about years ago. I don't even know if you remember." I handed him the portfolio I'd been working on.

Four hours later, I was surprised to find how amenable Matthew was to everything. I thought he'd give me more pushback, but he shocked me with his open-mindedness and enthusiastic attitude about moving forward with my ideas. He'd even helped me fine tune things and pitched some of his own ideas, which added to what I'd already configured.

"We're going to have to work our asses off to get all this shit in order. But I think we've got something here."

"You do?" I asked.

"Yeah," he said, looking down at the scattering of papers and plans in front of us. "I think there's real potential with this. Seems like you've been working through all this for a while. Or working a shit ton of overtime."

"A little of both, I guess. I've wanted to try this for a couple of years now. You know how we used to talk about doing our own thing. I just never knew where to start. But coming here . . . Everything just kind of clicked and fell into place."

"No wonder Dad's so confused about what's taking you so long."

I laughed. "Yeah. He's gonna be pissed. But I think this is much better than the original design. I don't know." I dragged my hand through my hair, suddenly feeling uncertain. "You think he'll go for it?"

He shrugged. "Only one way to find out."

I checked the clock, drumming my fingers on the tabletop. "I'm going to get this shit in order, get Mos on board. You get the flights arranged."

"I'll book them as soon as I get back to my hotel. I know you want to have a sleepover with your little brother"—he laughed, looking around at the close quarters—"but it's kind of cramped here. I got a big ass king-sized bed waiting for me."

"Don't remind me, dick," I joked. "Text me later."

As soon as he left, I organized the papers, cleaned up, and

called Mosby. Then I made the other call I'd needed to make since my scuffle with Matthew. I said a silent thanks when she answered the phone. "Hey, beautiful."

"Hey." Her voice was soft and made me long to touch her.

I wanted her back in my arms. "Sorry it took so long. I was dealing with work and my brother all damn day."

"It's okay. I'm sor—"

"No, I'm sorry. I was a jerk." Her little chuckle lightened the gut-wrenching knot in my stomach. "Forgive me?"

She sighed. "Yes."

"Can I see you tonight? Please?" I was begging. I knew I was. But I wasn't doing it out of weakness or guilt. I was doing it out of a genuine desire to make up with her.

CHAPTER Thirty-Three

SIENA

I KNEW I WAS ACTING like a cliché—a girl consumed by "what ifs." Michael's earlier words had stung, but he was right. His fight with his brother had nothing to do with me. His family issues were none of my business either. Just because we'd been sleeping together and had essentially admitted our feelings for one another, I had no right to butt into his family affairs. I would've reacted the same way if he'd done the same to me.

He was waiting for me when I pulled up, looking at the pink, red, and orange sky of the setting sun. He was so sexy in his jeans, and the tight black T-shirt showed off his sculpted arms and muscled torso. I was so familiar with his body now that I knew precisely where each ripple of muscle was, each dip and bulge.

"I brought leftovers," I said, lifting the bag.

"Finally." His smirk made me want to smack him, but the gleam in his eyes made me laugh. "I have a nice bottle of wine, open and breathing on the counter. Welcome," he said, kissing me before I crossed over the threshold.

He handed me a glass of wine. "Before we eat, I just need to say sorry. Look you in your eyes and apologize again for what I said. I didn't mean it like it sounded."

"I know that . . . now. At the moment, I thought you were being the typical rude, self-absorbed asshole I first met."

"Hey! I'm not any of those things."

"Really? Exhibit A—"

His mouth stopped me. Hot and urgent against my lips, his kiss stealing my words. He pulled away to look straight into me. "Let's just agree that we both jump to conclusions a little too fast sometimes. Okay?"

"Okay," I conceded. I wrapped my arms around him. "I do have one favor to ask. That is if you can wait to eat."

"Maybe." He brought his hands up to my shoulders. "Depends on what your favor is.

"Well"—I twirled his hair in between my fingers—"you see . . . I have all of this pent-up anger inside me."

"Anger?"

I shrugged my shoulders under his hands. "Well, more like frustration."

"Mmm," he murmured against my neck as he lowered his hands and began pulling my shirt up my body.

"And there's only one person who can help with what I need."

"Uh-huh," he said, reaching around and unfastening my bra. He slid it down my arms, slowly, my nipples already hard in anticipation. "And what do you need, Ms. Moretti?"

I reached for his jeans, unbuttoned them. "Mr. Blaire . . . I need you to fuck it out of me."

"With pleasure," he said, lifting me. I wrapped my legs around him, sucked at his neck as he walked us to the bed.

I was naked moments later. He leaned over me, already protected, his hand splayed over my stomach. He bent down, his lips on mine, the tip of his dick right at my entrance, rubbing and pushing me open, but not taking me. "Tell me what you want, and I'll give it to you. I'll give you anything you ask for." His eyes darkened, pulsing with a hedonistic desire, but there was longing there, too. Like he wanted to say more, ask more, but couldn't find the words.

I wrapped my fingers around his neck. "I want you to fuck me."

He slammed into me once and stilled. "Damn, you feel good." He pulled out, slammed into me again. He lifted my legs over his arms, trying to get as deep as possible. He held me like a glorious barbarian who wanted to be so far inside me that we were almost one. His body was pressed to mine, my legs bent, my knees up by my head. We were entwined in each other, our limbs like vines climbing a trellis. I was lost to the feelings he brought out in me. Like that first sip of a fine wine, lingering on my tongue, hitting the throat as I swallowed, a smooth intoxicating warmth spreading slowly through my system.

He was rough, raw, and wild as he buried his cock deep inside me, his strangled sounds against my ear. He bit my neck, sucked. His breath hot against my ear, skin against skin, both of us slick with sweat and need.

"Too rough?" he asked, checking my face for any indication that I was not thoroughly gratified.

I slipped my legs out from under his arms, scratched my nails down his back, and dug my heels into his ass. I begged him for more. Begged him for harder. Begged him not to stop. My fingers kneaded his tight, round ass, nails digging into his flesh. He told me to keep doing it, to mark him, brand him. His words pushed me over the edge. I came once, then again, as he continued to thrust into me, biting my neck and chest. I dug my teeth into his biceps as I came undone around him one more time, calling out incoherent nonsense, my mouth and body quivering from our storm of passion.

He wasn't done. Still hard inside of me as my legs quivered. "Jesus, Siena. I love—it."

His stutter stopped my heart. *It? Did he just stop himself?* I thought, but I was so gloriously unraveled that I didn't question him.

He turned me over and pulled my hips higher. My ass high in the air, my head on the pillow. He palmed my ass with both hands, pulled my cheeks apart, and entered so slowly I thought I could come again, right then and there. "Fuck, that looks good." I could imagine his face, his eyes, watching himself as he pulled out and then pushed back in, watching how my lips wrapped around his cock as he slid in and out.

I felt his hands move up to my hips, grab and hold on. His thrusts became rhythmic, my ass shaking from his onslaught, his balls hitting my pussy as he plunged roughly.

"Yes, just like that," I said, bringing my fingers between my legs. This animalistic fucking was undoing me. "Don't stop. Almost there. Harder." I was rubbing myself as I took two of my fingers and clamped onto his cock, sliding back and forth, deep inside me.

"Yes, baby. Keep doing that," he said as his hand came to my breast. "God, you feel so fucking good wrapped around my dick."

His voice above me, his scent surrounding me, his hands holding my body caused every one of my senses to shoot into overdrive.

"Fuck, it's so deep like this. I'm gonna come." He pushed into me violently once, twice more, then stilled, his chest pressed to my back, his arms on either side of my body, his breathing like he'd just run the 400-meter dash.

He kissed my shoulder as he moved over my body still under him.

I turned my head and kissed his wrist. It was the only part of his body that I could reach.

He collapsed onto his back. I turned onto my side, and he patted the mattress until he found my hand, dragged it to his mouth, kissed it, and laid it on his chest.

I relished the fact that he had fucked my brains right out of my head.

When our breathing finally returned to normal, Michael cleaned himself up, dimmed the lights, lit some candles, and brought dinner to us in bed. The sight of him naked, walking around so I had a perfect view of his body, made my mouth water. My stomach growled, and I slapped a hand over it. "Someone's hungry," he chuckled, giving me a cocky look.

"I'm hungry for food. Not you," I joked. I was starving now, having worked up quite the appetite despite having eaten with my grandparents earlier.

"Sure," he teased right back.

We sat on the bed: him in his sweats, me in his shirt. The bowl of pasta, steam rising, sat in between us, the spicy scent making my mouth water.

I sipped the wine he poured me. "How is it?" he asked.

"Good. Nice label. You're becoming quite the wine snob," I snickered. He had Moretti wine on hand, claiming he "knew the owner."

He bent forward, kissing my lips, sucking my tongue into his mouth. "Mmm. Does taste good." He took a forkful of pasta. "So, how was your day?"

"Good. I saw the girls, relaxed, made dinner."

"Did you talk about me?" His broad grin split his face, making me want to reach over and take his face in my hand and squeeze.

"Actually, I did. I needed to vent. They all took your side, by the way." I took a bite. "Assholes," I said, my mouth full.

"Hmm," he murmured thoughtfully.

"Told me I was taking things too personally. That I needed to hear you out."

He smirked, then chuckled. "Have I told you how much I like them?"

I speared more pasta onto my fork. "Yes. Smartass."

"They're great. Beautiful, devoted, and *smart*." I knew that the last word referred to them coming to his defense, but I let it slide. I wasn't going to divulge to him that we had gone round and round about how pissed off I was about what he'd said. How they'd told me to put myself in his shoes and finally helped me see things from his perspective. He'd apologized, so had I. All in all, everything worked out.

"They've always got my back. Always." We both went for another bite, playfully going after the same tube-shaped pieces, playing out a battle with our utensils. "And how was your day?" I asked, grinning after I successfully got the bite he'd been fighting for.

"After you left, Matthew and I worked a bit, hashed some things out, and are planning on moving forward with some new ideas."

My interest was piqued. He'd caught my attention. "New ideas?" I asked, trying not to sound overly eager. I was genuinely interested in what these new ideas were. But I was also nosy.

"After finding out that Walter came out here, I had some things I needed to take care of."

"Who's Walter?"

"He works for us."

I tilted my head in confusion.

"He's the guy who talked to your grandfather the other day."

My fork dropped into the bowl. "What guy? What are you talking about?" My heart was racing. Why did he know something that I didn't? Especially something involving Pops.

"Shit," he muttered. "You didn't know?"

"Know what?"

"I thought they'd told you. Jesus. I'm sorry."

"Told me what?" I demanded. "What do you know that I don't?"

"My father texted me, threatened to send that fucking

vulture out here. And he did. He sent Walter here to convince them to sell."

"Sell?" My throat was dry. "When? When did he come?" I asked, my heartbeat racing, my temperature rising.

"I had no control over it. You have to believe me. My father—"

"When?" I demanded, cutting him off.

He exhaled in disgrace. "Matthew told me today it was the day Pops had his heart attack."

"What the fuck?" I jumped off the bed, the bowl tipping over, spilling onto the comforter. I didn't care. "How could you do this?" My arms were flailing with my yelling. "How could you let this happen? How could you not tell me?"

Michael slipped off the bed, grabbed my shoulders. "I didn't do anything, Siena. I didn't know until after it happened."

I yanked out of his hold, stomped over to where my pants lay in a heap on the floor, and shoved my legs in. "The hell you didn't! This was all part of your plan. Part of your selfish, scheming, cheating plan."

"What are you talking about?"

"You, Michael." I rammed my finger into his chest. "I'm talking about you. Your father. Your brother. The minions who work for you. Everybody who does anything you tell them in order to get you what you want. Even if it means killing my grandfather to do so."

He flinched like I had struck him. "Where the fuck do you get off saying something like that?" His voice was hard, but he didn't yell.

"Pops could have died!" I screeched.

His chest was rising and falling, his breaths short. Just like they had been after we had made love. But now, the movements didn't have the same meaning. Instead of passion and what I thought was love, they were the breaths of a conniving, two-faced piece of shit. I had been right about him all along.

"Siena. Wait."

"No, Michael." I held my hand up. "I'm not waiting for one more attack against my family. You, your brother, and your father can all fuck right off."

He reached out to take my hand, his eyes looking lost.

"I'll never forgive you. Never." I turned and ran, leaving him standing in the flickering candlelight.

CHAPTER Thirty-Four

MICHAEL

SLEEP ELUDED ME. THERE WAS a ghost in the empty space. A ghost of someone who was very much alive. There was no point in even trying. I'd considered chasing after her, but I knew I wouldn't get anywhere with her. Not now, anyway.

I agonized over whether she felt the same thing I was—gut-wrenching loneliness, unbearable emptiness. Despite being completely distracted by what happened between us, I tried to do some work. I needed something to keep my mind busy, to keep myself from going crazy. The silence in the space was excruciating.

Ten hours later, I was on a plane, heading to New York with my brother. Sitting in first-class brought back memories of the last time I'd been on a plane. With Siena. The seats were spacious, but I felt like a sardine crammed into a tight tin can. It was almost suffocating, even though last time, with Siena, I'd felt like there'd been too much space between us. Back then, just a couple of weeks earlier, I'd thought, *"You should have booked regular seats. Then you'd be closer to her, be able to touch her easily."*

Matthew attempted to make small talk, but I stayed in my bubble, claiming to be going over our presentation. He knew something was up. I was disconsolate, unresponsive, distant. Instead of badgering me, he let me be, knowing I'd snap out of it when it counted the most.

Standing outside of Blaire headquarters, I inhaled a deep breath. This was it. Time to face the man who'd ruled over me my entire life. In his office, Allan Blaire, my father, sat tall and rigid in his executive chair, behind his enormous desk. It should have made him appear smaller. Instead, he seemed colossal. He owned the place, and in his mind, he owned the fucking world too. Confidence exuded from him, out of every pore. He carried the success of his business and his empire on his shoulders like a warrior.

And I carried the weight of his mistakes on mine.

Still, business was business.

And it was time to suit up.

Time to take charge of my own life, my own future.

Make a name for myself, out from under the shadows of Allan Blaire.

He grinned, showing no weakness, no worry. "It's great to have you both here. Matthew has informed me that you have some things you'd like to run past me."

Run past him? Like we were fucking hourly workers trying to pitch a new idea.

"After we're done, let's grab lunch," he said, as the door behind me opened. My dad's face lit up. "Steph, just in time. The boys were just about to fill me in on their next venture."

"Great. Michael, Matthew, I'm so glad I could join you. Your father's been keeping me apprised of all the progress."

"Yes, and what a great way to get your feet wet. Start with people you know. Practice makes perfect." He kissed her hand, then looked at us.

"What are you talking about?" Matthew asked before I even had a chance. Neither of us had any idea what was going on, and clearly, our father didn't value our opinion enough to make us part of his decision making.

"I'm guiding her on how to branch out. She'll be helping with Monarch."

"Jesus Christ, Dad," I huffed out in exasperation.

He held up an authoritative hand. "We are all family now. And Stephanie has some great ideas. Things I think will make a difference for E Enterprises and our future."

What the hell? "You've been married for about five minutes. What are you thinking?" I couldn't contain my anger. I was lashing out, and I needed to rein it in. I knew I did, but I was being pushed over the edge.

"I'm thinking that she is my wife, and we want to build a future *together*. That means being a part of each other's lives in every aspect. Thus, bringing her on board here."

"You're already making her a partner! I've had to claw for every inch of what I've earned. How can you do this? Haven't you learned a damn thing from your past?"

"You've earned everything you have, Michael. Both you and Matthew. No one denies that. But everything you have is because of what I've built with my blood and sweat since you were little. I've done everything, everything I could to create a business you could be proud of."

The intense repulsion I had for him was almost physical. "How could I be proud to be tied to a cheater. Why would I believe anything you say to me?"

"Those are some crude accusations, *Son*. I get that you're taken aback, but you should watch your tone and choose your words carefully. I am still your boss. Regardless of our relationship, you will show me some respect."

"You want respect? Of course," I laughed menacingly. "You, the very man who cheated on Mom, would demand respect. Like you showed her respect?"

"That's enough!" he roared, leaping to his feet, hands pressed to the top of his desk, anger flashing in his eyes. "You will not speak to me that way!"

"Michael, stop it!" Matthew yelled. "What the hell are you doing?"

"Stay out of this, Matthew. I'm doing what I should've done years ago." I glared at him, then turned back to my father. "Right, Dad? Why don't we just have it out, right here and now, once and for all? You cheated on Mom. You've never admitted it. Don't you want to come clean? It'll probably feel good to do something *respectful* for once." I shoved his words back in his face. He straightened himself, his back rigid, his face red, his lips pressed together. "You're nothing but a manipulative liar," I finished.

"He never cheated on Elyse!" Stephanie shouted, then slapped a hand over her mouth, realizing her mistake in stepping into our family feud.

My father silenced her with a touch of his hand. Her eyes welled with tears. "Oh, Allan. I'm so sorry."

A myriad of emotions crossed my father's face—irritation, disappointment, sorrow, guilt. But he remained mute, sitting down with a heavy sigh.

Matthew met my eyes, his own wide with shock. Like he'd never in a million years imagine that I'd have the balls to say what I did. "Why would you say that?" His disbelief and dumbfounded expression astounded me. Was he seriously this delusional, in this much denial?

"Because it's true." I looked at my father. "Admit it. For once in your life, admit your faults," I demanded.

My father remained silent. Stephanie's hand on his shoulder created a united front.

"How could you say that?" Matthew pulled at me. "Dad didn't cheat on Mom. She—" He stopped himself, seeming to have misgivings about what he was going to say.

"She what?" I sneered.

My brother looked lost, his eyes darting from my father to me. "Michael, I thought you knew . . . Mom cheated on Dad, not the other way around."

I sneered at him. "You would say that, wouldn't you? You would take his side. Figures." They were both liars. Joined in harmony ever since our parents' divorce. I would never be part of the inner circle. I'd always be an outsider.

"Clearly, you don't know the truth, hiding your head up your ass, like you always do," my brother snarled.

"Give me a break, Matthew. You have to take his side. You're his favorite. His pride and joy. The golden child who can do no wrong."

His lips lifted into a sneer. "What the hell? Are you kidding me? You're his favorite! Always getting what you want!"

"What I want? I wanted to be in Florida! He gave it to you!"

"I don't even want to be there!" he yelled back. "I wanted to be here in New York. But you got that gig. Well, until San Diego. But still."

"Boys! Boys!" Stephanie screamed out. "Stop it! Going at each other like this, at each other's throats, will not solve anything. You're family, for god's sake."

Suddenly, something clicked in my brain. In all these years, I'd never actually asked either my mother or my father about the divorce. I just remembered my mother calling him a liar from time to time when she was ranting and thought I wasn't listening. I'd just assumed. "Is what they said true, Dad?"

He sat heavy in his chair, closed his eyes, and exhaled a deep breath. He slowly opened his eyes, brought his hand to his mouth, drew it away. "I've never spoken ill about your mother. At least, I've tried my best not to."

"No, you haven't," I agreed. "You've never really said much about her. But I guess that's normal, considering. I need to know, Dad. I need to know the truth."

He sighed again. "I've never wanted to come between you and your mother. Either of you," he said, looking at Matthew too. "I hope you both know that. But, yes, Michael, it's true."

I felt like I'd been sucker punched. All this time. All these years, I'd been blaming my father for us not being a family. "Why does Matthew know this and I don't? Why'd you tell him?"

"I didn't tell him. Not until he confronted me one night several years back. But I made him swear to keep it to himself because I didn't want things to get worse between you and me. You idolize your mother. I didn't want you to think I was trying to sabotage your relationship with her. Maybe it was foolish. Maybe I should've talked to both of you together. But at the time, I thought I was doing the best thing for you, and for Matthew."

"And why didn't Mom tell me?" I asked. I felt like I was in a therapy session, asking questions, seeking answers, yet worrying I'd be no better off when I left.

"Maybe because she was protecting you too. Maybe because she didn't want to upset the balance. Who knows? That's something you'd have to ask her."

"Right." I stared past him. Like the answers might flash in the vast open space behind the windows.

"I know this is a lot to take in, Michael. But please know I didn't keep it from you to hurt you. I'd never want to cause you pain. For so long, I've known something was boiling just beneath the surface. I figured you'd come to me if you wanted. Maybe I should've pushed you to talk, to open up to me. But you're a grown man, and I just . . . I'm sorry. I thought I was doing the right thing."

I sat in the empty chair. Matthew sat beside me. For once, I felt like a part of the family that made up my dad, my brother, and me. Like the biggest burden I'd been weighed down by had suddenly been taken off my shoulders. "Jesus." I dropped my head in my hands and closed my eyes.

"I know, bro. It's a lot to deal with. Hard to accept. But at least you know the truth. I thought you did, but it makes sense now, knowing that you didn't. All this time—believing one thing. And it turns out to be a lie."

I cocked my head toward him. "Have you ever talked to Mom about all this?"

"No way. I figure, live and let live. It's all in the past. Why dredge it up?"

"Part of me feels like she should've told us. Well, me, I guess."

"Would that have helped?"

"I don't know. Maybe, maybe not. But maybe I wouldn't have had so much anger and resentment toward you," I said, meeting my father's eyes.

"I just hope that we can move forward. If you want to talk more, we can. I'm not trying to keep you in the dark." My father's voice sounded hopeful, less sure of himself than he ever was in business.

"Not right now. I need to think about everything, process it and deal with it."

"Just know, my door is always open."

"I think I need a drink." I laughed shakily.

My father went to the cabinet where he kept the liquor, poured me two fingers. "Matthew?" he asked.

"Sure, why not."

"Steph?"

"Just a smidge," she said, her fingers close together.

"To new beginnings," my father proposed. We clinked our glasses together, echoing the sentiment.

The scotch warmed me. My body had turned ice cold from the news I'd just received. I would need to talk to my mother. I just didn't know how I was going to deal with it, deal with her. I let the liquid slide down, smooth and warm.

It reminded me of Siena, drinking with her, and feeling the same warmth from Moretti wines. I missed her even more now. I wished I could talk with her about all of this, let her help get me through it. But what if she wouldn't be there for me when I got back home? *Home?* This was the first time I'd thought of Monarch as my home, and now everything was fucked up. I needed to get things back on track, and the only way to do that was to convince my father to change his mind.

"Okay," Matthew said, bringing us all back to attention. "Should we get back to what we came out here for?" His chuckle helped to lighten the mood.

"Yeah," I said, snorting. What the hell? Another thing reminding me of Siena. I'd never snorted once in my life. Why wasn't she here to make fun of me?

"Did you just snort?" Matthew asked, laughter escaping him.

"Yeah. Siena's clearly rubbed off on me."

"Oh, really?" he asked, smirking.

"Yeah, don't ask." I grinned.

"Whatever you say, bro."

I directed my attention back to my father. "Let me"—I looked at Matthew—"let *us* show you our ideas."

Matthew brought our presentation up, synced it to the projector. "Welcome to Monarchessa. A Blaire Brothers Hotel."

"Blaire Brothers?" my father asked, raising an eyebrow.

"Yes. After doing a lot of research on the area, Michael and I—mostly Michael—have revamped your original idea, creating a hotel we feel reflects the people and ambiance of Monarch."

My brother flicked through the images Mosby had recreated as I continued, "We want to build on your enterprise, our enterprise. Our name. But we want to branch out on our own."

"I see. And does this vision include the winery?"

"Allan, I told you to leave the winery out of this," Stephanie cut in.

"I know. But I know how much you loved it."

"And I told you that it would be part of the hotel's appeal."

"I wanted to surprise you . . . A gift."

"And I told you no. I wasn't being coy when I told you I didn't want it, Allan. The hotel is already more than enough."

"But—"

"We'll discuss this later," she cut him off with a raised eyebrow. The look she gave him dared him to rebut.

He looked like a fish gulping for air until he finally shut his mouth. He clasped his hands and sat back with a proud grin. "You can see who's really in charge around here." He chuckled, daring a glance at Stephanie.

Her stance didn't falter for one instant.

Knowing she had him by the balls, he cleared his throat. "Please, continue."

"As you can see, the new design uses a more open concept. This design merges the luxury of the E Hotels our patrons expect with the Moretti Vineyard. We plan to use Italian inspiration to unite our properties."

Matthew presented our ideas with expertise and confidence. I stepped in occasionally, expanding on his words, demonstrating our alliance.

"I love it," Stephanie said, a quiet sense of awe in her tone. "I've always thought there should be a different feel for this property, but I just figured, *what do I know?* You know?" She shrugged with a chuckle.

"I'm glad you like it," I said.

"I do. You captured what I loved about the area."

"Everything ties together now. The properties complement each other, and there's a smooth transition from one to the other."

"You'd never know they weren't connected."

"Exactly," I agreed, my frustration with her from earlier completely purged. I was relieved that she could see what Matthew and I envisioned. The potential we anticipated.

But our father held all the cards. If he didn't like it, we were screwed. "Dad?" Matthew asked.

I sent up a silent prayer for his approval.

"I'm impressed. I've been hoping you would do this at some point . . . for a long time."

"You did? You have?" Matthew and I asked in unison.

"Yes. Why do you think I sent you to properties that weren't your first choices?" When we didn't answer, he continued, "To get you to open those stubborn minds of yours and realize the potential you had. I didn't think you'd come up with something like this, a subsidiary of E Enterprises. But I like it."

"You do?"

"Yes. But—"

"I knew there'd be a *but*. Didn't I tell you there'd be a *but*?" I said to Matthew.

"You did." He patted my shoulder. "At least we tried, man."

I went to close the laptop, feeling defeated. Feeling cheated.

My father's hand blocked me.

I looked up, wondering what kind of game he was trying to play with me, with us. Was this a punishment over the winery deal?

"You didn't let me finish," he said, meeting my eyes. "I said *but*, not no. Because, well . . . ultimately, it's really not up to me."

Now I was thoroughly confused.

"Stephanie, I think you should take over from here."

My head whipped around to her. "Oh, because he bought the land for you." Now I was getting it.

"No, I didn't buy the land for her," my father said, confusing me even more.

"Jesus. I feel like I have whiplash from all this," Matthew said. "Would someone please explain what's going on?"

"I didn't buy the land. I haven't put one cent into it."

"What?" we asked simultaneously.

"You heard correctly. I didn't buy anything. Stephanie did." He swept his arm toward his wife. "She is sole proprietor. I'm just the name behind it. Being the up-and-coming entrepreneur she is, she saw an opportunity and asked what I thought. I saw great potential. But, not having any experience—"

"And seeing that we're married," she interrupted, taking his hand in hers. "I asked your father to put the Blaire name on it. Your name, my money. A true union."

"Seriously?" I asked.

"Seriously," she said. "I don't feel like I really have the name to put behind something this big. But I do have the money." She smiled gleefully, then brought her hands together in a clap. "I bought it, but this is a partnership. We are partners." She looked adoringly at my father.

He gave a satisfied nod. "So, you see, gentlemen, if you want to move on this, you'll have to convince the *real* boss."

"Holy shit," I said. Every lie I'd told myself about my father seemed to unravel. And I found myself truly relieved. Happy. Actually happy, for once. I had a lot of shit to work through, but I finally felt like everything was falling into place. My only concern was that maybe this was all a dream. That I'd wake up and realize this had all been fabricated in my subconscious. *Go with it, Blaire. You've been waiting for this your whole life.*

After another hour of going over everything, we went out for a celebratory lunch. Stephanie was on board with our plans, and my father backed my brother and me up, telling us we had done a phenomenal job. He assured Stephanie that she was in good hands and we'd all be at her disposal throughout the entire process.

Matthew and I returned to my suite at the hotel—the one provided for me while I lived and worked in New York—

and celebrated some more with shots and brotherly exuberance.

Hours later, I went to sleep, stupidly drunk. I was happy with how everything had worked out for us today. Happy that I finally felt some semblance of normalcy regarding my family. Happy that I would continue to make amends with my father and establish a real relationship with him. Happy that Stephanie made him happy. She was everything I didn't expect her to be and was genuinely invested in him and his children.

As I slammed into my mattress, all this happiness was great, but I still had a hole in my heart and a knot in my stomach. None of this would matter if I didn't have Siena.

CHAPTER Thirty-Five

Siena

I COULDN'T SLEEP. I TOSSED and turned all night. Again. It was the morning of day three. Two long, dreadful, and excruciating days had come and gone since I'd left Michael's place. Two days, and not a peep from him. I was relieved he hadn't chased after me that night. I'd been seeing red and was out for blood. When I'd gotten home, I went straight to my room and cried myself to sleep. I'd been foolish enough to think that things between us had changed for the better. But I was wrong. I had been right about Michael *fucking* Blaire all along.

How could he have let someone hurt Pops?

The next morning, after storming out of Michael's trailer, eyes puffy, and my hair looking like a crazed lunatic, I wrapped myself up in my old college sweatshirt. The one with frayed cuffs, baggy sleeves, and a hole in both armpits. I didn't care though. Who gave a shit what I looked like? I was still wearing Michael's T-shirt. It smelled like him, and I couldn't bring myself to take it off . . . not yet. I didn't care that I looked like a hot mess. My heart was broken. Again.

I thought what I'd experienced after breaking up with Tim was horrible. But this thing with Michael? I was at a whole other level of brokenhearted. It all happened so fast. One minute I insisted we have no strings attached, and the next minute I'm letting him pull at my heartstrings so tightly that I honestly didn't know if I could ever get him out of my system.

I'd plastered a fake smile into place. I didn't want my grandparents to suspect anything, and I certainly didn't want to add any stress to Pops. I knew I had to get some answers about this whole Walter thing, but I'd have to be especially delicate about asking them what had happened that fateful day.

Pops had been sitting at the table, a grumpy scowl on his face. Grams took one look at me and rushed right over. Instinctively, she knew something was wrong. I shamelessly broke down. I couldn't help it. She'd let me sob on her shoulders, the way I had many times in my life—from wondering about my parents to nursing a skinned knee to fighting with one of my friends. Like every time before, she held on tight, whispering how much she loved me and how everything would be okay.

When I'd calmed down, I tried to explain myself. It was difficult. While I'd pretended to myself and to everybody else that this thing with Michael wasn't a big deal, I'd gone and fallen in love with him. Neither Pops nor Grams was surprised by my admission, claiming they could tell from the first moment that there was a certain special spark between us.

Eventually, with my stomach in a giant knot, I'd asked about Walter and this whole winery business, explaining that I didn't want either of them to be upset, but I just needed to know the truth. They told me everything. About how Walter had come over declaring he'd been sent by Mr. Allan Blaire himself and was ready to make any offer necessary to purchase the winery. Pops had shut him down, telling him in no uncertain terms that our land was not for sale and that the only Blaire he'd deal with was Michael. Grams had gotten involved too, asserting herself as the matriarch of Moretti Vineyards, cussing him out in Italian, and finally sending him on his way, telling him to "never step foot on our property again."

I was proud of them: for standing up to him, for standing up for us. When I'd asked about him causing Pops's attack, they both denied that he had been the reason for it but agreed that it was eerily coincidental. Pops told me, "That man is no more cause for my heart attack than a bunch of butterflies. He didn't intimidate me one bit. I was just pissed that Blaire sent some underling out to us. I understand your concern, but honest to goodness, you've got nothing to worry about."

Grams then told me about contacting Michael about the original offer, that she and Pops had talked it over and decided that maybe it was time for them to consider their options. With the doctor's orders to take things easy and avoid stress, maybe they should sell and get a head start on an early retirement. With me going back to San Francisco and no one else to take over, what choice did they really have?

Talking with them had me considering my options and my future. Yes, San Francisco was where I wanted to be. I'd always imagined myself up there, opening my own restaurant, making a life and name for myself. And, of course, they were right. I had to follow my heart and do what I always dreamed of doing.

But laying here now, under the covers, huddled in the warmth of my childhood bed, I felt hollow inside. I needed to see Michael. Maybe then I'd feel better. Even if things didn't work out with us, I needed to apologize for the things I'd said.

Putting on a brave face, I walked to his trailer. I used the extra time to go over what I wanted to say and how I would fix my mistakes.

I was shocked that his car wasn't there. I don't know why I tried knocking on his door. It was obvious he wasn't inside. Instead of feeling relief, being able to prolong my begging and pleading for his forgiveness, I felt deserted. Like he had listened to everything I said and had taken me at my word.

And why shouldn't he? I hadn't been fair. I hadn't been willing to hear him out. My words, *I'll never forgive you*, reverberated in my mind. Tears pooled in my eyes and slipped down my cheeks. *You've supremely screwed things up this time.* They were my words in my head, but it was Michael's voice I heard saying them.

I got to the end of the line, the property line that divided Moretti from Blaire. I took a last look at his trailer, sitting empty and alone, just like I was. I pulled out my phone, said a silent prayer, and pushed Michael's icon.

It went straight to voicemail.

"H-Hey. It's me. Um—I'm over here at your place. I was hoping we could talk. I know I said some really awful things." My voice trembled. "I'm s-sorry. I don't want to do this over the phone, on voicemail. But I just needed to talk to you. Please, Michael. Call me when you get this."

I hung up, feeling defeated still. There was no sense of relief. Leaving him a message hadn't helped. I knew it wouldn't. Talking to an empty line, not hearing him on the other end, made me feel like we were worlds apart, that I might never see him again. Hearing his voice on his voicemail only made me feel worse. Where was he? Where could he be? *What the hell had I done that he'd just up and leave me?*

My phone rang and I was instantly relieved. *Thank god!* I went to answer it and saw Jenny's face. Jenny, not Michael, was calling. I slipped the phone back into my pocket, letting it go to voicemail. I wasn't in any mood to talk even to my best friend.

♥ ♥ ♥

Four hours later, still no call from Michael. I kept myself busy, cleaning, stocking, checking the wine barrels. Everything was tedious, and I was losing my mind. I kept checking my phone, hoping that maybe I had missed his call.

But every time I looked, there was nothing there to ease my fears.

Back at the house, I sat at the kitchen table, keeping Pops company while Grams cooked. I wasn't in the mood to help today, and she didn't push. Pops and I worked on putting together a puzzle of Florence. We had a large piece of cardboard laid out over the table, puzzle pieces organized on the outer edges, the design we'd been working on for a while pieced together in the middle.

My phone rang, Michael's name popping up. My heart stopped, then began beating erratically in my chest. "Hello?" I answered.

"Hi," he said, "I just got back. I was on the plane." He sounded so far away. Not physically, but emotionally.

"Plane?"

"Yeah. I just dropped Matthew off at his hotel. I couldn't understand your message. It was all garbled."

"Oh." He didn't even know that I was sorry, that I had called wanting to apologize. My head dropped, my eyes threatening more tears.

"We need to talk. I'll be back in about half an hour. Will you be around?"

I swallowed. "Yes," I said, my voice low.

"See you then," he said and hung up. His words, formal and detached, twisted the knife even deeper into my heart.

The wind was knocked out of me. I was completely crushed. I made excuses to Pops and Grams, and then I escaped to my room. The tears came on fast and hard as I slid to the floor in utter despair.

I must have been crying louder than I thought. A gentle knock on the door, then Grams peeped her head in. She stepped forward, offering her hand. I hiccupped, placed my hand in hers, and lifted myself up and into her open arms. "Oh, *Cara*," she crooned as I wailed. She patted my back, rubbed gentle circles, and rocked back and forth with me. I remembered how she would do the same thing when I was little. Hold me in the crook of her arms, swaying back and forth in her rocking chair, trying to bring me comfort.

My crying subsided. "He sounded so cold, Grams," I said into her shoulder.

"You have to have faith, Siena." She pulled back, took my hands in hers. "*Tutto accade per una ragione. Sì?*"

"Yes, Grams. I know. But what if he doesn't forgive me?"

"But"—she cocked her head to the side—"what if he does? You won't know unless you try, *Cara*."

I leaned my head back heavenward and took a deep breath. "You're right. Thanks, Grams." I smiled, even though I felt like curling into a ball and hiding underneath the covers on my bed.

She patted my face. "Go on. Fix your face. No sense in seeing him with your eyes all puffy and black."

I washed my face and tossed my dark locks into a ponytail. I changed into an oversized, soft knit heather gray sweater over the top of my jeans. I felt like a wreck, but at least I looked more presentable now that I had cleaned myself up.

I walked downstairs with my feet insulated in fuzzy socks. The sound of Michael's voice coming from the kitchen made my heart jump and the butterflies begin to dance. He was sitting, his back to me as I came in. My insides churned, and I felt like I might throw up.

I touched his shoulder as I passed him, letting him know I was here.

"Hey," he said, his voice hoarse. He cleared his throat. He looked tired. Dark shadows sat heavy under his eyes. He hadn't shaved in days, judging from the scruffiness of stubble that had grown in. He still looked sexy, but he looked like he needed at least a day's worth of uninterrupted sleep.

Grams brought him a cup of coffee over, fixed just the way he liked it. He took a few quick sips and sat back with his eyes closed. "Thanks, Sophia. I can't tell you how much I needed this."

"By the looks of you . . ." She held up her hand. "No offense."

"None taken." He chuckled, took another sip. "It's been a crazy couple of days."

His laughter froze my blood. Was he happy? Had he been having a grand old time while I had been sitting here miserable? Images of him with other women, many other women, began flashing in my mind. My stomach clenched in revulsion, and I had to swallow the bile that was clawing its way up my throat. Even though I was mad, ice was running through my veins, freezing me to the core. I huddled into my sweater, tucked my hands into the sleeves, and folded them in my lap.

His dark eyes met mine, his face unsmiling and somber. "We need to talk."

"I know."

Grams waited for Pops to stand. "We'll give you two some privacy."

I secretly wished they would stay and be the armor I needed right now. The room that always brought me such warmth and comfort suddenly felt cold.

"I actually needed to talk to them," he said as their footsteps faded away. "But I guess *we* should talk first."

My heart sank. He wasn't here to talk to *me*, about *us*. He was here to talk business.

I felt the sensation of being at an interview—or on trial—me the guilty, him the judge and jury. His eyes were flat and hard, not anything like they were a few nights ago when I thought he was going to say those three little words. I had no idea how badly I wanted to hear them. From *him*. I swallowed the huge lump, pleading with my tears to stay unshed.

"I'm sorry. I don't know where exactly to begin," I said at last, agony ripping at me from his obstinate silence.

"I'm shocked. Normally you have an arsenal of words at your disposal."

I winced. Okay, I deserved that.

"Seriously, Siena. You know how to inflict the right amount of pain. And then twist the knife just enough to make sure I'm still suffering."

He was right.

"You can't continue to jump down my throat and berate me and accuse me of things that I didn't do."

"I know." I was a small child sitting in the time-out chair being lectured by my lover. Everything he said was true. I couldn't deny it. I couldn't argue my way out of it.

"And to boot, you insulted everyone in my family. You have absolutely no right to say anything about them."

I cast my eyes down. "I know," I agreed again.

"How am I supposed to do this? Work like this when you think I'm such a piece of shit?"

My head snapped up. His words pierced me, immobilized my vocal cords. I couldn't find the words I needed to say. I had so much I needed to tell him to apologize for, but I felt that all I would do is cry if I opened my mouth. All over again.

"Are you going to answer me?" His words sounded demanding, and I shrank even more into myself.

I willed my brain to work, tried to think of something eloquent to say, to explain how sorry I was, but intelligent words eluded me. "I'm an idiot, Michael," I finally said. Simple, honest words. And wholeheartedly true. "I don't know what else to say other than I'm so sorry for being such a giant fucking idiot."

He waited a breath, eyes unblinking. "We were both idiots," he said at last.

The corners of my mouth wanted to turn up into an almost smile. But I wasn't sure if he was trying to be funny or if he was just rubbing salt into the wound.

"Obviously"—he gestured between us with his finger pointed—"some of us bigger than others."

A tentative laugh escaped me. "I deserve that, I suppose."

He was deadpan still, solemn and serious. Unreadable. Michael ran a hand through his messy hair, and my tortured heart ached with memories of running my own hands through it just days ago. How I wanted to just crawl into his lap and do that one more time, feel him beneath my fingers.

"I'm so sorry, Michael."

He remained stoically silent.

I continued, my arms wanting to reach out and have him hold me. "I need you to understand how sorry I am." I tried to read any emotion in his eyes, but I couldn't see anything. No sign of sadness, regret, or even anger. He seemed irrevocably lost to me. "I was so angry with you. Thinking you were some master manipulator, doing all of this"—I pointed between us—"trying to take advantage of me so you could get to my grandparents. It wasn't until I talked with them that I finally understood everything."

He rolled his eyes. Not in amusement or relief like I'd seen him do countless times before. This time was different. He huffed out in frustration before saying, "I'm glad you can see the truth now. But that doesn't change much. There's a lot that's happened. And a lot I need to tell you, explain to you."

My heart dropped to the floor. Okay, this was it. He was going to tell me that he had slept with someone else. Just like Tim. Or that he'd gotten back together with his stupid ex. He had broken my heart and was now going to step on it and grind it into the floorboards. I swallowed, trying to moisten my mouth, told myself to handle whatever he had to say with dignity and decorum. I wouldn't yell. I wouldn't cry. I wouldn't be weak.

"Can I get some more coffee?"

"Sure." I refilled his mug and added the cream and sugar.

What the heck? Why was he putting this off? Just to torture me? Make me feel pain? How much more pain could I take?

I set his cup down, took my seat, and tried to stop the shivering. It was warm in the house, but my insides were ice cold. Even the coffee I was drinking wasn't warming me.

"First off, I need to tell you that Sal and Sophia"—he looked back through the doorway they had left through—"they've been nothing but nice to me since I arrived."

A heavy weight descended upon me, waiting for him to tell me how he had drafted a more than generous offer for the winery to show his appreciation for all their hospitality.

"And sending Walter out here to try to cut a sleazy deal with them was uncalled for. My father allowed his ego to get the better of him. He didn't believe in me, in what I was doing."

"What are you doing?"

"I'll get to that in just a moment," he said. "But, first, I need to apologize to you too. You were right. I should have told you what happened."

"I'm the one who royally screwed up. I allowed my anger to cloud my better judgment, to get the better of me. I let my fear take over and pushed my feelings for you aside. I was scared. But I get it now."

"You don't understand everything. That's what I'm trying to tell you. I should have handled things better. It was foolish of me to just assume you knew. But I was so consumed with everything that I was trying to do, to get done, that . . . Well . . . Jesus . . ."

"What? Just say it, Michael."

His eyes latched onto mine, distant and unsure. He let out a held breath, waited another beat. "I did lie to you Siena. Right from the start."

I tried to remain strong, but my words faltered. So, he had lied to me, from the very beginning?

"My father did tell me to get the winery. From day one that was the mission."

"I knew it," I said, my voice weak and broken, just like my heart.

"I told him you guys wouldn't sell, told him there was nothing we could do. But he kept pushing me. And, for a while, I did think that maybe, just maybe, I could convince you."

"I see."

"I kept thinking there had to be a way to get it. But the more I got to know you . . . and the more I spent time with you all—" He reached across the table for my hand. I gave it to him without hesitation. "Siena, I realized that getting the winery from you would be the most backstabbing, callous thing I have ever done."

I was stunned. Speechless. Before, I was at a loss for words because of the guilt I was feeling. Now I was at a loss for words because him holding my hand, confessing his mistake, literally stole my breath.

"I know you've received two amazing offers in San Francisco. But I have a proposition for you. A better offer," he said.

I wasn't sure where he was going, but my heart told me to hear him out.

"We've been fighting about this whole hotel and winery thing, for what seems like forever." A cautious chuckle escaped him as he continued to hold my gaze.

"I know."

"I went to New York. To talk to my dad. Face to face."

My palms started sweating. Hearing this new confession made my chest pound.

"Matthew and I went to see if we could make a deal that would benefit all of us."

"All of us?"

"Yes. I think I found a way to make everyone happy."

My hackles raised on high alert and I took my hands out

of his. "Anything having to deal with your father is probably not going to make me happy."

"Please don't shut me out. You need to hear what I have to say."

"Do I? After you just admitted that you lied to me? After going to New York without talking to me, to talk to your father about my winery?"

"Your winery?"

"Yes. I am a Moretti. And the name reads Moretti on the sign, on the building, on the deed. I am Moretti."

"God!" He shot a hand through his hair. "You are a stubborn, dig in your heels, and don't budge an inch woman."

I glared at him.

A shit-eating grin crept onto his face. "And I wouldn't change a thing."

My lips quivered, a laugh threatening to gush from my mouth. I bit down on the insides of my cheeks, trying to keep it stifled.

He rushed to my side, took my hands in his. "Siena, I'm sorry. Please don't cry. I meant it as a good thing."

He must have mistaken my trembling lips as the beginning of tears. His seriousness and genuine concern about my feelings melted me. Having him on his knees, holding my hands in his warmed me from head to toe.

"I'm not going to cry." I smiled, taking his face in my hands. "For goodness' sake, get up."

He stood. "Shit." He raked a hand through his messy hair. "For a minute there I thought you were going to lose it." He dragged his chair closer to me, took my hands again.

"I guess I should let you finish," I said.

"You gonna interrupt me again?"

"Probably," I laughed.

He quirked a brow, narrowed his eyes, pressed his lips together. "So be it. But the more you interrupt the longer it's going to take for me to ask you to be my partner."

"Partner?"

"Yes. Damn it, woman."

"What do you mean?"

"Being away from you was hell on me. Watching you walk out my door . . . thinking you were walking out on me forever . . . wrecked me. Completely destroyed me. I want you, Siena. Don't you see that? Don't you understand what I feel for you? When I hold you? When I'm with you? When we're together?"

My mouth fell open.

"Jesus. Now you're silent? Twice in one day?"

"I-I don't know what to . . . What are you saying?"

"I'm asking you to take a look at the new plans that I had Jenny help me with."

"Jenny? Wait, what?"

"I called her . . . I don't know . . . a week or so ago. Had her draft up some rough ideas. I sent them to Mosby who worked like a dog to redraft and finalize them. Then Matthew and I went and pitched it to our dad."

"You did?"

"Yes. After we went up north and you said what you did about Jax's place . . . Well, I realized you were one hundred and ten percent correct. So, I had everything redone. Everyone working like madmen trying to perfect the image I had. That you had. And, well, it's pretty fucking amazing."

The excitement he felt was tangible. I could feel it coursing through him.

"I can't believe you did all that," I said.

"Well, when I realized how right you were, I had to take a chance. I hope I didn't overstep myself."

"You did all of that for me?"

"No."

My breath hitched. "Oh. I—"

"I did it for *us*."

My breath hitched again. "Us?"

"Take me back, Siena. Be my partner. In business. In life. In love."

My hand came to my mouth. "Love? Oh my god."

"I love you, Siena Giuliana Moretti."

He sat for a moment waiting for me to respond. "Fuck, Siena. Please. I'll do anything to make this right between us. Just say you want to be together and build a life with me."

I'd never seen Michael like this. So unsure. So on edge. I was so used to his cocky smile, his obnoxious confidence. This was a much welcome change. I should really sit here and enjoy this for a moment. I giggled at my own thoughts. I smiled, leaned forward. He leaned toward me, his mouth beckoning me, begging me for a kiss. I leaned even closer, less than an inch away from his lips. "Let me see these plans of yours, first," I teased.

He grabbed me, pulled me into his lap, and kissed me.

He broke away, just for a second. Just long enough to say, "I'll show them to you when I'm good and ready, partner. Right now, I've got something else I'd like you to see."

I laughed, squirming in his hold. "I love you, Michael."

His lips were on mine again—a delicious, silent agreement to start new.

To start fresh.

To start *us*.

Acknowledgments

There are many people I'd like to thank! I am eternally grateful to everyone who has been a part of this journey! It's been a long time coming—and if I miss someone, please know your love and support did not go unnoticed!

To my **READERS** (yes, **YOU** who are reading this book) and **Bloggers**: THANK YOU!!! Thank you for taking a chance on me as a debut author. It means the world that you took the time to read, review, and help spread the word. Your time is valuable, and I very much appreciate the dedication and sacrifices you have personally made to help me. From the bottom of my heart, thank YOU for all you have done! This has been a long, fun, and sometimes overwhelming and bumpy ride. Writing and being a published author has been a dream of mine since I was a young girl. Now that dream is a reality because you are reading this book!

Thank you to my BETA readers ***CAROLYN, DEBBYE, HEIDI, KRISTAL, MELISSA,*** and ***TERRI***! Your friendship means so much to me, and I appreciate your open hearts and willingness to read and give honest feedback to help make my debut novel everything I hoped for.

To my besties: ***DINA, JENNY, KRISTAL,*** and ***LIZ*** . . . You have been there through the thick and thin. Years upon years of friendship, the ups and downs of life and everything in between. I wouldn't have made it through the past twenty years without each of you. I could never repay you for everything you have done and continue to do. Whether it's a shoulder for me to cry on, an attentive ear to listen to me, or having my back in countless ways, you have each proven—time *and* time again—what true and everlasting friendship looks like. You are not just my best friends—you are my sisters . . . my family.

MICHELLE FERNANDEZ: We started off as email buddies touching base every few weeks. Then in July 2019 we met up in NYC – and well, all hell broke loose! We became instant BFFs and since then have become pretty much inseparable. Thank you for ALL of your help, guidance, support, and encouragement—for talking me off the ledge (many times), for making me laugh, for getting my sense of humor, and for welcoming me into your family.

Thank you to **MARY** for being a friend and confidant—for answering my endless questions, for offering advice, pointing me in the right direction, and being available whenever I called, emailed, messaged, or texted!

A huge thank you to my editor, **MISSY BORUCKI**, who helped me transform this book into what it is now. You helped me create the perfect blend of *sassy*, *sexy*, and *seductive*. Your patience is truly appreciated, and I have had a blast working with you! Thank you for supporting me from the very beginning and helping to make this dream of mine a reality.

Thank you to my proofreaders **MICHELE FITCH** and **JANICE OWEN** for your polishing and helping to put the final shine on my debut novel. Your support and encouragement to continue to do what I love is truly appreciated.

LAINEY DA SILVA: Awesome PA and Friend! Thank you for your devotion: for reading, helping strategize, for creating and sharing posts, and for all the chatting and laughs we've shared. Time zones may be crazy for us; but you've proven your loyalty, friendship, and commitment!

JULIA CLAIRE: Thank you for your suggestions, feedback,

and constructive criticism. You thickened my skin and helped me to re-believe in myself and my dreams.

To **TIFFANY BLACK**, my cover designer and formatter, and **LINDEE ROBINSON**, my cover photographer: Thank you both for your help, artistry, and attention to detail. The cover and design are everything I imagined and more!

KAILEY MARIE and **DAVID TURNER**: THANK you for helping to bring Siena and Michael to life! I was thrilled to find your pictures and be able to use them as my inspiration!

TO MY FRIENDS and ***EXTENDED FAMILY*****:** Thank you for being the best cheerleaders and support system . . . for the extra strength, the prayers, the laughter, the patience, the unconditional encouragement, and for being there when I needed you!

MOM**:** I miss you every single day and take comfort in knowing you are watching over ME. You have been a part of this journey and have been with me every step of the way. You always believed in me—even when I didn't believe in myself. Your love, friendship, support, and encouragement helped make this dream a reality. Thank you for being an amazing woman, friend, and mother and teaching me the love of reading.

DAD**:** Even though you will probably skip the "sexy parts" – know that none of this would have been possible without you as my #1 fan. You have always believed in me and encouraged me to live life to its fullest and never settle for less than I deserve. You have loved me unconditionally and unselfishly—always putting my needs ahead of your own. Thank you for reading me stories when I was little and using your funny voices and impersonations to bring characters to life. I will forever be your little girl.

To my family: ***ANNIE, DANIELLE, GMA & GPA, GRAMA, KIKIBUG & ALLIGATOR, AUNTIE DONNA & ROBIN, UNCLE DENNIS & RON*** – THANK YOU for believing in me! Thank you to my grandparents for supporting my love of the written word since I was little and for supporting my obsession of reading with books as gifts. Thank you ALL for asking about my writing and progress, for supporting the craziness, pushing me to follow my dreams of being a writer, and for reading my early snippets and encouraging me to finish because you liked what you read.

I love you with all my heart.

My (wine) cup runneth over.

XOXO,

Leigh

ABOUT THE *Author*

Leigh Adams resides in sunny southern California. As an avid reader and English major, she's always been passionate about literature. She is never without a book in her hand and never leaves the house without something to read.

Growing up, she always planned to be a writer. That was until college and the adult world locked her into a role and career she came to love. With writing on the backburner, Leigh worked hard honing her skills, creating her life, and focusing on helping others to find their passion and pursue their dreams.

After several years of working hard at her day job, she decided to redirect her focus onto her personal passion and picked up the pen to write. While she still loves her day-job, Leigh also enjoys creating worlds and characters for readers to utterly fall in love with.

Her novels contain a mixture of sweet, sass, and a whole lot of sexy. She writes heroines who are smart and snarky; and while some of them have been broken and bruised, they still have a backbone. Her heroes are strong, sexy alphas who are sometimes sweet and sometimes brass; but they always win the heart of their leading lady. While some of her characters may be damaged, as a hopeless romantic, Leigh's stories contain no cliffhanger endings because she firmly believes in giving each of her characters their own Happily Ever After . . .

When she's not writing, Leigh can most often be found

laughing and living it up with her family and friends, trying a new recipe, or simply relaxing with a good book or movie.

Leigh is currently working on *Enamored*, Book 2 in the Monarch Series. *Enamored* is Siena and Michael's duet. Her other books in the Monarch Series are also on her list of projects to come.

Stay in the Loop and Connect with Leigh—

Email→leigh@leighadamsbooks.com
Website→ https://leighadamsbooks.com/
Newsletter→ https://landing.mailerlite.com/webforms/landing/o5p8l3
VIP Reader Group→ https://bit.ly/LeighsLoversofRomance
Goodreads→ https://bit.ly/LeighAdamsGoodreads

- facebook.com/LeighAdamsAuthor
- twitter.com/LeighAdamsBooks
- instagram.com/leighadamsauthor
- bookbub.com/profile/1710799736
- pinterest.com/leighadams78